PRAISE FOR . ⎯⎯ URE

"A captivating thriller written in beautiful prose, providing an insightful, unflinching portrayal of institutionalized sexism and oppression of women and other marginalized people."

—Stephanie Scott, author of *Come Back Alive*

"*The Ascenditure* is a gripping feminist mountaineering tale wrapped in a compelling mystery."

—Natalie Wright, author of *Season of the Dragon* & *The H.A.L.F. Trilogy*

"Klarke Ascher is the next Katniss Everdeen, with a climbing rope instead of a bow."

—Dr. Samantha Schinder, Ph.D, author of *The Deliverance* Series

"Exquisitely written with characters to die for and a plot that is both intriguing and inspiring. I LOVED THIS BOOK!"

—Darynda Jones, *New York Times* best-selling author of *The Darklight Trilogy*

"It is a world for the senses, rich with lore, and navigated by a heroine who is strong, vulnerable...and determined to conquer the innumerable odds she faces in her quest for equality, for truth."

—Sandra Waugh, author of *Lark Rising* & *Silver Eve*

"*The Handmaid's Tale* meets *Free Solo* in *The Ascenditure*, a heart-pounding story of one girl's courage in the face of incredible danger, both on and off the mountains she loves to scale."

—Ellen Parent, author of *After the Fall*

"Klarke's harrowing quest to uncover the king's violence and corruption, to advance women's rights over their own bodies, and to live fully and authentically is described so vividly that we feel it in our tendons, lungs, and muscles—and in our hearts."

—Karen Holmberg, author of *The Collagist*

THE ASCENDITURE

Robyn Dabney

Fitzroy Books

Published by Fitzroy Books
An imprint of
Regal House Publishing, LLC
Raleigh, NC 27605
All rights reserved

https://fitzroybooks.com
Printed in the United States of America

ISBN -13 (paperback): 9781646034758
ISBN -13 (epub): 9781646034765
Library of Congress Control Number: 2023942951

Cover images and design by © C. B. Royal
Maps by Adam Bassett

Regal House Publishing, LLC
https://regalhousepublishing.com

For Shannon, my Ellias.

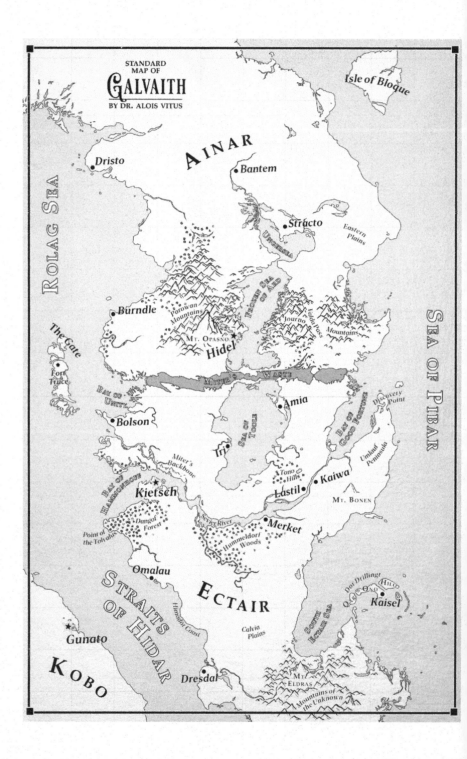

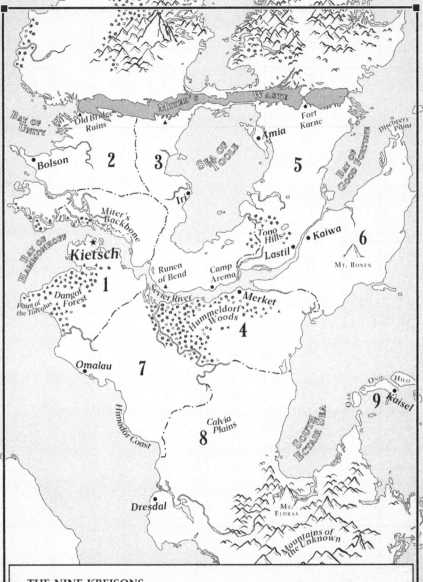

THE NINE KREISONS
OF

ECTAIR

BY DR. ALOIS VITUS

1. Capital
2. Western Shoal
3. West Inland Sea
4. Hummeldorf Woods
5. North Inland Sea
6. Umlauf Peninsula
7. Himadôr Coast
8. The Calvia Plains
9. Dor Drillingt Islands

1

Thick drops of cool water splash against my skin and against the fifty-foot cliff face I am about to climb. Each mossy handhold grows more precarious as the storm persists. No matter. I could make this climb with my eyes closed and one hand tied behind my back. I would do anything to make it to the top today.

I tighten my harness—a quad-coil of spiral-braided rope looped around my chest. My fingers move without thought, securing a sisal sling from my harness to the rope dangling from a pair of iron pitons high above. This setup will catch me should I fall. I tap the sling three times for good luck, a superstition inherited from Ellias Veber. He taught me everything I know about climbing.

In case charms and chance aren't enough, I whisper a silent prayer to Orna, the goddess of the mountains. "Protect me on this climb. Help me defeat my competitors."

Surely, from lady to lady, she understands. Based on my failed attempts to get ahead, I can only imagine what she must have gone through to reach god status.

In the forest at our backs, under the cover of a large sheepskin marquee beneath the oakenwood and fizhte spruce canopy, sit the men who will determine my fate. To my left, seven other figures dressed in woolen sweaters and dark hosen tucked into knee-high leather boots are visible through the misty morning, standing at the base of Vether's Fel.

The male climbers also wear woolen coppolas—flatbrimmed caps—on their heads to shield their faces from the rain. Beneath my straw hat, my hair is tied into a braid with ribbons wound through the plaits. A single strand of beads called an ilice hangs from each of our necks—a token of gratitude we will present to Orna once we reach the top.

Directly behind each competitor, in position to belay, stand the eight remaining Ascenditures, the kingdom's elite climbing team, which I am so desperate to join. Seven moons past, exactly one week ago, the ninth and youngest member of the team tied a faulty sling that came loose on a dicey descent. It took only seven days for us to mourn his loss, send his bones to sea, and start foaming at the mouth to replace him. How quickly our humanity flashes out the door when opportunity calls.

Unfortunately, these exclusive climbers aren't the ones who select their new partners. The real judges are three men who pretend justice and fairness reign supreme.

I glance at the judge's table. The oldest, a bent and gnarled man I know who frequents one of my bunkmates at her brothel, narrows his eyes at me. Squares his jaw. The other two notice his expression change and turn. One sneers as he wipes a bit of jam from the corner of his mouth. The other shakes his head and laughs.

"Good luck, Fram Ascher." He addresses me with the formal title of an unwed woman and lifts a mug of ale into the air. Rain tinkles against the pewter of his cup. "Maybe today Orna will favor you with fortune."

They laugh and go back to their banter. Exhaling slowly, I stretch my neck to one side and then to the other. I keep climbing, despite it all. The only place I truly feel free is pressed against granite. Dangling from a thin rope, with no guarantees. It's worth the pain of rejection, the broken bones, the sick feeling in my gut when I know I am about to be passed over yet again. It's the only thing I've done in my short life that is worth it all.

Besides, my other option is to work in one of the textile or machine factories, breathing in smoke and chemicals until my body succumbs to pulmonosis. Climbing keeps me outside, in the open air, away from pestilence, abuse, and the horrible afflictions that plague most of our citizens.

A long, slender alpenhorn blasts, signaling the sixty-tikt mark. When the horn sounds again, I will race to the top of this cliff, hoping to beat the seven climbers next to me. It is not just about time. I have to follow a specific route, touching certain holds and using the proper technique. My route is marked with rose-colored paint. Of course it is. I plunge my hands into my dust bag and then rub them together, knocking off the excess white powder. It lands like softly fallen snow on the ankle-length skirt I am required to wear. I can't afford a new pair of climbing boots, so the rain soaks through the worn and faded sheepskin of my knee-highs.

"Ignore them, Klarke," Ellias whispers from behind. Ellias Veber is the lead climber of The Ascenditures and my belayer for the day, the person I must count on to save me should I slip. As something of a surrogate father to me since my own passed beyond the darkened sea, I feel most comfortable with my life in his hands. "And *suertgût*," he adds.

"Suertgût" is the old Galvaithian word for luck. We still use it on the fel. We use anything that might keep us from ending up in a box beneath the tides. *Ash and wave.* That is our fate. Ash and wave and the darkened sea. Those words are carved in stone on the archway leading from the city to the port and etched into every tomb we set fire to and send to sea.

I nod so Ellias knows I heard, but don't break my concentration. My weight shifts from one foot to the other on the spongy ground of decaying forest detritus. The horn bellows again. I count down in my head, taking deep breaths I hope will fill my lungs so full of air my stomach won't have room to churn. Rain pounds my flesh in sharp staccatos.

Three. Two. One.

"Klettag," I say, letting Ellias know I am about to start climbing.

"Klettag und," he responds, letting me know he is ready to cradle my life in his hands.

The horn blares. Instinct takes control, sending me up the route with perfect ease. My hands touch each rosy fleck of paint and my feet follow. I know I look like a kefer beetle crawling up a wall. The urge to turn my head and watch the others is strong, but I ignore it as I encounter the first obstacle.

Until now, the rock has been almost vertical, but I've reached The Ankel, the obstruction where the cliff wall becomes a roof over my head, forming an overhang before returning to a vertical pitch. The only way up and over is to cling to the rock face with my body parallel to the forest floor and make sure I've got a good hold. Hitting the ground is not my worry. I am attached to a top rope, so a fall won't kill me if Ellias does his job.

I move onto the overhang using a heel hook technique, straightening my arms and bending my legs between moves to conserve energy. The wet rock makes it difficult to grip. The fabric of the skirt spilling onto my limbs adds an element of difficulty the others don't have to contend with. Each time I rest, my hands begin to slip. I reach for the next handhold— legs, arms, legs, arms. My fingers slide across the sharp edge of a crimper, and the skin peels away from the bottom of my pinky finger. This happens often. I'll feel the sting for the next week as the abrasion heals and reopens. Ignoring the discomfort, I plant the tip of my boot on a small nub of rock and propel my body upward. Next thing I know, I am pulling myself up and over the alcove and back onto the straight cliff.

The following challenge offers a sheer slab with few holds. I grip the nearest crimper, a thin ledge of rock no wider than a sprig of fluset grass, with just the tips of my fingers, curling my thumb up over my joints to lock my digits into place. Letting out a low grunt, I bear down to support myself, stretch one leg to an unnatural angle near one shaking hand, and find a sturdy place to push off. I know they are watching, which means they will see how perfectly I am crushing this route. I pass the final, near-invisible hold, and my eyes catch the rosen paint that will lead me to the top. I fly up the rest of the route as if I have wings.

I reach the top before the other competitors and yank on the long string, which sounds my bell. Clings and clangs ring out over the forest below. Shouts and cheers reach my ears.

From my perch atop Vether's Fel I can see Kietsch, the capital city of Ectair, through the rain and hazy smoke rising from the rows of chimneys, smokestacks, and weather vanes. Beyond the juxtaposition of dingy tenements and red brick multi-storied homes with vibrant shutters and hand-carved balconies, the Bay of Hammonhoff cuts like a jagged piece of broken glass into the land. Ships jostle about the port. Their brightly colored sails offer such vividness in this cloyingly earthen land.

A few seconds later, Russet Kamber reaches the top and sounds his bell. He gives me a smile and a thumbs-up as he squats to stretch and puts his hands behind his head.

I did it, I think to myself as my heart drums with celebration and fatigue. I watch Russet stretch, knowing I'd been first to the summit before and they still passed me over. "I did it," I whisper so only I can hear. "They can't say I didn't."

Russet leaps to his feet and walks to the wooden holzenschrein beyond the row of bells. "Tanks be to Orna. I almost forgot!" He removes the strand of ornate beads from around his neck and drapes it across the point of a chiseled pyramid.

The holzenschrein is carved into a hollowed-out triangle, adorned with small holes and filigree that let the light from the candles inside twinkle out. It is modeled after Fitzhan, the guardian mountain of our kreison. Each of the kingdom's nine kreisons, or regions, has its own protector, a natural landform that acts as a sentinel of the lands ruled by Orna, our high goddess of the mountains.

I pull off my strand of beads, one I made from mud collected along the banks of the Sevier River where it meets the Rolag Sea at the Bay of Hammonhoff. Bits of dried grass and dark pebbles disrupt the patterns I tried to carve. Next to Russet's varnished and painted marbles, my offering seems unworthy.

"Tanks be to Orna." I drape my ilice across Russet's and wonder how Orna decides whose beads merit her esteem. Hopefully she favors imperfection.

Another bell rings as a climber named Veit reaches the top. He gives an angry scowl and kicks the pebbles by his feet. "Foze," he hisses at me.

I focus on a krave nest at the top of the nearest pine. Five other bells sound, letting the judges know that all eight of us have reached the top. With a nod at Russet, I shout down to Ellias to let him know I am coming down. "Dirt me!"

"Beat you to the bottom," Ellias calls from below with his typical response that I am clear to descend.

"Helps when you're already there!" With a worn sigh and a half-smile, I lean over the edge and kick off, reaching the forest floor in a few swift seconds.

Ellias pulls me into a hug before I have time to untie my sling. He laughs his uniquely jovial laugh. I can't help but smile at the man who taught me how to climb—the man who chose me over every eager young person to train for this moment.

"Yes, Klarke! Yes!" He pumps his fist in the air. "They must give it to you this time. You were perfect. Clean. So clean." Ellias's rosy cheeks glisten with rain. His brown eyes twinkle. A beard that could be the tail of an obafox hangs from his chin. If he had any hair beneath his woolen coppola, it would be dark brown, the color of a fallen log in full decay, just like all of ours.

I nod, still smiling, and hope he is right. This is my second time trying out for the team. My second time making it to the top before anyone else.

Ellias wraps his arm around my shoulders and steers me toward the tent, where the three judges converse quietly, their heads together.

"I hope you had clear eyes today, Hannar," he says forcibly, giving them the courtesy title of Hannar even though they are far from gentlemanly. "She was perfect. You know she was perfect."

"Ah, Ellias," the thin, stringy one with drooping eyes says, his deep drawl marking him as one who hails from the Calvia Plains. "You are one to speak of clear eyes with such blinding devotion attached to your statements. We will do our jobs as we have been appointed to do. I suggest you focus on yours."

Ellias tugs on his beard and lets out a grunt. We turn from the judges. "You will always be the winner in my mind, always my first choice." He pats my back and then joins the crowd to await the decision.

"Fantish climb, Klarke." Russet pulls his untied harness from his chest and extends his hand. "You deserve this."

I accept the gesture. "You put up a good fight. And you know how it goes."

He shakes his head and lets out a frustrated sigh. Russet is short and wiry, which makes him light and agile on a climb. "You beat me. No questions about it. And I had a wee slip on one of my marked holds. That's a deduction heaped upon my slower time." He chuckles as he moves past me to hug his family. "We all thought the protests were wild before. Complete madness when they picked Kiel over you. Can you imagine the riots tonight if they do it again?"

Wiping the rain from my face, I take my place on the platform in front of the tent to wait for the other climbers to finish their greetings and join me for the results. They all have families to share this experience with. I have only Ellias and an inaccessible dream. Staring at my wet boots and the warped platform beneath them, I consider Russet's statement. The last time I was passed over, an entire street in the Eastlich burned to the ground. Two soldats were found naked and hanged from a crane at the docks. The king had women arrested and beaten for being out in the streets past dark. I bite my lip and pray for victory. For myself and for all that will burn.

From behind the judges' table, I catch Kiel Abel's eye. He gives me a wink and a sly smile. At eighteen, he is the youngest and newest member of the Ascenditures, being the most recent climber to beat me out for a spot. Kiel and I have been climbing together since he was ten and I was nine. I know he wants this for me as much as Ellias and I do. I wink back, hoping the misty rain masks the deep red coloring my cheeks.

The horn sounds again as the head judge stands, smoothing out his long, green ceremonial robe. He clears his throat and folds his hands across the stitched emblem of two intertwined golden knots at his stomach. With an insincere smile, he gives each contestant a nod before turning to the crowd of anxious onlookers on the other side of the marquee. Rain drips from the needles of the fizhte canopy onto their silken scarves and velveteen collars, but not even moisture can keep our people away from the sport of climbing. We covet it and our climbers like the people of Kobo covet song and dance.

"Geitsê, framen and hannar," the judge begins. "To be an Ascenditure is a great honor, one of the greatest honors this kingdom bestows upon its citizens. This elite group of champions risk their lives for the kingdom. They are beacons of hope and strength. They provide special food for the king and aid in times of great need. They procure medicine only they can retrieve from the heights of the Celebern Fields for our sick. They maintain our beautiful and historic Rektburg and keep our bridges and dams secure. Bestowing the title of Ascenditure is not an action we take lightly, and therefore only the best are selected. Three teams of three there will always be. Nine in total to represent the nine kreisons on which this kingdom rests."

I've heard this speech before. I'll hear it again soon, in a different, longer form, whenever the person chosen today is officially sworn in. King Adolar will deliver the words on the steps of his palace, the Rektburg, in front of the citizenry of Kietsch and whoever else from the kingdom journeys to the capital for the ceremony.

"Now, without further delay," the head judge continues, "I am proud to announce the newest member of the Ascenditures. Please keep in mind that selection is based on the entire performance, not solely on speed."

My heartbeat stalls. I know what's coming. Beside me, Russet stiffens. He knows it too. The scraggly judge whom Ellias spoke to smirks at me beneath heavy eyelids. I want to run into the woods and cry, but I stand taller, trying to fight the scowl from consuming my face.

"Our selection was based upon speed, accuracy, and technique. So please, framen and hannar, put your hands together to welcome Russet Kamber as our newest Ascenditure."

Ellias's lips stretch into a thin line. His eyebrows knit together. Kiel shakes his head, his playful smile replaced with fury. My soul seems to have left the empty sack of my body and floated upward into the canopy of the oakenwood trees, perhaps where it can grieve in private.

Russet bows to the judges and waves at the crowd before turning to me wide-eyed. His hand flies to his mouth, and he begins chewing at the skin of his thumb.

I rush to him, an expert at masking disappointment, and pull him into a hug. "You are a great climber. You deserve to be on the team. Don't worry about me. Enjoy this moment."

"Klarke," he mutters into my ear. He quivers in my arms. "It's scheiz. I'm so sorry. The city will burn. It will burn because of me."

"It's not your fault. You don't run this kingdom or make these rules. Whatever happens is not on you. Remember that." I let him go to celebrate with the others and force my mouth into a polite grin. Thin clapping permeates the forest, mocking me. Faces sway in and out of focus.

"When are you going to give it up, Klarke?" Veit, the competitor who came in third, strides toward me. He is nearly a foot taller than I am, with piercing blue eyes and dark hair. His climbing hosen are brand new. Swirls of flowers have been embroidered in snow-white thread across the wool.

"I beat you, Veit. Give it a rest."

"Russet beat me. Not you. You don't belong here." He balls his fists. His eyes bore into me like a chisel into the wall of a salt mine.

I shake my head and glare at him with the most severe look I can muster. Brushing past, I sneer at the judges and wave to the glowering faces in the crowd—both the ones incensed on my behalf and those who wish I did not exist.

Someone breaks out a bellowkord and begins squeezing the box-shaped instrument. The rich, reedy sound of an organ cuts through the jubilee and dissent pressing in around me. An already drunken man with a feather in his felt cap leans back and shouts the first line of a famous stanzllied, a classic and overly simplistic song chanted by drunks and joyfuls. After each line he sings, the crowd responds with the words "ho di oh di el," clapping their hands and clanking the bottles they've pulled from their rucksacks. Nausea builds with the fervor of each verse.

Come drink with me and toast the king.
Ho di oh di el.
From Fitzhan's fel to Laren's sea.
Ho di oh di el.

Today wasn't just about making the team. My time has run out. At seventeen, the kingdom considers me of age and will soon pick a man I must wed. Selection as an Ascenditure today was my one opportunity to escape becoming someone's brideprize. The lump in my throat swells. The air in my lungs dwindles. The only thing I can think of is my need to get as far from this clearing as possible.

From Kaiwa's wine to Orna's peak
Ho di oh di el.

Before anyone can reach me, I've secured my gear to my pack and am running through the woods, trying to find a safe space where I can scream and not be hanged for it.

2

I stare at the ceiling, cursing whoever is snoring in the dark. And yet I know their puttering noises are not what keeps me awake tonight. The true culprit is anger. As much as I try to shoo its annoying presence from my brain, the emotion lingers as if it has hooked itself into my heart with deep barbs.

I slide from my bed—a bottom bunk in a decrepit six-story tenement house—and slip through the door. Somewhere outside, a river aiwl hoots. Shifting my weight slowly on the gnarled floor in the hallway outside the room, I pray one of the landlords doesn't wake up and find me slinking through the building. As much as I like to say I don't care for rules, I am afraid to get caught breaking this one.

Ellias worked hard to get me into the all-female tenement after I turned seventeen a few months back and was kicked out of the orphanage. If I am caught breaking curfew, they will move me into one of the mixed buildings. I cringe. The women in the mixed slums face miserable existences. At least here I don't have to deal with unwanted hands pawing at me in the dark. I also don't have to work in one of the factories because Ellias pays me from his coffers to train.

"Keep her safe, Ell. If I ever cross the darkened sea, let no harm come to my Klarke." Those were outstanding orders from my father, according to Ellias. They had been friends.

Despite my dire circumstances, the privilege of having someone to care for me is not lost.

Sneaking out of a building is like climbing a wall of rock. Just as there are footholds you must find to ascend, there are silent places in floorboards you must seek to sneak around. If you miss the hold on the rock, you slip. If you miss the exact spot on the wood, an old building echoes and groans so loudly a deaf old fishmonger down at the port could hear. I knew every inch of the orphanage. I am still learning the mechanics of this tenement. Cringing, I place a toe in the wrong spot, sending out a careening moan of wood.

"Klarke, wait."

I turn to see Rayna, the one person outside of the Ascenditures whom I call friend, tiptoeing toward me. Her dark hair is tied in a long braid. She looks sleepy and innocent as she peers questioningly at me from behind her glasses. A small crack bisects the left lens. "Wherever you're going, it's not worth it. I shouldn't always have to tell you that."

"I know." I touch Rayna's thin arm and try to convey my desperate need to distance myself from the hovering rage that won't let me sleep. "I need to clear my head. I'll be quiet and return before dawn. I promise."

Her innocent eyes soften the edges of my anger. Rayna is the warmth in my life. The glow from a dying ember. We were two urchins, cast from sheltered stability at the death of our parents, when a boat cook named Obid who worked for my father introduced us. Desperately searching for something beyond a scrap of rye and a dry bed, Rayna needed my brawn, and I needed her compassion.

"Plus, maybe if I train a little harder, they'll give me a spot. I can buy both our bride-freedoms and get you a new pair of glasses." I grab her hand, stained black from the tar she produces twelve hours a day in one of the factories, and spin her once as if we are dancers in a ballroom finishing a grand waltz. The crumbling walls and derelict tapestries absorb her soft giggle. Someone coughs from the floor above.

She scans my face before nodding. "I don't want to lose you."

"I won't let that happen. Not ever." I give her a hug, her body so thin I worry it might not withstand the next frigid slumber. Then I am gone, quietly shutting the front door behind me. Ducking behind a row of feldenberi bushes heavy with inedible purple fruit, I pull out a small wooden box from an old skunk hole.

Rayna's mother was killed by a gang of marauders from beyond the island called The Gate many years back, somewhere west of the Rolag Sea. A mooncycle before that, her father had too much ale and fell off the gangway at Pohle Pier on his way home from work.

The sea welcomes a good sacrifice. Ash and wave for us all. Sometimes just waves.

Rayna's dark eyes are shaped like almonds. Her skin is tanned like the leather from the kuhkas grazing in the fields near Iri. It is no secret she carries blood from Ainar. Usually being mixed is enough to get you sent to the labor camps north of the Tono Hills. While the labor camps are ostensibly intended for criminals, most of the people sent there are those the king takes issue with—mainly women and dark-skinned foreigners. Rayna has never stepped a toe across the line; she has done nothing to give them a reason to take her away. Ellias got her into this women's home as a favor to me.

Rayna's deepest secret, though, one I will never share with another soul, is that she was born a twin to a baby boy. Twins of the same sex are fine in Ectair. Twins of opposite sexes are not. They are seen as bad omens sent from Laren, the god of death and the god of the sea. Warnings of plague, famine, drought… It is a sign that one's family line has come to an end.

To stave off impending destruction, the entire family to which twins are born is banished to a commune in the Mountains of the Unknown at the southernmost edge of the Calvia Plains. Both twins are killed in a ceremonial sacrifice. Most families who have twins dispose of one at birth before anyone knows of their arrival. And most of the time they dispose of their girls. Rayna's brother was stillborn. Otherwise she would have been thrown into the sea.

The small box I removed from the bushes contains two pieces of clothing. I strip quickly, pull on a pair of hosen I stole from a shop window, and button up a boy's shirt I traded for a stale loaf of bread. Lacing my boots, I jog down the slick cobbled street on the south side of Kietsch.

My story is different. I lived in the Westlich, which some would consider the "good part of town." Through my bedroom window I'd watch ships come and go from the Bay of Hammonhoff. I'd sit by that window, day and night, waiting for my father to return from Kobo with some exotic souvenir or spiced fruit. When his orange sails would come into view, the green flag of Ectair with its knotal insignia raised high on the main mast, I'd sprint down the staircase, out the front door, and down to the pier. As the captain, he was always the last man to disembark, so while I waited for his hug, I'd watch each sailor touch land. I'd giggle as they pretended to wobble back and forth as if they were still out to sea. It was a silly act, but I know they enjoyed it as much as I did.

I inhale deeply and run faster. Past the lumberyards stacked high with naked pine boards and piled logs, past the salt factory and the tar factory.

I hook a sharp left down another empty street crammed full of silent multistoried buildings in various states of decay. The candles in the streetlamps have burned to lifeless lumps of wax. Only Azura, our moon, guides my way with a soft blue light. I tread lithely through the shadows. Silent and invisible like Death's Whisper.

In other parts of town, in the Westlich for instance, freshly painted shutters cling to red brick walls. Intricately carved wooden balconies drape off the fronts of homes, overhung by exquisite eaves. Rope stone arches cover doorways. Flower baskets hang from windows. Weather vanes spin in the wind atop sharp rooflines featuring our kingdom's bird, the mountain turkas. Gilded in punched tin and emeralds, the birds fly freely in the westerly winds.

Here in the Southlich, where I now live, and in the Eastlich, and all the boroughs away from the waterfront, the metal turkas no longer fly. Bent and beaten by time and rain, they hang in various states of collapse, topping homes where anything carved or inlaid has been removed and sold for a sack of flour or a log of salami. Here in the Southlich, the smoke puffing from the chimneys provides the only sign that life resides within. The smell of horse manure, soot, and piss radiate from the street. I step into something warm and slimy, but I care little. Mud and animal dung are as common in this city as boils and poverty. It must be sometime between two and four in the morning, after the pubs have closed but before the sailors and merchants have begun their day. I love this forgotten period, the time between life. Only those willing to rebel against the norm slither through the streets. It is the only time we are exactly who we seem to be—the misfits, the overlooked, the wicked. Those with dreams too big for the daylight and motives too dark to hide in the afternoon shadow. Good or bad, we are free.

I'll give myself an hour, and then I must be back in bed, pretending I am content with life and grateful for all the world has given me.

My destination for tonight looms, an old wax factory with four massive smokestacks jutting into the sky. It is crammed between a coal refinery and a glue factory. I don't have a key, but I know of a broken window on the second floor.

I approach the stone wall and glance in all directions. No shadows move. No forms appear in the doorways or from behind the chimney tops. I do not fear Ignaz, the evil statdamen haunting the streets of Kietsch, but I can't help looking over my shoulder all the same. Ignaz comes out at night, his long, clawed fingers scraping down the sides of brick walls, looking for a maiden to disembowel. No one knows where he came from. Maybe from Laren's hüle. Maybe from the woods outside Merket. Our omies waste no time filling our bedtime stories with tales of Ignaz and other dark legends when we are old enough to understand their words. I don't believe in demons though. Only in men who behave like them.

Satisfied I am alone, I move to the wall beneath the window. I start to climb but pause when a pebble drops onto my head. I look up and stifle a scream, letting go of the bricks. A pair of feet dangle out of the window above. The person they belong to leans forward, grinning down at me. He drops silently to the ground.

"Who are you?" I ask. He looks to be around my age. His eyes, one dark and one light, sparkle in the light of Azura. Long hair brushes his shoulders. He is dressed in black hosen with a black coat and a black alpine hat. I have never seen him here before.

"Boo," he says in a deep voice. With a smirk, he turns and runs down the street, disappearing into the shadows of an alleyway. I wriggle the fear from my shoulders and move to the wall. He looked innocent enough, probably a street urchin who found a safe place to sleep. If he were Ignaz, my insides would be spilled upon the ground.

I scramble up the wall to the window, flick open the broken lock, pull back the shutters, and stick my head through the opening, wiggling down until my hands touch the dusty wooden floor and I am propped in an awkward handstand. It is not the most graceful way to break into a place, but it works. Once in the hallway, I jog down the rickety stairs to the first floor, conscious that the hour is floating by and I'll have time for only a few therapeutic climbs.

From an old cupboard, I pull out a small oil lamp and strike a match. Carrying the light in one hand, I push open the wooden doors and suck in a deep breath. The air is thick with the smell of sweat, dirt, rope, leather, and faded wax—smells that calm me quicker than a warm bath in winter. My lantern illuminates a cavernous room full of rock walls with various paint colors snaking their way from floor to ceiling. In four corners, the climbing routes snake up and out of sight into the charred and vacant smokestacks. Those routes are the most fun and require a multi-pitch setup, something I don't have time for right now.

I close my eyes and allow the smells to permeate my senses. This is my home now—not my childhood dwelling overlooking the bay in the Westlich, not the women's shelter where I now sleep—this old wax factory converted into a climbing space, these smells, this hard-packed floor that has broken my bones.

A smile returns to my face. I race to my trunk and grab some rope, quickly fashioning a harness. I plunge my hands into the dust sack and rub them together. The dust we use is made from a natural compound the king's scientists mix with oils, powdered rock, and drying agents to help give us traction against the ever-damp routes we must climb. I don't often slip, but because of the dust my hands are usually covered with cracks as deep as Miter's Waste and as dry as the storied deserts of Kobo.

I place the lantern on the floor and take a deep breath. Tying my sling onto a fixed rope slid through a pair of anchors high above, I tap it three times. One can never have too much luck. Then I am up and away, using a solo belay system Ellias developed so we could practice alone. Ellias once told me that self-belay is the purest form of climbing other than free climbing. It forces a person to rely entirely on themselves and their gear. Spiritual, he'd called it, though incredibly dangerous. Perhaps the two are linked.

The light from my lamp illuminates only the lower half of each climb—the rest I do in muted darkness. My brain clears as the aggravated fog dissipates, and I remember I don't need the title of Ascenditure to feel free. My father used to say that the only thing we could control in our lives was our attitude. A familiar sadness rises within me, and I pause to catch my breath, clutching at the fabric covering my heart.

I am now at the top of one of the higher routes, hanging silently in the darkness. From below, I hear the soft scrape of the wooden doors moving against the earthen floor. My breath catches. Footsteps travel to the sphere of light surrounding the lamp and then turn away. Footsteps retreat to the other side of the room and then return. Whoever is in the gym with me now is setting up to climb the adjacent route. Maybe it's that boy. Maybe he is back and not as unthreatening as I'd hoped.

"Who's there?" I deepen my voice to sound like a man. It is mostly Ascenditures who use this gym. However, wealthy Ectarian men have recently taken up the sport of climbing. What used to be an activity reserved for only the most dedicated and skilled has been co-opted by the rich adels. It is not uncommon for the Ascenditures to get a rescue summons to pull some dumtkof off the face of Treiger.

The person does not answer. Instead, the silhouette below grows more distinct as he climbs toward me. I place my feet firmly on the wall and release the rope as I descend. As I pass the other climber, a hand grabs my harness. I am about to chop at the man's wrist with my free hand when I am met with a familiar chuckle.

"Dammit, Kiel." I try to calm my beating heart as I hold the rope steady. "I thought you might be Ignaz."

"Come to steal your stomach, my fram." He smirks and sticks his hands into his dust bag. White powder drifts from his hands as he wipes them together. "You really need to work on your baritone. Woefully unconvincing."

He smiles. I want to smile too, but I am worked up. "Meet you at the bottom?"

We kick off and within seconds my feet touch the solid ground. I return my gear to my trunk and lie on the dirt in the circle of light. Kiel joins me. The lantern flickers between us.

"Couldn't sleep either?" I turn to face him. His eyes are the color of cinnamon, dark with hints of starlight illuminating a field at dawn. Brown hair is cropped close to his head, as you would expect from a member of the royal army. His father is the general of Ectair's northern forces.

"Just finished work at the Rektburg's Nied Tower. I couldn't sleep so I thought I'd get a few climbs in." He rubs a hand across his forehead, then wipes his eyes. "Broken bit of wall I had to rappel down to fix that ended up a nightmare to mend."

"Oh." I raise my brows. "Nied Tower. Did you catch a glimpse of our great leader?"

He chuckles and shakes his head. "Actually, yes. I wasn't trying to pry, but I had to lower past his window. The drapes were open, and he was sitting at the end of his bed."

"Clothed, I hope." I chuckle and feel warmth in my cheeks when he smiles back at me.

"Clothed, yes. But get this. He was holding a painting of a woman in his hands. I've never seen her before, but it definitely wasn't the late queen. She was beautiful. Must be some new secret lover."

"Poor lass." I stick out my tongue and feign a gag. "I'd rather work in the brothels than be the focus of Adolar's affection."

"I don't know," he says. "You'd eat well. Have nice clothes. Get to bathe a bit more often. Maybe it wouldn't be so bad."

"The man despises women, Kiel. I'd guess it more likely he was plotting to kill the woman in the painting than swooning over her beauty."

"Could be."

We are quiet for a minute, and I imagine King Adolar alone in his tower. I pity the woman in the painting. I really do. I pity us all. Digging my fingertips into the dirt floor, I let out a heavy sigh.

"Something else that might interest you." He pokes my shoulder with his finger, and I laugh.

"What?"

"I think Adolar has a black diemant."

"He can't have," I scoff. "The diemants were stolen just before Hildegroth laid waste to the kingdoms. If they ever existed. Without the darken mages, there couldn't be any more."

Kiel shrugs. "All I'm saying is that on the bed next to him was a really large, shiny black stone. What else could it be?"

I roll my eyes and look at the ceiling. The darken mages allegedly forged the black diemants using black magic and river stones. King Miter—the ancient ruler who founded the great kingdom of Galvaith, now split into Ectair and Ainar—supposedly had an extensive collection. They were the basis of his fortune. Of his power. But the darken mages were destroyed long ago, cast back into the sea from whence they had come. Their black magic, if they had ever possessed any, ended with them.

"I'm worried about you." Kiel's tone changes. The easy lilt to his banter vanishes. "We should be celebrating, not climbing in the shadows."

I grit my teeth, preferring talk of myth to chatter about feelings. "Russet is a good climber. He'll be a great asset to the team," I say.

"You don't have to be diplomatic with me, Klarke. Russet's good, but you're better. He could take the next open spot." His finger digs into the dirt floor between us. "You should have beaten me too."

I feel his stare, but I am afraid to meet his gaze. It has an effect on me that I am not yet ready to confront. "I doubt there will be another opening anytime soon. And besides, I will never pray for that opening. I will never hope one of you dies so I can climb." It's the first time I've said it aloud, but the thought has reverberated since they selected Russet over me. Minus Ellias, the team is young. A person must be under twenty-five to be selected. My odds aren't good. "You know as well as I do that in the next few months, I will be pregnant and baking bread for a drunk sailor who is off whoring in Kobo."

He lets out a sigh. His eyebrows draw together. "Maybe it won't be that bad. Maybe they'll give you a good home."

I laugh, a laugh so hollow it makes me feel even emptier. "I live in the tenements, Kiel. My parents are dead. I have no standing. You really think they will marry me off to the son of a businessman? A member of parliament? Grant me my bride-freedom? I have nothing to my name. I'll be lucky if they place me with a drunk sailor. They could always say to hell with me and force me into the brothels."

He scoots closer and takes my hands in his. He bites his lip, and I can almost feel the anguish radiating from his soul. "Marry me, then."

"What?" I jerk my hands back. My heart dives into my feet. I am not certain I heard him correctly.

"Marry me."

I'd laugh again if his expression weren't so earnest.

"I'm serious."

And I know that he is.

"I'm allowed to take a wife. I can save you."

"How romantic." I roll onto my back and wipe my tears before he can see them. "You can save me. Poor, helpless me." "Klarke, stop." His features harden. "I am not calling you weak or saying you need help. As a friend, I am trying to give you an option other than the dark tunnel ahead. I know better than anyone that you need nobody but yourself to survive. But would you seriously rather be married to a stranger than me? Or worse?"

I stare at the ceiling of the old factory, an artificial sky looming high above. Kiel's right. And his offer is more than I could ask for. But I am not asking, and I am not willing to accept a future determined by everyone but myself. It hits me what I must do.

"Kiel, what you are offering is so kind, and the fact that you would throw away a chance at finding love is the nicest thing anyone has ever offered me." I hold up a finger as he tries to interrupt. "But I won't let you chuck your life into Miter's Waste for mine. And I won't let the kingdom take away my life from me. There are still men loyal to my father. Tomorrow I will head to the port and find someone to take me to Kobo. I'll bring Rayna. They don't have the same laws there. Women are free in Kobo. I can have a life."

Sadness fills his eyes. "I don't want you to go. Can I say or do anything that would make you stay?"

My breath catches, and I search for an answer. What would make me stay in a place like this? In a place where I am unwanted? Where I have no hope. Ellias, maybe. But he would understand. Rayna. I would take her with me. Kiel. My stomach tightens, and I imagine a future with him—climbing together, summiting new and uncharted cliff faces, sharing in the glories and triumphs of our sport. But that's not how it would be. I would be home while he was doing those things. I would be his property, even if he wanted to pretend otherwise. I shake my head. "No. At this point, there's nothing for me here."

He nods slowly and swallows hard before standing. I follow him up the stairs, through the window, and into the still night.

We walk down the street in silence. I keep glancing in his direction, but he won't meet my gaze. Kiel just proposed to me. I think. But he didn't mean it. Not in the way someone should mean it. A gull flies overhead, breaking the calm night air with a screech. Behind the trailing caw of the bird, I realize the night is not as still as I'd initially assumed. Light illuminates the surrounding streets and buildings from the center of town where the Rektburg, King Adolar's palace, sits. Voices rise, angry and hostile, screaming and shouting. A low rumble, like a sailor's mourning melody, thrums beneath the commotion. I take one look at Kiel, and we run toward the chaos. We turn a corner. I crash into someone's back, nearly losing my balance.

A horde of people, mostly women, but some men as well, crowd the road as far as I can see. In the distance, the Rektburg looms atop Revolution Hill. It is made up of two main structures and ten imposing towers. The outer structure of the palace is called the Pentengen, with one tower positioned at each of the five corners. Miter's Tower, the point of the Pentengen, extends onto a stone platform visible from Revolution Square. Inside the Pentengen, and separated by courtyards, lies the Geistich, a diamond-shaped fortress surrounded by four towers. The Nied Tower, the location of King Adolar's chambers, rises from the center of it all. The palace is ancient, built by the fabled King Miter a millennium past when slaves filled the granite pits in numbers mirroring flies at a feedlot.

The Rektburg has always looked cold and forbidding to me, a stone relic in our world of wood and iron. Tonight, lights flicker along the parapets and in the small windows of each tower. Guards swarm the steps, their bodies erect, muskets at the ready. A sea of candlelight undulates from the streets of the Southlich to the base of the stone platform and beyond to the east and the north, rhythmically moving to the tune of some muddled chant.

"Scheiz." I cover my eyes and remember the smell of the cheese factory burning in the Eastlich.

Kiel grabs my hand and charges through the crowd. We force the mob out of our way as we head for a better view closer to the hill. The people cheer louder and smile when they see my face. The words from their doleful melody become clear. The voices resonate. My heart splits.

"They're holding down my sister; they're holding down my mother; they're holding down Klarke Ascher; we won't be silent anymore."

I dig in my heels and pull Kiel back.

"What's going on here?" I ask the nearest woman, knowing the answer but hoping I am wrong. She turns a toothless smile at me and points a shaking finger at my chest. A pink piece of twine has been tied in a knot around the sleeve of her shabby dress. Rosy ribbons wind through her braids. An ilice of pink beads drapes around her neck. She lifts it over her plaits and places it around my neck as if I am a holzenschrein to a guardian mountain. "We are here for you."

"No," I whisper. My eyebrows rise and my shoulders drop. Pink ribbons. Pink beads. A song of freedom. These images don't equate to liberation here. They just mean bodies will hang and streets will burn. The cheese factory smolders in my memory. Bodies swing from the gallows seven moons beyond their passage over the darkened sea.

"Excuse me." Kiel taps another woman's shoulder. The woman spins around, scowling. She too has a pink knot of silk tied around her arm and an ilice against her breast.

"It's goatsscheiz, all of it," she spits, pointing accusingly at the Rektburg. She wears pants instead of a dürmel and a blue tunic—rather than the required white to represent she is married and belongs to a man, or green to represent she is single and needs a bride handler. Blue means nothing. Blue means she is whatever she wishes to be. Her hair is chopped close to the scalp. "You should be the climber getting sworn in tomorrow. You should be standing there as a beacon to all the framen of this kingdom, a sign that someday they too can break the chains this kingdom binds to their feet. You deserved to win. And until they make this right, we will not be silent."

She grasps my shoulder and gives a stern nod. "Rosalie, by the way." As the woman before her did, she places her ilice around my neck. "A name helps. More than just a face blending into a crowd. A name gives identity to a person. Humanity. Agency. It is not the faceless behind you, Fram Ascher. The unnamed. The forgotten. You are anything but alone."

I open my mouth to speak but am silenced by gratitude and fear. The surrounding women follow her lead, and soon I am bent by the weight of rosen beads around my neck. The chanting grows louder. I hear my name. It dances from the lips of the soot-covered faces of factory workers from the Southlich. It cascades from the tongues of oily cheese makers from the Eastlich. It even flows from the mouths of women draped in velvet and fur from the Westlich. Most of the beads around my neck are handmade, but some contain pearls from the Crassots harvested from the reefs surrounding the Dor Drillingt islands.

My feet move but not from my direction. I am being ushered toward the palace on a wave of pink water slowly eroding the stone walls of tradition, borne forward on a swell as fierce as the waves in the Rolag Sea during an orkansturm.

Kiel moves beside me, his head high. As much as I want to fight it, as deep as my fear runs, I hazard a smile. The pink knots are everywhere, on the arms of men and women alike. Pink strands woven through hair, pink beads strung around necks.

I've hated that color for so long. It has been a color to demean me—to keep me down. Tonight, we've taken it back. We've redefined it. Dreams of Kobo and its waiting freedom vanish in the din rising from every direction surrounding Revolution Hill.

I was born in Kietsch in the kingdom of Ectair. I'll be here for the rest of my life. I will die here. But before that day comes, I will help to set it free.

A shot rings out somewhere ahead. The blast rattles the rows of glass in the windows and rebounds through the carved eaves, snaking through geometric cutouts and carefully detailed florals. A few in the crowd drop to their knees. Others bellow louder, chasing the boom from the muskets with their reverberating cries of freedom.

"They're holding down my sister, they're holding down my mother, they're holding down Klarke Ascher, we won't be silent anymore. Nevermore, nevermore, nevermore."

Another shot. And then another. Someone screams. Someone shoves me, and I fall to the ground. On my hands and knees, I peer up at the Nied Tower before a woman's tear-streaked face blocks it. I look frantically for Kiel, but he has been swallowed by the wave washing back out to sea. The retreating tide of dissent pulls away from the palace with the force of a greedy moon.

Behind the wall of protestors come the greencoats, a special-forces unit of soldats from the northern brigade. Candles drop to the ground, flimsy flames and squat wicks quickly subdued as protestors scurry into the protective darkness of side alleys and narrow passages. Pink ribbons and rosen beads are quickly cast aside. Cries ring out, louder now than the chants. The greencoats carry muskets. The palace guards assisting them carry clubs. Women fall like children's tears as they try to escape and are hit from behind or shot in the back. Rosalie storms forward, trying to usher an old woman to safety.

"Get her out of here!" she screams, pointing first at me and then at someone behind me. "Get her out of here now!"

Hands pull at me, lifting me from the ground as a man to my right goes down under musket fire. Our eyes meet—his full of fire, mine full of fear. I am dragged away.

"I'll take her."

Kiel shoves his way forward and hooks an arm around my waist. He steers me away from the Rektburg into the streets of the Southlich where I belong, even though I sometimes forget it. We jog in silence as the clamor is swallowed by each street we leave behind. I strip the ilices from my neck and cast them into the shadows, not wanting any part of what they symbolize. Ilices should be used to worship Orna. To submit before Laren. Not for me.

"It's starting," he says, balling his hand into a fist. "Ellias kept saying it would happen soon, but I didn't believe him. This is it, Klarke. This time is different. They've turned you into a lighthouse."

"I don't want to be a lighthouse. I just want to climb."

He stops and spins my body so I am looking into his eyes. Silhouetted behind him, the stone ridgeline of Miter's Backbone rises like jagged fangs toward the stars, making the Rektburg and all of Kietsch look like a city for mites. A single ilice hangs from my neck—the one adorned with pink pearls and blown-glass beads. I kept it for Rayna.

"Fair or not, you don't get to be the person who simply climbs. If you forge ahead, she—whoever she is—some ruddy gal asleep in her bed dreaming of becoming anything other than a brideprize will get to simply climb." He removes his coppola and wipes sweat from his forehead. His cinnamon eyes blaze with the fire that lit the thousands of candles moments ago. "Not you. You've had to weather the storm. Be their lighthouse, Klarke. Scheiz. Did you see them? Did you even see what happened?"

I shake my head and finger the ilice. "I saw people die because of my selfish dream."

"Nide." He points back toward the palace. "You saw people awaken to their dreams because you've dared to follow yours. They didn't go there to die so that you could climb."

I meet his gaze. "So now what?" My hands drop to my side, and all the anger I've felt over my lifetime warps into the blackest fear. "What can I do against thousands of years of convention? Against musket balls and clubs? Pull out my mother's handkerchief from beneath my bunk and wave it in their faces? Because that's all I've got."

He reaches for my wrists, his smile extending into my darkest corners. "At the risk of contradicting myself, climb. Just don't let them stop you. Simply climb. That's all you have to do. That's all you've ever had to do."

3

I hide in the crowd with Rayna, trying to be invisible. The power I felt last night has slipped away. Darkness makes heroes of us all, but daylight always reveals the faces of the vigilantes. Of the cowards.

Wagons loaded with barrels of wine from Kaiwa and gunpowder from Iri clog the streets. The dissent is muted. Except for a few smashed beads and pink bits of ribbon lying in muddy puddles at our feet, the symbols of freedom have vanished.

Someone will have to pay for last night's protest. The piled bodies of the dead on a wooden raft to be sent out and burned at sea are not enough. The king will need to demonstrate his power. I stand helpless in the crowd while someone takes the fall, even though my existence triggered this rockslide.

The crowd stretches well beyond where it marched in the early hours of the morning, diluted by loyal citizens and groups who would never turn against the king. Adels—ladies and gentlemen of higher status—climb delicately from their horse-drawn carriages, staying well away from those of us who smell of sweat and poverty. They strut down a path through the mob lined by armed guards to a special dais near Hadrian's Monastery, elevated above the rest of us. Fur collars line the velveteen dürmels—traditional Ectarian dresses worn by women consisting of tight bodices with low necklines, a blouse beneath, and a high-waisted skirt with an apron. The adels wear soot-free white gloves and strut with their arms looped through the elbows of their bride handlers. I watch their procession, pitying them. They have everything, and yet they are as caged as we who smell of tar and cheese.

No one wants to miss Russet's ceremony, even if they must travel all the way from Amia in the east or Omalau on the southern coast. We are a people who like to know what our heroes look like in the flesh and what our traitors look like swinging from a rope.

Guards form a tight circle around the base of the Rektburg. Others march back and forth through the streets with muskets poised and clubs swinging from their belts. Their tunics are the color of the oakenwood canopy, their hosen the hue of cobblestones. On their heads, shiny metal helmets reflect what little starshine creeps through the cloud cover. Like the Rektburg, these costumed guards are cultural remnants of a long-forgotten time. Nowadays, people are more concerned with how they will feed themselves and what to put on their boils than with what happens within the castle walls.

The greencoats are lined up at attention between the guards and us as if to protect the protectors from the brutes in the crowd. Like the palace guards, they wear the green and gold of our kingdom, but unlike the guards, they also wear thick green coats and are protected by metal breastplates.

In contrast to this sharp show of force, the steps to the mighty palace have been decorated with vases, banners, and fabrics in the ceremonial colors. The streamers might snap proudly in the wind if not saturated by the unending rain. Carved chairs weighing as much as a dock krane have been placed beneath a canvas tent for the judges, parliament, the king, and Prince Otto.

A wooden statue of Laren, our god of the sea and death, stands erect atop the steps next to the largest holzenschrein in all of Ectair, an homage to Orna. Beautiful ilices of intricately blown glass beads, polished shells, and painted seeds adorn the carefully whittled pyramid. We are ruled by two gods in Ectair. Two gods and one man who acts as if he were such.

Behind Orna's holzenschrein stand three päters. Per tradition, no skin is visible beneath their dark robes and draping hoods. Carved wooden masks painted white depict a generic man's face. Expressionless. Pale. One päter carries an ornate box that holds the golden silenote Russet will present during the ceremony. One clasps a copper bowl full of smoking herbs and incense. The third raises a crystal pitcher full of heilvater collected from the sky and blessed inside the walls of the monastery.

Three empty nooses swing from gallows erected to the left of the palace. I close my eyes. Dark clouds grumble above. A light rain falls. Overhead, a flock of gulls squawk and cry out as they fly from the sea to the dump on the outskirts of Kietsch.

Nobody flinches or reaches for a coat, not even the high-class women in their flowing, soot-free dresses. We're used to sodden boots and dripping foreheads. It could always be worse. We could have been born in Ainar to the north, where the rain falling from the sky is frozen, and the people resort to cannibalism to survive the worst of the winters. Not for the first time, I am glad Miter's Waste, the fifty-mile-wide ravine of wasteland dividing Ectair from Ainar, was sealed off and travel and trade to Ainar suspended.

An alpenhorn sounds. All faces turn toward the palace. Ladies on the dais raise pearl-handled binoculars to their eyes. Men in the crowd lift their children onto their shoulders. I strain on tiptoes to watch the procession. First, the three judges wearing the same long green robes they'd worn on competition day stride forward, waving jovially as they take their seats. Following them are the nine members of parliament representing the nine kreisons of Ectair, their sets of green robes distinguished by gold inlay depicting the kingdom's insignia: two knots, one representing our sailors and the other our climbers, intertwined around a ship's mast. Surrounded on three sides by ocean and connected west to east by the mighty Sevier River, Ectarians are a water people, a boat people. My father's face floats across my thoughts.

A trumpet blares, and a drum beats. Mumbles and murmurs from the crowd add to the percussion, heralding in our leader. King Adolar emerges from behind the palace doors and steps forward with a smile too big for the occasion. He is tall and strong, with dark hair like the rest of us and a matching beard highlighted with red. He too wears green robes with the golden seal of Ectair, but the gold is also sewn around the lower hem and the ends of his sleeves. Even though it is not cold, a thick white fur drapes around his neck—another sign of power as it came from an animal in the forbidden lands north of the Waste. The emeralds in his crown must weigh thirty pounds alone. I wonder how he holds his head so high. Polite clapping from the dais and from the men in the crowd fills Revolution Square. The arms of the women around me hang at their sides.

Behind the king, Prince Otto moves forward in a matching robe but without the fur and gilded crown. Tall and muscled like his father, he is the cause of swooning and useless day-dreams of many of the kingdom's young women. He waves a hand and offers a more modest smile before taking a seat next to his father.

Missing from this procession is Queen Eleonora, who was taken from this world many years ago by Death's Whisper, shortly before my own parents' deaths. I have a memory of my mother sobbing on the day our queen died; of my father holding her as tears spilled from his eyes as well; of frantic con-versations in the cellar and forlorn glances cast in my direction. A blanket of hopelessness draped over the dinner. Based on those recollections, I assume the queen must have been a great woman. I wonder how different our world would be if she were still alive today.

The Ascenditures appear on stage next, with Ellias in the front, followed by Aedan, Gio, Burkhart, Feiko, Dieter, Tiz-ian, Kiel, and then Russet, who stops at the top of the steps between Laren's statue and the holzenschrein and faces the onlookers. Many in the crowd cheer, shout, and fervently clap. Some remain stoic. Boos and jeers also rise around me. I join the celebrators, even though this is a sad day. It is not Russet's fault. The fight can begin again tomorrow.

King Adolar rises to his feet, lifting a hand for all to be si-lent. He moves beside Russet to the center of the decorated platform. At a nod from the king, guards drag three people, all women, to the front. Rosalie's short hair and pants are unmistakable. Someone has thrown white paint across her blue tunic. She glares at the guards grasping her arms. My heart clenches. I reach for Rayna's hand. She squeezes back with trembling fingers.

"Geitsê, my kingdom. Last night, a disturbance broke out before these steps. A crowd of treasonous souls came together against *our* kingdom. We are all one, and an attack on any of us is an attack on all. I will not let such harm come to you, my people. I will protect you from these traitors. I will always protect the kingdom above all else. It saddens me greatly as your king that a few bad seeds have tainted what was supposed to be a joyous occasion."

He puts a green and gold shrouded arm around Russet's shoulders. Russet's face has turned from pale to red. A hiss issues from some of the people around me. Soon it sounds like a swarm of bees has invaded the square.

"Yes! Shame on them," the king says, twisting the moment in his favor. He motions for the guards to take the three women to the gallows. Only now do I realize the ropes hanging from them have been painted pink.

All have fallen silent. Only the rain dares to speak.

"I have eyes and ears everywhere," the king intones. "I will hang someone every day if need be. Let this be a warning to the vermin in the crowd."

I stand far enough from the gallows that I cannot make out the exact words of the women. I see their mouths move angrily. Their hands are bound behind their backs as the sickeningly pink ropes are slid around their necks. All noise has been sucked from the square except for the gentle patter of rain on heads and cobblestones. I focus on Rosalie's face and force myself to watch. The alpenhorn, that stupid, awful horn, blares, shattering the quiet and sending shards of pain through my system.

A guard pulls the lever. A horrible *thunk* follows as the floor disappears beneath the women. One woman's neck snaps. Rosalie and another writhe and kick out their legs. Rayna trembles and whimpers next to me. I grow dizzy but don't turn away.

Finally, it ends. The bodies sway back and forth like three pendulums in a clock that refuses to stop keeping time even though the world has ended. I watch in horror as Rosalie bumps into the woman next to her. Arms that only a few hours ago directed protestors to safety now hang by her sides as limp and lifeless as the soaked banners surrounding the palace.

A woman beside me pulls down the sleeve of her white blouse to cover the pink ribbon braided around her wrist. Another leans forward and vomits. The hiss in the crowd rises again, but it is softer. Beside me, Rayna lets out a small sob. I squeeze her hand, warning her against further displays of outward emotion.

To my left, a man sidles closer. A frayed cloak covers his head and drags in the street muck. His eyes are homed in on my face. Green streaks jut from his pupils to the edges of his eyeballs like tiny rays of starshine. He is on drugs. Veisel. A dangerous drug at that.

Someone jostles forward, knocking the man to the ground. I take a few steps back, shielding myself and Rayna from his view. For a while, veisel could only be found in Kietsch, brought here from Ainar by smugglers or made in the veisel dens in the slums near the tar factories. Over time, it has spread across Ectair and infected all leiten cities and their wards. If pulmonosis doesn't kill you in Ectair, veisel surely will.

I shift my gaze back to Rosalie. I repeat her name over and over in my head. A name gives identity to a person. Humanity. Agency. I will never let her name slip from my mind.

Rosalie.

The king moves to the row of päters, taking the box from the first. He returns to Russet's side and pulls the silenote, a piece of climbing rope embalmed in gold leaf, from its vessel. He begins to speak, but I cannot hear his words over the mixture of sobs and cheers from my fellow citizens. It doesn't matter. I know what he says and what he holds. In a few seconds, after King Adolar shares the honor he is about to bestow, Russet will take the object and recite his vows.

Russet grabs the rope and lifts it into the air. His hand sways like the vacant bodies on the gallows. His mouth moves as he delivers from memory the oath that should be on my lips.

"This rope is a symbol of strength and courage. Bestowed upon me by a great king, it embodies the trust he has in me to be a hero for this kingdom and a loyal servant to the crown. By holding the golden rope in front of you today, I accept the responsibility, danger, and honor of an Ascenditure.

"I will never falter or show weakness. If injured or saddened by the loss of a teammate, I will get back up and continue the climb. My kingdom expects me to be physically and mentally stronger than the rest of its citizens. When I feel that strength has left me and my muscles can climb no higher, I will remind myself that weakness is for the cowards in Ainar and that an Ascenditure never runs out of stamina.

"We expect greatness and demand nothing less. The success of our climbs and the lives of our fellow Ascenditures rely on my skill, strength, and fortitude. If I fail, we fail, and if we fail, then I fail.

"I am an Ascenditure now. I will persevere in honoring those who have fallen before me, fighting against those who wish us harm, and above all, serving my benevolent king.

"I will not fall. I will not fail. I will not betray my kingdom."

I finish whispering the words just as Russet's lips stop moving. Ellias steps forward and pins the small knotal insignia of the Ascenditures on Russet's chest, finalizing the ceremony. The adels on their viewing platform cheer and clap, but around me a sea of discontent swells. It is a small wave hidden beneath white sleeves and ankle-length skirts. Simmering beneath stoic expressions and vacant eyes. I wonder if the king can see the tsunami building.

"Coward!" someone shouts. It is met by a cry of "pathetic!" and one of "spineless!"

I shrink in on myself. Why can't they just leave it alone?

King Adolar scans the crowd with a look of disgust. He leans over to Ellias. My mentor's eyes grow large. When the king backs away, Ellias raises his hands and motions the crowd to be silent. A hush falls. Everyone in this kingdom respects Ellias Veber.

King Adolar clears his throat. "Congratulations, Russet Kamber, on your new appointment." The king rests a hand on Ellias's shoulder. "Before we all go, I have one more announcement to make. While Hannar Kamber was clearly the best man for the job, I have decided there was another climber who shows potential."

Ellias's mouth hangs slightly open. I wonder if my expression matches my mentor's. King Adolar can't be daft enough to select a second male teammate in front of this mutinous group. But I can't fathom the other option.

"After discussion with Hannar Veber…"

At this, Ellias cocks his head to the side, and I know from his body language that no such conversation ever occurred.

"…I have decided that talent, even in the most unlikely places, can be rewarded."

The blood leaves my extremities. I am afraid I might fall to the ground, giving credence to the suggestion of inferiority leaving his mouth. This time it is Rayna who provides the warning hand squeeze.

"Friends and countrymen," he continues. "Please join me in welcoming Klarke Ascher as a guest climber on the next ascent up Fitzhan to the Celebern Fields. It's time we move forward in this kingdom, and I am proud to be the one to take that step."

The crowd parts around me as if they have just discovered I am sick with the plague.

"Please, Hannar Veber." The king sweeps his hand out to where I stand. "Do me the honor of retrieving our guest."

I swallow. The heads in the crowd sway as people step back, opening a path for Ellias to walk. Rayna wraps her arm around my waist and leans her head against my shoulder.

"I will pray for you," she whispers, squeezing my side. "Stand tall, Klarke."

I straighten my back. A cold hand clasps around my elbow.

Whirling around, I come to face the cloaked man with green-streaked eyes.

"You were meant for the sea," he hisses. "You were supposed to go to the sea."

I pull my arm away. Bruises cover the man's cheek and snake their way down his neck. He smells of sweat and kimmeron and something fetid.

"The sea," he wails. "Ash and wave. She should not be here."

"Get him out of here." Ellias reaches me and points over my shoulder to someone in the crowd. "Hurry. Take him to the docks."

It is as if the world moves in slow motion. I watch a drop of rain crawl from the sky until it thuds in a leisurely splash against the cobbles at my feet. Someone tackles my heckler and drags him away. Claps and cheers reach my ears. Hollers and taunts. My name. *Klarke*, they shout. The square fills with diametrically opposing forces of support and ridicule. My gaze never breaks from my mentor's.

"What?" I reach out my hands and grab his. I stare into his eyes. "What's happening?"

Ellias smiles and waves at those nearest to us. He pulls me into a deep hug. "Not here. Show them your strength, Klarkey. That's all."

He places a hand between my shoulders, and we move. Someone throws a pink ilice at my feet. Another spits on the sleeve of my blouse. Remembering Rayna's words, I straighten, trying to exude the confidence Ellias recommended.

"Go back to the hearth, woman!"

"Give 'em hüle, Klarke!"

"Ye shouldn't be here. This is madness!"

"Tanks, ye. Tanks, ye."

Trembling legs somehow carry me to the platform. King Adolar grabs my hand and lifts it into the air as the assemblage erupts in shouts and celebration. This stunt, while hollow, seems to have worked for some. I turn to Ellias, who casts me a warning look before cracking the largest smile I've ever seen him give. I know what thoughts lurk behind his familiar eyes.

"Something rotten lies beneath the water, Klarke," he would tell me if he could.

With a deep, slow breath, I wave and bow to the onlookers and to my king, knowing I have just become a pawn in a treacherous game.

"Rosalie," I whisper under my breath.

King Adolar turns to me and narrows his eyes. "What did you say?"

I bow my head. "My king."

4

I'd like to think my physical abilities and fortitude put me on the team today, heading upward toward Miter's Backbone to make history. But it is nothing more than a political stunt to make the king look magnanimous. I am just glad Ellias is here. My demeanor might appear to be steel, but it is mere parchment.

The horse-drawn coach stops at the base of the first pitch, the end of the road for anyone who can't maneuver up the fel by their own power. We jostle as the carriage comes to a halt. The horses whinny and stomp their hooves. I step out through the flapping canvas. Sheer cliff faces dominate my immediate view. Soaring over where I now stand is Miter's Backbone, a granodiorite ridge of seven jagged peaks and steep climbs.

Today we will summit Fitzhan, our guardian mountain. If I ever make the team, I will have the opportunity also to climb the curved and steep pinnacle of Hansba and the rocky thumb beneath it, Hansdaum, which lie to my right. To my left stand Treiger, Vilmer, Beck's Ridge, Shiendoff, and Kara Do. All pinnacles I yearn to reach. I grab my gear, shoulder my rope and haulbag, and place my straw hat onto my head. My nerves quake.

Lying at the feet of Fitzhan and Treiger, the muted blue waters of Lake Eisenturks stretch out like a mirror for the sky. Large boulders, loose rock, and glacial dust cascade in a sloped moraine stretching from where the rock towers jut from the earth to the edge of the cerulean water.

"Beautiful day for an ascent." Ellias smiles at me with his endearingly crooked smile. His bald head glistens with the softly falling raindrops. I return the grin. Staring up at the dark clouds, I reach into my pack for wire-rimmed goggles. It will rain on us even harder than it already has. Kingdoms like Kobo count inches of rain and cheer when they have enough to grow food. We count days of light and cheer when we have enough to burn our pale skin for a few days each year. The only reliably bright place in this land is the Celebern Fields—an elusive location two thousand feet above us at the summit of Fitzhan.

A chill hangs in the air today, the first hint of vintazite approaching. Once the rain turns to ice and snow, the Ascenditures will no longer make the climb to the Celebern Fields.

The Ascenditures climb for three reasons. The first is to assist in various jobs that require laborers who can climb and rappel to do things such as masonry work on bridges and towers and window cleaning in factories. The second is to retrieve the king's sacred food item—the bright orange root called a solan that grows only in the fertile soil of Celebern Fields. Only the royal family and the adel friends they deem worthy are allowed to consume the tubers. Even the climbers risking their lives are not allowed a bite. The third and most important task for the Ascenditures is to collect pollen from the ulrind flower. The soft pink powder is the only substance that can ease the symptoms of pulmonosis, the painful and slow disease that claims most men and women working in the factories. As with the solan tuber, the ulrind flower grows only in the meadows at the summit of Fitzhan, several thousand vertical feet above the city.

"Gather 'round, crew." Ellias's joints crack as he squats and rests a canvas map over one knee. "While the solans and ulrind powder are a top priority, as always, we have an important, historical task to accomplish and also a new teammate to welcome."

He winks at me. I stand tall, trying to feign bravery and strength.

"Today, Russet joins us for his inaugural climb. Congratulations, Russet. We are proud to have you on the team."

I smile and give three loud claps. It hurts always having to balance happiness for another with my sorrow.

"Neuba!" Gio Vinzenz shouts, then lets out a high-pitched whistle. Even though the term signifies a new climber who doesn't know what they are doing, we all know Gio is just having some good-natured fun.

Everyone claps and chuckles as Aedan Pfaller, the second oldest climber, pats Russet on the shoulder. Aedan's long, dreadlocked hair is pulled back with a dark ribbon. His skin has leathered from so much time on the rock. He is the only team member with children, which might contribute to his compassionate and patient demeanor.

Ellias joins in the celebration before raising a hand to silence the group. "Today is important for another reason." He pivots to face Tizian Crites, the one member of the team who is not dressed for the ascent. "I want to thank Tizian for agreeing to sit this one out so our guest climber could have her day."

Tizian's eyes narrow. They flash to me before quickly returning to the ground. He didn't volunteer to sit out. It's no secret some team members sympathize with the kingdom's subjugation of women. My guess is Tizian was the loudest dissenter. This is Ellias's way of setting a standard. Luckily, Tizian's respect for Ellias outweighs his contempt for me.

"I'd feel better with Tiz on the rope." Burkhart Craddus fashions his harness from a loop of sisal cord. He doesn't look up. Scars cover his face and arms. His dark hair is pulled into a tight knot at the back of his head. "Bad luck to have a woman on the fel. Orna won't like it."

"Orna's a woman, you arsch," Kiel snaps back. He loops a few slings across his shoulder and hooks his haulbag to his harness with a bolt and pin karabiner.

I am both flattered and annoyed at his move to defend me.

"She is probably wondering what took us so long," Kiel adds, looping his dust bag through a woven belt.

"She's probably wonderin' why Klarke is suddenly too good to be at home." Tizian breaks his silence. "Probably wonderin' what makes Klarke and all a ye' think you know better than tradition." He spits on the ground and turns away from us. "I didn't agree to scheiz. I think we're all going to pay for this somehow."

"Come on, guys." Feiko Cremlin moves next to me and rests a hand on my shoulder. "What can it hurt? Klarke's worked hard, and she is a strong climber. I think Orna has better things to focus on."

"Yeah, like setting us straight for breaking the natural order." Burkhart throws his pack over his shoulder and begins draping slings across his body. "Something's starting in this kingdom, and it ain't good. I feel it in my core. Tanks to this lass I'll be watching my back. You should too, Feiko."

"Enough." The fire flares in Ellias's eyes. "This order came from the king. You will all respect it."

My cheeks burn. I keep my eyes trained on a moss-covered stone by Russet's feet. Even this family I so badly want to be part of is fractured. This is the greatest day of my life, and yet it is soured.

Ellias lifts the map again and sets clear intention with his tone. "Klarke will make the first female climb to the fields, and we need to make sure she gets there. This is a big step forward for the kingdom and for us as Ascenditures. People look up to us—believe we occupy high moral ground. We will live up to that. I won't tolerate another word about whether or not you think a woman should be on the fel today or ever. This is my team, and if you don't like my rules, you can turn in your ropes when we get back to Kietsch."

No one speaks. I hold my breath and risk a glance at the others. Burkhart and Tizian both eye me with hatred. Kiel winks. Russet gives a nervous smile. Feiko, Dieter, and Gio's eyes are trained on the map in Ellias's hands.

Ellias is making his five-hundredth ascent of Fitzhan today. He implies that today is about Russet and me, but I find it hard to believe that our fumbling up a cliff is more significant than someone summiting the second most dangerous peak in Ectair for the five-hundredth time. He has also summited the deadliest peak, Mount Bonen on the Umlauf peninsula, more than any climber in history. His grandfather, Lars Veber, was the first to summit all seven peaks of Miter's Backbone and Mount Bonen.

Ellias says he also led the first team up Mount Opasno and Himmelisle in Ainar to the north. We know Lars Veber as the father of modern climbing, which means all of us are in the presence of Ascenditure royalty this morning.

"We'll take the Disillusion Route," Ellias says.

I follow the line his finger traces on the map.

"Klarke and Russet, you'll be lead climbing for your teams. Show us what ya got. Prove you deserve to be here. You too, Kiel. You'll lead kletshot three."

Russet and I give each other a quick smile and a nervous laugh. Kiel shrugs as if it is no big deal.

The other climbers secure their quad-looped ropes around their chests. I follow suit. I try to look confident as I straighten my ankle-length skirt and tie my haulbag to my harness. The thing is nearly as big as I am, and I wonder how I will carry it loaded with solans down a quarter-mile rappel. Draping a handful of slings across my shoulders, I clip a bundle of karabiners to a rope belt around my waist. I will need the slings and biners to lead this route.

I've trained for years now, competed for a spot on the team for almost as long. But climbing in the old factory is different from having nothing but a sisal rope, chest harness, and several hundred feet of air between you and the Sevier River far below. I must look up. Today is my first official climb—a woman's first official climb. I cannot fail.

"Three teams of three, line up." Ellias hands a rope to Kiel, the lead climber of kletshot three. Behind him are Gio and Aedan. "Feiko and Burkhart, line up behind Russet on kletshot two. Dieter, take middle on my rope. And, Klarke, make sure kletshot one makes it to the top."

I turn red from the pressure. I know I can do this. I lead climb at Vether's and at the gym all the time. Suddenly, I don't know what to do with a sling. Or how to thread the rope through a karabiner. Kiel meets my eyes and flashes a smile. The three of us in the lead will place protection in the rock and set up the rope for the rest of the team to climb. The Ascenditures in the rear of each kletshot also carry a rope for emergencies. Fitzhan is divided into a series of ledges. I will lead to each ledge, belayed by Dieter on the shelf of rock below me.

Just like the gym, I tell myself. Just like Vether's.

Ellias walks to the front of the line where I stand. He places a calloused hand on my shoulder. "I am proud of you, Klarke. This moment, right here, is my proudest moment ever."

I lean in for a hug. The rope coiled around his chest scratches my cheek. His long beard tickles my nose. "What if I fall? What if I can't do it?"

Ellias throws his head back and laughs. It echoes through the jagged folds of dark rock and skips across the lake like a smooth stone. "Klarke, you are braver than most. And if you fall…" He tugs at my harness. "This will catch you, as it always does. And here's another little secret." He leans in to whisper in my ear. "I'm scared too. Every time I wonder if this will be it. But that's the best part. We have the greatest job. We wake up every day, living life to the fullest. Understanding more than anyone how precious each breath is."

He brushes a loose strand of dark hair behind my ear, pulls his flat cap from his back pocket, and straightens it on his scalp. "Head up, darling. Always head up, for that is the direction in which the mountain grows."

I smile at his favorite saying and lift my chin skyward. The summit is up there somewhere. It beckons to me.

Ellias pats my shoulder and then walks to the back of the line. "Siec moldon." He motions toward one of the waiting coaches. The door opens, and a solitary päter steps out. Dressed in his long black robe and expressionless white mask, he carries a ceremonial pewter bowl. The rim of this bowl is shaped into patterns of undulating and jagged metal, mimicking the waves of the sea. A twisting stem in the shape of a metallic tentacle reaches from the base of the vessel to the basin of the bowl. Looking like giant wine goblets, Laren grails like this are used in ceremonial practices to carry objects blessed by the päters.

Inside the grail rest nine small balls wrapped in fabric. The päter hands each of us one of the spheres, uttering the words "May Orna and Laren be with you," as he places them in our open palms. I close my fingers around the bundle and tuck it into my pocket. I won't need it until I reach the summit.

"For glory, kingdom, and the wench waiting for me in the Krieg's Mast." Feiko lets out a series of hoots and hollers, cheered on by the rest of the team.

Gio taps his chest two times with an open palm, then raises it by his side, as soldats in the military would do. "For honor, valor, and Burkhart's mother."

The others laugh. Burkhart sneers and throws a small stone at Gio. I feel as though I am standing on the other side of the river from them all, unable to safely cross.

"To Klarke," Ellias shouts. "To Russet. To King Adolar."

"Here, here," Kiel, Aedan, and Dieter say.

Burkhart snorts.

"Take us to the firmament, leads." Ellias taps the sling on his harness three times. "Take us to the sky. And remember rope management is key."

I copy Ellias's gesture, tap my sling three times, and then stick my hands into the dust bag. Stepping forward, I grasp the slick rock and turn to Dieter. "Klettag."

"Klettag und," he responds. He has the rope set up for a standard belay. "Don't let the felfee find you."

The felfee, or rock fairies, are treacherous little imps who live on cliff faces and delight themselves by breaking holds just as a climber finds a grip. As long as one has an anchor in place, the felfee damage is minimal. A few scrapes, bruises, and abrasions. Occasionally a concussion if you let the rope get behind your leg and end up upside down when you fall. But if the felfee break one's hold before they have placed their first sling…

I free climb fifteen feet to an iron bolt in the rock and pull one of the slings from my shoulder. Threading it through the bolt, I then pull a length of the main rope up and secure it to the sling with a bolt and pin karabiner. My first line of safety is in place.

I lift my leg, finding a small groove to place my boot. My toe gets hooked in the fabric of my skirt, but I kick it away. What a pain in the arsch. One leg up, then another. My hands search for crevices in the rock and years of training soothe panic. I don't even have to think. Up I go, like a spider on a wall.

Rain begins to fall, slickening the already dicey holds. Droplets bead down my hat brim on their way to Lake Eisenturks.

There are a few iron bolts permanently secured in the rock, but most of the spots where I place protection are ones I have to decide upon. Just below the first ledge, I come across a hole in an arête and loop a sling through. Once again I pull up a length of rope and clip it in. Dieter has done a good job feeding me slack, so I don't have to waste energy tugging on the rope.

A few more feet and rock shelf number one appears above me. Stretching my right leg up, I hook my heel onto the ledge, bear down with my fingers, and thrust my body upward with a grunt. I secure the rope through a pair of iron bolts at the base of the next pitch and unclip from belay. This will allow Dieter to top rope, which is safer and easier than what I just did.

Kiel reaches the ledge ten meters to my right about a minute later. Russet joins us shortly after. I give them each a knowing grin and a wink.

"Yeah, yeah, yeah." Kiel fixes his rope to the pair of bolts at the top of his route. "Wipe that smirk off your face. We know you're the best."

I toss my hands in the air in mock surrender. "I said nothing of the sort."

"Your smile speaks for you." Russet laughs and takes a sip of water from his canteen. "Maybe someday I'll beat you on a climb."

"Only if the felfee find me." It feels good to be on the rock. Despite the rain. Despite Burkhart and Tizian wishing I would vanish. I am in my element, and I am showing I deserve to be here.

Dieter, Feiko, and Gio reach the ledges next. They take over the second belay and switch their gear to assist from above instead of below. Ellias, Aedan, and Burkhart eventually haul themselves up.

"Glad to see everyone alive and well." Ellias pulls the rope through the top anchors and piles it neatly at the base of the next pitch for me to climb with.

"How're you holding up, Russet?" Aedan nudges the newest recruit and chuckles.

"Nursing my pride as Klarke yet again beat me to the top, but otherwise fantish."

I smile appreciatively at Russet. He doesn't have to do this, take every opportunity to let the others know how good I am. And yet he does.

"Just wait." Gio adjusts his haulbag and untwists a pair of slings on his chest. "I reckon twenty years from now, this whole team will be women, and us blokes will be down at the docks prayin' someone will pay us for a good time."

Feiko fakes a gag and rubs his stomach. "I wouldn't pay scheiz for you, Gio. You'd have to pay me to take those hosen off."

We laugh, except for Burkhart, and all drink from our leather canteens. It amazes me I still need water to survive when my skin receives so much of it from the sky. I am surprised Ectarians haven't evolved like our forests—that we aren't covered in algae and gleaning our food from Cleos's rays. I bet in a thousand years, my great, great, however many times, grandchildren will have sprouted roots, and their hair will have turned green. I wonder if women will be equal to men by then.

Ellias stands and the rest of us follow. I stretch my arms, hoping they will last. I reach the next few rock shelves without issue and continue the climb. The rain pours harder, and the clouds thicken, but I am in a rhythm now. The moisture feels good in my lungs and on the fabric clinging to my arms. I am the moss on the rock, growing slowly up the mountain.

I reach the final ledge, grunting as I haul myself over. My arms shake and my shoulders beg for a break. The air is cool. My breath comes in heavy gasps as if I've been running. Dizziness rattles around my brain, and I put my head between my legs after I've secured the rope through the double anchors.

"It's exhausting your first time, climbing for so long. Much harder than the smokestacks even." Kiel laughs and offers me a biscuit. "Actually, it's always exhausting."

"No way." I turn my head from the bread, nauseated. "Food sounds awful."

Ellias sits by us. He pats my knee and pulls a slab of salted mutton and a small, bruised apple from his pack. "You're doing fantish. And you're almost there. It might help to eat something, though."

The sight and smell of the mutton make me ill. I breathe deeply through my nose and open my pack to find something to force down.

Kiel hands the biscuit over once more, and I take a reluctant bite.

"They don't really prepare you for this piece. The 'climb so high your body aches and lungs scream' part." I sit back. Rain pummels everything in its soggy path.

"Hah!" Ellias lets out a raucous laugh. "By 'they' you mean me? I couldn't give everything away, now could I?"

"Just wait until *they* send you up Mount Bonen." Aedan tosses a nut into the air and catches it in his mouth, grinning as he chews. "Then you'll really understand exhaustion exacerbated by no air."

"You could always stay home." Burkhart shrugs and rips a chunk of stag jerky with his teeth. "Plenty of air in Kietsch."

"Burkhart." Ellias snaps and glares at his teammate. "I won't hear it again from you."

I worry the biscuit in my hands. Little pieces crumble and fall into my lap. I try to shake away Burkhart's comment, but every time someone says something like that, it coats my insides like creosote inside of a chimney.

But creosote is dangerous and flammable, and so am I. Let it build.

Dieter walks over and prepares himself for the final belay.

He is a man of few words. I've never gotten the feeling he dislikes me. He is just quiet; that, or he dislikes us all equally. I brush off Burkhart's sentiment and stand. Tying a figure eight, I thread the rope through my harness and loop it back through the knot.

Dieter's eyes are dark and narrow. He is short and stocky, built like an ox. His skin is tanned. Like Rayna, his traits identify him as having blood from Ainar. Climbing keeps Dieter safe and out of the labor camps.

"One more push," he says.

"A hundred more feet, and you will see the most spectacular sight in all of Ectair." Ellias glances over Dieter's protection and my knots. He gives us an approving nod. "Even the starshine days below can't compare to the brilliance of the Celebern Fields."

I've seen paintings and heard stories, but I still can't get over the fact that I will be there soon. I imagine the color most of all. Up there, they say, are colors I didn't even know existed.

I stand, shaking the chills and fatigue from my limbs. Excitement has overtaken fear and discomfort. I will be the first female ever to make the climb. I will become part of the elite few to lay eyes on the treasure of Ectair. A squeal erupts from my mouth. I slap a hand across my lips.

Burkhart scowls. The others laugh.

"What a girl." Gio smirks and winks at me.

I throw a soft punch into his arm. He blocks it and spins away, pretending to teeter on the edge of the cliff.

Leaving him with his joke, I head to the wall. A narrow crack rises from this ledge, winding its way to the top. A different technique will be required to reach the summit, one that often removes bits of flesh from my hands. To avoid abrasions, I withdraw a few strips of linen from my pocket and wrap them through my fingers, around my knuckles, and down to my wrists. "Klettag," I say over my shoulder to Dieter.

"Klettag und," Dieter replies. "See you up there."

I twist my boot and jam my right toe into the crack. I wedge my fingers inside and constrict my hand. Straightening my leg, I stuff my left toe into the gap above my right and lift up. The crack requires a series of hand and foot jams. Sometimes my entire fist fits into the space. Sometimes just the tips of my fingers. About twenty feet up, I find a narrow place in the fracture to wedge a knotted sling. This device makes me nervous, as a constriction in the rock is the only thing keeping it in place. I clip a biner to the sling and pull up the slack of the main rope, making sure not to back-clip as I slide it through. Back-clipping is dangerous because the rope could pop out of the karabiner if I fall.

The wind gathers a new ferocity, and the rain pelts harder. Little wet daggers slash at my face and neck. I keep stuffing my hands into the dust bag. The linen wraps have soaked through, but the dust gives me some friction against the rock. Luckily, the dust we use repels water, so the rain does not ruin it.

I reach a small overhang and pause to catch my breath. I can tell from below that this is the crux move of the entire climb. The hardest effort I will have to make. I glance above to determine how to maneuver past the outcropping. The next iron bolt is over the ledge. If I slip up on this one before I reach it and secure a sling, I have a long way to fall.

A few small holds poke from the arête at my side, offering a second route option. The main crack continues onto a small ledge four or so feet above. If I can get onto the ledge, I will have a solid place to rest. I choose the crack.

Stuffing my right hand into the space, I create a fist jam and move my left toe out of the crack. As I try to wedge it into the rock above my other boot, the wet skirt hem gets in the way. My right foot slips. Both feet slide from the crack. I scream as the pressure on my fist grows with the weight of my entire body and gear. The linen slides out of place and my hand slips forward. Skin peels from my knuckles and joints. The pressure from my hand holds me in place, but I dangle fifteen feet above the last bolt. If I let go, I will have a thirty-foot fall.

Groaning, I lift my right foot, turn it sideways, jam the toe into the crack, and rotate it. The placement holds. I take a deep, shaky breath and put pressure on my leg. My left hand fits into the crack. I pull out my right but don't survey the damage. It goes back into the crack above the left hand. Legs, arms, slings, and rope. Those are my only points of focus.

Too many people expect me to fail. Too many people are counting on me. I picture the faces in the crowd as I hoisted myself into the carriage this morning.

Beaming. Proud.

Angry. Appalled.

Rosalie.

Brushing the skirt slip aside, I scan above. Streaks of light pop through the clouds. I must be close. I find my rhythm again, press on my foot, and turn my knee inward and down. Twisting my body from the dropped knee toward the other foot, I reach with my arms and move up the overhang. My legs quake and my shoulders burn. I keep my body as close to the wall as I can. With a grunt, I pass the overhang. My head bursts through the mist. Above me lies twenty feet of rock. Kiel's face beams down from the top with the rays from Cleos. Warm air hits me in a disorienting blast.

I climb faster, pausing on my hands and knees after pulling myself over the final edge. I lock eyes with Kiel. Tears brim at my eyes. I run to him and sob into his shoulder, not caring anymore about being tough. He kisses the top of my head, and I compose myself before the others can see. Russet reaches the summit next, gives me a nod, and the three of us set up the final anchors.

"You were brilliant." Kiel beams at me and begins removing his gear.

I untie my harness and pull the slings from my body. My arms and shoulders throb. "I almost got myself into trouble about halfway up. Foot slipped on this stupid skirt."

"Happened to me too." Russet drops his haulbag and gingerly removes the linen from his fingers. "Tore the scheiz out of my left hand, and I'm wearing hosen."

I peer down at the fabric covering my knuckles. Small patches of muddy blood soak through. I undo the strips and take stock of my hand. Three knuckles have been torn open, but just the upper layer of skin is missing. A raw spot oozes at the base of my thumb. I've had worse. It'll heal within fourteen moons if I don't reopen them. Hard to do when you're a climber.

Gio makes it up next. Dieter and Feiko climb over the ledge at the same time. Again, they set up their belay systems to assist the three remaining climbers below us. Ellias reaches the summit. His face beams as he pushes himself up—his dark eyes full of pride, the laugh lines at the corners of his lips turned upward.

He wraps me in one of his bear-like hugs. After a moment, he holds me at arm's length. "I am so proud of you."

"I couldn't have done this without you." Gratitude wells inside me. I wipe at the tears before they can break. "Tanks ye, Ellias."

"Your dad would be over the oar right now if he could see this." His eyes sparkle. "Are you ready?"

Of course I am ready. Even if it is just this once, even if this whole thing is a stunt to calm the unrest plaguing Ectair, at least for today I am an Ascenditure, and I've earned a little starlight.

We walk around the blokkenshon, the giant boulder at the top of the pitch that blocks our view of the meadow. I gasp. We learn from a young age that the Celebern Fields were where all life began, even the lives of our gods. I stare at acres of grass as high as my waist waving in the warm breeze. On the far edge of the field, trees of every shape and size form a complex forest. Scattered throughout the grass and on all sides of the mountaintop, tall flowers boast deep reds and warm lavenders. Yellow daisies, the color I imagine our star Cleos to be if I could ever see him, turn their faces skyward. I can imagine no holier place.

The wetness evaporates from my body and clothes. I throw off my hat. Shaking my hair with my hands, I turn my face to the heat of our star. The star looks close enough to touch, and even though it burns my eyes, I risk a peek. Yellow, just as I suspected.

I turn back to my companions to take in their array of emotions. Black spots dot my vision. Russet's face mirrors my dazzled expression.

"Before we continue, we must make the offering." Ellias motions for us to kneel and drops to the ground. He pulls the fabric ball the päter gave us from his pocket and opens it. The rest of us follow. I dig into the leather pouch resting at my waistline and untie the small bundle. It is full of dirt. There is no holzenschrein up here for us to adorn with ilices. Fitzhan is the guardian mountain, so it does not need a schrein. Instead, we bring soil from the humble surface and offer it to Orna—in gratitude for allowing us safe passage from the ground below to her kingdom at the top of the fel. The nine of us raise our hands in the air.

"Oh-me-augh," Ellias whispers.

"Oh-me-augh," the rest of us say.

"Tanks be to Orna."

"Tanks be to Orna."

We open our palms. The dirt is snatched by the wind and whisked away into the meadow. A chubby little bee buzzes past my ear and lands on a small pink flower. It bumbles around, gathering warm pollen onto its legs.

"Can we just stay here?"

Kiel laughs darkly. He unties his harness before coiling it into a small pile on the ground. "I would gladly stay here with you if it didn't mean the king would hang us for treason."

In the Cleoslight, everything about him brightens—his smile, his eyes, the way his still-damp shirt clings to his abdomen. I shake my head to dispel the disturbing flush of excitement racing through my veins. This is not the time for such thoughts.

"How would they reach us?" I imagine our elegant king clawing his way up the cliff we just climbed. Even in his worst rage, a need for retribution would not be enough to propel him up the side of the fel.

"He would send Gio after me." Kiel points an accusatory finger at Gio, who shrugs and nods in agreement. "Plus, I'd miss that little pub on Rainey Street."

"Treason is treason, even if I like the guy." Gio grabs Kiel and pretends to lock his arms behind his back. "If the king says jump off this cliff and aim for the Sevier River, I'd pray for wings. Speaking of the *Krieg's Mast*, wanna grab an ale after this?"

Kiel laughs and shoves Gio off. "You buying?"

I stop listening to their banter. Joking is a good way to deal with somber realities, but I am not in the mood to glaze over things. I finally reached this place that has only ever been accessible in my dreams. I am finally here to help the team gather food and medicine. But the more I stare around the meadow and feel the heat from Cleos, the more I let it sink in what this honor actually means. It benefits my life, but what does it do for members of the kingdom beyond the rich and privileged? Today I will gather solans for the king and his cronies to eat. But no one else is allowed to consume them. Today I will gather pollen from the ulrind flower to deliver to the apothekers to turn into a medicine so costly that most lung-stricken allow themselves to die from pulmonosis before plunging their families into debt. I look around at my fellow climbers. Laughing. Eating. Stretching. For them, this is life. Why would they question what allows them to rise above Ectair's unfortunate?

"So, none of you have eaten the solans?" I cross my arms and lean against the blokkenshon. "Not even once?"

Their laughter dies. I am met with heads shaking left to right. Feiko and Dieter cast fearful glances in my direction as if the blades of grass might whisper back to the court about my treasonous query.

Gio spits on the ground by his feet. "People have been hanged for illegally consuming solans. Only the king says who gets to eat them."

Rosalie's shaved head and vivid eyes pop into my head. She died so I could climb this rock.

"But why?" I ask.

"Troublemakers ask why." Burkhart shakes out his haulbag and tidies the rest of his gear. "Traitors ask why."

Sometimes I wish Burkhart would at least try to whisper. Or maybe just think in his head.

I brush a small round kefer beetle from my skirt and watch it lumber into the grass beneath a blooming purple heidle flower. "What makes the solans so special?"

"Solans are royal property, so they are automatically forbidden," Ellias says. "I am not sure what's special about them. Maybe it's just a way to exclude people and elevate weak men." He gives me a smile. "But we get to experience something better than forbidden food. Welcome to the Celebern Fields. Even the king will never lay eyes on the beauty of this place."

Ellias's open contempt for our leader shocks me. Burkhart casts Ellias an appraising look.

I clap my hands together, aiming for a new subject and not wanting Ellias to elaborate. "So, where are the solans, and which is the ulrind flower?"

Feiko gestures over the open meadow ahead of us. I part the tall golden grass and stare at the green tufts and unremarkable dirt below. "Here?"

"Kiel, Dieter, Burkhart, and Feiko, gather ulrind pollen." Ellias says. "The rest of us will harvest solans. And stay out of the woods. Beyond the meadow, the summit is littered with cracks and caves that would swallow you to depths no climber could reach. Best to avoid the belly of a mountain."

The men disperse. Ellias pulls his haulbag from his back and turns toward me. "Solans are not cultivated like plants at the surface. They only grow wild. We haven't been able to domesticate them as a crop. They grow at the base of the solanas grass. Each tuft grows as a nurse plant to protect the green sprouts and the attached tuber below from Cleos's energy. You'll have to get your hands dirty."

I look down at the mud caking my fingers and smile, remembering that despite the injustice of it all, what I've trained for has finally come to fruition. Running forward, I let the grass whip against my skin until I can't run anymore. I collapse onto my back in the dirt and stare at the bright sky.

A flock of birds flies overhead in an undulating ribbon of dots and wings. Something buzzes in my ear and crawls across my hand. Warmth. I am enveloped in a warm blanket of dry air. I peek again at Cleos, then close my eyes and watch the colors dance behind my lids.

Cleos is our star, Azura our moon. Together they make up the two Himmelorbs. The päters tell us that Cleos and Azura are the twin children of Laren and Orna. Long ago, Laren and Orna, who don't typically get along, spent an amorous night together that led to the creation of our Himmelorbs. Since Cleos—a boy—and Azura—a girl—were twins, Laren and Orna could never have more children. Their lines ended. That is why only two Himmelorbs grace our skies. That is also why baby girls are now cast into the sea. If the lineage of the gods can end in such a way, imagine the effect on people. I find the whole thing to be rubbish.

"We actually have to work up here, you know?" Ellias stands over me, blocking the starlight. I hear the smile in his voice. "Look." He squats beside me and digs in the dirt beneath one of the green sprouts before pulling out a bright orange root. "Ta-da."

I roll onto my stomach and then push into a sitting position. Dusty splotches and spiky burrs cover my front. I brush them off. Ellias pulls a small trowel from my pack and passes it to me. I dig carefully through the rich soil. The solans have reddish skin and are covered in small bumps that look as though they want to form spines but stopped before becoming sharp. Each one I pull from the earth has a different shape. Some are long and thin. Others are curved and bumpy. Soon my haulbag is overflowing with tubers. As long as Cleos continues to shine, I could do this forever.

"Your dad and I used to love coming up here."

I pause and look at Ellias. Any mention of my father draws

my attention. I am desperate for stories, for something that connects me to him.

"We snuck up here a few times." He sits back on his heels and laughs, staring out across the meadow. "In some of the darker, rainier times, when Cleos wouldn't shine for months on end, Anselm and I would climb the face of Fitzhan and spend the day lying on our backs in the warm light." His gaze drifts. His eyes wander to some far-off memory. "You can climb your way out of a lot of dark places, Klarke. Remember that."

I nod and stare at the solans poking out of my overstuffed haulbag. "Did you guys ever, you know, taste these things?"

"Not once. We were only keen on breaking one rule at a time." Ellias laughs and stands. He brushes the dirt from his hosen and lifts his haulbag onto his shoulder. "Finish up here. I am going to go check on Russet and Gio."

I watch him walk away, then continue digging. An odd-shaped solan catches my eye. It is curved like a scythe. Lumpy like a bog töte's back. Holding it in my hand, I stare down at the sacred potato. For years climbers have risked their lives for this small food item so the king could have something else that separated him from the peasants. My father risked his life for this. According to Ellias, he never tried one. I sit in the starshine, rolling the solan in my hands. Knowing this is probably my last climb, I am about to sneak a bite when Ellias's voice cuts through my intention.

"And just like that, it's time to leave."

"Already?" I sigh, stuffing the last unbitten solan into the sack. I am about to protest but refrain when I see Ellias's expression turn worried. "What's wrong?"

"Nothing." He waves me away. "Stay here and enjoy yourself a little longer. I need to check on something."

As soon as he walks off, I pop out of the grass and stare in his direction. He moves toward the woods on the far side of the field. Ahead of him the grass parts for someone, but I can't distinguish who it is from this distance. Curious, I am about to follow when a shadow crosses over me. I look up in time to see a giant white something soar over. It's the size of a canoe and silent. Another flies by. Two of them circle the meadow, leaving momentary shadows below. Graceful and giant, with wings that could be the fins of a great tolvalus in the sea. I watch in awe.

"Bessils. Aren't they incredible?" Kiel appears at my side.

"What are they?" My mouth is agape.

He laughs. "Birds. Ancient giant birds called Bessils."

"How are they so quiet?"

"I don't know. I've only ever seen them play with the wind like that, never flapping or calling out. Apparently, they're quite common over on the Umlauf peninsula. They love the mountains."

The birds soar off, nearly touching the tip of Treiger as they float along the thermals. "What else is up here that I don't know about?"

"Fissures that would swallow you and drop you across the darkened sea at Laren's threshold. Perhaps a new god hidden within the caves. Maybe a stash of diemants." Kiel holds out a small pink flower to me and winks. "Perhaps only simple beauty. Who knows?"

I smile, accepting the gift. "Do you give flowers to all first-time Ascenditures?"

"Only the pretty ones. Russet's out of luck today." He takes my hand and guides me to follow. "It's ulrind. This little flower has the power to save lives. Come on. I want to show you something else."

We run to the edge of the field, pausing to catch our breath under a large oakenwood tree at the brink of the cliff. He points into the distance. All I see is white upon white.

"You wanted to show me clouds?" I raise my eyebrows.

He laughs and shakes his head. "It's Ainar. This and the summit of Mount Bonen are the only places you can see it without going to the Waste."

I strain my eyes to see the forbidding, ice-capped north. "I still just see white."

"Always a pleasure to share in your amazement and enthusiasm." He crosses his arms, but playfulness skips across his face.

I peer at the horizon, straining to see some part of Ainar. Our teachings have painted a violent and dangerous picture of the northern lands. I'd love to glimpse the Parowan Mountains, especially Mount Opasno. Every Ascenditure dreams of climbing that dangerous snow-covered peak, but we all know we will never be permitted to cross Miter's Waste, the divide that separates the north from the south. Many years ago, before Miter's Waste was created, Ellias climbed Mount Opasno. He is the only one in all of Ectair still drawing breath who has seen Galvaith's grandest mountain.

Staring out at Ainar makes me think of Losan, the young boy from the north who worked with his father occasionally on my father's ship. During port calls in Kietsch, Losan and I would race through the market, playing hide and seek and throwing bits of discarded fish at the cranky fishmongers who'd raise their fists and scowl at us. We'd shout, "Fischbomb!" as we lobbed handfuls of beady eyeballs and stringy intestines at grumpy old men.

I didn't think much about the fact that we looked nothing alike. That people hissed under their breath for Losan to go back to where he came from, that I should behave more like a young woman. We were troublemakers. Losan with his copper skin and narrow eyes, me with pale flesh and oversized pants that dragged through the street filth. We were best friends.

Losan disappeared from my life the day my father did. Ash and wave for us all. Sometimes just waves.

Kiel leans against the oakenwood tree and sticks a piece of solanas grass into his teeth. "I wonder what it's like there. What it's really like. Especially the people."

I imagine Losan bending over in a fit of laughter as we slammed the front door to my old house before whichever angry fishmonger could find us and give us lashes with a whip. The sparkle in his dark eyes. The way he sometimes laughed so hard he cried. And then laughed at himself for doing so.

"Bloodthirsty cannibals." I shrug and twist the ulrind flower

Kiel gave me in my fingers, smearing the precious pollen across my skin. "If you believe the stories."

"Do you?"

"Do I what?" I scan the clouds in the distance, trying to find the summit of Mount Opasno. It must be visible from here on a clear day.

"Believe the stories."

I twist the stem of the ulrind flower between my thumb and forefinger. "All I can worry about is keeping myself and Rayna safe. They can do what they want up there. It doesn't matter to me."

Kiel kicks a stone at his feet. "I think it matters. What people say. People start to believe their words. I bet the people of Ainar are as cannibalistic as you are weak."

I turn my head toward him and catch his eye.

"Which is to say—not very," he adds with a soft smile.

I feel the depth of his gaze in my heart, in the air entering my lungs. It trickles through my body.

"Ah-lee-adl-oo. Ah-lee-adl-oo." Ellias's voice calls the familiar echosong from across the field. "Time to go back if we're going to make it down before moonrise."

Echosongs have been used by our people since the early days before King Miter. Shepherds in the valleys realized the narrow canyons and towering mountain walls created a natural way to communicate over distances. We still use them today. On the fel. On a ship. In the hills of Tono.

Calls of "ah-lee-adl-oo" erupt across the field as the climbers stand and shoulder their packs.

"Race ya?" I run through the grass. My hair blows behind me. Cleos's rays kiss each dark tress. The heat caresses my back and tickles my ankles where the skirt flutters. I feel as if I am nearing the end of a gratifying dream.

Ellias is scowling when I arrive. Something has altered his mood.

"Change of plans." He heads to the edge of the cliff and stares over. "Klarke, you will climb in second position on kletshot one with Aedan in front and Dieter in back. Russet, you'll climb second position with Feiko in front and Burkhart in back. And Gio, you'll climb second position with me in front and Kiel in back."

"Why the change?" Burkhart ties his harness and prepares the rope for keltshot two to rappel.

"Climb as you're told," Ellias snaps.

I try to read my mentor's mood, but he avoids me, instead focusing on the bag in his hand. After a moment, he lifts his head and gazes at each of us in turn. "'Though power and treason be the way of men, let them not be my guides. Though loyalty to kingdom be my duty, let me first be loyal to the light.' Can anyone tell me where those words came from?"

We fall silent. We all know who said this, including Ellias. He knows better than anyone.

"Lars Veber." Dieter takes a deep breath. He tilts his head to the side. "Your grandfather said those words."

"And when did he say those words, Dieter?" Ellias looks like he could strangle a bergbear. I've only ever seen him like this in private rants. Never before with so many witnesses.

"Before he was hanged." Dieter turns to look out over the cliff face we are about to descend. "For high treason against King Hammonhoff II."

"Treason," Ellias scoffs. His eyebrows draw together. Again I worry for his safety. It is no secret that Lars Veber, the father of mountaineering and the pioneer of the Ascenditure team, was hanged for treason.

I picture Rosalie swinging from a noose. Treason. Her face becomes Ellias's. Treason. Kiel telling me to be the lighthouse. Treason. I almost cry out but manage to swallow it in a near-inaudible whimper.

"Ellias?" I approach him slowly and drop my voice. "Are you okay?"

He draws me away from the team. His face relaxes as he pulls me into a tight hug. I feel him breathe into my shoulder. Emotion hitches his voice.

"You have grown into such an admirable young woman. I am so proud of you."

I am confused by the sadness in his voice and his sudden need to praise me. *Treason.* The air pulls from my chest. I gasp and draw away from him. "You can't say things like that, Ellias. Whatever you believe about your grandfather. You know you can't."

He sighs deeply and pats my shoulder. "When we get down, Klarke, there is something I must do. I know not what it will unleash."

"What do you mean?"

The darkness returns to cloud his face. He hugs me again. I normally feel safe in his arms. Now I am disquieted. He holds me out so that he can look into my eyes. "Give them hüle. No matter what. Just like you always have. No matter what happens in this life, Klarke, you must rise up. Always up, for that is—"

"—the direction in which the mountain grows," we say together. I smile at him even though I feel troubled. He smiles back. There is more warmth in his eyes than a hundred stars could cast.

We rejoin the group. I loop my harness around my chest, shaken by Ellias's flash of anger and his secret. I tie the hat onto my head and attach my sling to the rope with a karabiner. Ignoring Burkhart's eye roll and irritated cough, I step in line behind Aedan. Dieter steps behind me. Ellias takes his place at the front of kletshot three. Gio stands behind him, casting twitchy glances at our leader. His hands quake as he secures his harness. We are all clearly shaken by Ellias's mood.

"Watch for felfees. Wicked little things like to act up on the way down." Feiko looks around, trying to lighten the mood. Only Kiel gives him a half-smile.

Twenty feet separate each team. I hold my breath as the lead climber of each new group rappels over the edge. When it's my turn, I walk to the fel and take a deep breath. To my right, Russet gives an encouraging nod.

Ellias is already standing upon the ledge below the blokkenshon. I have no idea what he plans to do, what he thinks he will unleash. I don't have time to think about it. I lean back, perpendicular to the ground a thousand feet below. My life hangs on the threads of a thin sisal rope and the rusted iron pitons holding it to the rock.

Feet planted firmly on the stone, I walk backward past the permanent anchors holding our ropes in place. At first, the extra weight of the loaded haulbag hinders my balance, but soon I am descending with ease. Despite my earlier griping on the purpose behind our climb, I feel proud. Ellias's encouraging words ring through my mind. No one can ever take away that a woman summited Fitzhan. No one can ever put it back into the bag that women are not strong enough to climb.

We reach the upper ledge and the first rappelers and wait while Dieter, Burkhart, and Kiel finish their rappel. They take a little bit longer than the rest of us as they are cleaning our ascension protection from the route as they go. Once they reach us, they each tug on the length of rope dangling from the fel. The ropes slip through the anchors above and fall in a series of coiling thuds down to the shelf of rock on which we all stand. The leads take the ropes and prepare them for the next rappel. Aedan, Feiko, and Ellias double-check their connections, lean back, and disappear over the edge.

This pattern takes us to the final platform. Two hundred feet lie between us and the waiting carriages. The mirror-like surface of Lake Eisenturks reflects like opaque glass. I am sore and tired, and the open spots on my hands are throbbing. Still, I feel as if I could dance down the whole mountain.

Once again Aedan, Feiko, and Ellias drop over the edge. I pull out my canteen and take a long drink of water. Russet does the same. Gio fiddles with something on his harness. Burkhart, Dieter, and Kiel organize the protection they've pulled from the rock on the way down.

"I think that's my sling," Dieter says.

"Sure, yeah." Kiel hands him the piece of equipment. "You have three of my biners."

"Your rope is knotted. He said to manage the ropes!"

"Scheiz!"

I look up. Gio has knocked over his haulbag. Solans have scattered across the ledge.

He lifts his bag and shows us a tear in the fabric. "Looks like there's a hole. I'll try to patch it before it's my turn."

"We can gather the solans. No bother." I bend down and begin placing the stray tubers in a pile. Russet helps me while the three sweeps continue organizing their gear.

"We could always pretend one fell off the edge." Russet gives me a wink and mimics taking a bite. "I won't tell if you don't."

I gesture for him to pass me the tuber. He tosses it, and I catch it with one hand. I stick out my tongue and lick the skin. We both laugh.

An explosive noise erupts out of the quiet and ricochets across the face of Fitzhan.

"Rockfall!" Kiel shouts.

Dust and debris come crashing down onto the ledge. I cover my head and scoot my body backward until I am pressed against the face of the fel. Russet huddles next to me. I can't see the others through the dirt cloud. I hear shouts and calls, but don't know from whom they originate.

Calm and quiet settle over us.

"Anyone hurt?" Burkhart appears through the dust. "You both okay?"

Russet and I nod.

"Say your name if you can hear me," Burkhart shouts.

"Kiel."

My heart lightens.

"Dieter."

"Klarke."

"Russet."

"Gio."

Burkhart lets out a sigh and leans against the rock face. "We're all okay."

A pained scream leaps up to us from over the edge.

"Ellias!" I scramble to the brink and look over.

Aedan hangs about forty feet from the bottom. His shouts continue ringing up to us. Feiko hangs about sixty feet from the bottom. At an unnatural angle. Arms hanging at his sides. He doesn't move.

"Oh, gods."

I don't want to look further. I don't want to know the rest.

"Klarke."

I close my eyes. My fingers grip the edge of the cliff.

"Klarke," Gio says again.

"No." I allow my gaze to move down the fel. There isn't a third rope anymore.

Ellias must be sheltered somewhere. Maybe he is hurt. That is possible. He must have managed to grab the rock. I know it. He is the best climber there is. He doesn't fall.

I see nothing. No rope. The anchors are empty. No climber. My gaze travels down to the shore of Lake Eisenturks. Time freezes like the rivers of Ainar.

A dark shape rests on the moraine. "No!" I scream. "No, no, no!"

Someone drops next to me. An arm drapes around my shoulders. My wail mixes with that of the other climbers', ricocheting in an agonizing echosong across the seven peaks of Miter's Backbone.

5

My father and mother both died when I was eight years old. My father and his entire ship, including my dear friend Losan, were lost at sea in a terrible orkansturm. Maybe even devoured by the great monster Hildegroth. My mother was taken a few weeks after by Death's Whisper, the same culprit that killed Queen Eleonora. A person can be completely healthy one moment and lifeless as a river stone the next. The Whisper leaves no trace of infection or envenomation. It is as if Death himself came and sucked the soul from a body.

And now Ellias is gone. A sharp falling rock cut straight through the rope. He had no chance. We had to scrape our leader from the rocks. Pieces of a man we loved. No longer a man. And Feiko too. A stone struck his head, killing him instantly. We lowered him slowly from the pitch. After their bodies were swathed in linen and placed in the back of the carriage, we had to stand there next to Ellias's blood as it mixed with the rain and trickled down the boulders.

Everything I've ever loved has been taken from me or held just out of reach. I grab my knees and pull them closer to my chest as loud sobs echo through the climbing gym in the old factory. I didn't go back to the tenement last night, a choice that will probably get me evicted. I don't care. Grasping one of Ellias's old ropes and trying to catch a whiff of his scent—the smell of sweat, sisal, and moss—I simply lie on the dirt floor.

I keep thinking of the person whom Ellias had followed up at the Celebern Fields. He'd returned with a different attitude, switched up the teams, made that vague comment, and then fallen to his death.

I try to shake these thoughts from my brain. There was a

rockfall. Orna got angry. An accident happened. Something explainable. No one did this to Ellias intentionally. How could they?

Still, I've never seen a rope sever so cleanly. I picked it up, the sliced end, before the päters could whisk it away. The edges weren't frayed or jagged. The cut was clean, like a knife through a block of cheese.

I can't let myself venture too far down this shadowed path because, at the end, I might find one of my friends. It was an accident, I remind myself again. Accidents happen on the fel. It's part of the job. Part of what gives us a rush. I clutch my stomach as a fresh wave of pain undulates through my core.

I must have fallen asleep because the next thing I know, someone is gently shaking my shoulders. Aedan is seated next to me. I wonder if I look as bad as he does. His cheeks are blotched with red, and the flesh around his eyes is swollen and puffy. I sit up and pull him closer. We cry into each other's shoulders. Aedan is now the oldest climber and will be sworn in as the new Lead following the funeral this afternoon. He will make a great leader, but I know this is not how he wanted to take charge.

Or maybe it is. My mind wanders back to that dangerous tunnel with its dead end. I quickly pull away. Aedan didn't kill Ellias. Couldn't. Wouldn't. He was down below us when the rockfall occurred. If anyone is innocent, it's him. I have to stop this madness from planting seeds of doubt about my friends in my mind.

"Aedan." I lean away from him and stare into his eyes. Try as I might, I can't let this go. "I don't see how a rock could have cut the rope like that."

He takes a long breath and exhales slowly through his nose. "This is hard for us all, Klarke. I know you want an answer. I do too. But sometimes there isn't one."

I shake my head and plead with him to understand. "I saw the end. It wasn't a rock. Who carries a knife when they climb?"

"We all do." He rests a hand on my shoulder. His eyes fill with gentle pity. I see the face his children must get when they tell him they think there is a monster under their bed. "You should too. It's a useful tool."

Useful for many purposes. I stare at my fingers. At the joints still oozing from the scrapes they received on the climb. "Burkhart gave Ellias an odd look before we descended. When Ellias was saying…things he shouldn't have."

Aedan holds up his hand. "I won't entertain this. Take your time to grieve. And move past these reckless fantasies. Please don't bring this conspiracy before me again."

I nod and bite my lip. More tears form. I am not one to concoct drama. I do not fantasize about ways to further complicate my life. This is different. And if Aedan won't help me, I will have to uncover the truth myself.

"We need to get ready," Aedan says softly to me. He offers a smile. "King Adolar wants you with the team for the ceremony. I picked up your uniform on my way here. The king's seamstress sewed it for the occasion."

I wipe the tears from my swollen eyes and study the folded garments he places in my hands. "Why?"

Aedan shakes his head and stands, offering a hand. "No idea. When he says jump, we jump."

What else do we do on his command? I wonder to myself.

"You know this can't be good." I fight back a fearful sob. Intentional or accidental, the king will find some way to blame this on me. "What will he do to me?"

Aedan rests a hand on my shoulder and squeezes. "Ellias protected you. I will try everything in my power to do the same. I believe in Ellias's vision for this team. For our kingdom. Trust in me."

Regular bathing is uncommon in Kietsch as most citizens live in the slums where fresh, clean water is hard to come by. Today though, washerwomen have been brought to the climbing gym with basins and tubs to scrub us clean for the ceremony. The hot water feels good as it rinses nearly fourteen moons of filth into the tub. I wish it could wash away yesterday's misery, but that also sticks to me like a tick to a dog.

When I am finished, I dry off and then pull on the heavy black dress that buttons to my neck. Around the collar, a thin braid of pink rope has been sewn. I swallow hard and try to ignore the meaning. The dress is too big and hangs off me like a sack. I shake out my wet hair and meet the rest of the team by the main door.

The six other men who also lost to Russet in the recent competition at Vether's Fel, plus one newcomer named Gerd, stand with the group, also clad in black. I wonder which two men will take Ellias and Feiko's vacant positions.

Aedan leads us out to the waiting carriage. Rolling down the cobblestones to Revolution Hill and the Rektburg, I can't help feeling like an imposter. Burkhart and Tizian never take their eyes off me. They want me to feel their hatred. They want me to feel as small and useless as I am capable. I gaze at my tattered boots and try not to let the men see their tactics working. I imagine Ellias sitting next to me. While it gives me strength, it also nearly crushes me.

Kiel sits to my left. As if reading my mind, he grabs my hand from my lap and squeezes it. I return his sad smile. We hold hands all the way to the palace. He lets go before the guards pull back the canvas doors.

Aedan, Tizian, Burkhart, Gio, Dieter, Kiel, and Russet enter first, followed by me and the seven other hopeful climbers. We form two lines behind Ellias and Feiko's simple caskets. Feiko's mother, father, and younger brother drape themselves across the wooden tomb, sprinkling it with all the pain and love slipping from their eyes. Ellias's casket stands alone. He never married. Never had children. His father and mother passed long ago. I ache to throw my arms around his box. To give him warmth and family. But I can't.

Draped in black, we face a kingdom in sorrow. The adels on their dais. The poor in the crowd. We are a wave of black-clad mourners ushering our brothers across the darkened sea. To one side of me, Laren's statue stands atop carved wooden waves, a sword in one hand, a braided rope in the other. He wears a crown of barnacles and urchins. A collar of seaweed and pearls. All chiseled in fizhte wood. His eyes are cunning. Staring out at us. Promising ash and wave.

Orna's holzenschrein has been covered in ilices. So many we can hardly see the pyramid beneath it. We brought our soil. Said our prayers. And still, Orna let him fall. It's all I can do not to spit on the schrein.

Sucking in a breath, I turn from the gods to face Hadrian's Monastery on the other side of the square. The main spire, gilded in copper turned green from the unending rain, tilts greatly to one side. A giant clock has been set into the red brick beneath the spire, facing the Rektburg. Intricate spirals of white flowers and filigree have been painted onto the brick. It is said the architect who built this old monastery for King Miter was so ashamed of the misshapen work that he jumped from the window just below the clock. To his chagrin, he landed on a bed of straw in the back of a poor farmer's wagon. Unable to build a straight spire, unable to successfully take his own life, the architect fell into even deeper despair. One night he became so drunk he tied rocks to his feet and jumped from a small boat into the sea. Laren gleefully accepted his life. Now the failed architect builds crooked reefs and misshapen oyster beds beneath the tides in the Bay of Hammonhoff. On a quiet night beneath the star blanket of the harvest season, it is said you can hear the architect crying from beneath the water, still lamenting his twisted and failed work.

Ash and wave for us all. Sometimes just waves.

King Adolar steps forward, having exchanged his green ceremonial robe for a black one. His expression is a pantomime of melancholy. No tears fall from his eyes. Behind him stand three päters from the monastery. One carries a censer, smoking with the scents of pine, salt, and elderrose. Another holds a ceremonial oar as white as his mask. The final carries a torch, the flame that will set fire to these caskets once they are pushed out to sea. King Adolar raises both arms into the air. A hush descends. "It is with great sadness that we must lay to rest Ellias Veber and Feiko Cremlin. These men were honorable and brave. A terrible accident occurred, and I can promise we are working very hard to uncover what happened. What we do know is that something angered Orna. Something new and unnatural caused her to strike down these good men."

Burkhart turns to glare. Tizian coughs. I glance to where parliament and Prince Otto are seated beneath the tent, protected from the soft rain that begins to fall. Two stewards rush forward and lift a slick tar-coated canvas over the king's head. The rest of us are allowed to get soggy. The prince turns his head, and we make eye contact. He gives me a look of disgust so deep I turn away.

The three päters step forward in unison. In old Galvathian, they chant a prayer of good hope for the fallen souls in the afterlife. When they finish, the choir sings a beautiful dirge. A famous ballad called "Back to the Darkened Sea." Someone plucks at a harp. Another pulls a bow across a violin.

Out of darkness we have come. Back to darkness we must go.
Over wave we have drifted back to these familiar shores.
From Laren's kingdom to Orna's summit back to Laren we go forth.
Ash and wave for us all as we sail from this last wharf.

I look upward at Miter's Backbone and the seven peaks that guard Kietsch. The sharp fang of Hansba. Kara Do's jagged tower. The tiny summit at the tip of Treiger. The top of Fitzhan where the solanas grass waves in the starshine in the Celebern Fields. With a gasp, I turn back toward the square, unable to look a second longer at the main face of Fitzhan.

Flesh and blood are on loan as we breathe the mountain air.
Fragile bodies turn to ash, and the waves caress our hair.
As we breathe in the water where we came from long ago.
And the darkness wraps around us, welcoming each of us home.

Twelve päters in black robes and white masks approach the caskets, taking their places on each side. Six of them lift Feiko.

The other six lift the man who cared for me, who saved me. They follow the three leiten päters carrying the trinity of sacred articles toward the bay, where a small boat will bear these bodies to sea. Ash and wave. I want to fling myself across the solid oakenwood lid and sob for the future I no longer see. Instead, I plead silently for guidance, for Ellias's soul to linger and help me. It's a selfish request, but I know the world will be much less without him.

The procession disappears into the crowd of onlookers. King Adolar once again lifts his hands, motioning for silence. I peer down the line of my competitors and can almost see the foam forming at the corners of their lips, the desire for greatness clutching at their souls. I wonder what I would see if I held a mirror in my hand.

The king swears in Aedan as the new Ascenditure lead. The kingdom cheers and calls his name. Each time the name bounces around the square, I feel a stab in my heart. Ellias's name will no longer be spoken. He is a line in the history books now. A bit of ash floating on the surface of the Rolag Sea until some giant tolvalus surfaces and sucks him through its baleen with the krill and plankton.

A name gives identity to a person. Humanity. Agency.

"Ellias," I whisper. And I swear to whisper it every day as long as I draw breath.

King Adolar's booming voice pulls me from my reverie. "Two coveted spots have opened up on this team—two intrepid climbers will soon have the honor of retrieving life-restoring medicine for the good of our people." He clasps a hand over his heart. "I know some of you would like to see years of tradition crushed with the appointment of a female to the Ascenditures." He pauses and lets his eyes fall on my drenched form.

My heart stalls, but I don't let it show in my expression.

The king raises his gaze again. "I have heard your voices, my countrymen. Eight climbers stand behind me, wanting to serve as one of your champions. They will each have a fair and equal chance to oblige our great people."

An interested ripple undulates through the crowd. A few faces turn toward each other, eyebrows raised. Some cheer for my opportunity. Others are surely ready to place bets on who will win. Few will wager their dracals on me. I am the underfed horse.

King Adolar strides across the stone platform above the palace steps, clapping with the crowd. He raises his arms once more. The clamor subsides. "To lift us all from tragedy, this challenge will not take place at Vether's Fel. No, after losing Ellias Veber, we need something to restore our spirits."

My heart thrums like the harp strings that played during the funeral. If he plans to send us up Fitzhan, then I am not sure I will make it. Part of me no longer wants this—how could I want something that has done nothing but break my heart? If to claim a spot I must climb past the rocks that broke Ellias and Feiko's bones, I will fail.

"The weight of this loss calls for glory triumphant. A new test worthy of legend. I have promised you two new climbers. If I could allow these hannar and this fram to prove their merit on Mount Opasno in Ainar, I would do it. But as I would never send my people into that fetid nest of rats and scourge, we must remain south of the Waste. Therefore, the next two Ascenditures will be selected based upon a solo ascent of Mount Bonen. We will leave by boat in the morning. To those who would like to watch, I suggest you begin making your way east."

The *oohs* and *ahhs* morph into gasps. The color drains from my competitors' faces. Their bodies grow rigid. An expert at covering my true feelings, I remain impassive. The truth is, only one of the eight of us has ever been mountaineering. We are all fantastic climbers, and if thrown on a wall, we would beat anyone to the top. But to be alone on a vertical wasteland of crevasses and avalanches, with gusting winds and daily storms that blot out what little starshine we have—this is an experience none of us are prepared for.

Kiel spins to face me. His eyes are wide. Since I am facing the crowd, on display like a prized lamb, I smile and wave, briefly meeting his gaze. Only those closest to me could discern an undertow of fear. To the crowd, I look excited to take on the challenge.

Gerd, the youngest and newest contender, trots down the steps into his mother's arms. She pulls him into a tight hug. I walk forward in a daze. Searching for the comfort of ghosts.

"Mother, I can't do this," he says.

"You stop it now, boy." She wears a white blouse, signifying she belongs to a man. A girl around eleven with sharp eyes and a deep pout, clings to the hem of her dürmel. She looks fiercer than her brother. An even smaller girl clings to her older sister. Both little ones wear green to symbolize they are not yet wed. Already classified as chattel. "You will bring honor to your family. Think of the food you can put on the table. You will climb that mountain. You will get that spot."

Gerd sucks in a deep breath and nods. "Yes, Mama." His voice cracks. He can't be older than thirteen.

His mother pulls him into her arms and squeezes. He can't see her face, but I can. The doubt. The fear. Men who have dedicated their lives to the practice die on Mount Bonen. She is sending her son for the slim chance at some extra broth and bread. And she knows it.

These conversations surround me. All seven of my competitors stand with their families in various states of shock, fear, stoicism, and anger.

I gaze at Hadrian's Monastery with its crooked spire across the square and hardly dare to breathe.

Here's the truth boiled down to the marrow. King Adolar will never let a woman join the team. It sets a dangerous precedent. If a woman can climb, why can't she captain a ship? Why can't she rule a kingdom?

The king pretends to provide us all with a glorifying experience. The people believe him.

I feel bad as I glance at the men closest to me—the ones slack-jawed and the ones poorly feigning bravery. Because of me, they have all been sentenced to die.

6

My only possessions fit in a wooden trunk small enough to cram in the space beneath my bottom bunk. I own a few ratty tops, two worn skirts, a dür-mel with a faded apron, the hosen I stole, a moth-eaten coat, some woolen socks, a silver coin with the head of a hozierleon my father brought from Kobo, and a handkerchief embroidered with a ship bearing bright orange sails. My mother sewed this for me to carry when my father would leave so I could feel close to him. After he died and before she passed away, she stitched the words *Omen aum noche rialshan. Hûder amalaze onen hiab. Im lô la gurage omi alam warsen. Fonal Ramanata* along the border. When I asked what the words said, she told me I would understand when the time came to understand.

Stuffing the handkerchief and coin into my bag, I kick the trunk under the bed. "Take what you want." My bunkmates watch with ravening eyes. "I am either coming back in a box or with enough money to replace it all."

"You'll be back, Klarkey. We all know it." One of the older girls pulls up her green sleeve, exposing a piece of pink yarn tied around her wrist. I blush, partly from her gesture and partly because I don't know her name. I never bothered. I always just called her Ol' Salt because she was the oldest of us in the room and worked at the salt factory. I feel ashamed that that is the most respect I've given her.

Another girl with a perpetual cough so bad we call her Pulmy after the disease that is slowly killing her reveals a pink ilice tucked beneath the collar of her nightshirt. "Give 'em 'ell, Klarke. We're countin' on ye to show 'em we got more than tits and holes." She coughs and wipes the flecks of blood from her lips onto soot-dusted fingers. "And if ye don't die, would ye mind bringing me some ulrind? 'Bout sick an' tired of this bloody cough."

I nod. The other girls in the room scoot to the edges of their beds and show me the pink trinkets they've hidden beneath their garments. A hair ribbon stuffed into a sock. A single bead from an ilice tucked into an apron pocket. A small pink dot stitched into the inside hem of a waistband.

Rayna sits on my bunk with her legs crossed and arms folded across her chest. Behind her cracked glasses, her eyes are bloodshot and swollen. Each time I look at her, she turns away. When I returned from the funeral, she pulled me aside and begged me not to go. She thinks I am choosing my desires over the feelings of others. She is not wrong. But she is also not right.

I stand. The misfit girls on their lopsided bunks cheer and take turns clapping me on the back. Many are missing teeth or are covered in bruises from sour encounters with lousy customers. Some, like Pulmy, already show signs of pulmonosis. A few tramp in late every evening, their eyes flecked with green from veisel. Even though I wouldn't trust them with a used sock, I know they mean well. If they had better opportunities—something more than brothels and deadly factories—they would pounce on them.

"Rayna, can I speak with you?" I sling the bag over my shoulder. I hate leaving her like this.

She slips from the bed and shuffles behind me into the hallway. In the dimly lit corridor, her melancholy is suffocating.

"You know why I have to do this." I take her hands in mine. "Sometimes people have to take risks for change to occur."

She withdraws her hands. Hair falls from her usually tight braid. "It doesn't have to be you, and it doesn't have to be now. You're being selfish but wrapping it in ribbon to make it look heroic. You are a good person, but you have a stone on your shoulder that will someday weigh you down so much you'll sink to the bottom of the Rolag Sea and not have the strength to surface. You can do no good for us if you are dead." She points back toward the bedroom. "They need you alive. I need you alive." Tears stream from her face like rain down a pane of glass.

I want to argue, to get mad. How dare she mistake my motives as stemming from a bruised ego? Everything I do is for the betterment of others. For her. I bite my bottom lip and refrain from offering a cruel retort. A voice whispers in the depths of my mind that Rayna is right. By sheer luck, this just cause happens to coincide with my desires.

"But you need new glasses." I grab hold of this new strategy as if it is obvious and absolving. "And you need to be set free. I can help—"

"You have never needed to save me, Klarke." She touches the rim of her lens with a shaking hand. "I let you believe that because I knew it gave you purpose. I am quiet, but I am not weak. Please don't use me as a platform on which to martyr yourself. If you wish to die, it is upon your own ground, not upon my shoulders."

"I don't want to die." Anger builds in my chest. "But if death is what it takes, then I am not afraid. I will win. I will beat them all. And above all else, I will beat the king. And I'll do it alone on my own just as I've done everything else."

Rayna sighs and takes a step backward. "You've never been alone." Removing her glasses, she wipes the fogged lenses on her threadbare blouse. "Ellias. Me. Your mother and father. Kiel. Only in your mind have you survived alone."

I ball my hand into a fist and then walk forward and pull her into a hug. At first, her arms hang limply by her sides, but when I refuse to let go, she raises them. I feel their pressure against my back.

"I'm sorry," I whisper into her hair. She smells of burnt tar and stardried sweat. "I have to do this. I can't turn back now." My own tears begin to fall, and when she feels my chest contract, she pulls me closer. "I'll come back to you, Rayna. I promise. And when I do, things will be different. I'll be an Ascenditure. They'll move me into the granhaus. I'll take you with me, find some job you can do for us. It'll be better. You'll see. And I am not offering this because you need help. I am offering it because I love you."

When I pull away, she smiles sadly and reaches her hand beneath the green fabric of her collar. She lifts the ilice I smuggled from the riot, the one made of pearls and glass beads, so that the pink color catches the light from the wall torch. "I believe in you more than anyone possibly could. And if this is your decision, I will pray to Orna for your success. I hope you find what you're looking for up there."

My chest tightens. I sling the bag off my shoulder and dig into my meager possessions. The silver coin feels cool and insignificant in my hand. I press it into her palm. I am unsure what it's supposed to signify—maybe a promise to return or a token to show I care. Sailors make similar gestures of good faith to their wives before leaving for the sea. It seems like the right thing to do. Returning her glasses to her face, Rayna closes her fingers around the coin, turns, and shuts the door. The girls' noise retreats behind the oaken slab.

I take a deep breath and stuff my hand into my pocket where it finds the handkerchief. I am flooded with the notion that I will never see my best friend again. That I have chosen death over life to prove a point.

The gangway creaks under my soles. Dawn has greeted us with yet another cool, dusky day. I haul my gear onto one of the king's waiting boats at the mouth of the Sevier River where it meets the Bay of Hammonhoff. Heavy mist hangs in the air and, not for the first time, I wish it would turn to actual rain. I'd rather be pelted with droplets than stuck in fog. My feet slip across the mossy wood. I lug the new equipment I've been issued from the carriage to the boat. The rest of the team watches. They have been instructed not to help. Halfway to the ship, I trip over my skirt and nearly smack my forehead on the railing. Gerd, the young recruit who admitted fear to his mother at the funeral, catches me by the elbow before my head splits open.

"Tanks," I pant, bending to retrieve my straw hat before it blows into the sea. Men on the docks laugh and jeer.

"That wouldn't happen to you in my bed, sweetheart!"

"Go home, lass. Go home and wait for me."

"Look at 'er. She can't even carry a simple load across a wet dock. I wouldn't want her to darn me socks. Might spend a night between those thighs, but I don't think she's even worth bein' a brideprize."

I ignore them and the foul smell of fish guts and drop to my knees to gather the rest of my gear. This elicits a fresh caw of slurs.

Gerd bends down to help. His soft, round cheeks blush crimson through the mist. "I think they're right. You wouldn't be scheiz as a bride. It'd be wasted on ya if you were. Hüle, most of us would be better brides than you, just like you're a better climber than all of us put together."

A snort accompanies my laugh. Beneath the brim of his coppola, his round eyes twinkle. He is a boy. Barely more than a child. I remember his mother telling him to be brave. I remember her fear. My smile wavers. I can't make friends. I have one mission. We are all on our own from this moon to the next.

"Bloody hüle sucks you have to wear that." Gerd hands me a spare sling and points to my skirt. "What a pain in the arsch."

I lean toward him and wink. "Don't tell anyone, but I've got on a pair of hosen under this. As soon as we've set sail, I'm ditching the framwear. Hope that doesn't offend you."

"Not a bit. Man on up."

Grinning, I stuff the last stray sack of bartlenuts and dried gegenberries into my pack and stand. I have to keep Gerd at a distance, but it's still good knowing I have an ally. My spirit lifts the tiniest bit.

"I can't imagine what either of you find funny." One of the judges strides up the dock, grasping the slippery railing. His green robe clings to his skin like barnacles to the backside of a tolvalus. "Is it the crevasses or the lightning storms on Mount Bonen you find most hilarious?"

"Sorry," Gerd mumbles, his cheeks reddening.

I don't respond. We have nothing to be sorry for. And it's none of the judge's business where we find our joy.

Gerd shoulders his pack and lumbers forward beneath the weight. Water squelches in and out of the holes in his worn boots. He is so tiny I can't stop picturing the gusting winds of Mount Bonen ripping him from the ice and tossing him like a feather into the abyss of some yawning crevasse.

"S'cuse me. Pardon."

I move to the side as the ship's cook trundles down the dock, a large sack of flour flung over his shoulder. He is a sizable man with a booming voice and a reputation for burnt meat and drug smuggling. I only know him in passing, from his time working as a cook in the galley of my father's ship. He is the one who brought Rayna and me together in the fish market many years back. I think he feels loyal to my father's memory. He has always been kind to me when we bump into each other at the docks.

"Geitsê, Klarke. Ya well?" Drops of rain cling to his bald head. A wide smile stretches across the massive space between his ears. If I believed in myth and legend, I would think he was descended from the risants, giant-like creatures who live in the Mountains of the Unknown south of the Calvia Plains. Basically at the end of our world.

"Hey, Obid. I'm fine."

"Good, good." He keeps moving and disappears onto the ship. I peer ahead at the Ascenditures waiting along the railing. Kiel grits his teeth and glares periodically at the men making crude gestures from the adjacent pier. I try to conceal how heavily I am breathing beneath my load.

Julius and Tristan, two of the other men I will be competing against, pass by, each carrying two alpenstocks, hobnailed boots, and a coil of rope. They cast sullen looks in my direction but proceed in silence.

When all our gear is loaded, we board to join the Ascenditures and push off from the dock behind the ship that carries King Adolar, Prince Otto, a few adels, their servants, and the three judges who will decide our fates. Hovering thousands of feet above us, the seven peaks of Miter's Backbone cast dark shadows onto our transports from across the river. They look like massive stone fingers jutting from the ground or like the spiny backbone of some primordial beast. I stand at the stern, away from the king's ship, and stare down the Sevier River to where it meets the sea.

A cool breeze whips at my face, twirling my dark hair in a chaotic dance. Our wooden ship has two large masts, with canvas sails and an auxiliary steam engine to help move her forward. Smoke puffs from the solitary funnel, blending with the clouds and smog drifting in from Kietsch.

For the next week, this boat will be my home. I have never been farther east than the city of Iri, which rests on the Sea of Toole. The sea dominates the center of our continent, butting up to the north against Miter's Waste.

Mount Bonen lies on the other side of the kingdom, rising fifteen thousand feet from the floor of the Umlauf peninsula into the clouds. Although visible from hundreds of miles away if you are out to sea, the great peak will remain hidden from us by thick forest until we reach the village of Kaiwa, where the trees have been burned to the ground to make room for vineyards.

Our people and lands have been shaped by the hands of men for thousands of years. Long before King Miter ruled, Ectair was settled by nomads from the east who landed on our shores and discovered rich deposits of stone for making tools, forests for harvesting lumber, and mines for extruding salt and tar.

"Mount Bonen is treacherous, Klarke. You can always back out."

I whip around to find Kiel striding across the deck toward me. I lean against the ship's taffrail and shake my head. "I can't back out."

He rests his hands on the rail and stares at the ripples left by the propeller in the trailing water. "None of you have mountaineering experience. I barely have mountaineering experience. The mountain will sock in, and you won't be able to see. Afternoon storms will hit, and if you aren't in a safe spot, the lightning will strike you, or the mountain will send down an avalanche. The altitude will steal your oxygen. I could keep going, Klarke. This is a suicide mission."

I feel my lungs starving for air and a cold wind sweeping across my face.

"It's not suicide—it's murder." I glare at him, wanting to take my anger and panic out on someone. "I don't have a choice. This is my only shot. I will summit this mountain, or I will die trying. What choice do I have? Go home and marry the drunk sailor? Whore myself out in the tenements? I would rather die on Mount Bonen than rot in the slums of Kietsch."

"My offer still stands." His eyes drop to the warped wooden planks, and even through the haze, I see pink hues flush across his cheeks.

I sigh and rest my hand on his. Anger and heat leave my veins. My heart softens. I know the magnitude of what he is offering and know I would be lucky to be taken in by someone like Kiel. But I don't want a world that requires luck. I don't want his charity. I don't want Rosalie to have died in vain.

"You said it yourself." I lift his chin so he must look into my eyes. "After the riot in front of the palace when I asked you what good I could do against years of tradition. Do you remember what you told me?"

He shakes his head. I see in his eyes that he remembers exactly what he said.

"Climb." I drop my hand from his face and stare at the water trailing behind us. "You told me all I have to do is climb."

"At Vether's. Up Treiger. I didn't mean this." He flings his arm in the direction we are headed. Pointing toward the east. Toward the mountain.

"I don't get to choose. I can't just stop. I can't let the king win." Surely, he knows this. Not so long ago, he instructed me to follow this path.

"If you die on that mountain, Klarke, he will see that as a victory." Kiel grabs my hands. His eyes grow as they beg me to reconsider.

"Then I won't allow myself to die." I bite the inside corner of my cheek until a trickle of blood runs onto my tongue.

෴

Our ship has three decks, with the bottom deck reserved for storage, a galley, quarters for the crew, the boiler room, and the engine room. The middle deck provides our berth, and the top deck gives me a place to breathe and escape the shroud of doom that lingers over us.

The Ascenditures are bunked at the stern of the ship on the middle deck. Each climber has a small bed complete with a goose-down mattress and blankets. Their sitting area has chairs and books, and even oil lamps to read by.

We competitors must sleep nearly on top of each other in hammocks toward the bow that swing back and forth all night with the sway of the water. I have almost grown accustomed to the scent of body odor and the sound of retching. It is as if the king wishes us to be seasick throughout the journey before we gather ourselves for a climb toward death. Our common area consists of only a few off-kilter wooden benches, and even though the Ascenditures invite us to relax in their quarters, pride keeps us in the front of the ship, motion sick and terrified.

This, the third night of travel, puts us somewhere between the Runen of Bend and the town of Merket. Earlier I stood on deck, watching Cleos set behind the runen on the north shore of the river. A rubescent glow highlighted the tumbled stone and overgrown hallways—all that remain of our ancestors' ancient city. I wonder if their ghosts still linger or if the runen is as empty and forgotten as it looks.

We are nearly directly south of Iri and the Sea of Toole on our port side. Iri is the leiten city of the West Inland Sea kreison of Ectair. Known for its gunpowder, livestock production, and, above all else, cheeses. Our starboard-side view is completely obstructed by the Hummeldorf Woods, of which Merket is the leiten city.

Hummeldorf is an ancient forest full of oakenwood, tarnglebon, and hofaspen. And the creatures my omie decided to invent on a stormy eve next to the fire. My favorite was always the tale of the khatasol, the spirits of abandoned baby girls, mainly the sacrificed twins, who searched for unwary male travelers to latch on to and strangle. My mother's mother could leave goosebumps on your skin for hours into the night. I went through a profusion of candles trying to keep her monsters at bay.

Lying on one of the benches in our common area, I read a book on mountaineering I snatched from the Ascenditures' bookshelf. Kiel lent me one of their lamps and, even though it provides enough light to read by, the constant swaying of the ship makes it difficult for me to focus on anything other than my roiling gut. Someone gags in our sleeping area. I try to tune out the noise and smell. Somehow I must learn to survive in a high-altitude climate from the pages of an old book. Thank goodness my parents died after I'd been through my first years of school. If I'd been orphaned any younger, I would not have attended primary school or learned to read.

Another poor soul lets out his sickness, and before I lose my own dinner, I grab the book and lamp and sprint to the hatch that will take me to fresh air. I burst into the night rain, turning my face to the cool water. It washes the smells and sweat from me as I move to a place where the sail provides shelter. Setting down the lamp, I crack open the book to a section on alpenstock self-arrest, a technique I must master in case I slip on a glacier and plummet down an icy slope to the mouth of a bottomless crevasse. Everything I read tells me we should be climbing in teams, with each connected to a rope in case someone falls. Any doubt that this is a death sentence vanishes with each page I turn.

We should have been training for months to carry the necessary gear and food. Instead, I will be alone on the ice, with only my doubts and fears to keep me company. I have a feeling they will not attempt to rescue me should I fall.

"I'm glad to see you studying."

I jump from my sitting position, knocking my head against the rigging. "Scheiz, Gio." I rub the sore spot on the back of my skull and glare at him in the dim lamplight.

He throws his hands up in surrender and steps forward. "Well, geitsê to you too." He carries an alpenstock in one hand, a pair of hobnailed boots in the other.

"Oh, sit down." I fill my sigh with agitation as I pat the wooden planks next to me. "What do you want?"

"Just thought you could use some company. It's getting stale and stuffy down there." He turns up his nose and wafts a hand dramatically across his face. "As bad as I feel for all of you, the smell is making its way to the back and kind of starting to ruin this experience for me." He tries to smile, but only his lips turn up. His eyes remain heavy. Gio has also taken the deaths of Ellias and Feiko hard. We all have.

"Oh, poor you. Having to deal with a bit of bad smell. I get to go from seasick to altitude sick all in one week." I set the book down and lean against the mast.

He sits beside me, his eyes sparkling in the lamplight. "Advice from someone who has ascended Mount Bonen twice?"

"Please." I nod, eager for anything to keep me breathing beyond my upcoming summit pitch.

"Don't go."

"Excuse me?"

My mouth gapes, and I shake my head. "I've worked too hard for this. I can't believe you'd suggest such a thing."

He releases his fingers and drops his arms defeatedly by his sides. "You know this won't end well."

"I don't know that." I scowl and try to settle my shaking fists. "And I won't accept it."

Gio sighs deeply. Our silence is accompanied only by the sound of the ship cutting through the water. Rain patters with a different note on each surface it touches.

"Fine." He nods at his lap and then faces me with defeated eyes. "I thought you might say that. So pay attention. There is a place at about 12,000 feet called the Snag. It's a large outcropping of volcanic rock that forms a wall, leaving only one place to scramble over. It's hüle to climb, but it will block everyone's view of you for the remaining trip to the summit. Get over the Snag and find someone to rope in with—more than one person if possible. Beyond that rock, the crevasses are as deep and plentiful as the scars across Burkhart's face. If you don't secure a rope team, no one will find your body if you fall."

My eyes widen with each word he speaks. I don't know if he is trying to help or scare me. Maybe both. "I just read about this. I can use alpenstock arrest with a team. It should help, right?"

He nods and thrusts the alpenstock into my hands. It has a long, smooth wooden handle. From one end juts an iron spike, from the other a pointed pick and a dull adze. "When you pass the Snag, pause and make sure you know how to use this. And if you value your life, make sure everyone on your team knows how to as well. Two climbers can fall into a hole if the third can successfully stop them."

The wooden handle feels cool in my hands. I've been saved from falls by smaller, less impressive protection, but it was pro I was comfortable with. Pro I'd been taught how to use. This object feels foreign in my fingers. I set the tool aside and drop my face into my hands. A sick feeling unrelated to the motion of the river brews in my belly.

Gio grabs my wrists and pulls them away, forcing me to meet his gaze. "Klarke, you're one of the strongest climbers out there and, as much as I believe you could be successful despite the odds, you must keep something in mind. You are up against a powerful enemy. You are not supposed to survive this. None of you are. And once they send us up to pronounce you lost forever in a hole with no end, the king will tell the people that the gods were displeased with a woman leaving her place in the home for some unnatural desire. And having lost seven of its precious sons, the kingdom will agree with its leader. You will damn a century of girls to a life of servitude."

The sickness in my stomach rushes up my throat, but I swallow back the bile. "What are you asking of me? To give up this one opportunity to secure my dream?" I am suddenly cold to the core as if I am already standing on the summit. Darkness and the night air, previously peaceful, now slip in like a garrote around my throat. "And in case you haven't noticed, Gio, we're already damned."

A feral glow remains in his eyes. He wipes his dark hair across his forehead and takes a deep breath. "Forget about winning. You need to worry about keeping your seven competitors alive. Because if you survive and they don't, it won't matter that you made it to the top, retrieved your rosen banner, and easily glissaded to glory at the foot of the judge's table."

"What you are suggesting is treason. If I go up there and play nanny to those who can't fend for themselves, two of the strongest will reach the top, retrieve their banners, and return to the base before I've finished wrangling lost sheep. You know Veit won't join my team. Won't waste tears on weaker men." My heart is racing like the wings of a kolibarabird. My blood flows more swiftly than the river where it curved around the Runen of Bend.

A trumpet blares somewhere to the north. I whip my head around and see lights flickering along the shoreline. It could be a small city. Figures move between the shadows, but I can't tell if they are men or wisps of smoke molded by my imagination. "Where—"

"It's Camp Arema. The military outpost." Gio leans against a crate and closes his eyes.

"Your dad is stationed there, isn't he? With Kiel's father." I turn back to Gio, but he doesn't look at me, just nods. "It must be hard having him away all the time. I know you deal with a lot, having to care for your family."

He cracks one eye open and fixes me with it. "You know nothing about my struggles."

I glance at the shoreline and see a large fire. Music filters out to us. Someone is singing. Another is laughing. Someone squeezes a bellowkord. An invisible wall separates us from their delight.

I look back at Gio. "You're right."

He sighs and shakes his head as if to dispel a bad dream. "I don't know what's gotten into me. It's just Ellias... Feiko..." He trails off and stifles what could be a sob. "So much happening beyond our control. It's just hard sometimes—to feel like you have any control over your life."

I grab his hand and squeeze. "Which is why I can't do it, Gio. I can't quit, and I can't heed your advice. I won't go back to Kietsch as a failure."

He is silent, staring up at the few stars blinking serenely above us through the clouds. Someone at the camp lets out a large belch. The men around the bonfire hoot and cheer. The music increases in tempo, and slurred voices sing in joyous cacophony.

Come drink with me and toast the king.
Ho di oh di el.
From Fitzhan's fel to Laren's sea.
Ho di oh di el.

Gio thrusts the mountaineering book into my hands. "Then go back in a wooden box." He stands to leave, taking his axe and boots. "You have good instincts on the rock, Klarke. It's time to be more than an able climber."

I meet his hard gaze, angry and adrift in a place with no good options. He vanishes into the darkness. The wood scrapes as he lifts the hatch to the middle deck. Above me, stars peek through a gap in the clouds. I wish I could harness their warmth and light to melt the glacier that has formed in my core.

Rayna's words haunt me—that I am selfish, here to feed my ego. But to give up would be a betrayal of all those women at the protests, my bunkmates, my dreams...Rosalie. A moral battle rages in my soul, making me queasy. Unless I break the rules and persuade seven other contenders to rope up, we will all probably die. Or I can go it alone and be blamed for their deaths whether I win or lose.

Whatever my choice, whatever the outcome, I can't succeed. I will not be remembered as the first woman to become an Ascenditure, but rather as the curse that caused the deaths of so many innocent climbers.

7

We are on the final day of our journey, with plans to dock at Kaiwa—the leiten city of the Umlauf Peninsula—a half-day's journey to Mount Bonen to the southeast. My nerves grow more irritated each hour, prickling like a mosquito bite I can't stop scratching. I try to push the impossible task ahead out of my brain, but it rushes back in like the complicated and dangerous guest it is. I stand on the deck of the ship, trying to find peace.

Wayside schreins to Laren have been erected all along the riverbank from Kietsch to Kaiwa. Diamond-shaped wooden boxes sit atop fitzhe pine poles. Inside each, a carved statue of Laren, about the size of a child's doll, stands with his arms open, emerging from wooden waves that have been painted black. I lean against the rail and stare at one such schrein as we pass.

At the beginning of time, the world was a black ocean, what we now call the darkened sea. There was nothing but water and stone. Storm and chaos. During a fierce orkansturm, a bolt of lightning struck the water so hard it penetrated to the sea floor, hitting a stone and creating the first black diemant. Inside the diemant swirled the beginnings of life. Little particles of frenzied storm energy. Laren and Orna emerged from the chaos within the diemant.

Laren took over the sea, the sky, and the darkness. He was driven by destruction. Orna, on the other hand, was a creator. She created the land, the life forms, and the mountains. After her tryst with Laren, she created the Himmelorbs, and there was light.

Laren was furious that she kept creating new life. Each new plant or animal she concocted, he obliterated. As the world changed and shifted through these violent ages, the spot of creation on the sea floor rose into Miter's Backbone. It became the Celebern Fields.

After millions of years of war between the gods, they finally made a deal. First, Laren would let Orna's creations live as long as she created a monster for him so fierce it could destroy anything in its path. Second, she could create life, but it could not live forever. Eventually, her beings had to die, returned to him in the darkened sea.

That is why we still burn our dead and send them on the waves. We honor the pact made long ago that brought peace to our warring gods.

I move from the railing to head below deck. For the first few days I escaped the morbid sickness of the middle deck by going up top and watching the never-ending line of trees pass by. Now I take my mountaineering book to the bottom deck and sit on a barrel full of kimmeron—a smoky liquor hailing from the Himadôr Coast—reading fervently and listening to our cook, Obid, sing, spin yarns, and curse at the food he prepares. Obid is as salty as the eggs he serves for breakfast. I've grown fond of him during this voyage. The stories of his journeys at sea remind me greatly of the tales my father used to tell.

Knowing the one way to distract myself, I lift the hatch to the damp lower deck and crawl down the ladder to find the cook. Using my hands for balance, I drag my fingers along the dark hallway, heading toward the faint light at the stern of the ship.

Obid is bent over the large iron stove, throwing salt at a simmering slab of meat. Coals glow beneath the burners, warming the small space to an uncomfortable temperature.

"Oye, Klarke," he rasps, wiping his hands on a stained apron before shoving a pan of biscuits into the oven. "Fine day, eh?" His smile is as big as he is, nearly filling the entire galley.

"Sure." I shrug and hop onto my designated barrel, crossing my legs and leaning forward on my elbows. I have no desire to read today. My intentions are to stay as far from the mountain as possible.

Obid bustles about for a few minutes, stoking the fires and grumbling about weevils, before reaching for his empty flagon. He fills the cup with kimmeron from the barrel I am perched atop and plops down on some stacked sacks of flour. The flour sacks groan under his nearly three hundred pounds, or maybe it is the decking beneath them.

"So, ya going to climb that mountain?" He nods to himself and gazes at an open bag of beans. Something small wiggles through the legumes. "It's a tough 'un, I hear."

Great. Until now, Obid has graced me only with stories of smuggling, sea, and adventure. Today, when I need an escape, he brings up the mountain. "I hear the same. But I've got to do this. I've never wanted anything so badly."

"Not even to live." It isn't a question or a scolding remark. If I am not mistaken, the words contain a lilt of fondness. He grunts and takes a long swig of kimmeron. With a beefy hand, he wipes his sweating brow. "'Course ya do. Yer ya father's daughter. Ya shoulda seen that man climb when it came time to dam the Waste."

My attention piques. I've heard bits about my father's climbing days from Ellias, but no one speaks of Miter's Waste and what happened in that channel. King Adolar blames Ainar's King Gyalzen for the wreckage that occurred, a story reinforced by our school lessons. The climbers who helped during that time with the damming and sealing of Miter's Waste were forbidden to speak of it. Right after, my father quit the Ascenditures to try his hand at sea. He was the first and last person to leave the team voluntarily.

"Were you there? When they closed the channel?"

"Yuh." He takes the final swallow from his mug.

I hop from the barrel and offer to refill his cup.

"Course ya know the story. Hildegroth, Laren's great beast from the sea, found 'is way into the channel between Ainar and Ectair and wreaked havoc on the nearby cities, destroyin' the bridge that once connected our two kingdoms."

I hand him a brimming mug of kimmeron.

"Tanks ye!" He gulps half the vessel's contents. "Made it all the way from the Rolag Sea to the Sea o' Pibar, laying waste to every manmade structure he came upon. No one could stop 'im. After the Waste was dammed, Adolar told everyone King Gyalzen controlled the beast and released 'im upon Ectair."

"That isn't what happened?" I lean so far forward I nearly fall from my perch. Legend states there is always one who can control the beast. A power passed down through an ancient bloodline directly linked to Laren. We've always known King Gyalzen of Ainar held that power.

"No." He chuckles and rubs his belly. His eyes grow glassy and red as the kimmeron continues to fill his system. "Gyalzen can't control that beast. No man can. But a woman." He lifts a finger and wiggles it in the air. "Might be that a woman can. Might be that a woman's what set off the great beast in the firs' place. That's why ya mum worked so hard to get her out of there."

This time I lean too far and topple from the barrel. Wincing as my knee hits the ground, I look up into the cook's face. "My mom did what? For who?"

He smiles and closes his eyes. "Ya mum saved more women and girls than I can count. And I smuggled most of 'em beneath sacks of flour like these. Weevils and women and wee baby girls." He chuckles and claps a hand against the bags he lies upon. "Kobo. Ainar. Lands to the east and west ya ain't even heard of."

My mom was a brideprize. She stayed home. Cooked and cleaned and sewed and made sure I completed my lessons. Spoke only when spoken to. Never stepped a toe out of line.

"You must be mistaken."

"Mistaken? Hah. I remember the hazy morning when Mina Ascher strode down the pier an hour 'fore dawn, arms wrapped 'round a cloaked figure. 'Twas the Lady Genalt. Mental by that time. Totally cracked. Those darken mages he sicced on her did a number. Still don't know she even had the power they tortured her for. Don't matter, I s'ppose. We got her outta there. Fast-tracked to Ainar with a shipment of veisel and thirty barrels o' gunpowder."

I am not certain what I am hearing. Drunken slurs from a boastful cook. Mangled truth from a known smuggler. The darken mages were destroyed long ago, their blood magic returned to the sea. And my mother—I don't think I ever really saw her leave the house.

I have been taught to hate Ainar since birth. It has been beaten into my brain that King Gyalzen controls the beast. Dabbles in dark arts. Eats his own bastard children. I am not sure I am ready to let all of this go based on the words of a snockered boat chef. Part of my fondness for Obid comes from his farfetched stories and soaring imagination. But he called my mother by her name. Mina. And there is power and truth in a name. *Rosalie.*

The wooden planks undulate beneath me. The river rocks me into a focused trance. "Who was Lady Genalt, Obid? Who tortured her and why?" I don't bother to stand. On my knees, I plead with Obid for truth. For answers.

He closes his eyes and relaxes deeper into the sacks of flour. His eyebrows draw together, and he belches. "Can't say. Shouldn'ta said what I did."

"What does my mother have to do with any of it?" A bean weavil wriggles between my fingers. I flick it away and return an iron gaze to Obid. "I miss her."

A tear trickles down his red cheek. It drips onto the burlap and forms a small, dark splotch against the fabric. "We all miss Mina. But I swore I'd keep her secrets. Even from you."

Whatever floor has fallen from beneath my sense of reality drops even farther. I take a deep breath and lean against the barrel of kimmeron. Who was my mother? Not wanting to push Obid into silence, I shift rudders.

"What about my father? What role did he play in this?"

"Right." Obid perks up, clearly glad to change the topic. He struggles to sit, and I leap forward to help pull him up. "Took both kingdoms years a-workin' together under increasingly scheiz relationships to dam the Waste, first buildin' the Roudan at the Bay of Unity, and then the Schalk where it opened up at Pibar. Ya know every year we get two months or so when the tides pull the sea out far enough that the channel is near empty? That's when they did it. Engineers got it mostly figured, workers from the labor camps died in swarms to make it happen. For the firs' year or so after, the dam sprung some leaks. Goal was to make that channel dry as Kobo so no water beast could ever survive in it. Being that it was a stone wall a half-mile or so deep, the kingdom called upon the Ascenditures to rappel down to fix the leaks. Ya dad was a magician with a rope and a piton. It was a beautiful thing watchin' that man climb. Pretty as a tune."

"Why did he quit?" Something has started smoking. I take the towel from Obid's hand. The biscuits are blackened when I pull them out, and I feel bad for those of us who will have to eat burned bread for lunch—and I know to whom the scheiz food will go. Today, I deserve it.

Obid shrugs as he stands on unsteady feet to fill his mug again. I feel I should stop him, but he is a grown man. If there's anything I've learned in my experience with sailors, it's to never get between a man and his kimmeron.

"Didn't know 'im that well, actually." Obid plops down on the sacks. "Just made 'is food and watched 'im climb. No one knows why he quit. Really shocked the kingdom, though. Me, I think it had to do with Mina's work."

Having lapsed back into a conversation he'd tried to avoid, Obid leaps from the flour sacks and moves to the oven, busying himself with stirring the porridge and cursing the blackened biscuits.

"So what is the truth then?" I step forward, and my boot knocks over the bag of beans. "King Gyalzen didn't send Hildegroth? Instead, a woman named Lady Genalt did? After being tortured by nonexistent darken mages. My mother is what? A smuggler? A traitor? A hero? And my father quit climbing because of something she was up to?"

He stares at me with waffling eyes as if unsure whether I am asking questions or retching words. Wobbling on tree-trunk legs, Obid grabs the edge of the stove to steady himself and belts out a string of curse words. He yanks his hand from the smoldering iron and dunks it into a bucket of water. The scent of burning flesh mixes with the galley's other unsavory odors. I take it as my cue to leave.

"I'll see you later." I wave and make my escape before his anger, aided by drink, reaches a level I am not prepared to witness.

I move through the near darkness, past the boiler room and men shoveling coal, up the hatch to the common room where all seven men I will be climbing against are sitting smashed together on uneven wooden benches and laughing. My urge is to turn and find someplace where I can sit in silence and gather my thoughts.

My mother. I can barely remember what she looks like. Now I feel even my memories of her are false. Pulling her handkerchief from my pocket, I finger the lettering she stitched before she died. I never bothered to uncover what it said before. Now it is a mission second only to summiting Mount Bonen and securing my spot on the Ascenditure team.

"Join us." Gerd pats the open bench next to him. The others watch with a mixture of interest, apathy, and loathing.

I recall my conversation with Gio, and even though I have no intentions of throwing away my chance for a team slot by helping these guys, something tells me I will need their trust and friendship before this is all over.

I take a seat.

"So then she drops her skirt, and I just sort of panic. Black out, really. Next thing I know, there's three sets of wobbles hangin' over my face and a far-off voice askin' if I'm okay."

Julius finishes the story of his first time in a whorehouse to an uproar of laughter and knee slaps. I smile but don't have a lot to contribute. He is tall and lanky, from a family of tar miners in the Calvia Plains. His dark hair swoops across his forehead. He has good laugh lines for someone with deeply startanned skin and tar-stained hands. Tar mining is one of the nastier jobs in Ectair.

"So, did you do it?" Ingo, a stocky man in his early twenties from Bolson in the Western Shoal, asks.

Julius winks and makes a clicking sound with his tongue. "Best damn hour of her life, I reckon."

"You mean best ten seconds," Petrus says.

More laughter. Gerd giggles but casts a blushing glance my way. I am not sure if he is embarrassed or has a crush. For both our sakes, I hope the others don't notice and that he gets over it soon.

"Now, now, hannar." Veit takes a sip from a chipped mug full of what smells like poorly brewed kimmeron. "We've got a fram in our midst. I suggest we change the conversation to knitting. What have you darned lately, Tristan?"

"Come on, Veit," Achill exclaims—a gangly teen from the Hummeldorf Woods with freckles as big as splattered raindrops. "She beat you to the top of Vether's, and there's a good chance she'll beat you to the top of Bonen. Let it play out, and then spill your words."

Veit snorts and slaps his knee.

"I don't give a damn that she's a fram." Tristan narrows his eyes at me. Like Julius, his skin is deeply tanned. Tristan hails from Kaisel on the island of Ono in the Dor Drillingt. When he is not climbing, he helps his father dive for pearls and harvest oysters. "But I do give a damn that I'm being sent up this bastard mountain to die because of her."

The room goes silent.

"You all know it's true." He looks between faces. "Mount Bonen? A man's never been asked to climb an actual mountain to secure a spot. Doesn't even have to do with the job. They want her to die more than they want new climbers. You're all daft if you don't know it."

"It's not her fault, though." Gerd fiddles with his fingers and looks sideways at me. "It's not her fault they hate her."

I drop my gaze. My stomach grows woozy. It's nice to be defended, but I feel ashamed of the need for it. Gerd's hand grazes mine, but he quickly pulls it back. I want to laugh and also to shove him away.

"It doesn't matter whose fault it is." Julius sets his mug on the floor and turns to face me. "Drop out, Klarke. Drop out or look at every man in this room right now and accept that their fates are on you."

My head grows heavy. I want to fall onto the ground and slink away. Instead, I let my blood turn to steel. "I am not afraid to climb, and I am not afraid to die." I slowly make eye contact with every man in the room. "You all know the stakes. If you're so worried, go home. You drop out."

"I say give her a go." Veit puckers his lips at me and kisses the air. "I can't wait to finally shut her up. We just need to beat her one last time. A woman won't last on this mountain. Fill these spots, and she's done."

The air is heavy with tense silence.

Achill begins tapping his boot tip on the floor and changes the subject. "So, Petrus. What hints can you give us about Bonen? What do we need to know?"

Petrus lets out a low chuckle and a sigh. His long hair is tied into a knot atop his head. Tattoos of ships and sea creatures spiral up both arms. He hails from the Umlauf Peninsula, from a prosperous family of winemakers, and has dabbled about the base and lower slopes of Mount Bonen his entire life. If any of us has an advantage, it's him.

"Go home. Best advice I got. Klarke's not your enemy, boys. Worry about Bonen, not her."

"We're all going to die because of her," Tristan says.

Seven pairs of eyes turn to face me again.

I face them back. "Die if you will. I'm not going to die. I intend to win."

Veit scoffs so loud it makes Ingo jump next to him. Julius's eyes roll so quickly that he could be about to faint. Gerd's dimples become sharp pinpricks. Achill bites his lip and nods.

Tristan empties the dark contents of his mug. Petrus remains unreadable.

I glare at Veit, then turn my head to every attentive face. "If you don't believe you can win, you should listen to Petrus and go home. If you think you're going to die because of me or because of your own weakness, then why are you here?"

Gerd shrinks into himself and drops his head. I feel a brief moment of guilt but allow that to pass. If they are afraid, some may quit before setting out for the summit. In its own way, deterrence from ever leaving base camp is like saving their lives, right? If they don't heed Petrus's admonition and my warnings...well, at least I tried.

❧

I shoulder my gear and step from the boat on the same quavering legs those sailors pretended to walk upon for my amusement so many years back. Rising in the distance, Mount Bonen emerges like a waiting predator. I swallow the doubt that rises in my throat and continue lugging equipment from the boat to the wagon.

Kaiwa is everything Kietsch is not, or maybe it's the opposite. Streets are paved only in dirt—or mud—instead of cobbled with stones. Homes, shops, and businesses are all made of mud-brick basements with wooden upper levels and wooden roofs. Livestock live on the bottom floor, providing warmth for those above. The nicer homes have murals painted on the outer walls—images of fishermen on the sea, women picking grapes, and Cleos shining through the clouds.

Wayside schreins to Laren stand everywhere. Holzenschreins sit outside the farmhouses, bedecked in ilices and glowing with candlelight. Religion rules the day here.

Stretching out for miles from the town center—which includes a clock tower atop a monastery—to the base of Mount Bonen lie acres of vineyards. The forest has been cleared across the entire Umlauf peninsula to make room for the kingdom's wine supply.

While I freeze to death on the side of the mountain, the king and his cronies will be lounging on soft settees, sipping the finest vintage reds, and enjoying exotic dancers brought over from Kobo.

I shake the thought away and scramble into the wagon between Julius and Gerd. I want to be with Kiel and Aedan picking their brains about the upcoming journey and drawing comfort from their familiar faces. Instead, I sit with my seven rivals, wondering if any of them are so desperate to win that they would push me into a crevasse.

Eight of us ride toward the mountain—me, Julius, Petrus, Gerd, Achill, Tristan, Veit, and Ingo. I can't help but wonder if the two vacant Ascenditure spots will be filled with the two who manage to survive.

The mountaineering book I've been poring over sits on my lap. I stretch out my legs and lean against the canvas that forms a protective arc above us and to the sides. The rain lands with solid thumps as it hits the fabric and rolls down. We have a five-hour approach to base camp, and I intend to disappear into hopeful dreams for as much of that time as possible.

"Learn anything useful from your reading?" Petrus asks.

I crack my eyes and see everyone in the wagon watching me.

"Well…" I clear my throat and rest my hand on the book. "I've been reading a lot about avalanches. One of the most important things I've learned is that when a slide gets triggered, move to the side, don't try to outrun it. Also, the book says to swim in the snow to stay near the surface. If you can't do that and get buried, keep one arm raised high above your head so that maybe it will stick out and someone will find you. Don't cry out for help unless you hear voices. You'll need to conserve energy and air."

A hush falls over the group. We are all imagining what it feels like to be buried alive under immobilizing snow.

"How will someone find us if we are supposed to climb alone?" Gerd looks ashen as he asks the question. I give him an encouraging nod, still feeling guilty for snapping last night.

Gerd is only thirteen—small and afraid. I picture him crushed beneath an avalanche, the first victim of my need to win.

"I don't know how anyone survives without a climbing partner," I say honestly, shaking the guilt away. I didn't force him to come. He should have made the decision to preserve his own life before leaving Kietsch. I ignore the memory of his mother encouraging—no, instructing—him to leave.

"Hopefully, they will send the Ascenditures after us if we don't return. But truthfully, if caught under the snow, even with a small air pocket, you will run out of oxygen in about two hours."

"She's right." Petrus folds his tattooed arms. "Ask anyone in Kaiwa. They'd all tell you the only way to climb that mountain is with a team. Otherwise, you may as well climb with ghosts."

Achill taps his oar-blade-sized hands on his knees. "Some of us have never even seen snow before, let alone tried to climb in it. If it wouldn't kill my career, I'd have stayed back in Merket."

A vision of Achill's lanky figure plummeting into a crevasse flashes through my mind. "It's not too late."

"To leave?" Achill's head tilts to the side. He frowns. "Got nothin' to go back to."

Julius passes Achill a flask of kimmeron and shakes his head. "Who does, mate? S'why I'm here too, even though I know they're tryin' to kill us."

The rest of our journey proceeds in silence. A carriage full of corpses lumbering to our mountain grave. I nap fitfully, dreaming of avalanches, deep holes, and enemies lurking in a snowstorm. I dream of Ellias. The way his face lit up each time I mastered a new route. The rope that dropped him with its perfectly severed ends.

The jostling of the wagon wakes me, and I file out into the open air behind my competitors. Immediately I am drawn to the behemoth casting shadows on the tent village beneath it. Up close, Mount Bonen is even more forbidding than I imagine all of Ainar to be. It is not icy down here at base camp, but my heart freezes nonetheless as my eyes travel up the side of the mountain—from dirt trails to snowy fields and beyond to the volcanic rock and glaciers protecting the obscured summit.

It won't be just Gerd and Achill and the weak men who perish.

I no longer think I will die in Kietsch. My grave, too, lies somewhere on the side of this peak.

8

A feast has been arranged in our honor beneath a great marquee. The festival is really just an excuse for the kingdom's elite to imbibe Kaiwa's wine and mingle with its daughters. I nearly gag when a member of parliament forgets his family and moves unfaithful fingers across the body of a young server. I down my glass of wine and slam the goblet onto the long wooden table.

Beef stew, potato dumplings, fermented cabbage, and grilled white sausages cover platters and fill steaming bowls. Dark bread and spiced cakes give the air a warm, tantalizing smell. It reminds me of home when my mom used to bake pudding pretzels and cinnamon swirl bread dusted in sugar. My mother, the brideprize smuggler.

"He slipped. Wasn't paying attention."

The alcohol-boosted volume of a familiar voice snags my attention. Gio leans against a barrel of wine, grinning at the girls gathered around him.

"I heard his wrist snap from twenty feet above. Daydreaming about some lass he'd met at the Krieg's Mast the night before. Careful, ladies. Our Tizian here will break your heart."

Tizian grunts. His arm is draped around the nearest young woman, who giggles nervously and tugs at the hem of her green blouse.

"Not how it happened," he says. "I was rescuin' a lamb that had tumbled down the mountainside. Had to reach her quick. Forgot to put the proper piece of protection into the rock." He sighs and displays the jagged scar on his wrist. "Too focused on saving that poor animal."

My snort is so loud they all turn. I want to warn the girl that Tizian will never see her as anything but a piece of property. That he doesn't give a scheiz about lambs. Instead, I continue to clear my throat and beat on my chest as if I have choked on my wine. Tizian narrows his eyes and returns to their conversation.

"So, I had to rappel down and save his arsch." Gio gives Tizian a playful shove and dances away from Tizian's return push. "*And* the bloody lamb. Bit of a hero. No big deal."

Their laughter mixes with the guffaws and cheers leaping up across the room.

"And what about you?" A beautiful young woman with dark hair to her knees and an emerald dürmel made of fine silk leans toward Russet.

He inclines away, eyes wide. Burkhart pushes him forward.

Russet stumbles and finds himself in the arms of the bemused girl. Gio and Tizian laugh.

"I, uh. I'm new. Never saved a lamb or a teammate, but once I pulled my uncle out of the bay when he got drunk and slipped off the pier."

"Fantish." The girl runs a finger down Russet's cheek. His face grows redder than her lips.

Glasses clink. Laughs echo. I grit my teeth and look past my seven competitors huddled together down the way to the king at his dais on the far side. Men in woolen hosen and ladies garbed in shades of green and white fill the benches. A holzenschrein to Orna, modeled after Mount Bonen, has been placed in the corner. Ilices of every color drape across the wood. Candlelight dances through the carvings, which have been engraved to depict a scene of three men scaling a cliff face. The woodcarving casts an eerie shadow on the far side of the tent.

I dig into the pocket of my skirt and feel my mother's handkerchief. Tracing my fingers across the message, I watch Aedan talk heatedly with one of the judges. There is no comfort in the veins bulging from his neck or in the way he clenches and unclenches his fingers. His reaction to what is coming tells me everything.

Undisturbed by this lethal farce, Burkhart grabs a bellowkord from the bar top and gives it a squeeze. Conversations halt as the reeds inside vibrate together, sending out a joyful honking tune. The patrons recognize the familiar stanzllied, and soon the entire marquee fills with the words to "The Cobbler's Lonely Daughter."

Upon the slopes, my lass did sing.
Eerye-aye-o-la
In woolen skirt and blouse of green.
Eerye-aye-o-aa
Aye-o-la, aye-o-la, aye-o-aa, aye-o-la
Across the hills, she called to me.
Eerye-aye-o-la.
Come hither lad, my bower's empty.
Eerye-aye-o-la

I drop my forehead into my hands and exhale. The man beside me leaps from the bench onto the table, kicking empty vessels and dirty plates out of his way. I duck to avoid a spiraling pewter mug. Reaching a hand down, he pulls up the nearest young woman, and they lock elbows, dancing in a circle for all to see. Others do the same. Stomping feet and clapping hands add to the joyous atmosphere. The men sing louder. The elation in their notes rises.

Aye-o-la, aye-o-la, aye-o-la, aye-o-la
I hither now to fill her needs.
Eerye-aye-o-la.

"Tie your damn ropes, Klarke," I hiss to myself. "Get it together." Stepping away from the table, I go to the nearest oakenwood barrel and top off my mug with a blood-red wine made from a grape that grows only on the lower slopes of Mount Bonen.

The song ends. More wine is poured. Burkhart sets down the bellowkord and claps Tizian on the back. I search for Kiel. He has been absent since we reached base camp. Dieter, the only other Ascenditure unmoved by the festivities, walks toward the exit. Taking a deep breath to clear my wine fog, I move to follow. He has been up Mount Bonen once.

I slip through the doorway and trot after him before he fades into the night. "Geitsê, Dieter. Do you have a moment?"

He halts and glances around. "Not really. What do you need?"

"Oh." I rub my shoulders to warm them and take a step back. Music and cheer filter from the tent, but I don't feel any warmth out here in the mountain's shadow. "I wanted to ask you about the climb."

"Maybe tomorrow." He leans to the side to peer around me, then turns and begins to walk away. "I have something to attend to."

"Yeah, okay." I watch him move toward the forest, wondering what business a climber has in the woods after the moonrise. It could be veisel, but I don't believe Dieter uses drugs. His eyes don't carry the telltale green striations.

Footsteps approach from behind. I turn, and Prince Otto, the king's handsome and sullen son, brushes past me. He silently follows Dieter into the night. Shaking my head, I go back into the tent and to the wine barrels. I walk past the Ascenditures. Aedan, our new leader, now huddled by Gio and the rest of the team, stops mid-conversation. With a joyous, slurred tongue, he lifts his drink in the air and shouts, "To Klarke!"

The rest of the Ascenditures, minus Burkhart and Tizian who keep their drinks by their sides, join in. My cheeks burn as I try to smile. All I can think about is the target growing on my back. I return Russet's high-five and retreat into the anonymity of the crowded tables.

I plop into the vacant seat next to Julius and ignore the burning sensation in my throat as I chug my wine. Wiping red dribble from my chin, I find Veit sneering at me from across the room. As if mocking the earlier toast made in my name, he lifts his mug of ale, flicks me the fickson—a crude gesture made from the two smallest fingers raised, the others lowered, on one's right hand—then downs the entire thing and turns to speak with one of the judges. The last thing I need is another flesh-and-blood enemy when I've already got a mountain gunning for my life.

Veit hails from a wealthy family in Amia on the eastern shore of the Sea of Toole. They are King Adolar loyalists in every way. Like all of us, Veit's number-one goal is to reach the top of Mount Bonen and secure himself a spot on the team. I suspect his second goal is to make sure I don't.

I feel a nudge at my side and look up from my empty cup to see Petrus smiling. "Don't worry about him. He's threatened by you, that's all. Most of us don't feel the same."

Gerd, sitting across the table from me, nods. "Part of why I started climbing was because I watched you in the factory one day after Ellias brought you in. You were so good. My sister Marike is obsessed with you. I've been secretly teaching her to climb, and every time she makes it to the top of a rock, she shouts that her name is Klarke Ascher, the best climber who ever lived!"

I laugh, unprepared for such a compliment, and think of the young girl clutching her mother's skirt at Ellias's funeral. Me? She wants to be like me of all people.

"Hey, I'm serious." His face turns crimson. "You're a terrific climber, Klarke."

"Tanks ye. Both of you. And your sister…" I reach my hand across the table and rest it on Gerd's. "I wasn't making fun of you. I don't always know how to handle nice things being said about me."

"We're on your side," Achill, the tall, gangly climber, says from his place next to Gerd. "It's not about gender. That comes from the old men, not us. It's about the love of climbing and serving the people of Ectair with pride. I've never met someone with as much passion for the practice as you. That's all we see. Your ambition, not your tits."

My arms fly to cover my chest as the men burst out laughing. I throw a bartlenut across the table at Achill's face and chuckle. "Tanks ye, I guess."

"Why do you do it anyway?" Ingo asks as he slips into the seat next to Gerd. "Why keep putting yourself in a place where you have to deal with so much scheiz? Why not try and find something else that makes you happy?"

My lips tighten. I ball my hands together and stare at the cracked knuckles, some of which still bear the scabs from my last climb. "I guess it's the one thing I felt was always worth it, despite the hardships. It's the one place I feel at home, where every ache and pain and bruise mean something. The world drops away. It gives me hope. At least it used to." I trail off and grab my wine before I can say anything more revealing about myself.

"Look, what I said back on the boat…" Julius shrugs his shoulders. "I don't want to die because of you, but I get why you're doing it. Like Achill said, we're a new breed of climber. You just need to hang in long enough for the old men to die, and things will change. Let's just hope the old men die before we do."

"Here, here!" Achill raises his class, and we all chuckle nervously. A few of us glance over our shoulders to see who might be listening.

"To dead old men!" he whispers. We repeat with hushed giggles and clink our glasses together.

Guilt at my plans to ignore Gio's advice and instead let these men fight their own battles on Mount Bonen crashes over me.

We guzzle more wine than we should and laugh at things that probably aren't funny. At the end of the night, as I say goodbye, I am so torn by emotions and anxiety about the coming days that I try to run across the rocky ground to the safety of my tent on the outskirts of camp. The other climbers share their quarters, but as I am a "distraction," I am given my own place to sleep—something for which I am truly grateful.

Through wavering vision and an oncoming headache, I turn past the last tent before mine and crash into Dieter. The moonlight casts shadows onto his face, making it hard to read his expression. He grabs my shoulders to stabilize me as I teeter on one foot.

"Easy, Klarke. Why are you running?" He takes a step back and glances over his shoulder.

I scan his face, trying to see if his eyes are streaked with green, but the darkness hangs too heavy. "Why am I running?" The only thing I can think to do is to ask myself the same question.

"A little dunk, huh?" He smiles and takes my elbow, gently steering me toward my tent. "Be careful out here. A sprained ankle could end more than your summit bid."

I nod as I pull back the canvas door. Pausing, I turn toward Dieter's retreating figure. "How do you know Prince Otto?" I immediately feel uneasy. What if Dieter is dealing drugs? Plotting against one of us? Working with the crown against me?

"What?" He walks back to me, an alarmed expression on his face. "I don't know the prince."

"I saw you with him. Going to the forest." I release the tent flap and face him, telling myself it's stupid to be afraid. "I just wondered how an Ascenditure ended up taking a night stroll with the heir to the kingdom."

"You're drunk, and your eyes deceived you. Get some sleep. The coming days will be rough."

He ambles toward the center of camp, pausing once to peer back. I slide into my tent, collapse onto my bed, and shut my eyes on a swirling mind and the hint of a headache.

9

To combat the brightness of the snow, we have each been given a pair of goggles that make us look like kefer beetles. They are made of darkened glass surrounded by thick wires and leather that help to shield light from entering our eyes and causing snow blindness—an affliction that is usually temporary but up here could cost one their life.

We have hiked up about a quarter mile to where the snowfields begin on Mount Bonen to spend the day training with our alpenstocks and hobnailed boots. This is the only day of training we will receive.

Even though we are surrounded by snow, I wear only a high-necked wool sweater with my skirt, wool bloomers, chest harness, and boots. As long as I don't pause long enough for my sweat to cool, I feel warm.

The judges, royalty, and spectators have been left behind in camp, so it is just the competitors and the Ascenditures here on the mountain—eight of us, seven of them. We have been split off to partner with an experienced climber who will spend the day teaching us mountaineering tactics. Since Russet is new to the team and has never climbed here, he has been paired with Aedan and Tristan. Achill and Ingo are matched with Tizian, Veit is with Gio, Gerd has been paired with Burkhart, and despite my best efforts, Petrus and Julius are matched with Dieter. My trainer is Kiel, who finally showed up. Other than Russet, he is the least experienced mountaineer on the team.

I wanted to be with Dieter, but as soon as he saw my eager face, he grabbed the two nearest climbers and headed off toward a steep part of the slope before I could even say hello. When I get off this mountain, I will figure out what he is up to.

Kiel is far away in his thoughts. His eyes are hidden behind his goggles. He is slow to answer my questions, and after completing each exercise, I find him staring up at the summit or off into the distance—anywhere but at me.

I've just slid down an icy hill for the seventeenth time, using the stock to arrest my fall. It's hard work. A few times I landed on the back of the axe head—the adze—knocking the wind out of myself and bruising my chest. At 12,000 feet, if I can't dig my axe into the snow quickly enough when I slip down the slope of a glacier, I will become nothing more than a bad memory.

"What's wrong with you?" I finally snap and throw my alpenstock into the ground where it sticks.

Kiel points to the alpenstock. "Again."

"Maybe you can watch this time and realize I've got it down." I yank the metal pick from the ground and stomp up the hill. I drop onto my rear and begin sliding feet first toward Kiel. My skirt slips up past my knees, revealing my bloomers. If I showed this level of immodesty anywhere else, I'd be flogged.

I turn toward the snow, intent on ending up on my stomach, and grip the adze with my left hand, lower on the spar with my right. As I come over onto my hip, I dig the pick into the snow and swing my feet and hips up off the slope, making sure my boots are in the air and my knees are spread apart for balance. I must be a sight with my undergarments in full view. Now on my stomach, I dig the axe in as hard as possible, using pressure from my shoulder. The force of the axe sends snow and ice chips into my face, but I stop above Kiel and shoot him an irritated glare.

"Good," he says, crossing his arms. He adjusts his flat cap and glances to his side. "It looks like the hole is empty if we want to practice self-rescue."

"Lead on." I follow him across the snow, passing Gerd as he tries to arrest his fall. Instead, he builds momentum and crashes into Burkhart's feet, knocking the Ascenditure to the ground. I would laugh, but the scenario isn't funny. If Gerd can't learn to stop himself, he won't survive.

Unless I help him.

Kiel and I reach the edge of the hole I will practice climbing out of. I peer into the depths of the artificial crevasse. It is a narrow slit about five feet wide, ten feet long, and ten feet deep. No yawning chasm waits to swallow me if I make a mistake. I drop my gear to the ground and face Kiel.

He gestures at the equipment. "Pick it up. If you fall, you'll be carrying all that weight. You need to practice correctly."

I lug the pack back onto my shoulders and retrieve the alpenstock.

"On a real climb, you'd be roped in with at least one other person, if not more. If you were to fall into a crevasse, ideally your teammate or mates would stop your fall, and you could use your pick and toe spikes to climb your way out."

I glance down at the rusted iron spikes poking out from the front of my leather boots. Rawhide laces are wound and tied nearly to my knee. Lifting my foot from the ground, I gaze at the nail heads jutting from the sole.

"But alone and unattached to a rope..." He pulls his hat from his head, wringing it in his hands. "If that happens, we can only hope you land on a ledge."

Kiel passes me a length of rope. I attach my chest harness to it with a sling. He lowers me into the hole until I reach the bottom. Once there, I untie the rope and watch as he pulls it out of my reach, leaving me alone with only my tools and skills. I glance up.

Kiel squats above me and points to my hand. "Since this is just snow and not glacial ice, it will be easier to dig your tools into, but the snow won't hold as well as ice will. Reach up and jab the spike from the alpenstock into the snow above you. Then take one foot followed by the other and really force the nails in. Repeat. Got it?"

"Have I upset you?" I grunt as I kick the snow with one foot and then the other. My axe jabs into the powder, and I move up the ten feet with ease, hauling my body and heavy pack over the edge until I am kneeling next to Kiel. "I have enough people angry with me just for breathing. I don't need it from you too."

"I'm not upset with you." He pulls me to my feet and attaches the rope to my harness. "Do it again. Even if it seems easy, you need to practice until it is second nature."

I lean over the edge and drop down, baffled by his behavior. "I don't believe you. And if you don't tell me what's up, I will worry about this over the next few days while I'm on that mountain. You know as well as I do how dangerous a preoccupied mind can be."

He remains silent as I scramble up the snow wall. When I reach the top, he ties me back onto the rope. I repeat the exercise ten times.

Pulling the straw hat from my head, I wipe the sweat from my brow. We stand next to each other in silence until I can no longer bear it.

"I am about to head out on a climb that I may not return from. And this is how you want to leave it?" I keep my voice low as Aedan, Russet, and Tristan walk by, laughing at some joke. That should be Kiel and me. We've never had a problem making each other laugh. And that's what I need now.

Kiel cocks his head to the side. Beneath his cap, a pulse ticks at his temple. "That's exactly it. You might leave camp tomorrow, and that might be the last time I ever see you. How do you not know, Klarke?"

Despite the snow's glaring reflection, I remove my goggles and stare accusingly at him. "Of course I know the dangers of what I am about to do. But you, above everyone else, know how important this is to me. I need you to cheer me on, not bring me down."

He lets out a humorless laugh and tugs his goggles from his face. "You're out of your mind if you think I don't support you. You think I offered to marry you because I am some standup hannar? A good friend? No, I offered because I bloody meant it."

I suddenly feel naked without my goggles. I lower the lenses back down so he can't read my expression. "Oh," is all I manage to say. My mind races as I process his words. I wipe a cold hand across my face and try to maintain composure. "You know the second I marry someone I lose my edge. They will see it as a weakness, as me needing a man. I can't go down that path. With you. Or with anyone."

He takes a step forward. His body tenses beneath his wool hosen and overcoat. "Weakness? Your insecurity makes you weak, not your relationships with other people."

I fold my arms over my chest. "Don't talk to me as if you have any idea what it's like to be me. How wonderful you don't have to worry about the things I do. If you want a brideprize so badly, find one. I am sure there are a thousand women in Kietsch alone who cry out your name into their pillowcases. I won't give up my dreams for you or anyone else."

I storm past, half expecting him to follow me back to camp, but I don't see Kiel anymore that day or even at the dinner feast that night. I sit at the long wooden table with the men who will set out with me tomorrow up the slopes of Mount Bonen. I scan the faces of the crowded tent for Kiel, but he is nowhere to be found. I want to apologize, to clarify what I meant, but it doesn't look like I will have that opportunity.

All I want to do is to disappear into a drunken stupor, but I avoid the wine tonight. Tomorrow at dawn the alpenhorn will sound, and I will begin the deadliest test I've ever attempted. Some of the others are already drunk. I worry for their safety when they approach the snowfields hungover and exhausted. But it is not my job to nanny, to keep them alive, or to teach them responsibility. I think of Kiel's words that my insecurity is my greatest weakness. Questioning my relationships with other people.

I care about Rayna. I cared about Ellias. I cared about my family.

I stand from the bench and make my way outside. The summit of Mount Bonen is ringed in mist. I can make out the rocky formation of the Snag just beneath the halo of clouds.

Kiel secured his spot on the team, even though I handily beat him up Vether's Fel in that competition. He will never have to prove himself on Ectair's deadliest mountain. That is an obligation reserved for me and forced upon my competitors. Until he must sacrifice his life for a dream, he will continue to be as clueless as the rest.

I leave the din of the celebration and retreat to my tent. Sleep won't come easy, but I'll grab on to as much as I can. Tomorrow begins my ultimate test. It is not just about becoming an Ascenditure. It's also about beating the king and trouncing this backward society.

I cannot die, and I cannot lose.

Kiel is wrong. On all levels. My weakness is not my insecurity.

I have no weakness.

10

My pack feels heavier this morning, as if someone filled it with river stones in the night. I lug my gear through the village of canvas tents to a grassy gathering place. Here we will be displayed. Veit and Julius have already arrived. I plop my pack next to theirs and try to stand tall while we wait for the rest of our competitors. No one says a word, not even Veit, who I assumed would take this last opportunity to demoralize me. Nerves have silenced us all.

My pack contains a small acetylene stove, food, cloth and carpet for a floor, bedding, extra warm clothing, a spiral-braided coil of rope, a few slings, an extra bit of rope to craft a harness from should I need it, a large swath of canvas, my alpenstock, a lamp, and a short pole to support the canvas and craft a tent from.

Gerd sidles next to me. His breath comes in short, choppy inhalations. Only adels could afford to travel for such an occasion, so his mother and sisters are back in Kietsch. Probably spending every waking moment crafting ilices and praying to Orna.

I think about Rayna and the women in the tenement. Are they crafting ilices for me from river clay? Painting them in tar and rolling them in salt? We are not privy to glass blowers and bead makers. All we have in the tenements are the substances we work with our hands. And the materials nature provides us with.

Achill arrives next. He wears an ilice around his neck made of mud from the forest bogs deep within Hummeldorf. The beads are dark as night, filled with bits of grass and decaying leaves. He claims they carry the spirits of his ancestors. That they are filled with the essence of the bog people. The ancient peoples of Merket did not bury their dead. Instead, they placed them in the bogs and let nature claim them.

I stare at the beads and wonder if fragments of hair and bone also decorate his chain. His people might think of the bog bodies as gentle spirits, but the rest of Ectair does not. To us, they are another phantom haunting the deep woods of Hummeldorf.

Ingo, Tristan, and Petrus arrive over the next five minutes, completing our ill-prepared group of eight. Our packs lie in an uneven row before us—toppled, bulky objects discarded in the grass.

A breeze blows in, fluttering my skirt around the ankles of my boots. A tightly fitted jacket covers my blouse. Beneath my outer garments I wear a woolen bloomer suit and hose. It itches, but I am warm. A straw hat covers my woven braid. I've wound a pink ribbon through the plait, hoping to send the kingdom a message of my own. My canteen and a few spare slings dangle from a hemp belt tied around my waist. In a pocket hides my mother's handkerchief.

My mother. As mysterious to me now as the mountain. I want to linger on her secret, but I must stay focused until this task is complete.

The Ascenditures, minus Aedan and Gio, file in, some still drunk from last night's festivities. I try to catch Kiel's eye, to send some signal his way. He keeps his attention focused on everything but me.

The morning drags. The clouds drizzle rain, obscuring the great mountain hanging over us. My pulse rages. We were supposed to be out of here half an hour ago. Still, the monarchy and judges have not arrived. At this rate, we will not reach our camps until well after dark. As if we need another obstacle in our paths.

Finally, spectators trickle in, followed by parliament, Prince Otto, and lastly, King Adolar. The king strides to where we stand, a massive smile cresting his face, his arms wide to those watching.

"Today is the day!" he shouts in his booming voice to the cheers and hollers of those observing.

Their joy makes me cringe.

"Today, seven brave young men and one little girl will set out up the slopes of Mount Bonen in an attempt to secure one of the two coveted spots on the Ascenditure team."

Even though I am still on level ground, with plenty of oxygen in the air and no snow at my feet, I feel light-headed. The king prattles on. I try to focus.

"Their paths will be dangerous. Take a good look at the faces in front of you. Pray to Orna that our competitors will be deemed worthy of survival on these mighty slopes."

Kiel stares at his feet, scratching a line in the dirt with his boot. I need him to know I wasn't trying to be rude yesterday. I wish he could see life through my eyes. At least for today.

The king turns to us and pulls eight different colored pieces of fabric from his robe. He holds them in the air. They flap and twist in the breeze, gathering moisture until they are limp. He hands one to each of us—the soggy pink one to me—and we tie them to our packs. If only on the lower slopes, those below watching through scopes will be able to tell us apart.

I don't want to think of the women swinging from their nooses, but I do. It's hard not to while looking at the pink knot tied to my pack. Rosalie.

As if hearing my thoughts, King Adolar walks back to me. He takes my braid in his hand. My breath catches. My knees quake beneath my skirt. I know he loathes me. Still, he has never touched me. Never paid me any tangible heed. Eyeing the pink ribbon tied through my hair, he smirks.

"Fitting." With a swift and painful tug, he lets go and turns to face the crowd. My hand flies to my hair. I release the breath.

"Each of these contenders will begin at a different point along the base of the mountain. Each shall spend at least two nights upon the slopes before returning. Aedan and Gio left yestereve to climb ahead. They will place a colorful banner at the summit for each competitor to retrieve. They have taken the shortest route and are able men. We should be enjoying their company back in the victor's tent soon."

Clapping comes from the fifty or so spectators. Some wipe the sleep from their eyes. One man didn't bother properly dressing, instead arriving in a heavy velvet sleeping robe with matching slippers. Most have already filled mugs with ale and have begun clinking goblets and placing bets.

"Veit, my boy." A man wearing a dark felt hat with a feather poking from the side pounds the base of one fist into the palm of his other hand. A short coat with brass buttons covers a green vest. Black leather hosen embroidered with green thread sewn into patterns of florals and shadow stag cover his legs. He has probably never set foot in a tenement in his life.

"Make Amia proud, boy," he says. "'Bout time a lad from the North Inland Sea made this team."

Cheering follows from a group of men and one woman surrounding Veit's father. The woman must be his mother. Her face is stern. Everything is pulled tight—her hair, her clothes, her lips. She wears a burgundy dürmel with a white corset and white lace apron. White stockings and shiny black shoes. She has everything in the world, and yet staring at her now, I can't help but pity her.

The king smiles at the wealthy Obeldorf family and continues. "Selection of our two new Ascenditures will be determined by who follows the rules and makes it down first with their corresponding banner. You have each been given a signal flare to light in case of emergency."

One of the judges rushes forward with a pewter bowl and passes it to the king. Inside the bowl are eight small squares of fabric that match the flags attached to our packs.

"We will now determine which climber will attempt each route. The first and last names I call will be the farthest away from the entrance point to the Snag and will therefore require more effort in climbing. The two names I call in the middle will begin with the most direct routes to the summit. May Orna direct my hand to choose each of your paths."

The judge lifts the bowl high into the air. King Adolar turns his face away and pulls the first square. Tristan's face drops as the purple fabric is held high, and he resigns himself to a nearly impossible win. Ingo bows slightly as the yellow piece is drawn next. Petrus steps forward when black is shown.

The next two spots will be the easiest climbs. I am surprised to find myself not rooting for pink to be selected, but rather for Veit's red not to be. The king shuffles the fabric before pulling out a bright red patch of color. Veit cheers under his breath. I pray that I have the spot next to him. I don't. Achill takes the fifth spot when green is selected, followed by Julius and his blue flag.

Gerd and I are the only two left. Standing beside him, I hear the moans he tries to hide. King Adolar raises his hand, plunges it into the bowl, and removes a bright orange square of fabric. Gerd releases a relieved grunt. Even though we all know what remains, the king pulls my pink square and lifts it into the air.

Now that our paths have been chosen, cheers ignite from the crowd. I am in the eighth position, which means that I, along with Tristan in position one, will be the last to reach the Snag.

A päter steps forward holding a Laren Grail. Probably the same one they presented to us before the climb that ended Ellias and Feiko's lives. Twisted metal mimics the sea. A metallic tentacle connects the bowl to the base.

Inside the grail rest eight small balls wrapped in fabric matching our assigned colors. The päter hands each of us one of the spheres, uttering the words, "May Orna and Laren be with you," as he places it in our open palms. I close my fingers around the bundle and tuck it into my pocket next to my mother's handkerchief.

"The gods have spoken," King Adolar pronounces. "Now all that is left for us to do is watch and see who wants this most." He turns to us, nods slightly, and presses his hands together. "Suertgût to you all." The king meets the gaze of every competitor except me. "May your feet find firm footing and your heads a clear sky."

He accepts a mug of wine from a servant girl and raises it to the sky. "Let the competition begin!"

The onlookers cheer. Vessels clink and laughter abounds. Flags of various colors are raised on wooden poles into the sky from spectators hoping the contestant from their kreison will be elevated by Orna. I am the only competitor from the capital today. The flag of the capital, a black outline of the Rektburg set against a stripe of pale blue and a stripe of white, is oddly absent. It has even been removed from the top of the marquee. Yestereve, ten flags topped the tent: the flag of Ectair and the flag of each kreison. Now there are only nine.

As King Adolar moves to join the celebration, he rests his hand briefly on the wayside schrein of Laren, feigning piety. A holzenschrein for Orna sits on the table next to Laren's statue. Candlelight and incense smoke drift through the carved filigree, this one cut out with designs of men and women working in the vineyards.

I should be praying to our gods. But what good has that ever done?

"This way, please." The thin judge who'd exchanged words with Ellias at the competition at Vether's waves us toward a waiting wagon. Servants take our packs and load them onto an empty cart.

My breath sticks in my throat. It's happening. I look around for Kiel and finally hook his stare. He doesn't look away.

"I'm sorry," I whisper, hoping he can read my lips. My heart twists in a painful knot.

Suertgût, he mouths to me and places his hand over his heart.

I mouth a *Tanksye* in return, and clamber into my seat, trying to convince myself that this wasn't our final goodbye. Reaching into my pocket, I touch my mother's handkerchief, running my thumb over the stitching of her words. I want to scream but hold it in, letting the pressure balloon inside my soul.

The ride is bumpy and silent. I jostle into Gerd as the wheels pass over rutted roads and meadows. His eyes don't leave their place on the wooden floor. Against my better judgment, I take his hand and give it a squeeze. He looks up with a shy smile.

Tristan is the first to be dropped off at starting point one.

I give him a knowing nod as his handler joins him to make sure he doesn't begin before we are all in place. One by one, the others exit the wagon until I am alone. When we reach the eighth spot, I scramble from the wagon and set my pack on the ground in front of me. I wish my handler would say something because the silence is excruciating. At any moment, a series of alpenhorn blasts will ring out, signaling the beginning of the climb. I don't have a strategy and know nothing about this route.

Fizhte spruce form a tight circle around my imaginary holding corral. I can't see the mountain beyond their boughs, but I know which direction is up. I double-check that my bootlaces are tight. A numbness creeps through my body, like the feeling one gets after crying themselves empty.

Somewhere in the trees to my side, a herd of kuhkas graze. Their heavy bells jingle. Finally, deep booming fills the air, rippling toward me through the clouds. I shoulder the heavy pack. The pole for the tent juts into the air. I carry the alpenstock like a short walking stick.

I tap one of the slings hanging from my rope belt three times and take my first steps toward the summit. The ground is hard-packed soil covered in pine needles. My hobnailed boots keep getting stuck. Occasionally, I have to stop and remove clumps of dirt and detritus. The boots will work great on the snow; here, they are scheiz.

I move up gradually with the slope. Squirrels squeak from the forest canopy as I pass beneath. They are right to feel protective of their harvests. If I wanted to, I could easily climb these trees and steal their stashes. I smile, imagining a small army of squirrels and chipmunks defending their larders from me, in my skirt.

"Don't worry." I look up with a chuckle. "I have better things to go after right now. Enjoy your hofnuss, you silly creatures."

They peep and chirp back at me. One throws a bit of bark that hits me in the cheek. I laugh even harder and keep moving through the trees in what feels like the right direction. I come across a lone kuhka, this one the color of burnt butter and at a height level with my shoulders, and brush my hand across its back. The kuhka lets out a deep moo before trotting off to the tune of her rattling bell.

Eventually I poke through the wall of trees and finally meet the mountain's intimidating façade. "Orna," I hiss the goddess's name. It comes out in a foggy breath that coils and swirls in front of my face. "I need you to listen. Not just as a god, but also as a fram. I can't help wondering why you let Adolar pull my name last. But no bother. Now that we're here help me, damn it."

I know it's bad to end a prayer with a swear word. It was also bad to put me in the eighth position.

My boots crunch the white snow. I look around at the few remaining pine trees that will soon vanish behind me with the rest of the living world. The quiet up here is both relaxing and alarming. It allows me to get lost in a groove but also reminds me how very much alone I am.

I pull my glacier goggles over my eyes. Far below, people mill about at base camp, filling their drinks and assembling large scopes to watch the drama above unfold. I am certain many are praying for an avalanche or some other riveting disaster. I hope this whole trip was a waste of their time and dracals.

I pause, staring up at the snow and rock ahead. Ancient lava flows of basalt and andesite have shoved their way through the white powder, creating dark gray masses in the otherwise stark landscape. It feels like I am staring at some lifeless, frozen world. I wonder if this is what Ainar looks like—white silence and forbidding rock. The peace that normally accompanies a climb eludes me on these barren slopes.

At first my energy is relentless. I've even shed my overcoat down to my blouse. My mittens and outerwear remain at the top of my gear pack. I feel like I could reach the summit by evening.

The angle steepens. The snow increases and turns to knee-deep powder. My legs and lungs begin to burn. I consider checking my pack for rocks. Veit would have done something like that to me. Burkhart and Tizian probably helped. I don't have the energy to stop and unload everything. My muscles and joints, unaccustomed to so much weight, tremble with each step. It dawns on me that to make one vertical foot of distance, I must take three steps forward. Gritting my teeth, I try to expel air from my lungs in forceful blasts.

I think of my father, the Ascenditure-turned-sea captain, and wonder if he ever climbed Mount Bonen. Endless stories of his heroism have been shared with me through the years, but I am not sure which are real and which were concocted threads of truth sewn together to mend a little girl's broken heart. Especially with Obid's recent revelations. My father is as much a myth to me as the snow monsters in Ainar or the three-headed snakes in Kobo—my father and my mother both.

I remember the hazy morning when Mina Ascher strode down the pier an hour 'fore dawn, arms wrapped 'round a cloaked figure. 'Twas the Lady Genalt....No one knows why he quit. Really shocked the kingdom, though. Me, I think it had to do with Mina's work.

Most memories I have of my mother are of her in the kitchen baking cakes or fileting fish my father brought home from the sea. Quiet afternoons of her reading poetry while I played on the floor with my dolls. Her long, dark hair cascading down her shoulders as she stitched images of tolvalus, starsets, and mountains onto pieces of cloth she shared with her friends and their children. Twice a week, she went for prayer at the monastery, once a week for tea with the women's society. But every night when I went to bed and every morning when I awoke, she was there.

Fog rolls in, blocking my view of the route. I stop to pull on my coat and mittens as first rain, then sleet and snow bite my exposed flesh. In a matter of minutes the temperature plummets. I shiver uncontrollably. Removing my canteen, I take a few quick sips, then stuff a handful of gegenberries into my mouth.

I resume my climb, unsure how far I've come or how far I still have to go. The mist and snow blur everything. I trudge ahead, hoping my competitors have given up fighting the weather and taken shelter for their first night. I have more ground to cover, so I don't have that luxury. At some point I will hit a wall of rock and follow along its edge until I reach the Snag at 12,000 feet. My goal is to get as close to that ledge as I can tonight before resting.

I've lost track of time, but hours must have passed. Maybe four at this point. Or seven. The wind intensifies, whipping cold air against my face. My goggles fog over. I tuck my head low and lift my weary feet over and over again. The snow is so deep an ox would struggle to plow through it. I fall, and it takes me five minutes to gather the energy to rise. At one point I think I hear a scream ring out from across the mountain. I ignore my initial reaction to search for the distressed climber. We are on our own up here. We must climb alone, and if it comes to it, we must die alone.

Even though I typically prefer to be solo, the strangling loneliness soon becomes too much. I am lost, accompanied only by the sounds of the wind, my puffing breath, and the long-gone echo of someone's cry. I am heading in the wrong direction—up and away from safety, up and into the mouth of a waiting beast.

Darkness falls. With it comes a roaring wind so powerful I have to focus my energy on not getting swept off my feet. As the temperature drops, it becomes clear I must find shelter if I hope to be more than a block of ice come morning. My only comfort lies in the fact that the others will also have to stop.

There is no refuge on the side of a mountain, only endless stretches of unrelenting snow and rock. I flop my pack onto the frozen ground and carefully remove the canvas sheet, gripping its edges with all my might so it doesn't take flight. Once the tent is erected and staked down, I spread out an oil-covered cloth as a floor and unroll a threadbare rug on top of it to provide insulation between my body and the snow. I toss the rest of my gear—there are no rocks—and my body inside and pray for the center pole to be strong enough to combat the violent wind. I have no idea where I am, and for the thousandth time, I curse this mission and the men who sent me on it.

Even though I am not hungry, I pull the stove from my pack, light it with a match, and melt snow. First, I fill my canteens with the hot water, thawing what had earlier frozen, before stuffing them into the bottom of my feather-filled sleep sack, where my body heat will hopefully keep them from refreezing during the night. Next, I remove a tin of dehydrated beans and rice and add boiling water, shaking with cold tremors as I wait for dinner to rehydrate. When moisture has expanded the food, I scarf it down, desperate for the warmth from the nourishment.

I have to pee. I decide to hold it until morning. After staring at the canvas for a miserable hour thinking only of my over-filled bladder, I yank on my boots and step from the tent. It is as if every gust of wind carries with it a handful of knives. They slice through my bloomers and blouse, cutting at the soft skin below. Dropping my pants, I groan as the frigid air assaults my nether regions. When the urine comes, it flies in every direction, splashing my thighs. I want to wipe it away, but I don't have the energy to clean myself. I crawl back into the tent and collapse in my bag, freezing piss and all.

The wind whips the canvas so ferociously it smacks me in the face. I have no idea what time it is or how many hours have passed, but I lie awake with the tent popping me in the cheek and the cold twisting its fingers through my veins. I want to scream at my body to fall asleep, but the more desperate I become, the more my mind refuses to relax. Resigned to a restless night, I close my eyes and think of Kiel down in base camp, probably assuaging any feelings of rejection with a Koboan whore. I don't know why the thought bothers me so much, but surprisingly the rage that fills my body makes my blood boil. Even if it is in my head, I feel warmer.

My mind drifts into that strange place between wakefulness and sleep. I dream of Kiel. But instead of a strange woman, it is me who joins him in his bed. Up here, away from the prying eyes of condescending men, it is safe to enjoy these thoughts. The dream is more than pleasant until Kiel presses a pillow to my face. I can't breathe. But it is not Kiel, and it is not a dream. I open my eyes and stare directly into the canvas crushed against my face. The wind has gone quiet. I push lightly on the fabric, and a new horror takes over.

The tent has become a coffin buried under the heavy weight of snow. If I don't get out soon, I will suffocate.

11

I thrust my body upward and realize that only a few inches of snow lie above me. Last night's storm, rather than an avalanche, toppled my tent. I kick the powder from the canvas and drag my gear out into the misty morning. As I load my pack, I listen for another voice—something to let me know I am on the right track. The wind has ceased. A quiet fog cradles me in its hands.

It's still fairly dark. I imagine the fishmongers back home filling their tables with fresh catches. The cod and salmon might still have some flop in them. Sailors are stumbling across the pier. The factories have started buzzing. Rayna's hands are covered in warm tar. Pulmy's hacking up her lungs alongside the stamping of pistons and the blazing of incinerators.

I pull out a boiled potato and gnaw on the tuber. I load my gear, shoulder my pack, and trudge through the snow and dense fog. My daydreams turn to Ellias's horrific fall. I clear my head of all thoughts to avoid going there.

My muscles ache. My shoulders protest under the weight of the pack. Each time I lift my foot from the snow to step forward, my calves and thighs tremble. I am strong and athletic, but mountaineering is a whole new game—one I have not trained to play. The morning progresses, and my limbs begin to loosen.

I concentrate on breathing and what it will feel like to finally hold the golden rope and recite my vows. I find a rhythm. Through loud exhalations and the occasional grunt, I make progress. Mist prevents me from seeing more than twenty yards ahead. I wish there would be a break long enough for me to glimpse the wall of volcanic debris that will guide me to the Snag.

An hour passes. Then another. Panic rises. Veit and Achill have probably already scrambled over the route to the upper slopes and the glaciers. I think of yesterday's scream and hate myself for hoping it came from whoever was in the lead.

Something appears through the fog ahead—a dark silhouette pressed against the white backdrop. I approach the mass and place my hands against its hard surface, smiling. The dark rock wall extends as far as I can see in both directions. I turn left toward the Snag and drag my mittened finger along, humming a tune my father used to sing when I was trying to fall asleep.

There's something in the wind, it blows in from the sea. Carrying the voice of a long-lost daughter and the failings of her great dream.

Even before I associated the notes with my dead father and my own experiences, it was a gloomy tune. Now the song breaks my heart. I hum anyway to keep from feeling so alone.

A lass with so much beauty, a lass above the rest. Her father he betrayed her, at Laren's cruel behest.

Legend states that long ago, Laren fell in love with King Miter's youngest daughter, Layal, and was driven mad with longing. He begged Miter for her hand. Initially, Miter refused the request. After all, what kind of father would abandon his daughter to such a brute? As long as Layal did not touch a single bit of her flesh to a body of water, she was safe from the ruthless god.

But Miter proved as merciless as Larin. He made a deal with Larin—control of the god's great seabeast Hildegroth for his daughter. On an evening stroll along the Straits of Hidar, Miter shoved Layal into the sea. She was pulled beneath the waves, never to be seen again.

We are all Layals now, our spirits traded for the monsters of this world.

Lost in the past, I bump into what I thought was a boulder. The object jumps. A high-pitched scream bounces from the rock wall down the slope of the mountain. The climber spins and slumps to his knees, laughing hoarsely.

"Miter's arsch, Klarke. You almost gave me a heart attack!"

Gerd lifts his snow goggles from his face and wipes the sweat from his eyes.

I join in his laughter and pull him to his feet, helping to dust the snow from his pack. Never in my life have I been so ecstatic to see someone. "I wasn't expecting you either." I remove my canteen and gulp at the water. Not a lot comes out. I shake the bottle and hear bits of slush.

"You must have moved quickly." He takes a swig of liquid and pops a few bartlenuts into his mouth. "I started a good distance away from you. Did you not get stopped by the storm?"

I swallow the water I've been swishing around my mouth and pull my wool coat more tightly around my body. Resting at this altitude chills one's muscles quickly. "I stopped. I'm not sure where because the fog was so thick. Did you hear a scream yesterday?"

Gerd nods. His brow furrows and he frowns. "Came from my left. I don't think we would have heard anything from the guys on the far side. Must have been Julius or Achill."

"Damn." I kick the ground, hoping he's wrong, hoping it was Veit who got into trouble and not one of the nice guys. "Well, I hope you can keep up. I plan to overtake Julius in the next hour—if he's still…okay."

"I can keep up." Gerd nods. Ice crystals coat his eyelashes and the tips of his hair.

He pushes himself to his threshold, fighting to keep pace. Following the rock wall is straightforward but time consuming. It infuriates me that I drew the farthest spot from the Snag. If I had started square in the middle, I'd have a guaranteed spot on the team. Now I am traversing while several others have a straight shot to the summit.

At 12,000 feet, my lungs begin to scream for oxygen. My brain teeters upon the thin edge of oxygen-starved sanity. The wind joins us, throwing bursts of snow into our faces and cutting into my garments. Occasionally I peer back at Gerd, and even though his hunkered form is a little farther behind each time, he keeps up. Someday, after I have made the team, he will be a great addition to the Ascenditures. I think of his little sister, Marike, learning to climb from her older brother and watching me from afar. Perhaps she too will make a good Ascenditure.

We overtake Julius in what I determine to be about two hours. My heart relaxes at the sight of his lumbering form.

"Julius!" I shout through the wind, trying not to sneak up on him like I did Gerd.

He stops and turns slowly, waving a gloved hand.

"You're okay," Gerd notes, clapping his friend on his shoulder. "We heard a scream yesterday."

"Oh, that," Julius says, his voice tight. He shudders. "I kept feeling like something was stalking me. Got wicked creeped out. Let out a wee yelp when what looked like a bergbear ran across my path. Too many stories from my omie, ya know? Mind goes strange when you're at these heights."

I recall my dream of Kiel pressing a pillow into my face.

"Yeah. It does." A shake of my canteen reveals even less sloshing. We will need to melt water soon. "So, you're well then?"

Julius shrugs. "Not exactly. This morning my tent was completely soaked. Water dripping onto me like it was raining inside. Everything I have is wet. It's like someone came and dumped a bucket of water on me."

A rack of shivers suddenly shakes him. Stepping closer, I remove my mitten and feel his clothes—they are soaked. Blue hues tinge his lips.

"Julius. You've got to change. You'll get hypothermia."

"I'll be fine as long as I keep moving," he says, swaying on unsteady legs. "Besides, everything is wet. Can't stop now."

Gerd and I exchange a concerned glance. The selfish part of me is glad Julius doesn't want more help. We're too far behind to stop for wardrobe changes. A smaller part of me catches the way his eyes can't seem to focus.

We are each responsible for our own well-being up here. I was not put on the side of this mountain to make sure Julius keeps his hosen dry, and Gerd remembers to melt snow.

Achill and Veit will already have made it over the Snag, but there is a good chance we will bump into Petrus, Ingo, or Tristan. I have no idea how the conditions have been on their side of the mountain.

Lifting my boot from the deep powder, I trundle ahead. Julius lags. Each time we pause to rest, he struggles more to form sentences. Even though he has yet to accept it, he will not reach the summit. I pause and wait for Gerd to catch up.

"We have to leave Julius at the Snag. He's done. If we take him onto the glacier fields like that, then he will die." I have to whisper loudly for Gerd to hear my words over the roar of the wind. He gives me a nod and follows when I march on. We get strung out once again.

The stretch of sheer rock we've been following morphs into a series of ledges about five yards wide. Nature's staircase. The Snag. On the far side, a figure stands above another who is laid out on the snow. I race across the bottom ledge, sucking in gulps of the thin air. Tristan stands over Ingo, who lies curled in a drift, gripping his leg.

"Found him," Tristan says between breaths. "About a quarter mile back. He fell and twisted his ankle."

I drop my pack to the ground. Tristan was in the first position and Ingo the second, which means Petrus, Veit, and Achill have probably already headed toward the summit. I crane my neck to look up the rock steps for movement, but a groan pulls my gaze back down. Julius has collapsed on the ground next to Ingo. I peer back up the foggy steps. Half of me wants to wish these guys luck and begin my climb over the Snag, leaving them behind in the heavy mist.

"Fiek all," Ingo groans. His breath catches, and I realize he is crying. "It's over for me."

His words, his emotion, hit me like a punch in the gut. I know what it's like to lose your dream.

Gerd kneels next to Ingo and pats his head with a gloved hand. "We'll have you safe and warm soon."

Every curse word I know flies through my brain. I imagine

Gerd, quite possibly the kindest soul in all of Ectair, out on the snow by himself. Thirteen years old. Blown about by the wind. His screams echoing into the abyss. Sent here to die by a desperate mother. Gerd, who has been so kind to me. To everyone.

"Fiek all." I repeat Ingo's words beneath my breath and turn away from the Snag. After donning warm clothes, I join Gerd and Tristan in pulling Ingo's tent from his pack and setting it up.

Julius doesn't protest as we strip his wet clothes and move him and Ingo into their feather-filled sleep sacks next to each other. We try to make them warm and comfortable, taking time to melt snow for their canteens and rehydrating their food so they have something to eat. An imaginary clock ticks away in my brain. Each second is a step on Veit's way to the summit.

Outside the tent, the wind has picked up and is screaming so loudly it could be Hildegroth laying waste to the kingdom again. Ingo and Julius are down. Petrus, Veit, and Achill are somewhere ahead. Gerd, Tristan, and I are prepared to move beyond the Snag onto the glacier fields, where we will spend the night somewhere at higher altitude. I remove the flare from Julius's pack and light it, sending the flame high into the air. Hopefully, someone below will see the signal through the fog.

Clenching my teeth, I look at the two remaining faces staring at me as if I am their leader and they are awaiting my command. I hate myself for what I am about to do, but I think I would hate myself more if I let these two wander into the darkness alone. I curse the mountain, the gods, Gerd's stupid mother. Then I take a deep breath and hope neither of these climbers is in the pocket of the king.

"We have been sent to our deaths. We all know that. No one climbs Mount Bonen alone. Sure, Petrus, Veit, and Achill are ahead of us, but that doesn't mean they aren't a thousand feet down at the bottom of a fissure, wishing they'd done something different."

Gerd flinches. Tristan has no visible reaction.

If it gets out that I've colluded to cheat, then so be it. At least I didn't let these boys, decent men, die. I raise my voice

above the shrieking wind that seems to taunt me, building in
ferocity. "I know we are all gunning for the same positions,
and we want to win above all else. But the truth is, we don't.
We want to survive, and then we want to win." I pause to take
stock of their expressions. I pause to take stock of my feelings.
Do I really mean that? I think of Rayna's words that I can do
no good for women if I am dead. Yes, I mean it. Win or lose, I
will not die on this mountain.

Gerd and Tristan look at each other and nod.

"Once we climb beyond these ledges, we are out of sight of
even the most powerful scopes the judges will be using. Above
the Snag, the crevasses multiply. Without a rope team, we will
be heading to our deaths. I know what I am about to suggest
goes against the rules, but we are being sent for slaughter, which
means the rules must change. If you two will join me, we can
rope up as a team and, more importantly, survive. None of us
have mountaineering experience, but we stand a better chance
together than alone."

"It's treason." Tristan leans forward, his sharp eyes cutting
into me. He doesn't look mad, just afraid. "If we all go up together, how can a winner be determined? And we will be slow.
It's a great plan if your goal is to lose."

I nod, not moving my eyes from his. He is right, of course.
By proposing this, I have shot my dreams with an arrow and
am watching them bleed out onto the snow. But what good
is a dream when you are dreaming from the sweet slumber of
death?

I shrug. "By all means, Tristan, strike out across the Guale
glacier alone. I hope you find the glory you are looking for. But
at six foot five and two hundred-plus pounds, nature will not be
kind to you when your foot breaks through a snow bridge and
you plummet to your death."

Tristan looks up over the rock steps. "I want to live," he says.
"Rules be damned."

The three of us shake hands through our mittens, glance at
the tent with our injured comrades, and crunch our way up to

the Snag. The rock ledges are jagged and high. I have to remove my pack, heave it up one step, then lug my body behind. Small slits cover my jacket. My cheek is bleeding. The nails sticking from the soles of my boots get stuck in small cracks. I have to yank my legs to and fro to free them. By the time I reach the top, I am so out of breath and strength I consider taking a nap and letting the elements claim me. Face down on a pebbly shelf, I feel a hand rest on my shoulder.

"Almost there. We can rest soon."

I push myself to my knees and stand, following Gerd down the back side of the Snag. We pause behind the rock shelf, finally safe from prying eyes below, although I can't imagine they've seen much through the mist.

A break in the clouds offers a peek at the summit. Scattered rays of starlight fall from the sky, lighting up the slope in a dazzling sparkle. Slopes and ridges block the path ahead, but I can make out the crown of the summit. The edges of the crater. Still so far away. I could stare at the magnificence all day, but we have work to do.

"Gerd, remove your tent and leave it here." I pull the canvas and bamboo pole from my pack and discard them onto the ice. "Tristan, give us each something to carry. It'll be tight sleeping for one night, but if we shed the extra weight, we will make better time."

I take the rope from my pack and stretch it out across the snow, taking a deep breath as I try to recall everything I read in the mountaineering book. Moving to the center of the rope, I tie the first figure eight knot, then walk thirty feet in each direction to tie the final two knots. I coil the excess rope on each end for the leader and last climber to carry across their bodies. Finally, I turn to Tristan and Gerd, sizing them up.

"Gerd, take the lead. Tristan, take center. I'll bring up the rear. Keep space between each other. You don't want the rope to pile in front of you." I try to keep my voice confident and steady, despite feeling like a fraud. "Alpenstock in hand at all times. Yell if you fall."

I loop a rope around my chest, fashioning a harness. The clouds glow above us. The beams of light shift, but they have yet to vanish. It must be sometime after noon, which means fierce storms could be building. "Let's see how far we can get in an hour. Then we'll make our second camp."

"But the other three are so far ahead already." Tristan ties into the middle knot and stares at me through his bug-like glacier goggles. "If we don't push ahead, we stand no chance."

I shake my head, tie in, and pull the alpenstock from the snow. Now that I've decided to sacrifice my dream for my life, I am all in. "If we continue today, we could get caught in a lightning storm. Afternoon thundersnow is common. Rather than take the risk, we will build camp early, get in a few hours of sleep, and make our pitch for the summit after the moonrise. If all goes well, we will be marching into base camp by tomorrow evening, ahead of the others. Because, you know, we don't die."

Tristan wants to argue, but he keeps his mouth shut. We space out, leaving slack in the rope to give each other time to react before we too are pulled into a crevasse should someone fall. I give Gerd a thumbs-up to proceed, even though my legs are shaking, and a deep fear has mounted. I have never traveled over a glacier, but I know how dangerous their hidden crevasses can be—vertical chasms of unforgiving ice waiting to swallow you whole, as treacherous and deadly as Hildegroth and Ignaz, the wicked statdamen from our omie's stories.

We begin to move, passing in and out of the light rays falling from the sky. Our boots crunch the icy snow. I hope to have made the right decision.

Our hour of climbing passes without incident. Even though I still have energy, I call for a halt. Gerd and I erect the tent while Tristan lights his stove and melts snow. After filling the canteens, we rehydrate dinner and sit on our packs outside the canvas structure, silently eating our ration of food.

Our camp is wedged against an outcropping of boulders protruding from the whiteness. From our perch we can see down into the next valley, into the deep blue cracks of the crevasses that have become exposed on the glacier there. Ice, snow, and jagged folds of rock. Those are the skeleton, muscles, and skin of a mountain.

I take a bite of the warm oatmash and swallow. What are the others thinking? Or plotting. What visions do men have above 13,000 feet when their lives and dreams are at stake? Do they think of camaraderie or betrayal, life or death, and if death, whose? Unless any of the other three have fallen, there are six of us headed for the summit now. It's hard to imagine all six climbers will retain their humanity when no one is looking and when no one will hear a scream.

Wind roars down from the summit, swirling snow in a flurry around us. The gaps in the clouds close. Starlight slips back into the firmament. Goosebumps prickle my skin as a round of thunder and lightning electrify the sky. The three of us exchange glances and head for shelter. I send a prayer to Orna for the safety of the men farther up the mountain—the ones who decided to dance with fire—and climb into the tent behind Tristan and Gerd.

12

I toss and turn, as much as one can while sardined between two bodies. Occasionally the night and elevation steal my breath, and I wake up gasping. As my mind fights to fall asleep yet remain alert, it becomes harder for me to determine what is real and what is a phantom fashioned by a spiraling mind. Wind becomes a human scream. Snow falling from the sky becomes a roaring avalanche. Canvas flapping against our faces is a snow unger trying to claw into the tent.

Eventually, even though all I want to do is find peace in sleep, it is time to rise. I sit and wipe my eyes, fighting the nausea of altitude sickness. The darkness carries a cold so dense it penetrates the marrow of my bones. Shivering, I shake the two climbers next to me until both Gerd and Tristan are sitting.

I pull a carbide lamp from my pack and attach it to the front of my hat. After igniting the acetylene gas, I yank the canteen from my sleeping bag. It is slushy. Stuffing it uncomfortably into the front of my bloomers, I pull on my layers and steel myself to leave the tent. Even though the wind has died and the storm has been swallowed by a crack in the sky, cold and darkness make the calm night perfidious. I take a moment to stretch, hoping warm muscles will heat the rest of me.

While the others dress and prepare for the climb, I melt snow and concoct a breakfast of mashed oats and bartlenuts. We shovel the food into our mouths, then strike camp and take our places along the rope.

"Make sure the rope is tight around your chest, and your alpenstock is in hand." I raise my voice so both of my teammates can hear. "Suertgût, and don't forget to yell if you fall. The other two of us will drop to the ground and dig axes into the snow. If you are the one who falls into the crevasse, do everything you can to stop yourself."

As if on cue, the wind moans. I take the first step and force my mind into a groove. Lack of oxygen and the cold air keep me from finding a rhythm. My legs must weigh a hundred pounds each. Every pathetic step feels like it will be my last.

My lungs catch fire. My head throbs. Tristan hunches ahead of me. He weaves in and out along an invisible line. I wager he is experiencing the same troubles.

Why do we even want this?

Azura finally peers from behind a cloud, providing the first view of the summit, still a few thousand vertical feet away. I spot something else—a single light like a distant fire bug moving upward. Scanning the behemoth, I look for the lights of the other two climbers but find only darkness. My mind goes to the worst possible place, but I remind myself that the other two might already be at the summit, blocked by the crater walls.

We all knew the risks. If their lights were extinguished by death, then at least they died fighting for their dreams.

My muscles turn to stone. My lungs are useless sacks. I have always prided myself on being strong, but this is something entirely different. My mind must remain resolute long after my endurance gives out, or I will be stranded up here with the ghosts of those who fell before me.

A soft glow rises behind the mountain. Through the dawn mist, my companions trudge, still with energy enough to lift one foot in front of the other. The small lamplight has vanished. Its bearer has reached the summit. At least one spot is no longer available. The other two must still be up there. Or injured. Or gone. How do I even feel about Petrus and Achill? I don't know them well. I don't want anything to happen to them but if it does…

A scream assaults me, so close and guttural it raises the hair on my skin. The rope snaps. I am jerked to the ground, face-planting on the hard-packed snow. Pain shoots through my skull, and I am yanked forward. A trail of blood smears the white snow behind me.

"Scheiz!" I flail with the alpenstock.

Another scream reaches me as my body gains speed. I maneuver the pick of my axe into the snow. It skitters over the compact white. My fatigued arms can't deliver enough pressure. Dread plummets into my core. I am going to die. I know it.

I hack and slash. Kick my boots. Shards of ice bite into my skin. I can't slow myself. Ellias pops into my brain. His body broken on the moraine. "Nide!"

My legs crest the edge of something with no bottom, and the alpenstock digs in. The rope harness around my chest pulls tight as the weight of two climbers dangling beneath nearly severs my torso. Something in my ribcage crunches.

"Ahhhh!" I whimper. I need to scream, but I don't have the air. One of the men lets out a horrible shriek.

Gasping for breath, I let out a pained sob. I tremble with a force no cold can deliver. The taste of iron fills my mouth. I spit red onto the snow. I run my tongue across my teeth. They are intact, but my mouth tastes like raw meat. I try to find my breath and crawl to the edge of the crevasse, terrified to look over.

"Miter's arsch!" Tristan shouts. He rests on a steep slope thirty feet below me. His alpenstock is stuck into the ice.

He is secure. I let out a relieved breath and grasp my side. I feel like I've been kicked by a mule.

"I'm okay!" Tristan holds on to the base of the stock and peers out over the abyss. "But Gerd is hurt. Looks like he hit a ledge about twenty feet down. Maybe broke something."

A whimper drifts up. Stifled sobs. "My leg. It hurts so bad."

I imagine Gerd's mother standing next to me, screaming into the void for her son. I owe her nothing, yet my only goal now is to reunite mother and child. Losing one or the other is the worst of all feelings.

"Gods be damned." I scan the ground, unsure of what to do next. Confirming that the pick is secured, I sit back and dig the heels of my crampons into the snow for extra protection. "Do you think you can climb up?" I yell down to Tristan in a shaking voice. "I can't pull you guys to the top."

"Maybe." Tristan digs the spikes on the front of his boot into the cerulean wall of ice. With the alpenstock in hand and the hobnails jutting from his boots, he manages to stick himself to the wall. "Aren't there better and more precise ways of doing this?"

It's not a sheer drop he has to ascend, but it's steep enough to make my heart race. "Of course there are." Irritation flares both at the king for sending us up here unprepared and at Tristan for expecting me to somehow magic myself into a mountaineer. "But as we were not provided with proper gear, as this is my first time up here, and my only practical experience came two moons ago in an artificial hole, this is what we've got."

I hear a grunt and a few choice swears. Gerd cries out in another long wail.

"Hey, Gerd!" I shout. "Can you climb out of there?" The taste of blood makes me woozy. My cheekbone throbs. My tongue is swollen and tender. Every time I open my mouth to speak or breathe, my ribcage tightens.

Gerd's moan reaches my ears. "I can see the bone!" He trails off with a throaty wail.

"Gerd, you have to figure it out." I try to sound comforting, but it's not my greatest strength. Ellias's face appears again in my mind—before the fall. And after. I promise myself I won't leave Gerd to the same fate.

"Okay." I turn my attention back to Tristan. "There's thirty feet of rope between you and me and twenty feet between you and Gerd plus ten feet of slack. You should be able to make it at least ten feet before his weight becomes an issue. Maybe together we can pull Gerd out from there."

"He's fifty feet down in this hülehole, Klarke, and I'm exhausted!" Tristan presses his body against the icy slope and breathes hard. "By the time I reach you, I'll be completely out of fuel. He's got to do this himself."

Gerd's frightened sob echoes upward, mixed with desperate words. "Don't leave me!"

I bite my lip to keep from panicking. More blood leaks onto

my tongue. I spit and take in a greedy inhalation of the thin air. My ribs punch back.

I can't live with another climber's death bouncing around my head. I have too many of those already. "Climb as high as you can, Tristan. We'll figure it out."

Tristan begins his ascent, digging first his axe and then the sharp spikes on his boots into the ice. He closes the distance between us quickly. When Gerd's weight becomes an issue, he stops and glares up at me. "What now?"

I want to be angry because I am not a mountaineer, and I am not their leader. I sure as scheiz don't want this responsibility. But getting mad won't save Gerd. I rack my brain for a solution.

"Untie your sling from the rope and free climb."

"Excuse me?" Tristan glances down into the dark pit where the ice wall fades from turquoise to black, dropping to a place the light cannot reach. "Have you lost your mind?"

I shake my head and wave my hand for him to hurry. "You're a good climber. You've got it. Besides, if you fall on this, you don't deserve to be an Ascenditure anyway."

"What the hüle, Klarke?" He stays quiet for a few seconds. Gerd's muffled sobs issue from deep in the crevasse. My lip throbs.

"If I die, it's on you," Tristan says in a low voice.

"Fine. Whatever."

He unties his sling. The rope dangles free against the ice. His arms shake.

I keep myself from closing my eyes, from holding my breath each time he pulls the pick from the ice. When a boot leaves the wall to kick a new step, I feel dizzy.

A few feet below me, Tristan slips, but he manages to get the axe in place before losing a second foothold. I lean forward and take hold of his backpack shoulder strap. We clasp hands and spend a few seconds choking down our sobs.

"Fiek this mountain," Tristan says. He punches the snow next to where he lies. "And fiek the king."

My head whips in his direction. I cringe at the flaring of my ribs. Resting my free hand on his shoulder, I nod. That's when I notice tears in his eyes. Tough, bullish Tristan is so afraid he allows himself to shed tears in front of me, a woman.

"Fiek the king," I whisper back to him, sharing every iota of his emotions. "The biggest way to stick it to him is for us all to make it out alive. Help me save Gerd so that his life is not lost in that sadistic bastard's games."

Tristan removes his goggles long enough to wipe his tears, then grabs the rope in front of me. His expression hardens. "Ready, Gerd?" he shouts into the pit. Gerd answers with a bellowing howl when the rope comes taut.

Together we heave Gerd from the crevasse. It takes us several minutes of pulling, breathing, and recovering to get him out. Each time I tense my abs to wrench the rope, my ribs catch fire. Gerd's blood-curdling screams echo and reverberate. It sounds like there is a legion of victims. By the time we pull Gerd onto solid ground, he has passed out from the pain. His right leg bone looks like it has snapped in half and juts through his skin and ripped pants. I cringe at the sight of the marrow seeping through the hole in his body.

"We have to leave him." I pull Gerd's sleeping bag from his pack and try to get him warm and comfortable. We don't bother with a tent. We don't have the energy.

Tristan lights the fuse on Gerd's flare. It shoots into the sky, above the height of the Snag. Above the tip of the summit—a bright ball of orange flame hangs in the clouds above us for thirty seconds. Someone will see it. They have watchers around the clock. And they will know it is Gerd from the color of the flare. Rescue climbers will already be on the mountain. They would have come as soon as they saw our first flare yesterday. It shouldn't take them long to reach Gerd.

I close my eyes, pray to Orna, and sever every emotion that commands me to stay with Gerd. Whimpering in his bedding. Alone. Clutching his leg. Afraid. Weak.

Gerd is not my responsibility. Tristan is not my responsibility. Julius, Ingo, Petrus, Achill, Veit...

Rayna. Rosalie. Ellias. Feiko... Living names mutate into the dead. Anguished faces float in and out of focus.

"Ugh!" I grab my skull and silently plead for the visions to go away.

"You okay?" Tristan drops the used flare onto the snow.

My hands fall to my sides. Panic is replaced by numb exhaustion. I forget why I am here. Why I want this. "Fine. I'm fine."

Tristan shrugs.

I reconfigure the rope for a two-person team. Silence guides us as we plow on. I am not sure what we're headed for. I won't make the team. Tristan won't make the team. Gerd, Ingo, Julius... I stop before the names can again take hold. Cleos is rising to a clear day, but my spirits are as cold as the heart of Mount Bonen.

"Lucky bastard," Tristan mumbles, breaking the quiet.

I step on a coil of rope. He has stopped moving. I look beyond Tristan to the imposing figure headed our way. The first climber, a bright red banner attached to his pack, tromps toward us from the summit.

Veit approaches, a nasty grin visible between his goggles and scarf. "Cheating to win, huh, Klarke? How womanly of you." He points to the red fabric on his backpack and lets out an annoying whistle. "Better hurry."

"Have you seen Petrus or Achill?" Petrus and Achill. Names I am not sure belong on the list of the living or the dead.

"Nah. Left them in the shallows from the beginning." Veit takes a sip from his canteen and eats a handful of gegenberries.

Petrus and Achill should have reached the Snag before us and continued up the mountain. That, or Tristan and Ingo would have come across them on the lower slopes. We should have seen their lights when we saw Veit's.

I glance at Tristan, who shrugs.

"We haven't seen them either," I say.

"Who gives a horse's scheiz? Just means one of you will win." Veit stuffs his canteen back into his pack and lifts it onto his shoulders. He points the end of his alpenstock at Tristan.

"If I were you, I'd grab my banner and drop her dead weight in a hole."

A sickness lodges in my gut as Veit walks away. I try to determine if it originates from jealousy at his clear victory or concern for myself and the others. Maybe both.

Tristan doesn't react to the comment. He stands still, his mouth in a straight line. His eyes hidden beneath his goggles.

I watch Veit descend and gesture for Tristan to lead on. Shoving away my concerns, I focus on breathing and the placement of each step. We fall into our rhythm. By midmorning we crest the ridgeline. At the bottom of the white crater, seven flags hang gently frosted from seven wooden poles. Only the red one is missing.

Something happened to Petrus and Achill.

We slide down into the crater and approach the banners. I untie the pink one and attach it to my pack. Tristan unties the purple one and ties it to his. We drop to our knees and pull out the small bundles the päter provided before we left base camp. Because Mount Bonen is the region's guardian, there is no holzenschrein for us to adorn with ilices. Instead, as we did atop Fitzhan, we will offer dirt from below, blessed by the päters, as gratitude for safe passage across Orna's slopes. Forgetting this measure of respect can have deadly consequences.

I untie the bundle from its pink sheath and frown. A glance at Tristan's offering shows me a handful of soil. I look back at mine. Ash and something small. White. Porous. A fragment of bone, perhaps.

"Ready?" he asks.

"Mmm-hmm." I nod and clasp my fingers around the offering so he cannot see. This message, this threat, has left me with nothing for Orna. Instead of living soil from the ground, I will give her ash. Death. Laren's realm. I will pay for this offense.

"Oh-me-auh," Tristan whispers, lifting his hand into the air.

"Oh-me-auh," I repeat. My fist remains clenched to hide the ash.

"Tanks be to Orna," Tristan says.

"Tanks be to Orna." I open my palm away from him and let the wind grab the ashes. The bone fragment falls into the snow.

∂⍟

Tristan and I sip water and chew the rest of our snacks. Something has happened to Petrus and Achill. Those behind us are wounded. Of our duo, only one can succeed, which means our descent will be an ugly, exhausting race through deadly terrain. But as no competitors nip at our heels, there is no hurry to leave the calm of the summit.

I take this brief truce to rest and regroup. I will need every speck of strength to beat the man next to me. Especially if he heeds Veit's suggestion. I keep glancing at him, trying to catch madness in his eyes. I see many things, but betrayal and murder are not among them.

"Burkhart once told me you were a bit of a foze."

I cringe at the offensive word and focus on the ice crystals that have formed along the edges of the five remaining flags. I don't need a lecture right now about my place in society. What I should wear. How I should speak. What I should do with my life. How I've offended his existence. If Tristan makes up his mind about someone based on the comments of a lizard-brained rock like Burkhart then—

"I believed him. But he's wrong. And I'm sorry."

I turn to face him, bereft of words.

"I'm sorry I thought you were a—"

I raise my hand and wave his comment away. "You don't have to say it again."

He takes another sip of water. "You could have left Gerd and me in that crevasse to die. You could have cut the rope and guaranteed yourself the second spot on the team."

I almost throw up at the thought of a cut rope. I grow dizzy and recall the perfectly severed ends that broke Ellias's life.

"I wouldn't leave anyone to die. I couldn't live with that. Plus, everybody knows that if anyone dies up here it will be blamed on me."

He doesn't argue.

I stand and move to the crater's edge, taking my time to walk the perimeter. It is about the size of Revolution Square. Clouds cover everything below the summit, so I cannot see the Bay of Good Fortune cutting into the northland. I cannot see Discovery Point at the tip of the Umlauf peninsula, where our ancestors landed so long ago. I cannot see Kaiwa or base camp or the Dor Drillingt islands. I cannot see Ainar.

That is the way of the mountain. She shares when she wants and remains veiled when she doesn't. I make my way back to Tristan. The judges will find some way to give him the spot even if I manage to reach base camp first. At least I made it. Up Fitzhan and Bonen.

"When we get down," Tristan says as his face brightens, "I'll tell people you're not a foze. I'll tell them you aren't like most women. You're basically a man."

My sharp laugh and wounded heartbeat meld to create an awkward snort. I bite my bottom lip. Tears edge in. Not for myself. For the world I live in.

I am special because I am *basically a man.*

I have worth because I am *not like most women.*

I am not a foze, *but the others…*

As if to be a woman is a derogatory, nasty thing. And in the goodness of Tristan's heart, he will free me from my innate shame. I look around the crater, the apex of Ectair. The highest one can go in my entire kingdom. I don't feel on top of the world.

I feel the ice. I feel the cold. The lack of oxygen. And I feel lower than the lowest trenches along Miter's Waste.

I have dreamed of this moment my entire life. To stand on the summit of Mount Bonen alongside my friends. Ellias by my side. His smile so warm and wide that it lights up the entire world. Kiel beaming. My team surrounding me.

Instead, five banners hang frozen from poles that will be left here until climbers from Kaiwa come to clean our mess from their mountain. Five men are missing or wounded. Instead of soil to offer Orna, I was given ash and bone. Terrorized even when I am beyond their reach. My only companion, a man who can't see me at all.

I close my eyes and picture the throngs of women in protest filling the streets of our capital. I picture Rosalie.

"I am not *basically a man*, Tristan." I think of my mother, whoever she was. I imagine Gerd's mother and the impossible situation she faced. Where her best options lay in sending her child into danger. "Please don't defend my honor if you need to denigrate all women to do so."

"I didn't mean—"

"I know you didn't. But don't you get it? I have done everything you've done. All of it. I've bled. I've broken. I've woken up before Cleos and fallen asleep well after Azura has crested the horizon. For the same dream you have. Precious few have cheered for me. Have acknowledged my talent. I've been antagonized. Even now. Veit didn't tell me to throw you into the crevasse. The king didn't pull your hair. Julius didn't tell you to back out.

"For Layal's sake, Tristan. The päter filled my offering with ash and bone, not soil. They want me to die. They want me to fail. They want me to feel afraid and alone. All because I had the misfortune of being born this way in a world that loathes this way. So please don't say I am *basically a man*. I am not, nor have I ever been, basically a man. If I were, this moment would be different. My whole life would be different. If I were basically a man, I would already be on the team. I wouldn't be on the summit of the highest mountain in Ectair defending my right to be here."

I choke back a sob and wipe angry tears from my eyes. "I would rather be a foze than *basically a man*."

At the top of Ectair, my soul splits. Falling to my knees in the snow next to the small hole where the fragment of bone disappeared, seventeen years of pain cascade from my face. My tears fall so fast they don't have time to freeze.

A hand awkwardly pats my back. "I'm sorry. I didn't realize."

I shake my head. Sobs rack my shoulders. "Now that you do, what will be different?"

He doesn't answer. A gust of wind whips through the crater, ripping my hat from my head. Tristan catches it with a quick motion. I grab the pink banner as it tries to fly from my pack. Thunder rumbles from a darkening blotch of sky to the east.

"We'd better go." I wipe my cheeks and reach for my hat.

Hesitant hands place it gently upon my head. "I don't know what I'll do. But I'll try. Something."

I nod and take a deep, slow breath. Something. I guess something is more than most men have offered. "Thank you."

We turn and take in the crater. I close my eyes and inhale the scent of snow—the smell of a thin cold veil at the top of the world. My father would be proud of me. So would Ellias. I smile and let out a soft laugh, imagining his toothy grin. His strong hug. The pride galloping through his eyes as I raise my flag into the air.

Maybe in another life.

I lift my pack onto my shoulders and walk beside Tristan toward the crater wall.

Head up, darling.

Ellias's words sing out to me from across the void. On the wings of the wind. In the urgency of the thunder.

Always head up, for that is the direction in which the mountain grows.

I look up into the heavy layer of clouds and smile sadly into the swirling mist and the incoming storm.

"I wonder what happened to the others." Tristan waits for me at the edge of the crater where we left the rope.

I attach my sling and pull the alpenstock from the snow. We have a long march ahead of us. I don't want worry for the safety of others to cloud my judgment. "I guess we'll find out soon. You ready?"

With a final glance at the summit of Mount Bonen, I step over the crater edge to the steep slope beyond.

We traipse in silence, downward momentum pushing us along at a much quicker pace than our ascent. To avoid crevasses, we follow Veit's footsteps and safely reach the camp where we left Gerd. The sleeping bag is still there, but no one is inside.

A set of footprints is visible leading to the bag. Two sets of footprints accompanied by a few droplets of blood are observable leading away.

"That was fast." I breathe a sigh of relief and feel my heart lighten. Gerd won't make the team, but he will make it home. And if I make it, I will send money to his mother in secret. I won't let them go hungry.

"Why didn't they take his gear?" Tristan nudges Gerd's backpack with his boot and cocks his head to the side. "A rescue party wouldn't leave this here to trash the mountain. Would they?"

I stare at the backpack, alpenstock, sleeping bag, and discarded food sacks. "Gerd was in bad shape. They had to leave quickly."

I am tempted to gather Gerd's gear, but I lack the energy. Someone else will have to remove the debris. Climbers from Kaiwa. Petrus's people. Something tickles my brain. Petrus. One of the two unaccounted-for climbers. The only one with mountaineering experience. There's no way Petrus didn't make it to the Snag. He wouldn't have struggled against the mountain like the rest of us.

We proceed. Even though I've convinced myself all is well, I begin glancing over my shoulder and whipping my head at strange noises. A shadow lurks at the corner of my vision. Each time I search for it, I find only snow and the occasional outcropping of black volcanic rock.

Gerd is fine. Petrus is fine. We're all fine.

Descending a mountain takes almost no time compared to trudging up the steep slopes. We reach the Snag by midday and untie from the rope. Our teamwork ends here.

"Tanks." Tristan shrugs his shoulders and coils his length of the rope. He stuffs it into his pack and leans against the

dark edge of the Snag. "Being an Ascenditure isn't about ac-
complishing something alone. It's about being part of a team.
Something bigger than yourself. You're the only one who ex-
emplified those traits on this climb."

I stop mid-coil and stare at him. A large drop of rain smacks
against my glove. The skies are about to open.

"You asked me what I would do differently. What would
change now that I know." He sucks in a breath through his nose
and meets me with a hard gaze. "I'm not going down there. Not
yet. If we arrive at the same time or even within minutes of
each other, they will give it to me."

"I don't want your—"

He raises his hand to cut me off. "This isn't my pity. You
beat me in every way on this climb. You beat all of us. I am
offering you nothing you don't deserve."

Tears build in my eyes. I swallow the lump that grows in my
throat.

"I don't want to give them any reason to deny what is right-
fully yours. I'll take the next spot. Maybe you can help me train
for it."

I stand dumbfounded before dropping my rope and moving
to Tristan. I give him a tentative hug and then squeeze tighter
when he doesn't resist. "You need a lot of work," I say through
a sob.

He laughs and hugs me back. "Apparently, we all do."

I chuckle and pull away. Maybe some good came from this.
The king thought he'd sent us up here to die. To turn on each
other. To cast me in a light of blame and liability. Just the opposite happened.

Storm clouds now hang so heavy I fear they might unleash
a sea upon our heads. We trek over the Snag, pausing at the
still-erected tent where we'd left Ingo and Julius. Sleeping bags
and bedding spill from the opening. Why have the rescue teams
left a mess on the mountain?

I reach the tent first and pull back the flap. It's empty besides
gear. A small splatter of blood stains the side of the canvas.

The hair on my neck rises. A chill washes through my veins. I step away from the tent and scan the surrounding snow. There are more footprints and places where the snow has been disturbed. Mounded. Moving to one of the upturned areas, I drop to my knees and dig with my hands. A few inches down, I find more blood.

"What are you doing?" Tristan calls out.

I ignore him, crawling across the snow to each jumbled patch, uncovering the trail of blood someone tried to hide. My shoulders tense. Who was bleeding? Who had been hurt? No one besides Gerd.

I return to Tristan and show him the blood in the tent. "It continues down the mountain. Gerd's blood on the snow makes sense because his bone was sticking out of his skin." I shake my head and try to force away the strangling fear. "But not Ingo and Julius. Neither of them was bleeding when we left, which means—"

"Someone hurt them. Veit? But why?" Tristan stares from the tent to the trail of footprints. "Wouldn't we have been his biggest threats? Why wouldn't he have attacked us? Why go after someone who's already down? They were never going to reach the summit."

A new wave of fear crashes through my system. I nearly collapse. I grasp Tristan's forearm and pull him close, aware that the king and his minions can probably see us now. I can think of only one reason someone would harm these injured men.

Me.

"Stay close," I whisper. "We can figure out a winner at the bottom. I don't think we should separate."

He nods and swallows. We continue our trek. Every roll of thunder frays my nerves. Tristan lets out a yelp when a stanblouk leaps across our path. We stop to catch our breath and lean into each other. The mountain goat's large body and curved horns disappear over the edge of the slope, leaving us again in white silence.

Far below, the tree line emerges from the snow like an army of evergreen soldiers. Beyond the forest, the base camp tents offer companionship and warm mugs of tea—steaming plates of food and sizzling fires. Kiel will be there. He can see that I made it, that I am strong enough. That I won. I beat the king. I whimper. Safety is within sight. We can make it. I take Tristan's hand and squeeze. He returns the pressure.

I feel and hear the crack of an explosion from behind. At first, I think it is thunder, but this thunder doesn't end. Turning slowly, I see a wall of snow rushing toward us. Large sheets of white billow and crash like clouds tumbling across the sky. Angry puffs of powder fly into the air. The entire mountain groans. There's something else on the left side, but I get only a glimpse.

"Run!" I scream at Tristan. I remember what the mountaineering book said to do in an avalanche. Instead of sprinting downward, I turn and move laterally across the snow. My thoughts drown in the sound of the disaster and even though I want to glance over my shoulder, I don't. I just keep running.

The noise finally fades. I gasp for breath, collapsing onto the ground in terrified trembling. Rolling my gaze toward the avalanche train, I find nothing but white.

"Tristan," I scream. "Tristan!"

I stand on wobbling legs and move away from the debris pile, my eyes trained on the ridgeline above. All I see now are snow and rocks. But there's more than that. The hairs on my neck stand up so swiftly that they might be trying to jump from my skin. I know what I saw. As instinct kicked in and I fled, I spotted something more disturbing than anything nature could conjure.

Someone stood above the raging snow. Watching me. Heaving something into the moving ice—something that looked an awful lot like a human body. Whoever attacked the other climbers higher on the mountain wanted it to look like an accident. Wanted both my death and Tristan's to also look like accidents. They probably started the avalanche.

I touch my face and feel the blood surging in my veins. I am very much alive. My eyes race across the ridgeline, but all I see is white. It doesn't matter. I am certain our tormentor is watching my every move.

13

I send up my flare as I move, even though I know everyone at base camp saw what happened. The pink ball of fire flashes into the sky, casting me in eerie, artificial light. The flare is for Tristan, not for me. I don't plan to stick around.

I think Tristan ran straight down, straight into death's gaping mouth. Unless the rescuers arrive quickly and figure out his exact location, he will suffocate beneath the snow, buried with the rest of our competitors.

Part of me yearns to find him, but invisible hands shove me onward. My brain screams to get away from this place. I silently apologize to Tristan and the rest of the group and continue stumbling through the thick snow. Guilt tugs at my soul, but my will to live reigns supreme.

Knee-deep snow slows my progress. I plow ahead like an ant swimming through a pool of molasses. Reaching the tree line, I glance behind. I feel *him* watching, calculating eyes determining how to end my life. Fear threatens to freeze me in place. I slap the fright away and disappear into the pines.

I thought I'd feel safe with cover, but wickedness lurks behind every trunk and protruding limb. Because I am no longer visible to the spectators below, someone could slash a knife across my throat, and no one would know the truth.

"Stop," I say aloud. "Breathe."

A mountain aiwl hoots from the branch of a nearby tree. With the canvas of the grand marquee just visible through the trees, I shove my way forward.

"Klarke! Halt!"

Unbidden, a scream echoes from my throat. My nerves have coiled so tightly since discovering the blood in the tent that the sound of another human voice snaps the wire.

My legs take over where my brain fails. I run without looking back, but the deep snow slows me to a crawl. The tone of the intruder finally registers in my brain. I know that voice. I collapse and sob.

A gloved hand prods my shoulder, not comforting and kind, but familiar. I look up at Burkhart's scarred face and wipe my tears, embarrassed he is seeing me this way. He pulls me to my feet.

"Someone's attacking us." I peer between holythorns and pines that surround us. "The others. Something happened to them. And it wasn't—"

Burkhart motions with his hands for me to slow down and takes a step toward me. "Stop crying. You're fine."

I stare into his eyes. Burkhart loathes me, despises the idea of a female climber almost as much as the king. My heart turns to frigid stone.

I move away, edging around the spindly trunk of a fizhte. Positioning the tree between us. "How did you get up here so quickly? And from above. You were above me. You had to have come from up the slope. The avalanche—"

"Flares have been going off for the past two days. We're all up here."

I wish I could see his eyes beneath his goggles. He remains unreadable.

"You're wearing dark clothing. So was the man I saw." I back away, knowing I can't outrun him in the dense snow.

He shakes his head and raises his arms in surrender. "What are you talking about? We all wear dark. Will it always be a drama with you?"

Another figure appears from behind a nearby tree. My arms fly protectively to cover my chest. I fear my heart will give out before it can get me to safety. The newcomer removes his goggles, revealing himself to be Gio.

Like a cornered doe, my gaze flips from Burkhart to Gio and back. They are wearing the same outfits, carrying the same gear. The man I saw could have been anyone. Even Kiel. They could all be in on it. Conspiring.

"Where did you come from?" I turn an accusing glare on Gio.

His eyes narrow. He takes a step back. "Up the mountain. With the others. As soon as the first flare went off, we left camp."

"You're all here then? All of the Ascenditures? Did you find the hurt climbers?" My fingers crawl to the shaft of the alpenstock. I am unsure of my hand's intentions, but I let it go there, willing it to do its job if necessary. Both men's eyes follow my movement.

"We're all here." Burkhart takes another step toward me. "And no. Tizian and I set out to check the first flare. When we got there, the tent was empty. Figured whoever it was decided to try for the summit."

"They didn't. Someone took them. Someone did something to them all." I sound like a lunatic. I am certain my heartbeat is echoing through the trees. "And then the killer tried to wipe their tracks with that avalanche."

"Killer?" Gio intones. Burkhart scoffs.

"Were you with someone this whole time, or were you alone?" I point a quaking finger at Gio.

Gio's eyebrows rise. He looks stung. "Why would I have given you suggestions back on the boat on how to survive if I wanted you dead? Why would I tell you to back out?"

This sinks in, and I let out a deep sigh. The blood returns to my extremities. I don't trust Burkhart, but if Gio is here, I feel safe. "Yeah. Okay."

Gio looks relieved as he moves toward me, rubbing his hand on my head as an older sibling would do to their younger sister. Gio and Burkhart's innocent acts don't negate that I survived when I wasn't supposed to.

I start moving uphill, back toward the debris field. "They need help. Tristan. He's in there. We have to go back.

"Aye-ah-ree-ah!" I shout into the wind. The wind carries my echosong across the slope. It booms through the valley and bounces around the trees. "Aye-ah-ree-ah!"

It is a call reserved for avalanches. It is a call rarely answered.

Burkhart catches up and grabs me by the elbow. "If he's buried, he won't hear you. The rest of the team is on it. We have to get you down."

"Nide." I jerk my arm away and grab my alpenstock again. "He can't die. None of them can."

Burkhart folds his arms. "Don't you want to win? Isn't that all you want?"

I can't see his eyes, but they're probably filled with disdain. Annoyance.

I look at the snow surrounding us. Ice crystals twinkle even though no rays of Cleos cut through the storm clouds. What I want…I want a world with men like Tristan in it. He was going to help me. He was willing to change his mind. He was beginning to understand. I want a world where good people aren't murdered at a king's whim.

"I'll go help." Gio pats me on the shoulder and trudges up the hill. "You need warmth and food."

Burkhart turns toward camp. Gio continues his traverse. I glance between the two. My ribs ache. My bones are icicles. My head throbs. Deep fatigue has set in.

"I'm so sorry, Tristan. Suertgût, my friend," I whisper the words up the slope. "Orna, please don't let him die. Please let him be found."

I follow Burkhart down the rest of the mountain and slump toward base camp just before Cleos sets. My mind is lost down the dead-end arm of a labyrinth. I can't stop imagining Tristan suffocating beneath the snow. Gerd. Oh, gods. Gerd unable to breathe as the avalanche robs him of life.

Cheers grind against my dulled senses. I lift my gaze and remove my goggles. Spectators, judges, parliament, and even King Adolar himself circle, roused from the boredom of waiting. Delight and awe color their faces. At least most of them. King Adolar exudes something darker. A tic near his temple and the inferno blazing in his eyes say that he is not happy to see me. His gaze flicks to a place in the crowd, but when I turn to investigate, I see only tipsy civilians, päters, and dumbfounded old men.

Someone slaps me on the back and shoves a mug of ale into my hands. Another drapes the white fur of a bergbear across my neck. Their expressions confuse me. I don't have the energy for their mad celebrations. Let them rejoice and leave me in peace. I just want word that my teammates are safe, and then I want to sleep.

The pack is lifted from my shoulders. One of the king's servants unties the pink banner from my bag. He moves through the crowd to a pair of poles erected in the center of camp. A swath of red fabric billows from the top of one. The servant ties my pink flag to a bit of twine and pulls. The pink fabric moves up the pole, rising above the crowd until it is level with Veit's.

I survived. Tristan is buried beneath the snow. No one else reached the summit. Which means…

"Congratulations, Fram Ascher." The king steps forward, his momentary flash of odium evaporating as the crowd rejoices. "You successfully climbed Mount Bonen and made it back with your banner in second place. You and Veit have secured your spots as Ascenditures. Welcome to the history books, girl."

Veit raises his goblet and gives me a wink. At first, I seethe at his gloating face. Did he hurt those men? Did he attack them? And why? It's not worth it. None of this is. My eyes travel down to his attire. Veit's jacket is light in color, not dark. Plus, he couldn't have been the figure I saw above the avalanche and have made it down in time to be so drunk and so relaxed. Veit is an arschole, but he is not the man I saw above the snow fall.

Feeling like I might pass out or vomit, I turn away from the flapping pink banner and suck ravenously at the abundant oxygen in the air. I have dreamed of this moment my entire life. I have never wanted anything more than to be an Ascenditure and to climb as a hero for the kingdom.

All I can envision is that abominable man in his wool coat rolling something into the avalanche. Gerd's broken leg. Tristan beneath the snow. Julius. Ingo. Petrus. Achill. Rosalie. Feiko.

Ellias at the base of Fitzhan.

The mysterious figure on the mountain was dressed as an Ascenditure. I am sure of it. Either someone is up there posing as one of us, or something is rotten within the team I've so longed to be a part of.

I imagine the rock slide on the face of Fitzhan. The perfectly severed ends on the rope. The enigmatic climber up in the Celebern Fields whom Ellias followed.

Glory and dreams be damned. I no longer want to be part of this.

14

A feast is held in our honor, but I am in no mood to celebrate or eat cheese-coated dumplings and dark forest cake. Inside the large tent, mead and wine flow as freely as the laughter and merriment bouncing between drunk and happy faces. I stand in the entryway, staring at the mountain. The search team's headlamps bounce and flicker at the avalanche site like nearby stars twinkling through a turbulent atmosphere.

After getting me to safety, Burkhart returned to help the rest of the Ascenditures locate survivors. Besides Tristan, they are wasting their time. I know in my bones that Ingo, Julius, and Gerd are dead. I never saw Petrus or Achill, nor did Veit, so I assume their lifeless bodies will end up buried in the snow as well. All I can hope is that Tristan survives, and maybe he saw something I didn't that will help bring the traitor to justice.

"Shouldn't you be celebrating?"

Veit approaches with an extra drink in hand. He offers it to me, but I shake my head and turn back to the mountain. "Celebrating what? Six people died up there. I don't feel like a victor."

"They were weak." He shrugs and sets my rejected ale on a nearby table. "You can't feel bad for being the best. I don't. They knew the risks."

I try to read his face to see if deception lies behind his boastful words. His eyes are glassed over from drink, but I don't see any sign that he is hiding anything. Veit is tall and imposing, with wide shoulders and lean muscles, but staring at him now, I don't see a killer, just a narcissistic fool.

I tug at the hem of my coat and lower my voice. "Veit, did you see anything strange up there? Anything out of place?"

"You mean other than you?" He chuckles and takes a long swig of ale. "I was in front of you jesters, so all I saw was wide open air and a straight shot to the summit. Nothing strange about that."

"I think—no—I know someone was harming climbers. When Tristan and I came back down, we found blood in the tents where we'd left Gerd, Julius, and Ingo. And then above the avalanche I saw someone roll a body down the slope." I sag against a nearby table and avoid eye contact. "I think we were set up from the beginning to be slaughtered."

He remains silent, then throws his head back in a raucous laugh. "You've got a wild imagination, Klarke. Must be a foze thing. Or maybe it was too much time at altitude. It can mess with your brain, and clearly did. You won. Quit trying to sabotage your victory and mine. It's a godsdamn deadly mountain—of course we were set up to die. But not in the way you're saying. That's insanity."

He belches, then slaps me on the back and turns to rejoin the party.

"Veit," I say. He pauses mid-stride. "Be careful."

With a wink and a disbelieving chuckle, he melts into the din of the party, leaving me alone to watch the futile searchlights dance across the darkened slope. All I want is to see Kiel and tell him everything. He'll believe me and take it seriously—he might even know something after spending the past few days up there. Maybe he can provide clarity to the fuzzy clues I am trying to piece together. Unless...

He couldn't. He wouldn't.

The joy bubbling from the party makes me queasy. I turn to head to my tent.

"Klarke."

The soft voice could have been a wheezy gust of wind. A rustling in the bushes draws my gaze. I lock onto a pair of eyes hidden within a cluster of Maidenhair Ferns. Before I can cry out, a bloody hand shoots through the leaves and beckons. "Help," the disembodied voice croaks.

My blood turns to icy sludge as the dead man's voice registers in my mind. Beneath my cotton blouse, my skin rises in terrified prickles. I ignore my intuition to run and instead rush to help.

It's all I can do not to scream. Petrus's coat is tattered and covered with blood. Every inch of him is lathered in the dark red liquid. He smells of copper and rust. Like the entrails of a fresh kill on a hunting party. His eyes are cloudy.

"What happened?" I reposition him so he is leaning against the trunk of a large pine. His head lolls forward, and for a second, I think he might have died.

"Water," he whispers.

I rush to the victor's tent, hoping no one notices the blood covering my hands. I try not to draw attention as I request a large mug of water from the barmaid. When I reach Petrus, I drop to the ground and lift his head, helping him to sip the cool liquid. He coughs, and a new line of blood trickles from his skull. That is when I notice what appears to be damage to the back of his head. Sliding up the sleeve of his coat, I find bruises and cuts covering his skin where tattoos do not. I press my hand to his heart. He winces. "Petrus, you have to tell me what happened up there."

"Hit in the head. My entire body." He coughs, and it sounds like something other than air gurgles in his lungs. "Right after I started."

He needs a doctor, but I am afraid to trust anyone. Petrus is a dead man either way, but maybe I can find some answers from him. "Who hit you? Where's Achill?"

His eyes roll back in his head as he sucks in another rattling breath. "Dead. On the mountain."

"Achill?" I fight the urge to shake his shoulders. He is concussed, dehydrated, and on the brink of death. I can't expect a more detailed conversation than this. "Achill is dead?"

"Blood everywhere. Hit. So many times."

"Achill hit you? You're saying Achill is behind this?"

He opens his eyes, but they won't track anything, just bounce around like marbles on the deck of a ship. "Achill is dead. The attacker. The man with the eyes. He hit me. Over and over."

The man with the eyes? I want to rip out my hair. Glancing over my shoulder, I see the entrance to the party tent, but no one is paying attention to where I went or what I am doing. "Petrus, I know you're hurt, and as soon as you tell me who did this, I will take you to the doctor."

He reaches a gloved hand up and grips my wrist. "I came back to warn you."

"Warn me of what?" My heart has slowed to a point that I fear it might stop. I lean closer to his face, desperate for him to utter a name so this nightmare can end. His eyes finally rest on something, and they grow wide. A crowd of people rush toward us, calling for a doctor. Without Petrus's help, I am at the mercy of whoever wants me dead.

"Tell me!"

"The eyes," he whispers. "Look for the eyes."

It's too late for more. Already men have crouched down and lifted Petrus in the air, hauling him away toward the infirmary tent. I try to follow, but a hand grips my shoulder, applying so much force to a nerve that I freeze in place.

"He needs help, Fram Ascher. Let him go." King Adolar's words are icier than the glaciers above the Snag.

I don't make eye contact, instead staring at the rawhide lace on my right boot. "Yes, my king." I feel like a deer surrounded by a pack of hungry volves.

"Go back to the festivities and celebrate. You earned it, and people will want to see you happy. Go be happy." It is not a suggestion. It is a threat, no matter the content of the words. He releases my shoulder and strides toward the infirmary, his long cloak billowing behind him. I enter the communal tent and make my way to the bar, ordering an ale and two shots of fermented horse milk. I down the shots and chug my ale, slamming the mug onto the table for a refill. Once I am too drunk to stand, I stumble back to my tent, collapsing in a topsy-turvy fog of intoxication. Behind dark eyelids, the world spins. I suck deep breaths of the cool air, trying to keep the vomit at bay and the world from flying off its hinges.

I awaken to learn that the Ascenditures have returned, having recovered the bodies of three of the missing climbers. Achill, Ingo, and Gerd. None were alive. Tristan and Julius's bodies were not found, but that is to be expected in such a large snowfall. Climbers from Kaiwa will find them next summer when the snow melts. News has also spread that Petrus died in the night.

Cleos is just peeking over the shoulder of Mount Bonen. The bodies of the four men are laid out across white canvas. Päters surround them. Blessings and prayers issue from behind the päters' masks. Incense fills the air with scents of sage and cinnamon. The holzenschrein has been placed between the bodies and the mountain. Men and women kneel before it. Weeping. Praying. Throwing hastily made ilices across the top.

They're wasting their time. Orna didn't do this. Orna can't repair this.

My eyes fix on Gerd's small form. I drop my face into my hands and take slow, deep breaths. The kindest soul in Ectair is dead because of me. His mother won't get to hug him ever again because of me. Marike won't learn from her brother how to do a heel hook or what the best way to wrap one's hands is to climb a crack. Because of me. Tears fill my eyes. I look again at the deceased. None of them deserved this. Julius was right. Because of me, they were sentenced to die.

My gaze falls upon the king and the three judges, draped in green and gold, goblets of wine in hand. They have the decency to cast their eyes downward, but I know it is a sham. They might not have been the man on the mountain who started the avalanche, but I know they are somehow behind this.

Gerd is not dead because of me. He is dead because of them.

15

On the journey from base camp back to where our boats are docked in Kaiwa, Veit and I are kept separate from the rest of the Ascenditures—forced to ride upon horses at the front of the wagon train so workers in the vineyards and merchants in the street might lay eyes upon their newest heroes. Veit grins and waves, bowing his head and blowing kisses. I glare sullenly at the road, feeling as much a victress as the men in the fields with mud up to their knees. I keep reminding myself I am still alive. The thought only frightens me more.

Nine päters draped in black lead the procession in lockstep. Their legs move together almost as if they are one giant insect. Eerie white masks lead us onward. Incense burns from the cooper bowls they carry. Sweet spice fills the air. The two on the ends wield long wooden poles. My pink banner billows from one, Veit's red from the other. I wonder which päter packed my offering bundle with ash and bone. I wonder if they are all minions of the king or if some aspects of our religion remain pure.

A man rushes up to where we canter. My horse steps back and whinnies. I lift my head as he waves a scythe in my face.

"They're dead because of you!" Veins ripple and bulge across his forehead. "My Petrus—" With a sobbing gasp, he falls forward onto his knees in the dirt, dropping the scythe to the ground. His fists clench into mud-stained balls. "Orna did this because of you. We're all missing our sons today because of you."

Gulping down sickness and guilt, I turn away, meeting Veit's gaze. He looks at the figure on the ground with disdain.

"Be gone, old man." Veit waves his hand in a rapid, swatting gesture. "Your son was weak. Weakness can only be blamed on those who wield it for themselves."

"No." I shake my head and turn to the grieving father. "Petrus was not weak. He was strong. So strong. I am so sorry for what happened to him. I wish I could have done more."

"Pft." Veit shakes his head and rolls his eyes at me. "You're weak too. Weakness all around. It shrouds this land like the mist."

The man on his knees glares with tear-stained eyes but says no more. A woman comes up behind him, wrapping her arms around his shoulders. Together they weep. Mount Bonen rises as an impressive backdrop to their grief.

I want to hug someone in this way. To share the burden of my pain with another. I haven't yet been able to speak with Kiel. The team stayed up on the mountain recovering bodies until late last night. I was able to wave from afar, but he has been kept from me. Intentionally, I assume.

When we reach the boats, I dismount from my horse, preparing to haul my gear back to the ship. Instead, a young man stumbles forward beneath the weight of my pack, his feet criss-crossing as he tries to stay upright.

"Here, let me get that." I rush to assist, but the boy spins away, losing his balance and splattering into the nearest puddle. When I pull my gear from the slop, he glances around with wild eyes and leaps to his feet.

"I have to take it." He yanks the pack out of my hands, again faltering with the burden. "It's my job. I'll get in loads of trouble if I don't do it right."

His eyes are wide and innocent. He reminds me of Gerd. I think of Gerd's smiles, his blushing cheeks, his bravery, and his tenderness. With a deep breath and a sick heart, I follow the boy and my mud-soaked gear to the gangway.

I can't bear to see the empty quarters on deck two—vacant hammocks swinging with the ghosts of murdered men—the lingering scent of their motion sickness hovering over the guilty survivors.

"Just set it by my hammock," I instruct the boy. "Tanks ye for your help."

Electing for fresh air over haunted decks, I make my way to the stern of the ship and hunker down between two large cargo boxes and a pile of rope. My eyes shut. I inhale deeply. The rain hits the river in loud plops, melding with the sound of water rippling over barely submerged boulders.

Across the river from Kaiwa, the Tono Hills rise and fall in rolling mounds of lush knolls and green valleys. When I was a little girl, my father told me stories about the magical beings that lived in those hills—appearing only when the rains subsided, and Cleos had shone for an entire week. Only then would they emerge, granting wishes to those who stumbled upon their miniature earthen kingdoms. Lecals, they were called. Peering at the far shore and the hills beyond, I grimace at the memory of my father.

Even though it is raining, and Cleos never shines for seven days straight, I implore the imaginary Lecals, hoping they will break the rules this once and give me what I am asking for.

"Keep me safe," I whisper from my hiding spot, my eyes on the distant hills. "Let me uncover who is behind this and bring them to justice."

I can't believe six men have died. Not died. Died could imply all sorts of fates. They were murdered. Slaughtered. Butchered like sheep. I gaze out at the Sevier River and the path home. How had the one thing I'd yearned for above all else become so tainted with blood and deceit? When did the mask of honor peel back to reveal a soulless corpse?

"Klarke?"

My body prickles. Crouching down lower between the two boxes, I try to control my breathing, heartbeat, anything that could give me away. They didn't succeed in killing me on the mountain, but there is a respectable chance their actions will drive me mad.

"Klarke, I know you're up here."

A relieved sob escapes my lips. "Kiel?" I peek over the box and meet his eyes. In them, I see the same torment that tumbles around my head.

He reaches me, and without a word, pulls me into his arms. Tears flow from my eyes like the springs that feed the river. I don't care anymore about weakness. I empty my emotions onto the front of his shirt.

"How did I not lose you?" he mumbles into my hair, pulling me closer. "When we reached the spots where the flares had been released, the tents were empty. There was blood. And then the avalanche. What the hell happened up there?"

I bury my face in his chest. Words stick in my throat. Dread ices my veins. It feels like I have been plunged beneath the water, held down by a million invisible hands. Unable to breathe. Unable to speak.

"It's okay." His hand strokes my back. He rocks me as if I am a child. "You're safe now. No one is going to hurt you."

"You're wrong." I almost don't hear the words as they slip from my mouth like wind through fingers. "I will never be safe again."

He doesn't refute my words. I am both grateful for his silence and petrified by his wordless agreement. The raindrops crash against the deck. Kiel pulls a large piece of canvas from one of the deck boxes and covers us. Even though it is all in my head, a sense of safety descends, the same feeling I'd have as a child in my four-poster bed when the drapes were pulled and I was secure beneath my blankets. An illusion, but sometimes that was all one had.

I fill him in on my experience on the mountain, deciding to believe in his innocence. I need a solid foundation on which to anchor. He runs his hands through his short dark hair, shaking out the raindrops. His eyes find my gaze in the muted darkness cast by the canvas cover. Dwelling in their depths are words I don't want him to say.

"You have to leave for Kobo as soon as we get home."

The words tumble from his mouth and attach to my heart like weights. "You were right. Take Rayna. If I can come for you, I will. I promise."

Even though I have had the same idea many times in the past, I have come to realize I won't run away. I would have already left if that had been what I truly wanted.

I fumble with a mixture of emotions. Fear, pride, accomplishment, betrayal, anxiety, terror…

Things I've craved are falling into my lap, but the price is one I am not willing to pay. But when I think of leaving it all behind, my heart digs in its heels. Freedom will come from heavy sacrifice. My dreams bathed in blood. How does one choose between such forbidding paths?

"I can't leave," I whisper. I reach for Kiel's hand with both of mine. He squeezes back. "I want to stay and fight so those who had a hand in such treachery can be brought to justice. It terrifies me, but I disgrace all who have fallen if I leave. Gerd deserves better. Those young men, who only ever wanted to climb, deserve better."

Kiel is silent. I feel his warm breath on my face. His exhalations come in contemplative puffs of air. "When we get back," he finally says, "you and Veit will take the oath. You will move into the Ascenditure granhaus with all of us. We can look out for each other. I don't like the danger you're in, but I understand, and I want to help."

For the first time in what feels like eons, my lips curl into a minute smile. A grateful smile, not a happy one. The ship begins to move. I scoot closer to Kiel beneath the damp canvas. The exhaustion of the past few days settles, and I know it is finally safe to close my eyes. I will find no sleep below decks in my hammock, so I rest my head in the crook of Kiel's arm and fall asleep to the rising and falling of his chest and the percussion of raindrops against fabric.

16

King Adolar, Prince Otto, parliament, and the esteemed judges sit beneath their tent, shrouded from the rain. Green and gold banners line the walled platform. Three päters stand between Laren's altar and Orna's holzenschrein. One carries the ornate box that holds the golden silenotê Veit and I will present after the funeral. The middle päter clasps a copper bowl full of smoking herbs and incense. The third holds the crystal pitcher full of blessed water.

The crowd jammed into Revolution Square is the largest I've ever seen: the poor in their rags; children covered in soot and grime; merchants in their long coats; women with parasols and lacy dürmels; the dais packed with adels and their families. Horses and carriages fill the remaining space. The spectators on the fringe must be pressed against the bricks of surrounding buildings. Päters line the street in front of Hadrian's Monastery. I search for Rayna's gentle face, but she will be toward the back, buried among the destitute.

I feel like an imposter standing at the top of the steps to the Rektburg in the same oversized black mourning dress I wore to Ellias and Feiko's funeral. Veit is beside me. Based on the smile stretching from one ear to the other, his feelings do not match mine. He knew these men. Climbed with them. Drank with them. Laughed with them. How can his achievement overshadow their loss?

Four coffins lie between us and the gathering of grieving Ectarians. Two smaller wooden boxes sit next to them, representing Tristan and Julius who have been presumed dead. Six men who didn't have to die. Gerd was only thirteen. I cough, fighting back sickness and tears.

Whispers and murmurs nearly drown out distant thunder.

Rain has not deterred anyone today. Who could be deterred from such carnage?

The Ascenditures are lined up behind us in front of Miter's Tower. I fight the urge to turn and find Kiel. I would rather see his face than coffins and the eyes of a suspicious crowd. I remind myself that if I can make it through the day, I will move into the Ascenditure granhaus tonight. The home is on the edge of Kietsch, butting up to the forest. I will get my own private area but will share common quarters with the rest of the team. It feels like the only safe place left in this world.

King Adolar stands. The square falls silent. Thunder echoes over the city. Lightning strikes the bay. Gerd's family huddles together at the base of the steps. His mother collapses to the ground, sobs racking her body. His two little sisters hold each other tightly. The older one, Marike, does not cry. Instead, she glares at her brother's coffin. Gerd's father stands tall, eyes full of pain. The other fallen climbers' families are also here. Their grief overwhelms me; it picks at a still-fresh wound.

I suck in a breath and fortify my nerves.

"My countrymen and framen." King Adolar moves to the center of the platform, blocking part of my view. Gerd's mother lets out a trailing wail.

"Tragedy has struck our lands." The king nods to Gerd's mother and all the mothers lined up in front of his castle. "Tragedy of the highest kind. Eight young climbers set out to achieve their dreams. Only two have returned to us. We still have many unanswered questions. Besides the dead, one person was on the mountain at the time of the avalanche. We hope she will be able to provide us with some answers."

A few gasps followed by a wave of chatter blanket the crowd. I feel the blood drain from my face. My eyes flash to the back of the king's head, to the enormous emeralds adorning his crown. What is he suggesting? That I had something to do with their deaths? I want to scream, but I clamp my jaws together and glare at the crooked steeple of Hadrian's Monastery across the square.

"The gods are set in their ways," the king continues. "Even though we may feel that progress is necessary, in the end it is not up to us."

Jeers, boos, and glares reach me.

"Selfish foze!"

"Murderer!"

"Whore!"

Someone throws a rotten melon that explodes on the stairs at my feet. Others lob rocks and clumps of dried hay and manure. I duck to avoid them. One of the greencoats steps between the angry mob and me. My heart races. My knees knock together beneath the black dress.

"Crybabies," Veit shouts at the masses. "Bunch o' sore losers."

I almost laugh. Veit might be the biggest arschole I know, but he is fair in his viciousness. It is not reserved for me alone. Somehow I have gained an iota of his stingy respect. I shoot him a sad smile. My breath evens out.

"Please." King Adolar holds up his hands, motioning for the crowd to settle. "There will be time to sort out details later. I will confer with the päters who will communicate with the gods. For now, let us lay to rest these brave young men."

Prayers. Songs. Music. I can't take my eyes off Gerd's coffin. Sobs. Harp strings. Rain. I barely register what happens around me. I waffle between grief and anger. White, hot, searing anger at whoever did this to such a gentle soul. When the ceremony concludes, the päters in their simple black robes appear—six at each coffin—lifting and carrying them through the square and eventually to the sea. The families of the dead follow. The wailing from Gerd's mother and the others bounce back through the narrow streets long after the coffins disappear.

I offer my own silent words to the dead men. It is not so much a prayer as it is a vendetta. *I will bring down every last person who had a hand in your deaths, no matter the cost.*

The king retrieves the box from the first päter, removes the silenotê, and summons Veit forward. An alpenhorn sounds.

Veit takes the golden rope, recites his oath, and bows slightly to the cheering crowd after Aedan pins the knot insignia to his chest. Even though the audience is delighted to witness the naming of a new climber, the normal glee and joy are missing from their applause. They are sad and angry, and the king has ensured that their wrath is pointed at me.

Veit returns to his position next to me. His wide grin doesn't fit the atmosphere of the moment. It makes me dizzy. I know what's coming. I think I might throw up.

"We have one more spot to fill." The king's voice booms across Revolution Square. It reverberates down to my toes. "Klarke Ascher, would you please step forward."

Noise erupts. A few cheers and hurrahs but many more hisses, boos, and taunts. Kissing noises and jeers weave through the displeasure.

"Hannar killer!"

"She-beast!"

"Go home!"

My dress is soaked, and my hair is plastered to my face. The pink rope around the collar feels as if it has shrunk, cutting off my air. I've given up wiping the rain droplets from my forehead. Instead, I let them run down into my eyes and beyond, taking with them the tears I am trying to mask. I should be grinning—filled with a joy so pure and light it lifts me from the ground. Instead, I feel guilty for being alive and indignant that this moment has been stolen.

Cold lead has replaced my blood. My feet won't move. My heart has stopped beating. I struggle for one breath of the collective oxygen that has been sucked from the gathering. Veit shoves me forward, and I catch my balance before I topple over. Next moment, I am standing next to the king of Ectair on the steps of the great Rektburg as he thrusts the golden silenoté into my hands. I thought I would feel something when holding it, some sort of buzzing magic. Nothing. It's just a wet rope someone painted gold.

I make eye contact with my king, knowing he can see my

fear and disgust. Behind his warm smile and sparkling eyes lies cool detachment—a message that I am as welcome as I am dry.

He knows the message has been received and turns back to his people. "Framen and hannar, I bestow the rank of Ascenditure today upon Klarke Ascher. As many of you know, before becoming a captain in the royal fleet, Fram Ascher's father, Anselm Ascher, was one of the greatest climbers the kingdom had ever seen, having assisted with the damming of Miter's Waste, which prevented countless deaths of innocents from the monster our villainous neighbors to the north unleashed upon us. Following his passing, Fram Ascher was selected by Ellias Veber himself to train for the possibility of this moment. And what better way to honor the late Hannar Veber than by bestowing this title upon his protégé?"

Mixed emotions ripple across the people before me like a wave crashing onto the shore along the Straits of Hidar. They loved my father. They loved Ellias. The mention of their names has brought the people slightly back from the edge of revolt.

The alpenhorn sings. The world grows silent. I murmur my vows, trying to wrestle the words from a paralyzed memory, trying to keep the hand holding the golden rope from shaking.

"I am an Ascenditure now. I will persevere in honoring those who have fallen before me, fighting against those who wish us harm, and above all, serving my benevolent king. I will not fall. I will not fail. I will not betray my kingdom."

When I finish, I hand the rope to the king. Aedan fastens the metal pin to my chest and squeezes my shoulder. I turn to join Veit. Kiel, standing with the other Ascenditures, gives me a thin-lipped nod. Seeing his face relaxes the grip on my soul. Tonight I will be safe.

A hand grabs my wrist. Bony fingers covered in jeweled rings press into my flesh. I freeze.

"Wait." King Adolar yanks me around to face the perplexed spectators.

The faces closest to us look as confused as I feel. I try to wriggle my wrist free, but he grips it tighter.

"I have one more gift of good tidings for our kingdom," the king shouts. "We've had nothing but tragedy. Great, terrible tragedy. It is my duty as your king to turn that sorrow into joy."

From the corner of my eye, I see Prince Otto stand and take his place on the opposite side of his father from me. His handsome features are muted by the angry veins bulging in his neck. He glances behind at the line of Ascenditures, and for a moment the anger dissipates, replaced by something mimicking sadness. His head whips around when his father begins to speak.

"I am growing old," the king says, resting his free hand on his heart. "And while I intend to live a long life and rule this great kingdom for the benefit of all, I will not be here forever. Someday my son, now seventeen, will be your leader. He has recently come of age, and it is time he takes a wife and creates his own heir."

My eyebrows draw together as I search the nearest face in the crowd for some explanation. Even though I am soaking wet, my skin is on fire. I peek over my shoulder at Kiel, whose jaw looks like it might grind his teeth to dust.

"I have held council with various adels and their daughters, but my son is not easily satisfied. Therefore, I have decided to offer him something fresh." The king drops his hand from his heart and wraps his fingers around Prince Otto's wrist. "Today, Klarke Ascher was named an Ascenditure, relieving her of a pauper's status. Her father, we know, was a great climber and a courageous sea captain. Her mother came from noble blood. From the Knezvic family of Omalau. Fram Ascher's line is strong."

The rings on his fingers cut into my wrist. His grip tightens. My brain grows fuzzy as it fights against forming his words into concrete meaning. This can't be happening. I try again to twist away, but he won't let me go.

"My countrymen, I would like to announce with your witness the marriage arrangement between my son, Prince Otto Ewald Adolar, and your newest heroine, Klarke Verena Ascher."

I haven't heard my full name spoken since the last time my mother scolded me after my father vanished. "Klarke Verena Ascher," she'd shouted as I sprinted down the dock at Pohle Pier on an exceptionally cold winter's morning. I'd hit the woodice and slipped onto my back. My body skidded across the planks. I would have crashed into the frigid sea if a sailor hadn't grabbed my dress collar just as my legs crossed the edge.

"Klarke Verena Ascher," she'd sobbed as she held me in her arms on that dock. "I can't lose you too."

I lost her not long after. Mina Verena Ascher.

There is power in a name.

King Adolar raises my arm and Prince Otto's arm into the air. I have never heard more noise erupt in Revolution Square. Clapping, cheering, singing. Pots banging together. Whistles being blown. Dogs howling at the melee. The bell in Hadrian's Monastery comes to life. Clangs dance between brick buildings and the castle. I jump as the alpenhorn booms from behind. Once, twice, three times. A total of nine blasts to represent the kingdom's kreisons.

The king bows to his kingdom, drops my hand, and makes for the main castle doors with Prince Otto. Two palace guards flank me and usher me to follow.

"Wait!" I shout, digging in the heels of my boots. "Please, nide!"

The guards march ahead, pushing me forward between them. My eyes widen as I scan the line of my fellow climbers, pleading with each to do something. I was supposed to move into their quarters tonight. I was supposed to be safe.

Aedan watches me with worried eyes. Gio stares at his feet. Burkhart looks at the crowd. Kiel might explode. His face is red, his body tense. Part of me wishes he would shove these guards to the ground.

I am thankful he remains in place. Any action on his part would lead to the gallows. Resistance would be deadly.

I am on my own for whatever comes next.

17

The four posters on my bed rise nearly to the ceiling. A thick white fabric woven with designs of tree branches, pears, lemons, and blossoms drapes across the posts. I've drawn the deep red curtains so that I am safe in my cage.

A chandelier hangs from the carved rafters, holding more candles in its arms than lit the entire tenement in the Southlich. Paintings of stags and hunts and Laren beneath the sea cover the gilded walls. Gold, blue, and turquoise paint coat the archways between my sleeping quarters and the bathroom. Archways are held up by detailed granite columns. It is a lovely prison.

I was given the title of Ascenditure today, something I should be rejoicing over. But to blame my womanhood for the deaths of the men on Mount Bonen, and then immediately remind the kingdom that I need to be wed to a man, defeats the purpose of that gesture. That was King Adolar's plan all along—give them their climber, give them a princess, and they will shut up and be satisfied. What just happened is not progress—it is not a step forward for the little girls of this kingdom. It is a reminder that even if you make it, a chain is tied to your ankle. I was given wings today, and then they were snipped.

I have been hiding in my bed now for a few hours. After the ceremony, two greencoats led me through the palace and up to this room, where a young woman insisted upon bathing me and dressing me in fresh clothing. I fought her off until I realized she was not at fault. She is as much a prisoner as I am.

The new clothes are the loveliest things to grace my skin other than my mother's touch. The blouse is white with lace sewn around the collar and cuffs, which fall mid-arm. The dürmel over the blouse is made of black satin with burgundy ribbon stitched across the breast and matching flowers adorning the base. A corresponding claret apron ties around my waist. I keep reminding myself not to be seduced by the fancy dresses and sparkling bracelets they will set before me.

A knock sounds at the door. I pull the covers over my head before tossing them back and sitting up. I want to hide. I want to be left alone. But I am a prisoner. I poke my head through the curtains.

"What?" I hope the question comes off as commanding as I intend.

The heavy wooden door scrapes open, revealing the tall, handsome figure of Prince Otto. He wears a red weskit with small dark buttons over an ivory shirt. Black pants and black boots up to his knees. His jaw is set. His eyes narrowed.

I must look ridiculous—a free-floating head surrounded by fabric, eyes goggling, mouth agape. Releasing the curtains, I slip from the bed and lean against one of the large wooden posts, hoping I look brave and unflinching.

The prince scans me with dark eyes, studying me like a hog in a butcher shop. I do the same, making sure he knows I am not impressed, even though his biceps push through his linen top, and his jawline could cut sea glass.

"Come," he says.

I look to both sides as if he is addressing someone else in the room.

"You." He points a finger at me. "Let's go."

"Where?" The last thing I want to do is disappear into the bowels of this place with a person who seems to loathe me.

His eyes flash, dangerous black coals ignited. The man with the eyes.

"Does it matter?"

I shrug and follow him from the room. He doesn't try to take my hand or even look at me as we walk down one corridor after another. Green carpets line the floors, covering polished wooden slats. The white walls are covered in garish gold reliefs of heavenly figures and woodland creatures. Portraits of somber, long-dead Ectairians hang in bejeweled frames. King Miter once walked these halls. His daughter Layal might once have stepped where I now place my feet. I pause at a painting of a young woman being pulled into the sea by hands made from waves. The tentacles of a great seabeast project from the water into the stormy sky behind her.

"I don't want to marry you," Prince Otto blurts. He pulls me through a door into a deserted room. The furniture is covered in dusty fabric. It is hard to see anything as the curtains of the windows have been drawn. Muted light filters through, casting eerie shadows across his face.

"Then why am I here?" I press my fingers into my temples and glare at the prince. I am surprised how his words sting, even though I share the sentiment. "I am sure there were lines of other women who wanted to marry you."

He sighs. His voice almost sounds sad when he speaks. "I don't want to marry anyone right now."

"Well, neither do I." I cross my arms across my chest. "I want to climb, and I want to be left alone."

He watches me without speaking. We stare at each other for a few moments, clearly confused at the other's reaction to all of this.

"I've told my father that I can be a king without a queen," Prince Otto says. "That I can adopt an heir from one of the orphanages, but that is no path he can envision with me."

I blink stupidly, then step back into a covered table and manage to catch a teetering porcelain vase before it crashes to the ground. I've never imagined the prince to have a shred of humanity within him, to harbor his own desire to break the mold set for him by tradition.

Unless this is a ruse. The ploy reeks of King Adolar trying to throw me off my game. To make me trust his son. To trick me into participating in something seditious that would allow him to be rid of me once and for all.

I'll play. But I'll do it with my eyes open. "All I wanted was to be an Ascenditure," I reply. "To be taken seriously as a climber and to inspire women. Now I am a brideprize, proving that no matter what, we will always be tethered to men."

I am certain my defiant comments will set him off. I search his face for clues that he is filing my words away to share with his father. I look for a tick at his temple. A clench of his fist. A flash across his eyes.

He smiles, and his face relaxes. "Do not let my father hear you speak like that. He's not one for forward-thinking ideas."

I nod. The prince is a good actor, if indeed this is a ploy. My face must betray my thoughts because Prince Otto laughs. He leans against a tapestry depicting six men on horseback hunting rabbits in the Dangof forest. A grin spreads across his face. "You and I are not so different. Neither of us fits the frame built by tradition and law." He moves to me and takes my hands in his. I flinch but don't pull away. His hands are warm. Soft. I was expecting ice.

"What a relief you are not expecting a doting husband." He stares into my eyes. I stare back, trying to match his intensity.

"We will wed," he continues. "And you will be my queen. But I will leave you to live your life if you leave me to live mine."

My gaze drifts beyond him to the hunting tapestry. Am I the hound, the stag, the hunter, or the horse? A weight lifts from my soul. I so badly want to trust it. To trust him. Do I dare? "What about the heir? What about the wedding night?"

He shrugs and offers a wry smile. "It takes months for most women to conceive a child, sometimes it isn't possible. We have time."

I pull my hands from his and walk to the window. Wiping a dusty space in the glass, I peer out at Miter's Backbone. The clouds have parted. I can see the seven pinnacles and ridges from Kara Do to Hansdaum. Mighty and forbidding. That is my realm. Right now, I am in the prince's dominion.

"I'll take you back to your room." He offers a hand.

Is he a snake or an ally?

I place my hand in his and walk with him through the gilded halls. Outside my room he kisses my forehead, making sure the greencoats down the way are watching. I smile, trying to play my part in whatever game this is.

"Until tomorrow, my sweet." He strides away.

For a second my heart races, and a girlish crush rushes through my system. But then Prince Otto turns a corner and takes my silly feelings with him. I close the door and head to my bed, shedding the black silk dress into a heap on the floor. I crawl into bed. The prince doesn't seem interested in me, which means in that regard, I am safe.

I glance beyond the bedposts at the opposite wall. Above the ornately carved mantel of the fireplace, the portrait of a woman with sad eyes and a round face stares back. Watching me. She looks kind. Timid. Fragile. I think of Rayna. I will go see her in the morning before practice.

I roll onto my side and face the window. Rain splats against the panes, running down like tears. When King Adolar announced my engagement earlier, I couldn't imagine why Orna had cursed me yet again. But a new thought has emerged, energizing me. Orna has not cursed me. She has given me a gift. An opportunity. Or maybe the Lecals granted my wish.

The avalanche was not an accident. That is certitude. I could believe Ellias's death was an accident until I saw that figure rolling a body into the snow on Mount Bonen. Someone is terrorizing climbers. And I am certain the murderer lies in one of two places—within the Ascenditures or here in the castle. Somehow I've infiltrated both.

I will figure out who killed my mentor. I will unveil who killed the others. And then I will gift them the same in return.

18

On my way to training, I stop by my old tenement to find Rayna and share with her the wonderful idea I had to bring her on as one of my helpers. A quick chat with the prince this morning, and my idea was approved. Having turned down a carriage ride from palace servants, I walk through the streets in one of my new dresses. Today is one of those rare cloudless days. I bake in the warmth of Cleos's rays.

Gulls screech overhead. Pigeons flock on the cobbles outside the bakeries. A woman sweeps the threshold of her shop front. A man beats a dusty rug on the side of a brick building. Two ladies carrying parasols that look like curved doilies on a tea table strut down the street, chuckling about something. They smile when they see me. I blush and glance away.

A dress. That is all it takes to make me visible to them.

Kietsch is alive today. Just as our people gather for funerals, hangings, and swearing-in ceremonies, so we gather for starshine. I hop over a pile of fly-covered manure and duck to avoid a man carrying lumber poles. I sidestep a herd of loose sheep. The shepherd follows shortly, shouting commands at the fluffy creatures. I smile as they keep trotting.

In front of the cobbler's house on Shusta Street, I am nearly knocked off my feet by two girls play-fighting with broom handles. They wear identical green dürmels, faded and discolored by soot, with torn aprons tied around their waists. Black smudges highlight their cheeks.

"Take that, ya pirate scourge," the younger one shouts while the older strikes forward, smacking her handle against her sister's. They break out in a chorus of giggles before spinning and advancing again.

The older one's eyes fall on me. They grow large. She pulls her sister close and whispers in her ear. The two grin. The little one waves and turns bright red when I wave back. They break out in a fresh wave of giggles and continue fighting. I stop to watch, cheering each time one lands a soft blow.

"Get back inside," a male voice shouts from the nearest building. "You two are behaving like rambunctious boys. What kind of lady imagines a broom as a rapier?"

The girls lower their brooms to the ground but don't move.

"Now!" he shouts.

One sister sighs. The other stares at her shoes and shuffles over the threshold. I watch the place where their imaginations ran free. They can't be more than seven and ten, and already the lines of what a boy can do, and they cannot, are being drawn. With a sad sigh, I continue through the city.

The greetings I receive from my old housemates are mixed. Ol' Salt, whose name is actually Luzia, pulls me into a congratulatory hug. Pulmy, whose name is actually Marlis, stops cheering only when her cough becomes so bad she can't breathe. A few others watch through squinted eyes from the dark corners of their bunks. I wonder if they believe I killed those men on Mount Bonen or if they are simply angry I've escaped the confines of poverty while they wait to be wed off to lower-class men.

Rayna's bunk is empty. Even her meager belongings have vanished. I turn to the nearest girl, a new arrival I've never met. "Where is she? Where have they taken her?"

"Who? Glasses?" The new girl stretches her arms into the air and yawns. I notice she is wearing a pair of my socks. "She got her bride summons."

My heart drops. I collapse onto Rayna's empty bed. The springs squeal. "To whom?"

Marlis scrunches her nose and frowns. "The butcher's son. On Fleeker Street." She pauses to cough, wiping blood onto her sheets.

"It's not good, Klarkey," Luzia continues where Marlis left off. "He's got a reputation."

"Hits me every time 'e visits," a woman named Tabea, who

works in one of the brothels, says. "Pays extra for it, but still. 'E's not a good man."

I picture Rayna's tiny arms, her birdlike bones, her sweet disposition. An image of Eugen Martus hacking a large hock of lamb with his giant cleaver pops into my brain. He is drunk, he is angry. I wrestle a wad of saliva that sticks in my throat, threatening to cut off my airway.

"They put her with Eugen?" The words trickle out in a faint whisper. My eyes search the dusty floor for a solution. Once a woman is wed, there is no dissolving the marriage unless one partner dies. The penalty for adultery, or a woman leaving, is the gallows. I want to intervene, but any meddling on my part would only harm Rayna.

"Aren't you about to be a princess?" Tabea asks, running a comb through her long dark hair. "Can't you just ask your beloved for a favor?"

My eyes light up. My heart quickens. I leap to my feet and race out of the women's home into the bright streets. The leather soles of my boots slap against the cobblestones as I sprint down the narrow alleys. I weave in and out of tables covered in spices and fruits, sidestepping around patrons sniffing perfumes and perusing aprons and leather goods. I don't care that I am missing my first official day of training. Blinking away tears from Cleos's rays, I skid to a halt in front of Martus Meats.

Headless, skinned creatures hang from their ankles in the windows. A rusted iron sow hangs limply from a weather vane atop the structure. The place reeks of death, blood, and sweat. All I can picture are the six lost climbers hanging in some shop window like slaughtered pigs. Fighting the urge to gag, I push open the door. A bell tinkles. From behind the counter, a frail voice says, "Welcome to Martus Meats. How can I...Klarke? What are you doing here?"

"Rayna!" I rush to the counter. Before I can open the wooden gate to hug my friend, I notice the bruises on her arms and the deep bags under her eyes. "Rayna, what has he done to you?"

She lifts a shaking finger to her lips and steps around the

counter to where I stand. "He's asleep upstairs. If we wake him, he'll be very angry."

I shake my head. Black, purple, and yellow splotches decorate her skin like lichen on a rock. She looks thinner, as though she hasn't eaten since I left for the mountain. "I'm going to get you out of here, I promise."

"Nide." Rayna takes my wrist in her bony hands. "It will only cause more harm. Leave me be, Klarke. You can't protect me from everything."

"Yes, I can." I swipe the tears from my face and glare at the nearest animal corpse. "I have to. Look at you. You're wasting away."

Rayna drops her gaze to the floor. Tears splash the wooden boards at our feet. "There's only one way out of this. Only one thing I can control."

It takes a second for me to grasp her meaning. I fight the urge to rush up the rickety staircase in the back and bludgeon the bastard to death. Closing my eyes, I scream at the gods in my head for the curse they've put on me. My parents. Ellias. And now they are trying to take Rayna. I'll be damned if they succeed.

A groan filters down from the room above. Floorboards creak as someone takes a step and then another. Rayna's face blanches. Her lips tremble.

"Woman! Get up here," a slurred voice shouts.

"Go," she whispers, shoving me with her thin arms. "Get out, Klarke. Don't come back."

I dig my heels into the floor. The meat cleaver lies on the counter, stained in old blood. My eyes flash, but before I can commit to the decision, Rayna has turned and fled, racing up the stairs.

Black hatred fills me. The king's face pops into my head, and the hatred grows. He has perpetuated this society. I hear Rayna's pleading voice, followed by a thump and a low scream. A vile creaking follows—the sound of an old brass bed moving back and forth. A man grunting. A woman crying.

I rip the meat cleaver from the butcher block and move up the staircase.

☙

Blood pounds in my ears, so loud it sounds like I am standing on the shore when a storm rolls in. A bell tinkles in the shop below. I pause at the top of the stairs. Boots stomp across the wooden boards. I hide the cleaver behind my back.

"Stop!" a voice shouts from the shop floor. "Get down here, Fram Ascher."

From the bedroom down the hall, I hear commotion and rustling. Tossing the meat cleaver into an empty room, I descend the stairs. Five greencoats stand in the store, muskets across their shoulders. I glare and try to push past them, but one named Silias, who was assigned to me by the king, straightens his arm and blocks the door.

"What business do you have here?" Silias demands.

I glare into his icy stare, wishing I knew how to wield a musket. "I needed meat. Obviously."

"Then go to the kitchens in the palace." He cocks his head and smirks.

"How did you know I was here?" I try again to force my way past him, but the greencoat to my other side grabs me by the elbow.

"When you didn't show up for training, I was sent to find you. As you have so few friends, it wasn't hard."

I feel trapped, like a horse tied to a tree. "I wanted to say hi to my friend. I haven't seen her since I left for the mountain." I maintain a calm exterior as I lie, hoping the greencoats don't search upstairs and find the misplaced cleaver.

Footsteps bound down the staircase. I close my eyes and try to calm my rage.

"What's going on here? The hüle is this?"

I turn as Eugen Martus fastens the top button on his pants. His shirt lies open, revealing a wide swath of chest hair. I am taken aback by his imposing size. Eugen is at least six foot five and built like a bergbear, with dark hair and a thick beard.

"Pardon the interruption," Silias says with a bow. "We have come to collect Fram Ascher."

Eugen narrows his eyes as he appraises me. Cruel and cunning. Streaked with green. He is already high on veisel. I feel the fear Rayna must experience each time he forces himself upon her. Not letting that dread show, I straighten and meet his gaze with a stony glare.

"Fram!" Eugen shouts. His voice scrapes across my nerves. "Get down here."

Rayna appears at the top of the stairs, wrapped in a blanket. Like a waif, she descends, quivering beneath her protective covering. Her left eye is swollen. When she stops, I see she is silently pleading with me.

Swallowing my need to protect her, I smile and say, "Geitsê, Rayna. It's lovely to see you."

My soul shatters.

She nods, her right eye blinking rapidly. "Geitsê, Klarke."

A silence hangs between us. Hidden beneath it, I beg her to fight for her life. She commands me to let her go.

"You've said your greetings, now go." Eugen throws his tree trunk arm around Rayna's twig-like shoulders and gives me a menacing grin. I am afraid her bones will snap beneath his weight. "She's a brideprize now. With duties. She han't time for friends and scheiz."

I stare pathetically because I don't know what else to do. Inside, a forest fire rages through my core. I think of the first time I saw Rayna when Obid brought us together so many years ago. She needed me then, and she needs me now.

With a desperate wave, I am escorted by Silias and the guards from the meat market to the training center. A forbidding orkansturm brews out at sea. The thunder rolls in. Waves groan and crash upon the shore. Cleos vanishes behind her mask of clouds.

I imagine the meat cleaver in the back of Eugen's head and plot my revenge against a growing list of enemies.

19

As soon as the guards leave, I turn from the old factory and slink into the anonymity of the crowded city streets. I am not ready to face Kiel. To receive his salutation on my engagement. I don't want to listen to Tizian's snide comments or feel Aedan's pitying stares.

Rayna needs me. Much more than I need to climb. Rayna is starving herself. Trying to take her life before Eugen Martus can. All across my kingdom, women are trapped in invisible cages.

Even me. I walk the streets of Kietsch a free woman. I am allowed to climb. I can come and go from the palace anytime I want between the star and moonrise. But just like the others, I wear unseen manacles. My wedding date has not been set, but when it is, I will be told what to wear, how to hold my posture, and how to spread my legs when the celebration is finished.

Freedom in Ectair is a mirage. From a distance, it gleams like a beacon in the wasteland. Up close, it vanishes, leaving one with a dry and aching throat. I think of my mother and wonder if she was happy—if her love for my father was real or if she was just pretending, hanging banners and ribbons from her tiny cage. Death's Whisper took her not long after my father. They used to tell me she died of a broken heart. I try to find comfort in those words.

I decide to find Prince Otto when I return to the palace. Surely he can do something about Rayna's situation. I am not sure why I assume he will show me pity or have any kind of loyalty toward me. He has made it clear he wants nothing to do with me. I will beg if I must. Sell my soul to the darken mages. Whatever Otto needs from me to make the command to save Rayna, I will do. No matter the query.

A rumble of thunder rolls in from the bay. The orkansturm has moved from the sea onto the shore. Before heading for the palace, I make for Pohle Pier. The ground is slick, but I am sure of foot. Merchants and shoppers scuttle inside and beneath the eaves of buildings. I continue my march through the rain. Water crashes down onto the streets, churning in quick rivulets along the gutters. The silk dress clings to my skin. My hair presses against my face.

The Bay of Hammonhoff stretches out to the Point of the Tolvalus on one side and to the southern edge of the Western Shoal on the other. Large ships with colorful sails loll on the turbulent sea. Salt mixes with the rain and sticks to my body. The docks are crowded with fishermen hocking their catches and with sailors trying to sell trinkets they picked up in Kobo and the lands to the west. Strings of shells. Teeth from a hairk. A lucky rabbit's foot. The painted shell of a sea tûndle.

Wet bits of canvas stretch across their stalls. Water pools on top and drips down onto their backs and wares. Unlike the city folk, seamen are not frightened by water falling from the sky.

"Hey, sûssa! I han't seen a woman in three months. 'Specially not a highborn one. Can you fix that?"

Sûssa is a much kinder word than foze. It's what my father called my mother.

I stop and face the heckler, casting him a hülish glare. He stands with four others in front of the old cargo krane. The krane extends like the trunk of a Koboan fontanl from a small hut that sits atop a rounded base. It is constructed from the bloodwood trees that grow deep within the Dangof forest. Two trade wheels, each operated by four men, allow weights of up to three tons to be lifted and moved easily.

"I am not Ignaz, my fram." The man laughs. The others sneer. Green streaks in their eyes glow through the dim light. Their bodies twitch with unnatural energy.

"I might be a statdamen…" He takes a step toward me. "But I'll leave your guts just as they are."

I flick him the fickson with the two smallest fingers on my

right hand and keep walking. From the corner of my eye, I watch to make sure the men don't follow.

"Hey!" one of the other men shouts. Stringy hair mats against his cheeks and forehead. His coppola is stained with grease and tar. "That man is speaking. It don' matter where you come from. Pay some respects, whore."

I move quickly, shoving my way into a cluster of fishermen squabbling over who caught the largest fish. Leaning against a wooden statue of Layal, King Miter's legendary daughter, I catch my breath and calm my nerves. I come to Pohle Pier when I need to escape. The smell of salt, fish, and men who have worked too long without a bath brings me peace. It's almost as if I am with my father when I come here. I just have to close my eyes.

"I will be back in twenty moons, my dear. And then I promise to stay for a bit." My father smiles with the warmth of a thousand stars. He wears a long leather coat. Boots to his knees. The five-pointed hat worn by captains. Five points representing the pentagonal base of the Rektburg.

I pout. Squeeze the stuffed fontanl he brought me from Kobo on his last voyage. I'd named her Sina. "Why do you always have to leave?"

My mother holds my hand. Black lace gloves cover her fingers. The statue of Layal towers over us. The cargo Krane loads the last bundle of salt boxes onto my father's ship. Obid carries two baskets—loaded and covered in canvas—onto the boat.

"Your father has a very important job, Klarkey." My mother squeezes my hand. She beams down at me, her brown eyes twinkling.

"They don't need salt at Fort Truce." I throw Sina to the ground. Before my father can retrieve her, a sailor steps on her trunk, leaving a muddy boot print. My father tries to wipe off the mud, but the stain runs deep. I grab Sina and whimper into her soft side.

My father bends down so he is at eye level with me. "Someday, my love, you will understand. Until that day, just know that I love you. More than Lecals love Cleos. More than Ellias loves rock. More than King Adolar loves his crown. His smile grows. "Be well, my darling. Look for my sails on the evening of the twentieth moon."

I open my eyes. The fishermen have finally decided upon a

winner. Someone snagged a six-foot thund far out in the Rolag
Sea. The others clap him on the back and take turns holding
the large fish.

I waited for my father on the twentieth, the twenty-first, the
twenty-second… I waited every night until news came of the
accident. Obid was the only survivor. He washed ashore hanging on to an empty barrel of kimmeron near Fort Truce on
The Gate. One of the orange sails washed up near Omalau. An
orange sail and a five-pointed hat.

*My mother and father embrace. It is a long hug. "Soon," he assures
her. "We will be together soon. Stay strong, my love."*

*"Soon," my mother repeats. She kisses his cheek and returns to holding
my hand.*

*My father walks down the gangway. He waves, removes his hat, bows,
and then disappears onto the ship. Gulls scream and fight over bits of fish
entrails. It is a bright day. Cleos shines through a thin layer of clouds.*

*"Let's go home." My mother pulls gently on my hand. I remain in
place, yanking my fingers from her grip.*

"Wait." I skim the men boarding the ship. "I have to say bye to Losan."

*She bends down and taps me playfully on the nose. "How could I
forget? Stay near Layal and say your farewells. I will be at Hannar Jager's
stall buying something fresh for dinner."*

I nod and stand on tiptoes, searching for a small boy among men.

"Fischbomb!" A wad of beady eggs and scales lands at my feet.

I jump back. "No fair! We do that to other people, not to each other."

*Losan bends over and laughs. The sound of his joy makes me smile.
I laugh too.*

"I wish you could stay longer," I say.

*"Did you hear that, lads?" he shouts and looks around, but no one
pays us attention. "The captain's daughter says she'll miss me." He grins.*

*I slug him on the shoulder. "I did not say that. I'll miss your company.
Not you."*

"Same scheiz." He shrugs and grins.

*I gasp at his swearing and peer over to Hannar Jager's stall. My mother
did not hear. I breathe out a sigh of relief. "That's a bad word. You can't
say things like that."*

His laugh is so loud and deep that it startles the nearest pigeons. The group of birds fly off in a flurry of wings and caws.

I open my eyes. A cluster of pigeons gathers around an old man who tosses bits of stale bread at them. They grapple with each other over the tiny pieces of food. It hurts. Ten years have passed, but the pain of loss still throbs in my heart.

I leave Layal's statue and wander farther into the market. I toss three silver dracals, the lowest coin in Ectair's currency, to a vendor, who passes me a skewer laden with smoked shrimp. Juice dribbles down my chin as I walk past wooden barrels filled with mussels, scallops, crabs, and oysters. Googly-eyed fish stare up at me. Hanging from wooden beams are long sheets of seaweed and thin tendrils of seagrass. Closing my eyes and inhaling the air around me, I imagine my father teaching me the names of each creature and plant.

"That one is a lungfish. Can you believe it has lungs? We aren't so different, are we?"

"Oye, Fram Ascher."

I recognize the booming, slurred voice. Obid, the ship's cook, stands in front of one of the nearby stalls, a basket tucked into the crook of each elbow. One basket is covered in canvas, the other is filled with fish and mussels. Bloodshot eyes gleam back at me, letting me know he is drunk. I smile, grateful to see a friendly face.

"Geitsê, Obid. You're well?" I move to where he stands. He thrusts the canvas-covered basket into my arms. I stumble but quickly regain my footing.

"Better 'an you, I s'pose, princess." His loud chuckle is matched by the toothless grin of the fish vendor. "Strange turn of events since I last saw ya."

I blanch at his words, embarrassed that the whole kingdom knows my life. "It's not what I had in mind." I want to say more, to vent, but I am not sure who's listening. "I will serve the kingdom however I am called to."

Obid narrows his eyes, then keels over, hugging his large belly as he guffaws. It reminds me of Losan. I clear my throat.

I did not come here to be mocked or to have attention drawn to me.

When he recovers, Obid pays and thanks the fish seller. He takes the basket from my hands. A beefy arm wraps around my shoulder, and he steers me down the pier to the end of the dock. The wind is ferocious. Rain and sea spray pelt my face. Obid no longer looks jovial and carefree. He gazes at me with eyes full of unease. "I can get ya outta here, Klarke."

I almost don't hear him over the sea's roar. My head cocks to the side. "What do you mean?"

He sets his baskets onto the wooden planks and swipes a thick hand across his forehead. "I hear what people on the street are sayin'. I hear whispers of what happened on that mountain. Somethin' stinks worse than that fish market. And ya at the center of it all. I'm on a boat headed for The Gate today. Sneakin' up to Dristo afterward to pick up a shipment of schneestone. The Gate is a seedy place, but Dristo's not bad. In a few days, you could be in Hidel if you don't like the portstat."

Heidel. Dristo. My heart grows heavy and cold. I look away from Obid. Out to the sea, in the direction of The Gate, though I cannot see the island from here.

The ruins of an old castle cling to a rocky peninsula next to the pier. Haradön. Only the stone base remains in places. The stone base and a narrow tower of rock that is actually the remnants of an interior wall. It pokes into the sky like the finger the schoolhouse mistress used to prod into my side when she caught me staring out the window at the gulls instead of memorizing Miter's Creed for the Kingdom.

I watch the waves leap over the rocks and kiss the runen. The memory of its purpose has crossed the darkened sea with those who built it. We think it thrived in the times before King Miter. Maybe as a fortress to keep out marauders from the lands west of Galvaith.

A seahound barks three times and then flops like a suffocating fish from the slick stone at the base of the runen. It slides into the waves and swims toward shore. Seeking refuge.

"Dristo?" I face Obid. Water sprays me from all directions. "Hidel? Those are cities in Ainar, Obid. You want to take me from one enemy to an even viler enemy?" I take a step back, careful not to move too far. A plunge into the raging, frigid sea could be fatal.

Obid shakes his head and holds up his hands. "Ainar's not so bad, Klarke. Been trading with them for years, even after King Adolar dammed the waste and outlawed trade. He's a liar, a light-skinned lover. Ainar has people from all over Galvaith and beyond. And they get along."

I snap my gaping mouth shut when a blast of sea spray grazes my tongue. The people of Ainar are heathens, monstrous barbarians who consume human flesh when the winters go too long. Men and women who speak to animals and control the monsters of the sea. "The things you are saying are treasonous. You can't mean this."

"Klarke, think about where ya information came from. Maybe ya learned it in school, but those ideas came straight from the palace. Do ya trust the palace? Do ya trust the men who make decisions for ya?" He places his hands on his hips. The wind whips his oversized linen shirt, creating a rhythmic pop-pop.

I peer up at the cliffs to my right. Miter's Backbone rises above Kietsch and the bay. Somewhere, high above the mist and rain, well beyond my range of sight, lie the Celebern Fields and the single place of starshine and warmth in my kingdom. I swallow. It is also the place of Ellias's death. His murder. How high does the betrayal go?

"I don't trust anyone." My whisper vanishes in the storm. I've thought of leaving so many times, and yet here I stand. I think of Rayna. Of Gerd. Of Rosalie. Of Ellias and Feiko. I can't leave. Things have to change. That won't happen if I raise anchor and flee.

I rest a gentle hand on Obid's arm and grit my teeth. "Tanks ye, but no. I have to see this through. This orkansturm is mine to weather."

Obid sighs and picks up his fish basket. "The offer stands. If ya need an out, ya know where to find me."

He reaches for the other basket. A cry issues from beneath the canvas when he lifts it. I stare between Obid and the basket, thinking I must have misheard. It was probably a gull flying in from the storm. The seahound signaling to its herd.

The cry sounds again. It morphs into a wail and then a gurgle.

"Obid, what are you doing?"

His eyes shift. He begins moving down the dock, trying to get away from me. The wooden boards groan beneath his stride. I rush to catch him and yank on the piece of canvas. It falls to the decking.

I gasp and reach for the canvas before it blows into the bay. "I don't understand."

A baby girl wrapped in green towels flinches against the raindrops. She is the tiniest child I have ever seen. She can't be more than a few days old. I fling the canvas back over the basket.

"They would have killed 'er." Obid closes the distance between us and drops his voice to a whisper. "I'm tryin' to save her life. Don' tell no one."

I recall Obid's words on our way to Mount Bonen. Down in the belly of the ship.

"Ya mum saved more women and girls than I can count. And I smuggled most of 'em beneath sacks of flour like these. Weevils and women and wee baby girls."

"She is a twin to a boy, isn't she?" I lift the corner of the fabric and stare at the child. Our kingdom would have her thrown into the sea. Because she was born like me. But now, because of Obid, this little girl will become someone's Rayna. "My mom helped you save twins, didn't she? That's what you were getting at on the boat ride to Mount Bonen."

"Ya mum was holier than all the päters in this kingdom."

I release the cloth and steel my gaze, knowing he won't like what I am about to say. "I want to help you."

"Nide." Obid meets me with a hardened look. He shakes his head so fervently the water clinging to his hair and beard fly back into the sea. "I won't have what happened to her happen to you."

"My mom died from Death's Whisper. I could come to that fate even if I never lifted a finger to help anyone." My hands clasp in front of my face. Maybe this is it. Maybe this is why I am meant to stay in Ectair. Why I can't flee. "I'll take the risk."

A wave crests the small outcropping of land to our side. I watch Haradön become consumed by water.

"An what the hüle is Death's Whisper? Huh?" Obid rocks the basket in his arm as if it is a cradle. What a sight we must be. A small woman glaring up at an imposing man embracing a basket of fish. Standing in the middle of a furious storm like two drunken botswein's mates.

"We don't know nothin' about it," he snaps.

"Lots of people die from Death's Whisper. It isn't unique to my mother." I lean in, pleading. I want to do something. I must do something more. "Nothing happened to her except tragedy and maybe a broken heart."

The baby begins to cry louder. Her small screams leap into the fury of the storm. Obid coos softly. An old lullaby my mother used to sing.

Sleep softly, my child, and journey with me.
'Neath rolling waves and 'yond lands in your dreams.
To a kingdom of seamachens, tûndles, and vadim.
To the place we all yearn for, in the deep, darkened sea.

The crying stops. I thought the song was beautiful when my mother sang it to me. Now I realize it is about death.

"Stay out of it, Klarke." Obid strides away, leaving me with the haunting words of his lullaby. "Climb ya mountains," he shouts over his shoulder, "an' come to me when ya need to escape. Otherwise, leave it alone."

I watch him move down the pier, feeling like I've been slapped across the face. He boards a ship. In one arm, he holds a basket of fish. In the other, someone's life. The krane lowers another load of gear onto the deck. Obid is blocked from my view by a stack of wooden crates.

The baby girl will go to Ainar. She will grow up in Ainar. How many of us are there in the frozen north? How many of Ectair's daughters live among the barbarians?

I have many questions. Many answers I've let slip past me over the last seventeen years. One line of queries burns inside me now, so furiously it warms me from within.

A wave crests the pier and splashes me in the face. I wipe the salty spray from my cheeks and walk with purpose back toward the market.

Who was my mother, really? And what actually happened to her the night she died?

20

The guards greet me with curt nods. I return the gesture as I step through the main doors into the palace. I am not such a fool as to think King Adolar is letting me gallivant around his kingdom unsupervised. Every step I take, both in the palace and on the streets, is monitored. I hope no one saw the contents of Obid's basket.

"Geitsê, Fram Ascher." The guard Silias welcomes me. His helmet sparkles from the candles in the chandelier above us. A club hangs from his side. I wonder if he has ever used it.

"I trust training went well." He lifts an eyebrow and rests his hand on the end of his cudgel.

"Fantish." I wipe the wet hair from my forehead and slow my gait. Water squelches from my boots. I know he knows I skipped, but if he wants the truth, he must admit that I am being followed. "Where's the prince?"

"The prince is not my charge," Silias says, sizing up the soaked dress that clings to my figure. Behind him two other guards stand still as holzenschreins, like suits of armor waiting for the darken mages to breathe life into their metallic joints.

While the outside of the palace is rustic and archaic, the inside looks as if all the gems and precious metals mined from the Tono hills were brought to the Rektburg, slathered in glupaste, and tossed into the air. The arched ceiling of the entryway is the color of the sea when Cleos shines through the clouds. The star has been painted in gold in the center of it all.

The rest of Ectair struggles to eat.

I stare at Silias to see if he'll say more about the prince's whereabouts, but he remains silent. "Okay, then. Tanks ye."

The prince is not in his room. He is not in the gardens that fill the space between the outer fortification and the inner diamond-shaped wall that supports the Nied Tower and the four towers of the Geistich. Prince Otto and his servants occupy one of the four towers. One belonged to Queen Eleonora. The other two belong to Orna and Laren. Only the päters and those deemed holy can enter.

I step from the gardens through a rough wooden doorway into the kitchen. Stone columns support a freshly painted ceiling. So much cleaner than any soot-covered galley I've been in. Copper pots line shelves and hang from hooks above cast-iron stoves. Carved wooden counters, barrels of wine and ale, stacks of flour and corn, and baskets brimming with onions, potatoes, parsnips, and carrots fill the space. Cooks and chefhands bustle about. Spoons clink against pots. Shouts to move, pass the garlic, and hurry up echo through the columns. I sidestep a frantic chefhand whose eyes widen when he realizes who I am.

"Can we get you anything, Fram Ascher?" He stops midstride, a heavy pot of potatoes weighing down his arms. He smiles, but I can tell it is the forced pleasantry of someone only following protocol.

"Sorry, no. Please just ignore me." I wave my hand for him to keep moving and offer a sheepish grin. I am no one special. I hate that there is a notion that I deserve superior treatment.

The smells of wheat and yeast baking in the oven escort me through the kitchens. Soup gurgles on the stovetop. A roasting rack of lamb sends tendrils of savory smoke into the air. My tongue trembles.

At the orphanage and later, at the tenement, food like this would have fed us for a month. I want to stand here forever, sniffing the sweet and spicy aromas of curcumin, zimtammon, cloves, and hünich that hang heavy in the air. The smells remind me of the feasts my mother would make to celebrate Ursprung, the day our people moved from the darkened sea onto land in the times before history.

I scan the heads of each servant, hoping to find the prince hidden among them, sneaking bits of lamb or bites of cheese. He is not here. Tearing my eyes from a mound of butter and a steaming loaf of bread on the counter, I move beyond the kitchen into a windowless hallway that drops beneath the earth. Tapestries cover the walls. Images of ships at sea and armored men fighting a giant tentacled beast have been stitched onto their facades. I stare at one hanging that features Hildegroth, the great monster. Thirteen arms reach from the waves and wrap themselves around a boat with bright orange sails. Three rows of teeth circle a gaping mouth filled with a dark whirlpool. My stomach clenches. I wipe a stray strand of hair from my forehead. My father's ship had bright orange sails. Rumors spread that Hildegroth consumed his vessel and all aboard. Obid claims he can't remember what happened, that he hit his head on the mast and was knocked out. His first memories are of waking up on the beach with children staring down at him.

Every old woman and drunken sailor will tell tales to those who listen. This tapestry is clearly timeworn. And Hildegroth hasn't been seen since his destructive tirade through what is now Miter's Waste. The monster didn't kill my father any more than felfees killed Ellias.

A bell sounds from Hadrian's Monastery somewhere high above and distant from where I now stand. Three gongs. I should still be at practice proving to Veit why I deserve to be an Ascenditure.

I won my spot on the team because my competitors were murdered. I don't deserve scheiz.

I come to a small door at the end of the hallway. The door is locked from my side with an iron bolt. I slide the bolt from its catch and slowly push open the door. Another hallway stretches out at a diagonal to my left and right. I leave the door cracked behind me. From this side, it looks like a fragment of the wall, painted a slick white and gilded in gold leaf. Murals of men tending oxen and women in traditional dürmels picking wheat stretch from floor to ceiling along the hall. At each end of the corridor, a rounded wall and oakenwood door sit. Towers. I am somewhere in the Geistich between two of the four turrets. The hidden passageway must be how the cooks and servants move unseen between the outer Pentengen and the inner Geistich.

Above the doorway to the tower on my left hangs the circular seal of Laren. Set against a black sky and deep blue sea, a lone bolt of lightning drops from the top of the circle to meet the tip of a tentacle that reaches up from the bottom. Laren's domains are the sea, the sky, and the darkness.

The other tower displays the seal of Orna. One mountain rises from the bottom. Another descends from the top. Their summits meet in the middle. Behind the junction of the peaks radiates Cleos. A yellow ball of fire. His rays streak out in golden bands. The sigil looks like an eye. An eye formed of mountains and light. Azura, our cobalt moon, hangs from the upper right bend of the seal. Those are Orna's domains—the land, the life forms, and the himmelorbs, her twins.

I have not been outwardly forbidden from entering the Geistich. Prince Otto's quarters are here, and I am allowed to visit him. Walburga's Library sits beneath the Nied Tower, as does the dining room and the writing room, and just above the cellars and dungeon lies the Maja Grotto. But sneaking in through a hidden entrance and tiptoeing between two sacred towers I am not allowed to enter feels prohibited. I glance in both directions to be sure I am alone, then move toward Laren's Tower. The prince could be in the library. I decide to check there next.

The door to Laren's tower scrapes against the stone floor. I duck into an alcove behind the carved statue of Rüdiger the Dumt, King Miter's famed jester, who, according to legend, saved Miter's life from an irate servant with his toy harpoon. The black hem of a robe appears first from behind the door. Then a dark boot. I press myself into the statue, grateful the bells around Rüdiger's collar are whittled from wood and not forged of tinkling metal.

A päter steps from the tower cradling the stalks of a plant I don't recognize. A purple fern, although such things do not, to my knowledge, exist. I squint for a better look but still don't recognize the cuttings. Many small violet leaves hemmed in white stick out from a bright purple central branch. Four päters follow the first from the tower, each carrying a bundle of the strange fern. Four of the figures pass by, their white masks staring expressionlessly ahead. I hold my breath. They move past me down the hall, pausing briefly at the cracked servants' door and whispering. The fifth päter locks the entry to Laren's Tower, then follows the others. When he passes the statue I notice a dark gem hanging from a thin cord around his neck. The gem is nearly the size of a ganzen egg, with impurities that make it look as though it fell from the night sky bringing with it a handful of stars. So beautiful and mesmerizing I can't take my eyes off it. It looks how I imagine a black diemant might look, but that could not be. The only black diemants ever found were sent to the palace for safekeeping. Just before Hildegroth lay waste to the kingdoms, the entire collection of Ectair's diemants were stolen. And without the darken mages…

I think of Kiel telling me he thought King Adolar had a diemant.

Before the fifth päter reaches the others at the doorway to Orna's Tower, he tucks the jewel into his robes. My heart drops when it vanishes. I let out an exhalation that is too loud. Over a silly stone? I clap a hand over my mouth until the five disappear into the turret.

To my knowledge, päters are forbidden from owning or wearing jewelry or anything precious. And a diemant of that size…would be priceless. I have never heard of such a gemstone being part of their ceremonial rituals. Shrugging, I slink from behind Rüdiger's statue and make for the library.

I find the prince a few hours before starset. He creeps up from the basement, straightening his crown as he walks. A servant saunters behind him, carrying two empty baskets. My mind sails to Obid and the baby girl on her way to Ainar.

"What are you doing here?" He folds his hands and rests them on his belt. His eyes are cool. Detached. The servant pauses behind him.

I glance around at the murals on the wall and at the blue and white vases set atop ornamental tables. What am I doing here? I have no business in this palace with this man. My resolve jumbles around my brain. I am taken in by the prince's eyes, which burn with a passionate gentleness I find captivating. I find it hard to meet his gaze. He both intrigues and intimidates me. I forget why I searched all day for him.

He nods as if my silence deserves a response and takes a long stride forward. I watch him move away with the grace of a canoe cutting across glassy water.

"Wait! Prince Otto."

He pauses and turns. I race to catch him. I will not let fear keep me from saving Rayna.

"I need your help."

He cocks his head to the side. One eyebrow rises. We stand awkwardly. Neither of us knows how to handle this relationship that has been thrust upon us. I am not sure how I am allowed to speak to him or what I am allowed to demand. I think he doesn't know how much kindness and warmth to extend to me. Neither of us knows if the other is trustworthy.

I clear my throat, wishing he would participate in this conversation. Help me along a bit. He says nothing.

"I have places to be." The coolness deepens in his expression. He sighs as if he is out of breath. "Gob it out or find me when you have located your tongue."

I imagine Rayna's black eye. Her ribs protruding from her skin. "My friend, the one I asked you about before." I run a hand through my hair and search for words on the floor between our feet. "She is in trouble. She has been married off to a terrible man. Please. I need to get her out of there."

A group of adels strut past us. Shawls made of fur cover the shoulders of the women. Their dürmels are made of silk, hemmed with lace and threads of gold. The men stand tall, wearing high leather boots that have never stepped in the street filth of Kietsch. They bow to Prince Otto as they pass and look at me like a slice of moldy bread.

Otto smiles warmly at them. He turns to me. "I said she could work for you when she was single. If she is married now, then there's nothing I can do." Irritation sweeps across his face, and his gaze draws away, down the hallway where he wishes to go.

I shake my head and fight the urge to be angry. "You're the prince. Can't you just declare that Rayna is needed at the palace and that her marriage is no more?"

The adels stop and peer back at us. One woman has raised a gloved hand to cover her mouth. The other holds her heart. The men shake their heads.

Prince Otto's lip lifts in a momentary smile. "Once a woman is wed, only death can end the marriage. But I think you know that. Are you asking me to kill your friend's husband? To commit treason?"

Murmurs come from the eavesdropping group of privileged swans. I want to throw the nearest vase at them. Tell them to mind their own business. Slap the women's fragile hands from their fragile figures and show them the horrifying aspects of this society they so comfortably sit upon.

"Of course I am not asking that." I tear my glare from the adels and plant it upon Otto. "I was hoping you would follow your own rules and save my friend from a violent peasant. I guess your authority only extends so far."

My anger surges like the vanguard wave of an orkansturm. My face must be the color of an apple because it burns like a winter hearth.

"You will not speak to me in such tones." He lifts himself to his full height and points a finger into my face. "I am your betrothed. You will remember you belong to me now. I demand your respect and loyalty, and I will have it."

My mouth gapes. My rage boils and pops. "You will have my loyalty and respect when you earn it, sire. Until then, you will receive only my truth."

We stand silent, glaring at each other. The adels watch with no regard for privacy. Otto should be scolding them for not having respect instead of turning his vitriol upon me. I brace for the prince's irate retort, ready to fight back.

Prince Otto smiles and places a hand on my shoulder. He shakes his head and clucks his tongue. I suck in a confused breath. "My love. My sweet, sweet Klarke. I know you are weary from your climb. Delirious even. Rest, darling." He leans in and kisses my cheek. His voice morphs into an urgent whisper. "You will either learn to play the game or not live beyond the next moonrise."

He pulls away. My heart feels like a stone in my chest, crushing down upon my lungs. An icy chill, as if I am back on the slopes of Mount Bonen, caresses my back. I can't tell if Prince Otto's words were a warning or a threat.

"To your room, sûssa." With a sugared smile, he points in the direction of my quarters. "You'll feel yourself again come supper time. Sail along, little bird."

In a daze, I walk to my room, flinching each time a door closes or a pair of eyes linger too long. I slam my door shut, fling the deadbolt into place, and dive into my bed. Beneath the covers, my heart somersaults. I gasp. It's too much. Being watched. Judged. My words scrutinized. I am no princess. I will never be a princess. Above all, I do not want to be a princess.

Something rustles in the corner of my room. I sink deeper into my sheets. Are there ghosts in this palace? Of course, there must be. The ghost of King Miter? Specters conjured by Walburga? With so much deceit in the hearts of the inhabitants, the spirits of the dead must be cruel and guileful. Like the prince, I wonder if they are here to warn me or come with a more malignant purpose.

Footsteps approach my bed. I whimper and pull back the covers. I am not greeted by the face of a long-dead adel or the claws and snarling teeth of Ignaz. Prince Otto stares down at me through the curtains. He places a finger to his lips and motions for me to follow.

ॐ

To the side of the hearth, Prince Otto slides a bookshelf across the floor as if it is weightless. I keep my face still. I don't want him to see how horrifying I find that secret opening into my private chambers. Who knows what eyeballs watch me as I sleep, eat, dress, and bathe?

"This way." He steps into the dark passage beyond. Only his hand remains, beckoning me toward it.

I glance at my bed, then harden my resolve and follow him into the tunnel. He slides the bookshelf back into place. My vision returns as he lights an oil lamp. I stare at the braided wick and the oil in the chamber.

The passage moves downward to my left and upward to my right. Prince Otto moves to the right. I follow in the flickering light of his lamp. After 352 steps, which I counted in case the lamp oil runs dry and I am forced to find my way in the darkness, we stop.

"If you do not wise up, you will continue to suffer." He sets the lamp on the stone step above him and sits.

I remain standing. "Is that a threat or a warning? It's hard to tell with you."

He balks and shakes his head. "Why would I threaten you? All I am saying is that if you haven't figured out that you have a target on your back, it's pointless for me to even try."

My lip curls. I sink onto the step beneath the prince and bang my head once against the wall. "Of course I know all of that. But I can't show weakness. I can't let them think I am afraid."

"Are you afraid?"

His question catches me off guard. Again, my gaze drifts to the oil lamp. To the dust on the steps. To the curvature of the stone walls. Anywhere but his face. "I don't want to be."

Prince Otto sighs and leans his head against the wall. His muscles press against the sleeves of his green doublet and the fabric of his tan hosen. His skin is pale, like mine, and his hair dark. Every feature on his face is sharp and angled like a climbing route on Vether's Fel. By every standard, he is handsome.

"You and I aren't so different." He whispers these words, gazing at the ceiling of the passage.

He'd said something like this before, but I'd let it sift through my thoughts and flicker out unaccounted for. I fold my hands across my knees and watch him. "How do you figure?"

He thinks, takes his time. Maybe he just said those words to gain my trust.

"Neither of us wants to get married."

"That's not true." I shrug one shoulder and glare at my hands. "I might want to get married...someday. When I decide and to whom I wish. I am not some hannar-hater."

He smiles and gives a small laugh. His eyes twinkle when they meet mine. "And I am no fram-hater."

His lightheartedness relaxes me. His smile warms my soul. "I just want to be able to climb mountains and not have every step I take questioned. Or always having some drunk demanding I sleep with him."

He frowns. Something new dances in his eyes. I don't recognize it. It is soft. Earnest. Kind.

"I can imagine what you go through every day must be hard."

Compassion. That is what it is. I chew at my lip and watch him. It might all be a ruse to get me to trust him. A plot with the king to destroy me. Right now, I don't care. It feels good. "Tanks ye," I whisper.

We sit together in silence, the light from the lamp casting peculiar shadows upon the circular walls. No tapestries hang here. No vases or filigree decorate the space. We are in some secret stairwell in one of the towers of the Pentengen. It feels safer here. Safer without the gold and opulence. I trace my finger through the dust on the step beside me. M. V. A. My mother's initials.

"I will help free your friend."

My finger freezes. I look up.

"I don't know if it is possible, but I will do what I can to relieve her of her duties." Otto's expression is sincere. There is no mockery in his eyes. No hint of malicious teasing.

A cry escapes my lips. I cough it away and fight back tears. I could wrap my arms around him in gratitude, but I don't know if I'm allowed to touch him yet. I don't know anything about our relationship.

"Be smarter, Klarke. Blend in. Don't make waves." He grabs my hand in his and holds it. Warmth spreads in places I wish to remain cool and unaffected. I nod, hoping the lamplight doesn't illuminate my blushing cheeks. "Prince Otto?"

"Just Otto, please."

I swipe an errant tear from my cheek and rock back onto my ankles. "Can I trust you? I know you might lie—will probably lie—but I need an ally. I am so desperate I am willing to take you at your word."

The prince gives a slow nod. He takes my other hand in his as well and looks directly into my eyes. "I may not want to marry you, but the truth is, it could be worse."

I wrinkle my nose at what sounds like an insult, but he winks and continues.

"I could have been assigned a miserable, stuck-up adel— someone who only cares about status and wealth. At least with you, I know you are genuine. I know your motives. As I said, I might not want to marry you, but if we are going to spend a lifetime together, I hope we can at least be friends and confidants."

My heart softens. A knot of tension releases in my shoulders; a bundle of nerves relaxes in my spine. For the first time, not all feels lost.

He stands and pulls me to my feet. "If you need help or need to speak with me in private, this is where we will meet. You know the way?"

I nod and brush the dirt from the rear of my skirt.

"We will need a sign," he says. "If you need me, cross both hands over your heart. Any bystander will think you are sending me a loving gesture. I will know you are in trouble." He picks up the oil lamp and descends the stairs.

I trot behind in his shadow. We stop at my door. "Tanks ye,

Otto. For everything. I was beginning to think the whole world is against me."

He rests a large hand on my shoulder and grimaces. "It is, Klarke. I will protect you to the best of my ability, but don't let that fool you into a false sense of security. My father is not a forgiving man, nor one open to opinions different from his. Your existence challenges him. He will try to destroy you."

I bite my lip. The momentary feeling of security floats back up the staircase where it belongs. Where I can find it when I need to. It does not exist down here. Down here I become a rabbit in a wood of volves.

"Then I must destroy him first."

I slide the bookshelf open and disappear into my room before the prince can respond. Instead of crawling into the false safety of my bed, I creep to the window and peer out into the gardens below. Dusk is falling. Heavy rain morphs my view, turning everything into hazy, shapeless blobs.

My eyes drift to the Nied Tower. Candlelight flickers in the uppermost window, in the bedchambers of King Adolar. I will go to training tomorrow. I will not disobey or slink around the palace. I will behave as if all is normal.

Meanwhile, I will plot my revenge.

21

The dining room table is as long as the entire hallway of the second floor of my old tenement. Crystal glasses, as clear as the spring water spilling from the rocks near Lake Eisenturks, hold wine so red and thick it could be blood. Three silver forks lie on a silk napkin next to my plate. Wooden boards bearing cheese and fig mustard accompany each place setting. Platters covered in grapes, pears, sausages, cabbage, and spätzen noodles with cheese fill the vacant spaces. Five candelabras provide glowing circles of light along the tabletop. I shift my gaze between the forks, trying to discern the purpose of each. My mouth waters.

From the head of the table, King Adolar surveys us. He smiles proudly at all who have gathered to feast with him. His face beams. His eyes shine with greedy hunger. I am reminded of a small child at school named Wilfried who was bullied until he finally got big enough to fight back. Once he grew, Wilfried became the bully. Wilfried would tuck sardines into other kids' lunch sacks or throw rocks at the girls. He did everything to others that he'd hated for himself. But he was so proud of what he saw as an accomplishment. To have shed the weak skin he was born in.

I know almost nothing about our king's past. I don't know if he was like Wilfried—rotting from the inside out over time from inflicted cruelty—or if he was born sour. I overheard Ellias speaking once with my father about a supposed friendship between King Adolar and my mother. She never spoke of him to me in any tone other than quiet respect.

Adels, dressed in their finest, sit closest to the king, laughing and fawning over each other's words. Prince Otto sits erect at the opposite end of the table, swirling the wine in his glass. I am to his left, thankful to be as far from the king as possible.

My servant—I use that word for lack of a better one as I loathe the term—dressed me in a silk dürmel the color of salmon, with enough frills around the apron and poofs under the sleeves to fill the seamstress's shop down on Takk Street. Beneath the fabric I have been strapped into something so tight it sucks the skin to my ribs. I don't feel pretty or elegant. I feel silly and out of place. Like a sheep in a wig. I keep pushing down on the fabric in my lap, but it bounces back.

Women dressed in oversized white smocks bring trays of bread from the kitchens and place them on the boards before us. The breads are all shapes and sizes, with the kind of crust so thick it sounds like ice crunching beneath your boots when you cut into it. Orange soup is ladled into a bowl next to my plate. I tilt my head. My breath catches.

"Don't you feel lucky, Fram Ascher?"

I look at the head of the table. All eyes turn to me. I swallow hard and force a smile for King Adolar. "Yes, of cour—"

He cuts me off mid-gratitude. "You are not only the first female Ascenditure but also the first climber in history to eat the sacred solans and keep their head. We must toast to this."

He lifts his wine goblet. A loathsome chuckle bubbles along the table as overfed lords and ladies giggle and raise theirs. I let my mind race through the insults and retorts it wants to fling before offering another demure smile and lifting my glass.

"I feel most honored and humbled for all you have given me." Maintaining my prim composure, I bow my head as I imagine a proper lady would.

"Yes, I am sure you do." The king narrows his eyes before raising his glass higher. "To gratitude and accomplishment," he says. The dinner guests repeat his words. We sip the wine. It tastes of gegenberries and soured grapes. With hints of vanilla and summer cherries.

The king reaches for his bowl and lifts it to his lips. He takes a long sip and then sets down the vessel. The solans must taste like warm butter. That is how I imagine them. Warm butter, brown sugar, and hofnuss.

The dinner guests lift their spoons and dip them into the orange soup, taking dainty sips of the liquid. The rest of my teammates would be punished if they tasted the soup. Ellias, Feiko, and countless others died retrieving these ingredients. I ignore the bisque. I don't even have the urge to taste it. Why should I have this privilege when my brothers do not? To blend in, I reach for a slice of bread and slather it with butter.

"He's watching you."

I turn my head slightly in the direction of Prince Otto. "What?"

The prince doesn't look at me as he dunks a warm chunk of bread into his bowl. "If you truly want to blend in, you'll have to eat it. He'll see your untouched bowl as a sign of ingratitude. He will use it against you."

"I don't want it. I can't." My voice breaks. I stuff bread into my cheeks to plug the sob in my throat. A piece goes down my windpipe, and I gag, coughing and drawing the attention of the room. One of the servants races over, but I wave her away. Clearing my throat, I smile at the guests. "Good bread." I shrug and wipe the unavoidable tears from my eyes.

"How are you enjoying the soup?" The king runs his fingers through his beard. The way he looks at me is the way I imagine a snake views a töte, or a volf contemplates a lamb.

Glancing at my bowl, I notice half of the liquid is gone. I flip my eyes to the prince, who stares ahead, ignoring me. His bowl was almost empty. Now it is almost full. A fist of gratitude tightens around my heart.

"Very much so. It is delicious." I bat my eyes like a child begging for sweets at the bakery. It infuriates me to see how these soft, clueless adels look at me with dead eyes and stony expressions. To them I am no hero. I am no princess. In their eyes I will never be anything but a girl from the slums who manipulated her way into the palace.

Prince Otto stands suddenly and pushes his chair back across the floor. "My lord," he says to his father with a polite bow. "With your permission, I'd like to take my leave before the rest of supper is served. I am quite tired and would like to take my future bride to bed with me."

King Adolar laughs and slams his fist against the table. The crystal goblets rattle. The blood-red wine wobbles. The women gasp. "It is improper to take a young lady to bed until you are married." He gives a devious smile to the lords closest to him and turns back to Otto. "But Fram Ascher is no lady, is she? She is an Ascenditure. She has chosen the life of a man. I am not quite sure what to say here."

My cheeks burn like the fire roaring in the hearth. I want to shrink into the depths of my gown and hide from the judgments being cast in my direction. Wilfried. King Adolar is just like Wilfried.

"Your parents didn't die, dumtkof. They left because you are ugly. Ugly Klarke Ascher is all alone with her ropes and rocks."

I never harmed Wilfried. I never mocked his size or picked on him for being slow. I was nice to him. I stood up for him. I defended him against the monsters. But bullies don't need sensible reasons to choose you. They find the easiest prey and give chase. They select those who have seen their weakness and try to destroy them.

"Nide." The king shakes his head and again turns his smirk on me. "Fram Ascher is no lady. She wants to be equal to a man. Show her what that's like."

I swallow and keep my head high. King Adolar is making the same mistake Wilfried did. I am neither easy nor prey. I did not pick the fight with Wilfried. But I ended it. He learned soon enough I am no shadow mouse. So will the king.

Otto pulls back my chair and takes my hand. On trembling legs hidden deep within the folds of salmon silk, I take a shaky step. The men make crude noises, the women disparaging *tsks*. My hunger is forgotten. We move from the dining room out into the stone corridor. I have so much to say, but I don't dare speak. When we reach Otto's room, he lifts me into his arms, opens the door, and places me on the bed. I cross my legs and give him the meanest glare I can muster.

He shuts the bedroom door and turns the key. A lock thumps into place. "You're welcome."

"For what?" I scoot off the edge of the bed and nearly trip on the hem of my gown. "For humiliating me? For giving them all another reason to hate me?"

He laughs and moves to a wooden armoire by the window. "Yes. For all those things. Don't you get it? They don't want to like you. They don't want you to win them over. They want to break you. And the sooner they believe you are broken, the sooner you know your life will be spared." He pulls out two glasses and a bottle of dark liquid.

I gape and search for a retort, wanting to fight. Instead, I sink into a chair by the fireplace. The adrenaline pumping through my veins dissipates. Otto passes me an overflowing glass, and I chug it like water. It tastes of smoke and zimtammon and burns like hot peppers. Kimmeron. High-quality kimmeron. A welcome buzz filters through my system. I pass him the glass for a refill, which he obliges. "You're right. Of course."

He lifts his glass and tilts it in my direction. "You picked a dangerous sea to sail, Klarke. An ocean you are ill-prepared for, but one on which I have had seventeen years of experience. And lucky for you, I believe in your cause. Someday I will be king, and the future I see for Ectair is much different than the world we currently live in. How fortuitous that you have been placed here with me. My father thinks he has backed both of us into a corner. Little does he know we have found a secret passage."

We exchange grins and clink glasses. Half the bottle disappears. I remove the awful pink gown and lie on a sealskin rug by the hearth in my white bloomers. Prince Otto lies next to me. I am not sure how much time passes. Most of it is spent laughing. I tell him about growing up by the sea, about throwing fish guts with my friend Losan, about my mother and father, about Rayna and Kiel, about Ellias. He tells me of his mother, a kind woman, of growing up behind the palace walls with servants and so many expectations. About not wanting to rule with cruelty and fear. At one point he stands and takes my hand. We dance or stumble around his room, singing a silly song from our youth.

Dumt-diddy, dumt-diddy, dumt dumt dumt.
Rüdiger! The hero of Galvaith.
Stabbed a peasant with a sword made of clay.
Saved the king, saved the day, made it home in time to play.
Rüdiger! The hero of Galvaith!

Otto bumps into a table, knocking off a stone bust of his great-grandfather, King Hammonhoff. We bend over, laughing. Tears fill my eyes. Maybe it's the words of rebellion, or the alcohol surging through my veins. Either way, I feel happy and hopeful, two things I never thought I'd feel again. We lie down by the fire. I watch the embers crackle and flame.

"What's Adolar like? As a father?" I roll onto my side to face Otto. He remains on his back with his hands beneath his head. His skin is so smooth. The muscles on his abdomen could be carved granite. I don't want to, but my attraction grows. "Is he even capable of love? Of kindness?"

"Hmm." Otto rubs his chest. Where his heart lies. His breathing stalls. That feels like all the answer I need. "I think he loves me. And I think he is proud. But I don't think he loves himself. I think his fear and pride are too strong a force for his love to compete with. Anyway, we don't really know each other anymore. We're just two breaths living under the same roof but never in sync. I don't know any other way a father should be, though. I suppose it could be worse."

I think of my father and how I never had to wonder how he felt about me. How I always knew how safe and loved I was. I suppose Otto's father could be worse, but I know with certainty he could be better.

"I think he once loved," Otto says, some strength and enthusiasm returning to his voice. "Like the real kind of love. There is a painting of a woman he hides beneath his mattress. I've seen him holding it and staring at her when I've snuck up to his tower. For an entire mooncycle, I snuck up to his tower, and each night, I'd find him staring at her. She's not my mother."

I recall Kiel telling me about the painting he'd seen Adolar holding after he'd done stonework on the Nied Tower the night after I lost to Russet at Vether's. It's hard to imagine the frigid heart of our king being capable of that kind of enduring love.

But we all have our secrets.

"Can I ask you something else?" Emboldened by drink, I don't wait for a response. "You keep saying you are like me, a misfit. I don't see it. You are a man in a society that worships men. You are the prince of Ectair. You have everything you've ever wanted. What is it that makes you feel like an outcast?"

He pours himself another glass of kimmeron. His face darkens. Pain creases his forehead. Sadness or maybe fear drifts across his eyes. "I'm tired," he says after a few moments of agitated silence. "I wish to go to bed now. Please see yourself out."

I sit up slowly. He may as well have slapped me across the face. "I'm sorry." I touch his arm lightly. "I didn't mean to pry."

He stands and moves to the window, staring out at the misty night beyond.

"Otto?" I rise from the ground and take a step toward him.

"Don't let these moments confuse you. I am still your prince. You will obey me and leave." He doesn't look back. He stands rigid at the window. Beyond the panes of glass, the jagged summit of Kara Do towers over the smaller point of Shiendoff. Azura glows in a blue circle in the crescent of Kara Do's slope.

I want to be angry. I don't deserve this admonishment, and I loathe the word obey. But I see and feel his pain. I know what it is like to be stuck with your burdens trapped beneath the skin. Bending down, I grab the pink dress and walk to the door.

"Goodnight, Klarke."

I pause with my fingertips on the handle. "Goodnight, Otto."

I slip through the palace to my quarters, making sure every guard and warm body sees that I am in my underwear, that I had premarital unladylike relations, and that I am broken. I hope I haven't pushed too hard or been inappropriate, because I need Otto. And it is clear he needs me too.

22

I suck in the factory air as if I haven't breathed since I last left. Dirt, moss, leather, sweat… These smells are Ellias. They are Feiko. They are Petrus, Gerd, and all the other boys who died on the mountain. My heart grows heavy. My stomach turns. Sorrow presses upon me so firmly that I fear my ribs might snap. I must figure out a way to reclaim this world into something positive. I can't bear dreading it for the rest of my life.

I've arrived early. No one is around. I head to my locker and change into my climbing dress. I loop the rope around my chest to create a harness and drape my dust bag across my shoulder. I slip into my boots, tie my hair back into a loose knot, and make my way to the rock walls. The smell hits me even harder. I close my eyes and try to recall life before Ellias died.

I have a vivid memory of being in this very room after my parents passed away. Ellias had his hand on my shoulder. He still had some hair then. He looked deep into my eyes and told me I would always have a family here. That as long as he, Ellias Veber, was an Ascenditure, I would be part of his team. I swallow back the ball of emotions.

"I know it hurts, Klarke. And it will hurt every day for the rest of your life. I wish I could tell you otherwise." Ellias's hand tightens on my shoulder. We stare at the wall. Tears drip down my face. I want to rip the holds from the rock. Light my ropes on fire. Toss my boots into the sea.

"The gift of life comes with the responsibility of carrying burdens." Tears fall from his eyes too. I glance at him. Men don't cry in Ectair. They aren't supposed to show weakness. I soften, feeling slightly less alone. He loved my parents too.

"Your burdens will grow over time, but so will you. You will become stronger."

I climbed with Ellias every day. I climbed my way out of

my misery over losing my parents. I climbed to a place where I was mostly happy. I breathe in and force out the impending sorrow. If climbing could relieve my grief, then surely it can do the same again.

"Welcome home." I open my eyes and see Aedan.

"I'm sorry I missed practice." I drop my gaze and search for a reasonable excuse. Thankfully he gives me the grace of not needing to lie.

"Don't apologize." Aedan shakes his head. "You were ill, and I marked you down as such. It happens to us all."

My lips pinch together in a sad smile. He pats my shoulder and moves to the center of the room. I stand beside him as the rest of the team filters in. Gio, Burkhart, Tizian, Dieter, Russet, Veit, and Kiel. My heart flutters when I see Kiel. He smiles at me—a smile that is filled with relief and sadness. I am certain my smile contains similar elements.

"Listen up, team." Aedan steps into the center of our circle. He looks like a leader. I am glad he was here to fill in behind Ellias. "We received notice that King Adolar needs another harvest of solans and ulrind. We will head up Fitzhan later this week. Use the next few days to strengthen your muscles and get your minds right."

My vision wobbles. I sway on my feet. I imagine Ellias's body smashed against the moraine at the edge of Lake Eisenturks, Feiko hanging limply from the fel.

"I know what this means for us," Aedan continues. His voice cracks. "I know what going back there will feel like. I wish we were given more time to grieve and process, but these are our orders." He wipes a hand across his forehead. "The king wants his solans, and we will deliver them."

I rock back and forth on my heels. I think I might be sick.

"Someone help the woman," Tizian sneers. He moves to the wall and sticks his hands into his dust bag. "She might faint."

"Don't be a dick, Tiz." Dieter drapes several slings across his shoulder and finishes tying his harness. "We're all struggling with this."

Dieter has never been rude to me, but he hasn't ever used his energy to defend me. The shock snaps me out of my daze.

"We're all sad. Doesn't mean we can't handle our scheiz." Burkhart sits on the dirt floor, preparing his solo belay system. He rarely looks at me when he casts an insult. "Shouldn't be an Ascenditure if you can't handle pain. That's half the job."

"Let's not do this now," Gio says. "It's been a rough time for all of us."

"Come on." Kiel takes me by the elbow and guides me to the far side of the room. I lean against the wall. He pulls at his chest harness to make sure it is tight and attaches a sling. I take deep breaths, purging my system of debilitating thoughts.

He doesn't try to comfort me or tell me everything will be fine. He knows that would be a lie. If there's one thing I can appreciate today, it's that I know Kiel will be honest. I watch him move up the rock face using Ellias's self-belay system. Seeing him climb eases my mind. He makes it look so effortless and clean. I want to feel what he is feeling.

Stepping to the route next to his, I tie in, prepare my self-belay, tap my sling three times, and place my hands against the stone. My toes perch on the edge of tiny ledges. My fingers grip whatever fragment of rock they can find. My brain switches from hyperactive sadness to freedom and joy. Kiel has waited for me at the top. We hang high above the dirt floor.

"How's everything at the palace? How's the prince?" He keeps his expression bland, as if he is asking to be polite but doesn't want the real answer.

I haven't forgotten his words on the side of Mount Bonen. I know what feelings live in his heart. "Fine. Everything's fine. The prince is kinder than I expected. Obviously, I am not thrilled with my situation, but it could be worse."

"It could be better." He turns away as if interested in Russet's actions to his other side.

"You're right. It could." There is no reason to hurt him. No reason to be snarky. I allow myself to imagine life with Kiel but pull back from the thought when I feel myself longing for him. "I would rather be here with the team."

He refocuses his attention on me. A sad smile lightens his expression. "At least we still have climbing. That'll always be our thing."

"Absolutely." I return his smile and lean back, rappelling to the ground. I move around the old factory, challenging myself with each route, forcing myself to climb with and interact with my new team. It's not that I don't like them or don't want to be here. I've just been told my entire life that I would have to stand on the periphery and watch. I am struggling with the idea that I've been brought in, no longer forced to ogle with my face pressed against the fogged window.

A grin the size of Miter's Waste has been plastered to Veit's face all day. I watch him as he moves up each route. He is good. Not as good as I am, but decent. As I climb the route next to him, carefully placing my hands on each hold, I can't help but wonder why his life was spared on Mount Bonen. Was he too fast for the killer? Was he in on the plot? I've already made the assessment that Veit is not evil, just arrogant. I hope my arrogance is not leading me down a false path.

We pass each other in the middle of the wall. I grip a strong flake with my right hand to stay in place. He does the same.

"The palace and the team all in one day, Klarke. I underestimated you." He smirks.

I roll my eyes and force my emotions to remain even. "Look, Veit, I don't know if your egotism is a defense mechanism or if you really are just an arschole. Either way, I need a serious version of you for one minute." His sneer lingers, but he doesn't interrupt. "You were the only other person up there besides me. Surely you saw something. Maybe after being separated from the situation, you've been able to process, to remember?"

"Oh, for Miter's sake, Klarke. This again?" A dark shadow crosses his face, and he bites his lip, scraping at the stone wall with a finger. "You think I had something to do with their deaths? I didn't. I earned this spot fair and honest. You lived too. Maybe you caused that avalanche so you could win. Whispers on the streets say so."

Of course, people are blaming me. The mob is eager to have my back when they think injustice is being done. They are also the first to turn on me when they need a culprit. I am just a tool.

"I'm not accusing you of anything." Faces below turn toward us. I lower my voice and move closer to Veit. "I want your help. You and I survived. Why? Why us?"

He shrugs and backs away from me. "Give it a rest. Has it crossed your thick foze skull that maybe we just weren't in the way of the avalanche? I was already down. You saw it coming. The other poor bastards didn't. Close the door on your imagination, Klarke. You're losing your mind."

A figure silhouetted against the blinding white snow. A body rolled into the avalanche. How I wish I were creative enough to construct such a horrifying story.

"It was murder, Veit." I grab his rope and pull him toward me.

"Everything okay up there?" Aedan stands below us, peering up. The entire team has homed their attention on us.

"We're good! Just teaching Veit how to improve his technique," I shout back. My attention returns to Veit. He looks like he might throttle me. The jab was worth it. I lower my voice. "I saw someone up there."

I don't know if he is innocent or not. My heart tells me he is. And if so, I can't imagine he was supposed to live.

"I think you're in danger, Veit. I don't know from whom or what they want. Just watch your back, okay?"

He rolls his eyes and shoves my hand away. "Laren's arsch, you're worse than I thought. Burkhart's right. You don't have the grit for this job."

We make eye contact. I can't tell if he is afraid or wants to punch me. Letting go of his rope, I rappel down and land softly on the ground. A few seconds later Veit joins me. He makes sure to bump into me. I almost lose my balance but catch myself on the wall. Tizian laughs. I pretend they don't exist.

Aedan calls the rest of the team over to where we stand.

"The upcoming climb will be a big day," he begins. His dark eyes are heavy. His strong shoulders sag. "Practice is finished. Dieter and Russet, you two are needed for a bridge repair at the Thirsten Canal at first light. For the rest of us, our next practice begins an hour before starrise. Get some sleep, clear your minds, and come prepared."

We move toward our storage trunks in silence. Despite their insults, I know Burkhart and Tizian are also rattled by the upcoming climb. They both liked and respected Ellias. At least, I think they did.

I watch them change and pack their gear. It is not just the emotion of seeing the fel that scares me. I am not looking forward to going up the face of Fitzhan with a potential murderer who hasn't yet finished the job. Which one of these men should I fear the most?

In the water closet, I strip out of my clothes and button up a coal-colored dress over cotton bloomers. I lace my boots, grab my satchel, and say goodbye to Russet and Dieter. Kiel catches me as I am pushing open the door.

"Can I walk you home?"

"To the palace?" I laugh. My heart warms. I've felt so alone over the past few days, so isolated from everyone and everything. "I would love that."

Dusk is falling, casting everything in a hazy shroud. Smoke puffs from the rows of chimneys, drifting down onto the chipped shingles atop the derelict structures. A lamplighter walks the street, stretching a long pole toward each iron beacon. Kiel and I proceed in silence. His footfalls are heavy. His breathing is audible. He walks with his head down, his lips moving slightly as if conversing with himself.

"I ate stuffed duck one moon past for lunch." I am not sure why I needed to share that. His silent solo conversation makes me nervous. Why did he ask to walk me home if we aren't even going to talk? "It was smothered in the most delicious tangerine jelly. Definitely not something I'd get in the tenements."

He cocks his head toward me. A fire rages in his dark eyes. It scares me. It excites me. I both want to run and stay to see what lurks in those raging depths.

"Have you had duck?" My question comes out in an awkward whisper.

Instead of answering, Kiel grabs my wrist and pulls me into a small alleyway between two buildings. He raises my arm over my head and presses it into the hard stone. The air stops in my lungs. The blood halts in my veins. His other hand rests against my face. For a second, I think he intends to kill me. Before I can process what's happening, he has crushed his lips against mine. I kiss him back, hungry for the same things he craves. The fire I'd seen earlier in his eyes races through my body. I wrap my arms around his neck and pull him closer. Footsteps pass by on the street. Kiel's lips leave mine, and we are left panting in the dark. His frustrated exhalations tickle my ear. I feel like I might pass out.

"I'm sorry." He leans his forehead against mine. "I shouldn't have done that. I know the danger it puts you in."

"I don't care about that. I don't care about any of it." I inhale his scent. My body aches. I don't want to listen to reason. I don't care about my well-being. "Let's leave. Let's go to Kobo," I say. "We can climb there. We can start our own team. I give up on this place."

"Really?" His body trembles. I feel his lips turn into a smile against my skin. "Let's go. Let's go now."

I laugh. Deep ravines of mixed emotions carve their way through my soul. Excitement. Grief. Anticipation. Fear. I imagine taking this leap with Kiel. Fleeing to freedom, to happiness, to love. I can be anything across the sea. I can be with anyone I choose.

Then I think of Ellias, of all he sacrificed to ensure a spot for me on the Ascenditures. Is my happiness selfish? Does it negate the significance of his death?

"Not just yet." I sigh and move away from him, pacing the

alley. "I need to climb Fitzhan again. I need closure from that day. Closure for Ellias. We can leave after the climb."

He lifts me in the air, twirls me in the dark. We kiss again, something fierce and passionate that feels more dangerous than all the climbs in Ectair.

"So much for being the lighthouse." I look into his eyes, feeling guilty. Guilty and free.

He kisses my forehead and then backs away. "You did what you could. It's too dangerous now."

I nod, then leave the alley by myself, practically skipping down the street toward the Rektburg. The stores are closed. The windows dark. Azura is absent from the sky. A bright glowing ball burns inside me, keeping the shadows at bay.

Something long and narrow flies out of the darkness. It crashes against my abdomen. I collapse to my knees and grasp my midsection. The hard object returns, smacking my shoulders.

"Whore," a woman's voice screeches. The object, which I've determined to be a broom handle, strikes my arm. "You filthy slut."

I roll out of the way as she swings the broom in for another blow. Her voice has drawn the attention of the neighbors. Others enter the street. Soon I am surrounded by inquiring eyes and the ravings of this mad woman. She must have seen us, though I am not sure how.

I hear commotion on one side of the circle. Silias and another of the palace guards force their way through. When they see me on the ground, they rush forward. Silias lifts me to my feet. The other snatches the broom from the woman.

"She was with a man in the alley. I saw them together." The woman points a shaky finger at me. "She is no princess."

Silias turns toward me. All eyes turn toward me. My mind races. I cannot out Kiel. They will hang him. They will kill anyone who is inappropriate with the future princess. I could blame Ignaz. Try to convince them all the statdamen cornered me in the alley, and I somehow escaped before he disemboweled me.

A better thought crosses my mind. It scares and excites me.

I drop my gaze to the floor. I conjure every bad thing that has happened to me or the people I love. This kingdom is built upon deceit. The foundation is forged of cruelty. The walls of fear. The roof of hate. Why should I be different from those who built this vile home? Why should I behave honorably in the face of ignominy?

When I raise my head, tears glisten in the corners of my eyes. The pools become too large, and the tears run down my face. "I wasn't willingly with a man. I was attacked. Assaulted. I did not wish for his advances. He came at me in the darkness on my way home from practice."

I cover my face with my hands, pretending to sob. I am treading in dangerous water. The kind that sucks you down and holds you there until your lungs fill with icy liquid. I am going down a path I cannot come back from. A path that will end a man's life. I continue sobbing into my hands, allowing myself time to grapple with my decision.

"Who hurt you? Who did this?" Silias's voice is deep and sullen. The club hangs from his waist belt. I wonder if he will use it tonight.

I hope he does. That hope makes me dizzy, nauseated.

If I utter my lie, I will lose a piece of my soul.

Am I capable of being like them? Am I no better than Wilfried? Than King Adolar?

Nide, I am not.

"Eugen Martus," I whisper. The crowd gasps. Silias narrows his eyes. "He must pay for what he's done."

23

The royal wedding has been scheduled for the next full moon. I have no say in the matter. Someone else will determine what I wear, who will attend, what food will be served. My only obligation is to show up, smile, and express to the kingdom how delighted I am to be their princess. I think of Kiel and our fiery kiss—the promise to leave. Wild hope fills me.

My servant, Lena, sticks pins into the heavy blue fabric of my wedding gown, occasionally stabbing the small needles into my flesh. I stand on a wooden platform in one of the rooms in the bowels of the palace. The mirror before me shows a dark-haired girl draped in too many layers of silk and lace. She looks awkward and crass, certainly not the princess she is supposed to be. I glare at her, then stare down at Lena. She can't be more than a few years older than I am. Her fingers move swiftly across the fabric, and soon the gown is pinned to fit me like a perfectly knitted sock. Even I don't scowl at the girl in the mirror. I allow myself to feel beautiful.

The silk hugs my body, showing off the right curves and sucking in the wrong ones. Against my pale skin it shimmers like the sea when Cleos peeks through the clouds and kisses the water. Lena stands back and rests her chin in her hand. She squints and motions for me to turn in a circle. I oblige. She remains silent for a few minutes before her face softens, and she claps her hands together.

"Beautiful, my lady." She smiles at her handiwork and bows her head. "You will make a lovely brideprize."

I step from the platform and reach for her hand. She trembles and pulls back from my touch. I hold firmly. "Tanks ye." I give a soft laugh. "It is no small task to make me look elegant."

"You are most kind, my lady." Her small hand twitches. Her

eyes shift between our touching flesh and the open door. "Too kind."

"Lena." I release her hand. She takes a deep breath and a step back. "A few days ago, I was a nobody. I lived in Harid's Tenement. I've been an orphan for years. I am no lady nor a princess."

Her hazel eyes widen. Again she glances toward the hallway. "Nide, nide, you are mistaken." She rushes forward and closes the wooden door. The hinges creak. The wood scrapes against the smooth stone floor. "A lady doesn't have to be from money or status. Any woman can be a lady, if she has the will to be."

I tilt my head. "What do you mean?"

Lena retrieves a few wayward pins from the floor and sticks them into a worn pincushion. "When I was a little girl, I knew my fate. I would marry a man I didn't choose, work a job I didn't want, and make babies I wouldn't have the money to feed. I knew this at four years old. My mother told me. Why wouldn't she? Why teach about the possibility of dreams only to snatch them away?"

Lena leans against the wall. White knuckles press against the stone. Her gaze travels to the ceiling. I want to hug her, to offer comfort. But the words she utters are the truth. Sometimes there is no comfort in the truth other than to listen.

"When I was ten," she continues. Her voice has a sing-song quality to it. "A young orphan was selected by Ellias Veber to train to be an Ascenditure. I remember where I was when my father burst into the room to tell the family the unnatural news. A young girl was training for a man's job. Not just a man's job, but the most coveted profession in the kingdom."

A knot constricts in my chest. I blink rapidly to keep the tears in my eyes where they belong. I was eight years old at the time. Sad. Alone. Excited. Looking at the floor, I swallow a lump and try to keep from choking.

"My father was furious. The rest of us remained silent. But inside my head, my mother's words erased themselves. The day Ellias chose you, he also chose me. He chose all of us. I learned to dream that day, and even if my dreams wouldn't come true, I knew yours would. And I knew if yours did, then maybe my daughters' would too. Maybe at four years old, I could tell her not what she couldn't be, but rather what she could.

"When I use the word lady with you, it is not to give you the same courtesy as the other women of the court. It is to give you something greater. Whether you are dressed in green velvet or rags, you radiate hope. When status comes from within rather than without, when it is defined by actions rather than clothing and by oneself rather than by others, then you have become a lady. The person standing before me is the only true lady in this entire palace."

I shake my head and stride toward her. Throwing my arms around her neck, I pull her close. Her hair smells of strawberries. My tears dampen the dark strands. "You're wrong, Lena. Based on your definition, this palace is full of ladies. You are one. Every woman serving here is one."

"We look up to you," she whispers in my ear. "We know you are the one who will set us free. We are on your side."

My knees weaken. I tremble. When I'd first come to the palace, I'd felt alone and afraid. Now I had Prince Otto. I had the women to protect me.

"I won't let you down. You have my word." I release her. She wipes tears and walks to the door, dragging the heavy thing open. When she returns to my side, her demeanor shifts. She helps me out of my gown and smiles blandly.

"Have a wonderful day, Lady Ascher. Please let me know if there is anything I can help you with."

My steps feel lighter as I make my way through the palace. Hope has filled me with air. I am almost skipping as I move across the thick carpets of the main floor. Out of the corner of my eye, I see Silias approaching with a scroll of parchment. He stops when he reaches me, bows, and thrusts the parchment into my hands. "The king wishes to see you in the throne room. Now."

I open the parchment. Eugen Martus's name glares out near

the top. The light air leaves my body. My heart skids to a stop. I crash back to the ground, all hope and happiness vanishing into the pit of my lie.

Green tapestries hang against the smooth walls. A thick mint-colored carpet lined with a golden stitch runs from the wide entrance to the foot of the dais the throne sits upon. From iron chains in the ceiling, crisscrossed wooden platforms hang, covered with oil lamps flickering barely enough in the massive chamber to cast shadows. More lamps line the perimeter of the room, situated on knobby pedestals. One window on the far side made of green and yellow glass shards fused in the shape of our kingdom's crest, projects a sickly muted light across the lumbering slab of oak beneath it. The throne is made of old wood forest, each plank knotted and whirled, exposing partial ages of the trees who gave up their lives for some long-forgotten king. It weighs as much as a small ship. Emeralds and refined hunks of gold imbue the dark timber. Unlike the rest of the palace, which has been adorned with colorful murals and gold, the throne room is dark, cold, forbidding.

"Come." King Adolar sits on the throne, his crown heavy upon his head. His eyes are narrow slits. His fingers rap impatiently against wood.

Swallowing, I try to ignore the blood throbbing in my ears and the face of Eugen Martus glaring from between two palace guards. To the right of the throne, the nine members of parliament sit stone-lipped and erect, watching me as if I am a thief come to steal their grain. Despite the clammy air licking my skin, I feel hot and sweaty, as if Cleos has finally come out in full force and is baking me from the inside out. I take a step. Then another. My feet sink into the carpet. It is quicksand, threatening to freeze me in place.

I reach the base of the throne. All eyes bore into me. I lift mine to the king and try to look confident. My knocking knees give me away, as does the sweat forming at my hairline.

"Klarke Ascher," the king begins, standing and folding his hands across his waist. "We are here to address your accusation that Hannar Eugen Martus attacked you in the mercantile district one moon past."

"Is this a trial?" I ask, incredulous that our justice system consists of a room full of men who always vote as one—for one. I think of Rayna and what will happen to her if Eugen walks free after my lie. He'll kill her because of me.

The king's posture stiffens. His lips tighten. He ignores my question. "You accused a man of a crime warranting death, should he be convicted. Do you swear on gods and kingdom and all you hold dear, to tell the truth today?"

A wad of heat roils in my stomach. I feel thirsty as if I need to dunk my head in the Sevier River and never stop gulping. "Yes," I whisper, thinking only of Rayna. "I swear."

"Lying foze." The cords in Eugen's neck flare. He cracks his knuckles and stares at me like a pig that needs to be slaughtered. I don't meet his eyes. I hate him, but I also hate myself right now.

"Tell us what happened, Fram Ascher. And remember, there is a penalty for lying in this kingdom. Justice will be served in some way today." King Adolar remains stoic. I expect him to smirk, to lean over to the judges and laugh knowingly. He doesn't. He sits straight and still.

I nod and take a deep breath. As I open my mouth to speak, the king raises his hand to silence me. "One moment." He motions to Silias, who disappears through a side door, returning with a wisp of a woman. She looks thinner and frailer than the last time I saw her like a sheet of paper left out in the elements. Silias seats her on a stool next to Eugen and takes a step back.

"Good," the king says. "Proceed, Fram Ascher."

I want to vomit. Rayna won't look at me. The stool wobbles beneath her, moved by her quivering form. My intentions were—are—to save her. But her fear is palpable. She must think I have compromised her.

I keep my eyes on the hand-shaped bruise on Rayna's left

arm and clear my throat. "I was walking home from practice. Down Sandial Street. Someone grabbed me from the alley and pulled me in. I tried to fight him off, but he held me close and kissed me. I finally escaped, and that's when the woman hit me with the broom. That's all I know."

The room is quiet. The air heavy with doubtful silence. I swallow my fear and lift my chin.

"And who grabbed you?" King Adolar narrows his eyes. He peers into me with a knife's-edge gaze. He knows I am about to lie. He wants to compromise my honor. Will delight in it.

Rayna's shoulders heave. She is crying. Please let me have made the right decision. I lift a shaking finger. I stifle a sob. "Him. Eugen Martus attacked me."

"Horsescheiz!"

The guards restrain Eugen as he fights to barrel toward me. I flinch and instinctively reach for my throat.

"She is a lying whore. A filthy lying scheiz." Spittle flies from his mouth. Bloodshot eyes bulge from his head. On the stool beneath his towering form, Rayna trembles as tears spill down her cheeks. He turns his focus to her. "Tell them. Tell them I was with you that entire day, woman."

Beads of sweat gather at Rayna's hairline. I close my eyes and waffle between the words I hope she will speak. Part of me desperately needs her to corroborate my lie so she can be free of Eugen and I can be free of this debacle. Another part of me wants her to save her own skin.

"He was with me that entire day and night," a whimpering voice says. "My husband is innocent."

My exhalation is slow and deliberate. Rayna chose Eugen. She chose a monster over her friend. When I glance up, Rayna has wrapped her arms around herself. Uncontrolled tears fall from her face, splashing the smooth stones at her feet.

Rayna did the only thing she could. She chose herself. I left her unprotected when I went to Mount Bonen, and then lied to save Kiel. In that lie, unintentionally, I threw her to Hildegroth. Eugen is not the only monster in the room.

I turn to King Adolar and pinch my lips into a thin, challenging line. Now I must try to save myself.

"So, you are saying Fram Ascher is lying?" He watches Rayna sob. Delight is evident in every syllable. I am cornered, and he knows it.

"Yes." Her voice could be a breath of wind.

I close my eyes. The numbness rushes in before I can feel any profound emotion. I am not mad at Rayna. I am glad she is trying to protect herself and still has some small will to live. I find hope in her declaration of truth. I am glad she didn't compromise her soul for the rapidly deteriorating soul of her best friend. I am not worth the lie.

"Tanks ye for your honesty, Fram Martus. It pains me that you have been forced to endure such trauma. Hannar Martus, you are free to go. I apologize for your character being called into question. I will see that appropriate punishment is served to the wrongdoer." King Adolar extends his hand toward the entryway and smiles as Eugen grips Rayna's wrist and storms from the throne room.

Eugen pauses mid-stride and turns to me. His eyes try to spring from his face. His neck muscles might tear the collar of his shirt. "You will not speak to my wife again." Spit flies from his lips.

I focus all energy on not letting them see me cry. It is too late to disguise my trembling.

"The rest of you may leave, including the guards." King Adolar's voice is calm, yet the ice in his tone makes my legs quake harder.

I turn to lose myself in the retreating queue of sentries.

"Not you, Fram Ascher."

A sour taste graces my tongue. I face the king. When the wooden doors close somewhere behind me, drops of sweat drip down my spine. Whatever semblance of a smile King Adolar wore when others were around, he sheds. I realize I am rocking on my heels and try to stand still and firm. Before he can dictate the conversation, I take charge.

"Why do you loathe me so much?" Even though my compulsion is to flee, I maintain eye contact and push my shoulders back.

He studies me, like one who might analyze a piece of art they dislike but can't quite figure out what about it offends them. His nostrils flare. I think once he might have been handsome, but years of treachery have so badly tainted his soul that the ugliness has seeped through to his exterior.

"You are a liar. And I do not take kindly to the dishonest. You lied today about Hannar Martus. You lie every day about who you are. You lie to the kingdom when you offer false hope. You lie in your dreams when you see possibilities you shouldn't. You dishonor the gods when you disobey the order they've set for the universe. You dishonor the women of the kingdom when you pretend what they do is beneath them. You dishonor the men by putting false ideas in their women's minds. Your very being is as disruptive to the kingdom as Hildegroth himself and as treasonous as King Gyalzen and his vile kingdom to the north. You are a disease, a plague, a monstrosity." Spit accompanies each word. His face grows as red as an apple and as taut as a tanning piece of hide. "And you must be treated as such."

Adrenaline courses through my body, nearly knocking me off my feet. Rage boils inside, mixing with my perspiration as it beads out of my skin. "Then why am I here?" I scream. My words echo around the dark chamber. "Why am I still alive? You have no problem killing innocent people. If you can take the life of a young man who has done nothing wrong, then surely you take no issue removing someone as ruinous as me?"

He squeezes the arms of the throne. White knuckles contrast against the dark wood. "I don't know what you are talking about. You are alive because I am a benevolent king."

"Nide, you are not." Emboldened by the faces of the dead fluttering through my mind, I continue. "You killed Ellias and Feiko. You killed those six men on Mount Bonen. You killed the women who protested for my right to climb. Maybe you killed my father. You are a murderer with no soul and no heart. You do as you please, unapologetic for the suffering you cause others. The only thing you care about is power and yourself."

I am certain I will die for this tirade. I no longer care. I storm forward until I am only a foot in front of him. "You have taken everything from me—my family, my life, my passion. I know I am only alive because you are biding your time. But know this. If and when you come for me, I will slip through your trap like sand fleas through a net. You have taken everything from me, and if it's the last thing I do, I will take everything you hold dear and crush it beneath my feet."

He hits me so hard across the face I stumble to my knees.

"You are just like your mother." He laughs. It is empty and devoid of humor. Maybe even sad. "She beat you to your revenge. She already took everything from me."

"What?" I clutch my cheek and breathe. The skin has split. He hit me with his ring. I feel the blood, but I will not cry. I will not show weakness. My mind races. My mother again. Her life woven through everyone and everything. What is he talking about?

"I have not taken all from you yet." He pauses next to my hunched form and drops something. Then he strides down the carpet, leaving me in a crumbled pile at the base of his throne. "But I will. I will take everything. Just as it was taken from me."

The wooden doors scrape against stone. Gasping, trembling, I sit up and take my hand from my face. My cheek is tender and wet from the tears I am unable to hold back. It is red with blood. I look over at what he dropped. A coin. A silver coin with the head of a hozierleon emblazoned on the front. The coin I gave to Rayna. With a sob, I grab the coin and wrap myself in my arms, burying my face in my knees.

I hear footsteps near the throne. Lifting my face, I am surprised to find Silias watching me.

"Come," he says, offering a hand. His expression is not harsh. It might even be sympathetic. "You will need to get that stitched."

I stand, ignoring his hand, and follow him from the throne room. He walks me to a chamber off the Pentengen I've never been to. It is some sort of hospital. Jars and vases sit atop stone shelves. A simple woolen blanket lies atop a stone platform in the center of the room. A drain sits in the floor, still wet from whatever was washed down it last. A plethora of windows let in natural light. The rest is made up of hundreds of candles atop a board hanging from the ceiling.

"May I help you?" A bent and gnarled man steps through an open stone doorway in the back. He wears black robes, like the päters, but no mask. He is bald, with hair forming a horseshoe around his scalp. He smiles, and the warmth feels real.

"Geitsê, Dr. Helmut." Silias places his hands between my shoulder blades and gently pushes me forward. "She fell in the garden and will need stitches."

I open my mouth to correct him but shut it when I see his expression.

Dr. Helmut gently touches my cheek. He makes a few murmuring noises. "You must have fallen quite hard to tear the skin like this. And onto a sharp rock. Poor dear." He eyes Silias over the top of his glasses and then goes to the back of the room.

Silias clears his throat and shakes his head. I receive the message even though I don't like it.

Dr. Helmut returns with a needle, thread, and something in a little blue glass vial.

"This will hurt a bit, but these stitches will keep you from scarring too badly. Now keep still." He rubs the contents of the vial onto my wound. I gasp and shrink back at the sting but then hold steady.

"I don't mind scars." I try to watch the needle from the corner of my eye. It stings as it cuts into my flesh. The pain is worse when he pulls it back through.

Dr. Helmut chuckles and finishes his work. "Of course you don't. You are a tough young woman." He pats my shoulder and hands me the vial. "Clean the wound twice a day with this, and come see me if infection sets in. Oleg to you both."

"Tanks ye," I say. "And oleg."

I like Dr. Helmut. I can tell he is a kind man.

Silias and I make for my chambers. I keep my head down, not wanting the passing adels to see me upset. Or to see my wound. Silias walks by my side. I didn't think he liked me, but right now, his presence feels, if not friendly, at least not hostile. He didn't have to take me to the doctor. He could have let my face heal naturally.

"Oft, the son pays for the crimes of the father," he says.

I look at him. His helmet comes to his eyebrows which are dark and thick. His lips are thin and naturally turned down. Maybe that is why I find him surly.

"And in rare cases," he continues, "the daughter for the misdeeds of her mother."

"I don't understand," I say. "What could my mother possibly have done to him that warrants this?" I point to the stitches.

He nods at a passing guard, waiting to continue until the sentry is out of earshot. "If it brings you peace, I do not think the king wants you dead."

"Oh, did he share that with you over tea?" I roll my eyes and then feel bad for being snarky. I think Silias is trying to be nice. Whatever nice means in his case.

He laughs. His chuckle sounds like rock sliding down a mountain slope. We reach the door to my room.

"Lie low," he says. "Keep your head down. Take your licks. Eventually he will be satisfied and will move on."

"Satisfied with what?"

Silias gives me the same nod he gave the passing guard and turns away without another word.

"Wait!"

He ignores my call and marches away. I open the door and rush to my bed. Tugging down the covers, I plunge my hand beneath the pillow and remove my mother's handkerchief. My mother is the thread binding everything together. The needlework of an image I can't quite see. If I can unlock my mother's past, maybe I can save myself.

"Omen aum noche rialshan. Hûder amalaze onen hiab. Im lô la gurage omi alam warsen. Fonal Ramanata." The words may as well be written in invisible ink. They mean nothing to me. I close my eyes.

"But what does it mean, Mama?" Tiny fingers trace the strange letters and words. I look up at my mother, confused why she would have ruined my hankie with this rubbish. I liked it better when it was just my father's ship with its orange sails.

She kisses her fingers and then places them on my forehead. I giggle. She smiles down.

"You will understand when the time comes. Think of it as a mystery. A coded message."

"How will I decipher the message?"

She taps my nose with her finger. Her eyes are so kind. Loving. Gentle. "Simple, my sûssa," she says, a glimmer in her eye. "You must find the queen."

24

Silias's footsteps echo behind me all the way from the palace up the cobbled streets toward the training hall. He doesn't speak, having resumed his demeanor of detached stoicism. A few blocks from the gym a woman steps through the doorway of her bakery, wiping her hands on the apron tied around her waist. Patches of flour cling to her face and arms. She shakes her head and scowls. I glance away, but my ears pick up the faint "liar" she whispers beneath her breath.

I pause at the door to the refurbished factory and peer over my shoulder, nodding to Silias. Since the incident with Kiel, I have been barely able to relieve my bowels without a sentinel's prying eyes upon me. I step across the wooden threshold. He follows. I move to my trunk and remove my gear before slipping into a cupboard to change. When I emerge, Silias trails me.

"What are you expecting me to do, run away?" I huff and finish tying my harness. Every ounce of freedom they take feels like an added bar to an already suffocating cage.

"Pretend I am not here."

Eyeing his helmet, his club, heavy boots, and stern gaze, I laugh. He doesn't smile, but he must see the humor in his statement. "Does the rabbit pretend the fox does not follow?"

"I am not the fox."

"What are you then?"

"None of your metaphors." He raises an eyebrow and maybe the corner of his lip. Is it a smile? I will pretend it is a smile.

I walk into the main room. Shivers attack my body. Breath fogs around my face. Spread across the floor, huge ice blocks are stacked into frozen pyramids. My teammates huddle in the center of the room. I find the back of Kiel's head. Our kiss had been so full of promise that for a moment I'd felt free. Now the king's eyes are attached to my every move. I could no more

escape with Kiel on a ship than I could free Rayna from Eugen
Martus. My life is a series of dreams and good intentions that
die. Someday, when they speak of me, it will be with downcast
eyes. My name will be synonymous with failure.

"Klarke, great to have you here today." Aedan beams. A wool
cap is pulled low over his forehead, and he rubs gloved hands
together. The rest of the team focuses their attention on my
approaching form. A few gaze at Silias standing in the doorway.

Kiel's face darkens. He must have heard the rumors. What
does he think of me? I am a liar. I told a lie that could have
ended a man's life. I did it to save him. Surely he knows that. As
I stare back at him, trying to help him understand, I realize his
gaze is not on me but rather behind me. His glower is meant
for Silias.

"He is not the fox," I want to say. I should not be so quick to
trust the words of a guard. Maybe Kiel's glare is justified.

I sigh and join the huddle, standing beside the man who'd
promised a new life. His pointer finger grazes mine. I move my
hand across his so he knows…something. That I still care. That
my lie was to protect him.

"It's payday, climbers." Aedan bends down and reaches into
a tanned leather sack. He pulls out individual bags tied together
with twine bands. Coins rattle as I catch the little bag he tosses
to me. Mine is the smallest, smaller than Veit's, even though
we started at the same time. I don't have the energy to cause
a scene. Peering into it, I see a handful of golden dracals. I've
never in my life held so much money. I decide to give it all to
Gerd's mother.

"We leave for Fitzhan in a few days. This will probably be
our last climb of the season. Vintazite approaches. We will soon
have snow." Aedan's voice draws me back. "It is imperative we
prepare for this mission as authentically as possible. If you hav-
en't yet noticed, I've had ice hauled in to make the temperature
more like it will be on our climb. Get used to the cold and discomfort. Choose your routes carefully. Stretch. Get your minds
right." He claps his hands together, and we disperse.

I stuff my gold into a pocket and follow Kiel to the far side of the gym. Silias lumbers behind me. I scramble up the route to the top, locking my rope to hang in the air and be free from his presence. Kiel reaches the top and locks himself next to me.

"I heard that someone saw us, but what happened to your face?" His shoulders hunch. He lightly punches the rock wall. "I am so sorry I put you in that position, Klarke. I had no right."

"Stop." I want so badly to reach out and touch him. "You gave me a taste of the one thing I've longed for my entire life— freedom. What we did was by choice. My choice too. What an amazing gift you gave me, letting me decide for myself what I wanted." I shake my head and peer down. Silias's head is tilted skyward. He looks confused as to what he should do. My gaze drifts back to Kiel's tortured eyes. "I'm sorry I lied. I did it to protect you."

His hands tremble against the rope. "I would have done the same. I would sell my soul to Laren if it meant saving your life."

I want to kiss him. I want more than that. I bite my lip to keep from crying or screaming. "I can't leave with you, Kiel. Not yet. Not until things cool down. They watch me night and day. If we try to leave, we will be caught, and they will kill you. King Adolar would probably make me watch." I tell him about the confrontation in the throne room but leave out the part about Adolar hitting me. I tell him I fell in the garden. He cannot change what happened, only get himself into trouble.

He flinches, turns red. Veins tick in his neck and arms. He leans his forehead against the rock and lightly bangs his head. "We can't live like this."

I think of Lena's words. That maybe I am the one who will set her free. That maybe because of me, her daughter will be able to dream for more. That I give her hope—that I give all the women hope.

"We can live like this." I shake my head up and down, trying to encourage him. "We can and we must. I am tough, Kiel. I've trained my entire life for this. I thought I was training to climb mountains, but I was really training to beat the king. The laws of this kingdom—the vile man who leads it—that is the greatest mountain I will ever face. If I truly wish to call myself Ascenditure, I must summit the peak that scares me most. I need you with me. And if that means biding our time and acting like everything is normal, then we must do that. Trust me. What Adolar wants most is to see me suffer. I must show him the opposite. I must flourish beneath his gaze. Rise beneath the crushing weight of his laws."

Kiel pulls his head away from the rock and turns eyes so full of passion and fire on me that I almost break a sweat in the frigid room. "You sound like a lighthouse. Ellias would be proud."

Grief threatens to loosen my grip on the rock. It hurts hearing his name, hurts that he is not here to tell me those things himself. "I miss him so much, Kiel."

"I know. I do too. It isn't right or fair." Ignoring the guard below, he touches my cheek, the uninjured one. "He believed in your journey before you even knew what that would be. I am a poor substitute, but I believe in you too, and I want to help."

I smile, feeling something earnest and new rising in my chest. Shaking my head, I rappel to the ground. I untie my sling, high-five a bewildered Silias, and move around the pitches, pausing to stretch my arms and legs and make sure I live up to Aedan's challenge of readiness.

At the hangboard I grip a tiny pair of holds for eight seconds before resting and repeating to strengthen my fingers and hands. When I first started climbing, I'd have to wait a week between sessions to let my tendons and muscles recover. Now I hit the board three times a week. I still feel the burn, but the torturous exercise distracts me from the king.

I move to the middle of the floor to stretch. I don't want to completely wear myself out, and I want to take some time to watch the other climbers. The day after tomorrow I will be on the fel with these men. I watch Burkhart and Tizian laugh and joke across the room. They both despise me, but would they harm me on the climb? They didn't hate Ellias, and yet...

I watch Dieter and Gio lifting stones. They look serious and focused. Russet and Veit climb contiguous routes.

Toward the end of practice, a jolt of thunder rumbles so loudly that the accompanying lighting strike probably hit somewhere within Kietsch. More thunder booms. Raindrops pelt the roof with a soothing staccato. Our typical drizzly day has morphed into a raging deluge.

"This is it." Aedan ushers us into a huddle and looks at each of us with his dark eyes. "Tomorrow, we will take it easy. Resting. Stretching. Meditating. Praying if that is your thing. The day after, we head out, and it is my mission that we all survive to climb another day beyond our task."

This is his first climb as leader. He wants to get it right, wants to be as good a leader as Ellias Veber. I can't imagine stepping into shoes that big and not tripping with each stride.

"Aedan." I smile and pat his shoulder. "You will be great. And we won't let you down."

A smattering of *here, heres* and cheers rise in the room. Even Burkhart and Tizian join. The mood shifts from one of impending doom to one of hope and joy. Which is how we should feel. Climbing is our lifeblood—water to parched lips and food to rumbling stomachs. It is oxygen to desperate lungs and fire to chilled hands. I cannot forget that. I cannot let that be taken from me. I smile as I look at the faces around me—eager, determined, happy.

My soul rises, and the nubs of my severed wings grow just a little.

Because of the storm, the palace sends a carriage to retrieve Silias and me from practice. I glance through the open door to the city streets thrashed with rain. Two white horses stand in front of the carriage. Water drips from their manes. Their hooves clomp and splash in the forming puddles. The coachman also sits in the elements. He stares straight ahead, ignoring the rivulets dripping from his cap.

"I am going to change." I look at Silias and then back at the patient coachman. I hope he does not catch a cold from this. "There's no need to join me. I will meet you here when I am finished."

I reach the upstairs bathroom with the loose window we sneak in and out of. I don't bother changing. All I can focus on is breaking this cage they've forced me into. The wind screams and fights as I open the window. I drop over the edge onto the slippery rocks. It's not my most graceful descent, but I am off as soon as my feet hit the ground.

I slink behind a row of hedges that block me from view of the entryway. The streets are empty except for the gullies of water streaming across the stones and the garbage and leaves blown around by the whirling wind. Weather vanes spin like angry whirlpools, the metal birds squeaking and cracking as they move. Water soaks through my dress and into my soles. Lightning and thunder battle in the sky above. I slip on a mossy stone and crash to the ground, feeling a bruise form on my hip. The pain makes me feel alive. Without a glance over my shoulder, I continue through Kietsch until I can barely breathe, and my side is cramping. Just when I feel like I can't go any farther, I burst from the man-made structures of the city onto a rainswept dune and beyond to the beach a few miles south of the pier. I run straight to the water, plunging my body into the salty, white-capped spray.

I hold my breath and force my head under, letting the waves break across my back. Releasing the air from my lungs, I sink to the sandy bottom and dig my fingers into the loose kernels and jagged shell fragments. Somewhere above I hear loud rumblings, but I couldn't say if they came from the sky or the sea. Behind my closed lids, beneath a layer of ocean, there is no difference between the two.

When I run out of breath, I resurface and gasp in a deep lungful of rainy air. Out across the choppy water, ships jostle and sway with the crashing waves and unrelenting wind. Amid the large vessels, I glimpse a small fishing boat being juggled through the waves like a jester's ball. The small boat crests a breaker, then disappears. I hold my breath until I see it again. The fisherman must be terrified. He must know death is closing in.

I don't want to know his fate. I am in the middle of my own life-and-death battle, and the one thing keeping me going is not knowing how the story ends.

Closing my eyes, I let the sea wallop me. The surge crashes over me. The salt burns my eyes and lungs. The lightning causes my heart to skip beats. Freedom. I am free if just for a moment. Pain and fear let me know I am still alive. And if stolen flashes away from my chains are all I get, I will revel in every rain-filled breath and every grain of sea salt that clings to my hair. I am a fisherman in a small boat. The world may be trying to sink me, but it hasn't yet succeeded.

I open my eyes as someone grabs my collar and yanks me from the water.

"Do not mistake my intentions for friendship. I am no fox, but I can become one." Silias lifts me to my feet. His voice is angry, sharp. "If it is ash and wave you seek, I am sure that can be arranged in a way that does not continually inconvenience me."

My gaze drifts back toward the sea. Just as Silias jerks me around to march toward the waiting carriage, I catch a glimpse of the still-floating fishing boat and smile. The storm has not yet won.

25

Practice was canceled today due to an explosion at the glue factory next to the gym. I spend my free time in a corner of Walburga's Library in the Geistich, perusing old books on the history of Ectair. I have internally declared war with the king and therefore wish to learn as much about my enemy as possible.

Silias sits in a wooden chair a few feet away, cleaning his saber for the umpteenth time and occasionally chancing bored glances in my direction. When he does this, I peer up from the pages and deliver an innocent smile. He will have a much easier day with me today than he did one moon past.

The library is larger than the abandoned factory and contains more books than all the schoolhouses and libraries in the entire kingdom. A forty-foot ceiling arches above me, and from top to bottom, every book written in our corner of the world forms a colorful pattern of leather and cloth. It smells of animal hide and old paper. I find the smells of dusty pages and earthen leather almost as soothing as the scents at the training facility.

The tome I am reading now is about the destruction caused by the monster Hildegroth, leading to the damming of the canal and the sealing of the Bridge of Worlds connecting Ectair and Ainar. We learned much of this in school. However, this particular volume, written by a man named Dr. Alois Vitus, goes into greater detail about the incident and the resulting political fallout.

Hildegroth, Laren's monster from the sea who, up until thirty years ago, was thought only to be a legend, emerged in the Bay of Unity, then began making his way down what was then the Unity Canal, wreaking havoc on small villages along the way. With thirteen long tentacles, teeth like a shark, and a mouth like a vortex, he tore through wood and stone as a knife slices through a rack of lamb. Thousands died. Millions of golden dracals were spent to mitigate the carnage.

In the wake of the destruction, King Gyalzen to the north sought an allied approach to rebuild, wanting to work with Ectair to protect both kingdoms from future attacks. King Adolar agreed to the plan, and teams were sent to dam the Unity Canal.

I lift my eyes from the page and think of my father. He was still an Ascenditure when this occurred. Immediately following construction, he left. A pitter-patter begins on the rooftop above as the skies discharge their daily rain. I sink lower into my chair and continue reading.

Shortly after construction was completed, Ectarian soldats uncovered a conspiracy that stated King Gyalzen was a direct descendant of the ancient and brutal King Miter, once the leader of a kingdom so large it encompassed all of Galvaith, the land that now makes up both Ainar and Ectair. King Miter built the canal hundreds of years ago to have easier access to future conquests across the seas.

Another theory states King Miter had the canal dug so that Hildegroth had better access to the villages and people in his empire. After trading his daughter for Laren's monster, Miter ruled through terror and violence. He could speak with the sea beast and force it to do his bidding. By bisecting his empire with bodies of water—the Frozen Sea of Ard and the Sea of Toole—stretching north and south into each kingdom, the monster could access and attack anywhere by command.

When news of this legend and Gyalzen's alleged family history spread to King Adolar, our king immediately shut down travel and trade across the Bridge of Worlds and condemned Ainar as evil and treacherous. King Gyalzen tried to reason that his kingdom had also been destroyed, but when Adolar realized how happy his citizens were to have a flesh-and-blood enemy, he latched on to the story and turned legend into truth. Myth into fact.

The Unity Canal, reclaimed from Miter's brutal legacy by

later generations as a symbol of trade and camaraderie between neighboring kingdoms, became Miter's Waste—a no-man's land of rubble and tragedy.

My hands tremble as I lay the book on my lap and try to process what I am reading. King Adolar must not know the full content of this work, or he would have had it destroyed. The historian was calling him a liar, an opportunist. I think of Obid's words that no man can control Hildegroth. Maybe a woman, he'd said. But not a man.

"Might be that a woman's what set off the great beast in the firs' place. That's why yer mum worked so hard to get her out of there."

If that was the case, King Gyalzen couldn't have led the monster to destroy Ectair. I don't know what to believe anymore.

Hildegroth. Lecals. Black Diemants. Darken Mages.

The Darken Mages were destroyed long ago. They are nothing but legends. But that is what we thought of Hildegroth before he returned.

Lady Genalt. Who is she?

I don't trust my king, but I don't know that I trust Obid either.

"Find the queen."

I am not sure I trust my own mother.

I flip the page and shake my head. The author goes on about how trade was affected by the Waste. How the villages along the channel were never rebuilt. The people who lived there were forced to find new homes, new jobs, new communities. Families who lived in both kingdoms were separated. Mothers in Ectair never again saw their sons in Ainar. Glancing up, I see Silias conversing with one of the päters who caretake the library.

"Find the queen," my mother's voice whispers again in my mind. *Darken Mages. Lady Genalt. Ya mum. Control the beast. Might be that a woman can. Find the queen.*

"She is dead," I hiss at the book. "You left me a fragile clue, Mother."

Silias and the päter turn to look at me.

Quidle dee und tra la la, Käthe on the mountain.
Odel le und tra la la, the volf is on the mountain.
I smile and pretend to be singing a song.
Echo, echo, echosong. Warn those on the mountain.
Take your sheep und tra la la, please get off the mountain.

It is a song for children. It is an absurd thing for me to be singing in a library, but it is the first tune that popped into my head. The päter lifts a finger to his lips. Silias scoffs. They return to their discussion. I return to my thoughts.

The queen is dead. Whatever message my mother intended to give me died not long after her. Whatever she, Obid, the queen, the Lady Genalt—and why not, the Darken Mages—were up to, died with the lot of them. I could no more speak with Queen Eleonora than I could with my father.

My gaze drifts out the window and rests on Miter's Tower, the point of the Pentengen. A locking mechanism clicks open in my brain. I tilt my head and analyze the stones that make up the wall. Holds, all of them. A few crimpers, maybe. But an easy route for a professional. The Ascenditures scale these towers to make repairs. There might already be protection in place and a discernible route. A hammer, some pitons, and a set of slings would be all I needed to reach the window. Or I could free solo.

But I am not interested in Miter's Tower. Somewhere above me, hidden from view, another turret stands. The one I want. The Geistich comprises four corners that form a diamond shape around the Nied. Laren's to the west. Orna's to the south. Otto's to the west. And the late Queen Eleonora's due north.

I don't bother checking if the door to the queen's tower is locked. It will be, and I don't want to alert Silias to my quest. We leave the library and head back to my room. The palace is quiet. We don't pass any adels. The prince and the king are absent. The guards we do see are silent as always.

"I need to go to the training center," I tell Silias outside the door to my room.

"What for?"

"I would like to fetch some of my gear. Since practice was canceled today, I fear losing ground in training if I don't do something. I'd like to gather some tools to prepare in my room."

I am proud of my lie. It sounds reasonable. I wasn't sure what my excuse would be, and then this slipped out. I am getting better at lying. Maybe my pride is misplaced.

"Very well."

He summons a carriage. We ride in silence to the training center. Smoke fills the streets. It pours from the glue factory. The explosion took out the west corner of the building, the opposite side from the climbing center. Chunks of stone and pipe lie scattered across the street. Feurmenn and gawkers crowd the structure. Eight bodies lie on the cobbles. Covered in soot. Some missing appendages. Others barely recognizable. I look away.

The gym is smoky but quiet. I close my eyes and thank Orna for letting it survive the blast. She probably had nothing to do with it, but I thank her anyway. I stuff a rucksack with my gear. Silias and I return to the palace, and he walks me to my room.

"Do you share my daily activities with the king?" I pause at the door and face Silias.

"I am required to give a report, yes." His heavy eyes watch me.

I have so much I want to say, so much I'd like to know. I want him to be my ally, but I cannot trust that. "Do you let him know how often I use the restroom?"

"Of course."

My jaw drops. He smiles and then laughs. A big booming laugh that bounces down the gilded hallway. I actually enjoy his rare laughs.

I open the door and step into my room. Turning my head, I offer a warm smile. "Well, good evening then."

Silias gives a slight bow. "Good evening, Fram Ascher."

∽

I open my window and stare down at the rain-slicked stones. My room is along the northern wall of the Pentengen. I will rappel from my window into the inner courtyard and free-climb the queen's tower. It should be straightforward. Rappel. Ascend. Find answers. Answers to questions I don't even know how to ask.

The evening is dark. Azura hides behind the clouds. Dinner will be brought to my room in about three hours. I fashion a harness, hang slings across my body, tie the dust bag around my waist, clip a few karabiners to the slings, and drape another satchel that holds a hammer and pitons across my shoulder. I hang a second rope across the other shoulder. I wear dark hosen and a silk tunic instead of a skirt. My mother's handkerchief is stowed in my pocket.

I hammer a pair of bolts into the wall beneath the window and pray no one hears. When Silias doesn't burst through the door, I secure the first rope through the anchors. Gliding the rope through my harness and securing it with a karabiner, I tap the sling three times and climb onto the windowsill. Street noises from Kietsch reach my ears—dogs barking, drunken men guffawing, wooden wheels scraping against cobbles—but inside the castle walls, it is still.

I lean back and lower myself. I am five floors above the ground and therefore must pass four windows. Behind the first window, a mother in a silk nightgown sits in front of the fire brushing her daughter's long hair. I hold the rope and watch, remembering how it felt when my mother pulled a tolvalus-tooth comb through my dark locks. I can almost imagine the tugging on my scalp when she reached a knot. I always wanted to cry out, but I didn't. More than anything, I wanted her to know how strong I was. How courageous.

The second window showcases a couple in the throes of passion. I think of Kiel and wonder what it would be like to share myself so intimately with someone. Blushing, I loosen the rope and pass quickly. I don't look into the bottom two.

My feet touch damp grass. I leave the rope in place. It hangs limply from the window five stories up. Phase one is complete. I look left and right and then dart across the courtyard, hiding as I go behind shrubs trimmed in the shapes of large eggs. I reach the base of the queen's tower and press myself against the stone. My heart races. I look at the windows of the Pentengen. Lights illuminate the rooms. Many of the drapes are open. Forms move about. Unless they look closely, they shouldn't see me.

I don't have a death wish, but without a belayer, I have decided it will be easier to free climb. I leave my slings and all but two anchor bolts, the hammer, a few karabiners, my chalk bag, and the second rope on the ground beneath the tower. I will need the items I retain for the rappel. Tilting my head back as far as it will go, I peer up at the window high above. A large drop of rain splatters against my forehead.

"Head up, darling," I whisper to myself. Closing my eyes, I tap the sling three times and press my fingers against the tower. "Head up."

I plunge my hands into the dust bag and rub them together. I find two jugs—good holds—and can almost grip them with my entire hand. The stones are uneven. Some lie smooth, but others jut out, offering solid places to plant my feet. I move up the side of the tower, occasionally dusting my hands to keep them dry. I don't look down. I am confident I won't fall, but I have never actually free-climbed outside the gym.

I pass the first piton about fifteen feet up. Repairs have been done on this tower. It has been climbed before. Another anchor protrudes around thirty feet. I keep climbing. The rain falls. The sounds of Kietsch prattle on. I find the chants of drunken sailors soothing, the cries of gulls a rhythmic cheering on my progress.

I reach the window to the queen's tower and find a double set of anchors already in place. I remove two slings and karabiners and use them to secure my harness to the bolts. With a deep breath, I lean back and rest. A small hole forms in the clouds above. The light of a solitary star twinkles through. I create a list of what I need to find in this tower. The meaning of my mother's words on the handkerchief. My mother's connection to the queen. My mother's link to the king. The identity of Lady Genalt.

I scramble onto the window ledge and push on the glass. It is locked. I glance at the Pentengen, scanning the windows for prying eyes. I see figures in their chambers and guards in the hallway, but none are interested in the outside world. With a deep breath I pull the hammer from my satchel and smack it against the pane. Large chunks of glass crash against the floor of the tower. They shatter into smaller pieces and skitter across the floor. I unclip the karabiners, pull myself up, and slink into the room before anyone can see what happened. Small cuts sear my skin. Droplets of blood bead across my hands. I pick bits of glass from my palm while my heart rate slows.

The round room is dark. I crouch on the floor while my eyes adjust. No lights will accompany my mission. I must find answers in the shadows. I stand and walk around the room. The door to the stairway and lower chambers is shut. Bookcases stand floor to ceiling, covering half of the wall space. A four-poster canopied bed, a fireplace, a sitting area, an eating table, a large wardrobe, a desk, and several large paintings occupy the rest of the space. I approach the desk first and slide back the rolltop cover. A brittle feather pen protrudes from a bottle of dried and cracked ink. A stack of yellowed papers sits neatly in one corner. A lone match is propped against a candle. A partially stitched handkerchief lies flat and dusty in the center. It depicts the beginning of what looks like Hadrian's Monastery with its crooked spire.

I rifle through the stack of papers. There are letters from women in the kingdom asking the queen what they should name their children, how they can be better wives to their husbands, what they can do to earn the blessings of the monarch. I find an order for silk napkins. A speech the queen gave at Fielshide, the annual celebration where ranchers bring their cows down from the hills for the winter. Flowers are woven into garlands and laced through the kuhkas' horns. Large bells hang from their necks. Little girls don their finest dürmels, small boys their nicest hosen. Parades are held in the ranching villages. We don't have kuhkas in Kietsch, but it is still customary for the queen to stand on the steps of the Rektburg each fall and welcome the cows back into the valleys. Since her passing, the speech has gone unsaid. I have no idea what the cows are up to. Not that it matters.

The desk doesn't contain anything useful. I didn't expect it to. I imagine anything that would shed light on my queries would have been removed unless it was well hidden. I move next to the bookshelf. I pull down each book and flip through the pages. There are ledgers containing the birth records for the residents of Kietsch. I wonder if my birth is recorded here. Most likely. I open them all in case something is hidden within the pages, but don't bother scrolling the lists. A book on the bottom shelf of the second bookcase grabs my attention. It is a book on ancient Galvaithian runes. A book that has translated the words of the ancient language into our modern tongue.

I remove my mother's handkerchief. "Omen aum noche rialshan. Hûder amalaze onen hiab. Im lô la gurage omi alam warsen. Fonal Ramanata." I trace the words and grab the candle from the desk. I push the book and the candle beneath the bed and then wiggle under, letting the bed skirt fall back into place to conceal me. I light the candle with the single match and inhale sharply.

"Omen." I open the book and flip through, hoping to find the proper translation. I find it.

Death.

"...aum noche rialshan." Back and forth, I move the pages. Tracing my finger across unfamiliar runes and familiar words.

...is no accident. Death is no accident.

The hair prickles on my neck. Goosebumps rise on my skin. I imagine someone rolling a body into the avalanche on Mount Bonen. I imagine the perfectly severed rope that dropped Ellias to the moraine. Death is no accident. I wriggle my shoulders and keep going.

"Hûder amalaze onen hiab. Im lô la gurage omi alam warsen."

Wax drips from the candle to the floorboards beneath the bed. My eyes dart back and forth across the contents of the old tome.

Someone always has a hand. Be it the gods' own might or the traitorous will of men.

I can't see the deeper meaning in this. Is my mother predicting her death? The queen's death? One died soon after the other from the same affliction—Death's Whisper. But Death's Whisper has no cause. Neither woman bore traces of poison or physical harm. The gods? Did my mother believe she'd angered the gods? Is that what Death's Whisper is? A curse from Orna or Laren?

"Fonal Ramanata."

Find...

I cannot find the word Ramanata anywhere. I spend twenty minutes scanning the pages. Nothing. Find what, Mother? Find who? She said I would understand the words when the time came. Now, even knowing what they mean, I do not understand. "Find Ramanata," I whisper.

I scoot from under the bed and return the book to the shelf. Slipping the candle behind a chair to block some of the glow, I continue searching through the books. Shipping ledgers. Histories on industry in Ectair. An illustrated guide to the plants and animals of Kobo. I was hoping for a journal. Something that laid out exactly what I needed to know. It's not here. Why would it be?

Near the bottom of the final bookcase, I remove an unmarked leather book. It falls open to the middle. Something protrudes from the crack. I pull it out and flip it over. My heartbeat stalls, and my stomach lurches. I rush to the candle and crouch behind the chair, holding the small painting to the light. Two women sit together on a chaise, smiling. One is the queen. The other is my mother.

"Who were you?" I shake the painting and hiss at the smiling face of my mother. I am angry. I am confused. I don't feel any more enlightened than when I entered this tower.

Taking the painting, I return to the book it fell from. Before
I close the cover and return it to the shelf, two words catch my
eye. My hand stills.

Death's Whisper.

My heart skips like a flat stone on the smooth surface of a
river. My gaze flies across the paper. Every handwritten word
elevates the hair on my neck and the pulse in my veins. This is
not an official tome. It is someone's journal or book of notes.

According to the author, the same Dr. Alois Vitus who
wrote the book about Miter's Waste I read in the library, Death's
Whisper is not an accidental and unfortunate end that befalls
unsuspecting victims. Instead, he claims that Death's Whisper
is brought on by the victim ingesting trace amounts of the mineral flüstodapul, an odorless white powder, perhaps originating
in crystal form.

I think of my mother, Queen Eleonora, and even Petrus,
who died before he could speak his truth. Death is no accident.
I know why Petrus was killed, but my mother? And the queen?
I must find out what they were up to.

*"An what the hüle is Death's Whisper? Huh? We don't know nothin'
about it."*

I have to speak again with Obid.

I want to blame King Adolar. He told me I was just like
my mother and that she had taken everything from him. Did
he have her killed? And his queen? My brain races to make
connections, but the bridges are missing. The canyons cannot
be crossed.

The king wants me punished. Maybe dead. If death is his
goal, the king will want no part in the deed. If he possesses this
so-called flüstodapul, and if he has used it in the past to kill,
then I must assume it could end up in my wine or porridge.

I slam shut the book's cover and tuck it into the satchel.
I blow out the candle, return it to the desk, and creep to the
window. Enough time has been spent here. I cannot risk being
absent from my room when dinner comes. I slide the second
rope through the anchors and prepare to rappel. Careful to

avoid shards of glass, I climb through the window and attach my harness with a karabiner and sling to the rope. I peer once more around the tower. It did not appear that anyone had been in the queen's tower for ages, so I don't worry about the broken window or the scattered glass on the floor. They will have no proof it was me if I escape now without notice.

A gaping black hole in the wall stares back at me, and my blood turns to ice. The door to the staircase is open. I know it was shut when I entered. I don't see movement in the room, but it is dark and full of places to hide.

I rappel quickly, certain the line will be severed on the way down. It isn't. I reach the ground and pull on the rope. It falls with a thud. Gathering the protection I'd left behind, I sprint across the courtyard to the rope dangling from my room. I ascend and scramble through my window.

I stow my gear in the rucksack and stuff it beneath my bed. Maybe the door was open all along. Maybe I am losing my mind. If an antagonist had entered the room, they would have had plenty of time to take my life. I find comfort in the fact that I am still alive.

I change into a simple dürmel, take a deep breath, and step into the hallway. I am not sure what I have discovered. If what the author says is true, then my mother and Otto's mother were murdered. By whom and why, though? I cannot solve this riddle on my own. I stroll casually through the palace. Just past the Balhalle—the great hall—I spot Otto and give him a timid smile. I place my hands over my heart and hope he remembers. His brow furrows. He returns the gesture with a nod. To throw off prying bystanders, I giggle and tuck my hair behind my ears, trying to appear like an infatuated girl rather than someone seeking a private meeting. When I reach my room, I lean against the wood briefly, catching my breath, before grabbing Dr. Vitus's journal and sprinting to the secret passage. I dash up the spiraling staircase, nearly crashing into my handsome betrothed.

He grabs my shoulders. His lips tighten. "What's going on?"

I bend over and place my hands on my knees. I am not out of breath, but I feel like I am suffocating. Leaning against the wall, I slide down to the steps and inhale deeply. "Flüstodapul. Have you heard of it?"

"Nide." He shakes his head and drops down to sit on the step above me. "What is that?"

"Death's Whisper." My eyes move to meet his. Pain creases his forehead. I open the book and pass it to him.

He scans the page. His arms flex. His jaw clenches. Finally he looks up. "I don't understand."

"I don't either, but if what this Dr. Vitus says is true, then you know the significance of his words as well as I do. Our mothers—"

"You want me to believe my father killed his wife? The mother of his only son?" He looks at me with aversion.

I meet his gaze with sad sympathy. "I don't know, Otto. But if so, then it might not just be me who is in danger. A man who could kill his own wife could kill anyone. I have my suspicions about others. I am convinced I am his next target."

Otto stares at his feet. He covers his eyes with his hands. "Where did you get the book?"

I tap my lips with my finger and hope he doesn't feel betrayed by my actions. "I found it in the queen's tower."

"What?" He drops his hands from his face and looks at me. "How? It's impenetrable. I've tried to go and can't get in."

"The window's not impenetrable." I offer a sheepish grin and shrug. "Locked, but not impenetrable."

"You broke in? How?"

"I am a climber, Otto. Reaching high-up things is my job."

"Wow. That's amazing." He rubs the back of his neck and eyes me with admiration.

I chuckle, pull the painting from the back of the book, and hand it to him. "Our mothers were friends. I don't know what any of this means, but something happened that involved both of them. Something that made someone—maybe your father, maybe not—want to silence them."

"I know of Dr. Vitus." He passes the painting back to me and meets my gaze.

I grab his hand with too much force. "We have to speak to him."

He shakes his head. "I don't know him or where to find him. I just know his name." He takes a few deep breaths. I wait. "Klarke, I have never told anyone what I am about to tell you."

I nod. My eyes widen.

He bites his lip. Rests his hand against his forehead. "After my mother died, I snuck up to her tower before it was locked and found an old journal hidden in the mattress. I took it. I've read it a thousand times."

I want to shake the answers out of him. He hesitates to tell me the rest. I wait patiently, even though I am erupting on the inside.

My head grows dizzy. I want to scream.

"Dr. Vitus was my mother's physician. He delivered me as a baby."

"Hmmm." I file this in my brain but don't yet understand the significance.

"I was not alone. There was a girl. My twin."

"Oh." My gods. My stomach lurches. My mind races. Otto had a twin sister. If the kingdom knew of this, Adolar would be shunned. His line would end. He would have had the baby destroyed.

Otto looks at me, wringing his hands together as he speaks. "Your mom helped smuggle my sister out of the kingdom."

I imagine Obid, a covered basket draped from his elbow. My mother. Giving him instructions on where to take the baby. How many baskets has the boat chef loaded onto ships? How many boys have sisters they will never know? "To Ainar," I whisper. "Your sister is in Ainar."

Otto runs his fingers through his hair. He trembles. "I wonder if my father knew. Maybe he found out. Maybe that's why…"

I nod again. If the king knew the baby had not been killed,

he would have had to destroy everyone who played a role in deceiving him. The risk of the kingdom uncovering the truth would be too great.

Dr. Vitus. The queen. My mother. They all had to die to protect his power.

The truth falls into place. I decide to speak with Dr. Helmut. Maybe he knows Dr. Vitus. Maybe he can help us find him. Not so deep down, I know Dr. Vitus must be dead.

But why did Ellias have to die? Why Gerd? Why the other boys on the mountain?

Why me?

"Otto, do you know the name Lady Genalt?"

He drops his hands from his head and leans back. "Of course. She was my aunt, my father's sister. Her portrait hangs in your room. That used to be hers."

My pulse races. The avalanche of discovery plunges forward. I hope I do not suffocate beneath the truth. "What happened to her? Where is she now?"

"She went mad. Killed herself."

So my mother smuggled the king's daughter and his sister to safety behind his back? I let out a deep, slow breath. I don't share the rest, not yet. I don't tell Otto that Obid thinks Lady Genalt was tortured for her power. That she was the one who controlled Hildegroth. I need to speak with Obid first. He is the key to everything. The bridge. No wonder Adolar despises me so. He might even think I know something I shouldn't. Which I guess is now the truth.

"Do you really think my father would try to kill you?"

My hand moves to my face. I touch the still-tender stitches and imagine the phantom pain of the king's hand against my skin. *You're just like your mother.* "Yes. I know he will."

"Just to keep a woman from climbing mountains. I don't get it." He shakes his head. His fingers graze mine.

I chuckle sadly. The laugh morphs into a sob. I cover my mouth with a hand, then bury my face in my knees. "To a man like your father, power is everything. He killed our mothers to safeguard his power. He doesn't want half the population of Ectair believing they are equal and can do anything. It's not about mountains, Otto. I threaten his power, and for that, I must be eliminated."

"Did he do that to you?" He gestures to the stitches.

I nod. I don't want to lie to Otto. I don't want to confuse him with falsities.

"Oh, gods." He drops his gaze and hits his fists against his forehead. "I am so sorry, Klarke. I am so sorry."

I lean my head against his shoulder. We sit for a few minutes in silence.

"We don't know that he killed them. We can't be certain." Otto's eyebrows are drawn together. He takes deep, slow breaths. He doesn't seem keen on his father, but I imagine it would be horrible nonetheless to learn your father had your mother killed.

I put my hand on his leg and squeeze. It's all I have to offer. "I understand how hard this is. Maybe I am completely wrong. But if I want to stay alive, I must proceed under these assumptions."

Otto sets his hand on mine. He lets out a deep sigh and shakes his head. "Dinner will be served soon. We should return to our rooms." He stands and pulls me to my feet. "I believe you, Klarke. Do everything you must to stay alive. We have to uncover the truth."

"I will. The truth is everything to me now." I watch the prince disappear around the spiraling stairwell and turn to retreat to my room.

As soon as I flop onto the bed to process what I've just learned, I realize I left my cloak in the library earlier. I exit my chamber, nod to Silias who follows, and walk through the cavernous halls. We pass the throne room. I am startled to see Aedan and Kiel strolling down the thick green carpet. Behind them King Adolar finishes conversing with Gio and shakes his hand. I smile when I see my teammates until I catch the expressions on their faces. Aedan's cheeks flush, and he doesn't meet my gaze. Kiel looks like he might explode.

"What are you doing here?" I pause and glance between them, waiting for an explanation.

"Last minute plans for the climb tomorrow. We'll see you bright and early." Aedan grabs Kiel's arm and steers him down the hall away from me, without making eye contact.

"See you later, Klarke." Gio and the king have reached the hall as well. Gio's face is pale, like the surface of Azura. With an embarrassed nod, he jogs ahead to catch up to the other Ascenditures.

I stare after them. A heavy arm drapes around my shoulders. "You may leave us, Silias."

I flinch as the king pulls me to his side. A grin that makes my insides curl stretches from ear to ear. "Are you ready for your big climb?"

Silias looks like he wants to retort. Instead, he bows and disappears down the hall.

I try not to choke on my nerves. I can't center my mind or gain control of my senses. Something is wrong. I need to know what. But the king mustn't know I am rattled. "I am excited to do my duty for this kingdom."

The hand around my shoulder slips down to my torso and rests uncomfortably beneath my breast. I fight the urge to retch. "That's what I like to hear. Good girl." His hand moves up until there is no doubt as to his intentions. He steers me down the hall, and I walk with him, afraid to breathe, afraid to blink. "I have some big news to announce to the kingdom when the team returns with the vintazite harvest."

"Oh," I say, focusing on not falling with each step I take. Basic movements have abandoned me. "Good."

"Mmmmm." He gives a squeeze to my chest, and I am certain he feels me trembling. "The kingdom loved when I announced your marriage to my son. They love a good love story, you know?"

I nod, keeping my eyes on the ground.

"Kiel's a handsome man, isn't he?"

There it is. My blood stops pumping. I stumble, and he grips me tighter so I don't fall.

"Easy now." His smile is so full of hot malice that I almost feel my flesh melting from my bones. "Anyway, my niece, the Lady Gelta, has just turned seventeen, and the only thing she wanted for her birthday was a husband. Specifically, one of my climbers." He shrugs, and his lips curve in a cold smile. "What kind of uncle would I be if I denied her that wish?"

My vision is going. My knees are rattling so hard I am surprised they haven't shattered. For a second, I think he must have slipped me a bite of Death's Whisper. But he hasn't. He has slipped me something much worse.

"And you know who she picked?" His laugh echoes through the hallway. It is sharp and cuts me. My soul bleeds. "She selected that handsome man, your friend, isn't he? Kiel." He whispers this last bit into my ear. His lips graze my skin. They feel like a dead man's lips. "He will make a fine husband for Gelta."

I stop walking and stand like a marble statue in the middle of the hallway, my face etched into a guise of horror and pain.

"Does this news trouble you?" He takes a step closer and slips a hand into the waistband of my skirt.

I pull away, eyes wide.

"Does it make you sad that your friend will be seeking comfort in another woman's arms?" He rolls his tongue across his lips.

I take a step backward and then another. A laugh erupts from his dead lips, and it follows me as I sprint away from him.

"And one more thing," he shouts at my back. I don't want to hear it. Nothing more from him. "Your comrade Julius, was that the boy's name? They found his body on Mount Bonen. Dead like all the others."

I knew Julius was dead, but it hurts all the same. There was always some hope he and Tristan managed to survive. Tristan's body will turn up next. I pump my arms so that I am nearly flying through the palace. Past mocking statues, up the stairs, down the hallways, and into the false safety of my bedroom. Flinging the bolt into place, I lock the door and dive into my bed, sobbing as my face hits the pillow. I scream and punch the pillow, trying to understand what happened.

And then it hits me.

King Adolar said I would be safe until he had taken everything from me. Until now he's taken everyone I'd loved and destroyed them. But there was one final person he could use against me. He did that tonight, which means only one thing. I no longer serve a purpose. I am broken, and it's time to discard the waste.

26

The breeze has shifted over the past few weeks, blowing Ainar's frigid air down onto our villages. Vintazite will be here soon, and with it, the ice and wind which make climbing nearly impossible.

I am frozen to the marrow, though I doubt wind is the sole culprit. I try not to think about the cold as we jostle up the rutted mountain road in the carriage. I try not to think about a lot of things. Kiel sits as far from me as possible. Each time we lock eyes, I see him fighting the same nausea that plagues me. He is to be married and not in an arrangement like Otto's and mine where the two partners agree to a façade. I swallow the swell of emotion in my throat and try not to think about death. Or Kiel in bed with King Adolar's niece.

Behind us another carriage rolls up the road. It is filled with greencoats from the Rektburg. Perhaps they are here to scrape my blood and bones from the rock when the king makes his final move on me.

I assume Adolar doesn't expect to see me after this climb. I wonder if he has laid the penultimate retribution to my mother by breaking my heart. That just leaves the grand finale. I rub my hands against my arm to fight off the consuming chill. Although goat-hair-lined gloves protect my fingers, the wind penetrates the leather.

Dieter sits to one side of me, Gio to the other. We are pressed so tightly that their shoulders squeeze mine. The warmth their bodies provide helps only a little. Only the death of my king, or my feet planted firmly on the deck of a ship bound for Kobo, could make me feel warm.

I look around at the faces of my team. If I am to believe my intuition, at least one of these men played a role in Ellias and Feiko's deaths and the deaths of the boys on Mount Bonen.

If the king is indeed finished with me, then I should be afraid. What better place to stage an accident than the face of Fitzhan? I shiver. Does one of these men carry the sentence, or is it someone else? Is there another climber in this kingdom who is as good as our team but hides in the shadows instead of standing in Cleos's light?

We hit a bump. My head bangs against Dieter's shoulder. "Sorry." I still haven't spoken much to him since I confronted him in the shadow of Mount Bonen. I haven't quite known what to say. Back then I thought he was colluding with the prince in some grand scheme or selling drugs. Now that I trust Prince Otto, does that mean Dieter is innocent? Or am I once again being too assuming? Could Dieter be the one who carries my death sentence?

He looks at me with dark, narrow eyes, then turns away. His eye shape is rare below the Waste. Some people revere those with tapered eyes as having some power left over from the old days. Others scowl at them in the streets, believing them to be descendants of the kings from Ainar. Dieter was born in Kietsch. His mother and father have dark hair and pale skin like the rest of us. His father owns the only business in Ectair that produces oil for our lamps. I don't think there's anything mythical or spooky about Dieter. He simply has narrow eyes and darker skin. Rumor has it that Yonas Abegg is not Dieter's birth father, but that is just speculation. He must feel my eyes on him because Dieter turns, raising a brow. I smile, then look away.

I gaze at Burkhart. I don't know a lot about him. He comes from Merket from a family of lumberjacks. He started climbing the trees in the Hummeldorf Woods at a young age and was a natural when they stuck him on the fel in Kietsch. He looks like he is forty from the scars on his face, but he is young. Maybe twenty-five or six. We've never had a conversation. Friendly or otherwise. He is a mystery to me. All I know is that if he had his way, I wouldn't be in this carriage.

I peer from the corner of my eye at Gio. He has only ever been kind to me. I have only seen him be light-hearted and helpful with the team. His father is away most of the time, stationed at Camp Arema along the Sevier River. Gio cares for his mother and sisters. He carries the burden of his family's well-being. I am sure that is not easy in this world.

As my gaze moves to Russet, Tizian begins to sing a sobering dirge. "The Fizhte Tree." An old folk song from the Tono Hills that cuts into my soul and makes me feel as if I am drowning.

O'er green hill and lonely valley,
Rests the soul, my heart does crave.
The tears I've shed cannot be tallied.
My love has gone, 'yond darkened wave.

His voice is haunting, like the creaking of a wooden board on a ship's deck. Like the howling of the wind through the trees by the river. Burkhart contributes his deep voice to the song.

I dreamed last night, she lay beside me.
Hand in hand, we shared the eve.
But when I woke, my heart was heavy.
I recalled her hanging from the fizhte tree.

I pick at the waistline of my skirt and try not to cry. We approach the base of Fitzhan. The rest of the team add their voices to the melody. Even I whisper the words beneath my breath.

To lose a love, it leaves one hollow.
Like a well, where the waters run dry.
My throat is parched, I cannot swallow.
I make my way to the fizhte to die.

I think of Ellias, of the emptiness I've felt since his passing. I feel the thirst. I feel it all. I glance at Kiel, and my throat tightens. I fight tears until I notice every passenger in the cart besides Veit is emotional. That is all the permission I need to weep. We all miss our leader. Coming to this place, for all of us, is like returning to the fizhte tree.

The carriage stops. Rain taps the canvas covering in a soft pitter-patter. The wind gusts, then rests, rustling the trees and then vanishing into eerie silence. Aedan is the first to stand. He moves to the back and lifts the flap to step out.

I am the last to exit. I can't be in this place. Not with the nightmares that still haunt me. Kiel takes my hand as he passes, squeezing warmth back into me. My legs wobble as I stand. My knees knock together as I descend the few steps to the ground.

Precipitation has washed the blood from the rocks. I turn away, sucking at the moist air for relief. There was no way around the bodies when we descended after the last climb. I was forced to look upon Ellias's smashed figure. Forced to see the strongest man I ever knew broken on unrelenting stone. And now I have to climb again as if their deaths don't matter, as if our lives matter less than some stupid root.

Russet wraps his arm around me. I turn into his embrace. We share a bond. Our first and only time up Fitzhan was marred by tragedy. I pull him closer, finding comfort in our shared grief. Should I warn him that I might soon be his next nightmare?

"We must get started." Aedan interrupts the sorrowful moment with a soft voice. "This is a tough day for us, and I know it feels too quick for some. This day would come sooner or later, and now that we are here, we must do our jobs. Ellias would expect nothing less. Feiko would be chomping at the bit to reach the top. Let us honor them with a successful climb. With joy in our hearts for the sport. With compassion in our souls for each other. This is a family. We climb together. We mourn together. Sometimes, we die together. But most importantly, we rise together."

"Here, here," Dieter says, lifting his fist.

The rest of us join him. I find comfort in Aedan's words. He is right. Ellias would be devastated to learn that climbing has lost its shine for me. It would break his spirit to know I didn't want to be here today. I can almost hear his voice.

"Klarkey," he would say. *"You've worked your entire life for this. So, there were some hiccups along the way. There always are. If you let those bumps determine your future, you will hate everything and will spend your life locked in a cupboard, avoiding all that brought you joy because maybe there was some pain mixed in. Head up, darling. Always head up, for that is the direction in which the mountain grows."*

I shake out my arms and stomp my feet. Our collective breath hangs in the air, swirling around in a light fog. I loop the rope around my chest and attach a sling. I hang the empty canvas bag across my shoulders. The brim of my hat catches in the wind, but I've secured it to my head with pink ribbons.

"Gather round."

We move to hover around Aedan. He pulls out a map, the same map Ellias used to use, and traces his finger along our route. "Same as last time. Three teams of three straight up the Disillusion Route. The weather is crummy, so I am not sending newbies in the lead. Kletshot one will be Gio in first position, Veit in second, and Tizian in third. Kletshot two will be led by me, followed by Russet and then Kiel. Burkhart will head up Kletshot three, with Klarke in second position and Dieter bringing up the rear. Any questions?"

I feel a temporary wave of disappointment at not being placed on Kiel's team. But Burkhart and Dieter are strong climbers. I think I trust Dieter now, and if Burkhart wants me dead, I am probably safest on his rope. Especially since I will be his belayer.

"Don't screw this up." Burkhart glares at me. His body reminds me of an oakenwood sapling—wiry, thin, and strong.

"Siec moldon." Aedan waves his hand at the second coach. A lone päter steps out. The ceremonial pewter bowl in his hand carries nine small bundles. Our offerings to Orna. The päter hands each of us one of the spheres uttering the words, "May Orna and Laren be with you," as he places it in our open palms.

I glare into the dark eye holes on the white mask as the päter hands me a bundle. He winks. One blue eye, one brown. I know those eyes. I shake my head, unsure if my eyes played tricks on me. I can't recall where I've seen them before, but I know I have looked into them. I notice a chain around his neck. Barely visible. I cannot see what hangs from it. But there is only one päter I've seen wearing a necklace. The one who left Laren's tower donning that beautiful black gem.

"Who are you?" I whisper.

He moves away without a response. I sigh as if I've been holding my breath and bend down to grab a handful of dirt. The päter turns but makes no motion to stop me. I stuff the bundle and the dirt into my pocket. If they once again provided me with ashes and bone, I will bring my own offering. It is time for me to outsmart the kingdom.

Those eyes.

"For Ellias and Feiko," Gio says, moving to the face of the fel.

"For Ellias and Feiko," the rest of us reply.

"For the men who died on Mount Bonen," I add.

"Aye." Aedan nods.

"For the men who died on Mount Bonen," the team chants.

We must not forget anyone who has perished in the climb, official team member or not. And if the murderer is standing here, I want him to be reminded of what he has done. Of the extent of his damage.

I double-check my harness and protection and prepare the rope to belay Burkhart to the first ledge.

"Klettag," Burkhart grunts. He stands at the wall, his fingers touching the stone.

"Klettag und," I reply, letting him know I am prepared to keep him safe.

He vanishes into the fog. I take it as a compliment that he trusts me to belay him. He doesn't think I belong here, but he knows I am good enough.

Kiel glances over from his spot on kletshot two. His eyes are full of longing and promise. Mine are filled with sorrow and regret. Behind me, waiting in the second carriage, are the palace guards and the päter. My way out is blocked.

Burkhart reaches the top. Dieter takes over belay, and I move to the rock face. Burkhart will have already attached the rope to the protection, so my climb will be easy. I tap the sling three times.

My prayer to Orna is quick and angry. Mostly I ask for safety against my fellow man, not against the mountain. I doubt she is listening. I gave up on her listening somewhere between the deaths of Gerd and Ingo on Mount Bonen.

I grab an undercling on the rock and find two good places to plant my feet. My mind clears. The feelings of fear and doubt that have plagued me vanish into the mist. This is why I love to climb. It narrows my focus. It challenges my body and spirit. Palace intrigue has no place here. Grief and anger don't belong on a cliff face. I am alone. I am free.

My arms extend. My fingers grip the slick rock. My feet find sturdy holds, and my legs push off, propelling me to the next hold. I plunge my hands into the dust bag and do it all again. The rock ledge materializes, and I haul myself over it, feeling as though I could conquer anything today.

Burkhart takes over a top belay for Dieter down below. I dig into my pack and pull out a small bag. Nibbling on a bartlenut, I peer around at the group. They wouldn't hurt me, not even the ones who don't yet understand. Someone else must have infiltrated our team when Ellias died and the massacre on Mount Bonen transpired. Part of the king's plan was probably to sew discord from the beginning—to make me question everything and find safety in nothing. I sip from my canteen and allow my body to relax. I need to enjoy this. For Ellias. The final three climbers from each team reach the ledge.

"How are you feeling?" Tizian asks Veit, giving him a hard slap on the back. "First time can be a bit rattling."

Veit sits up straighter and puffs out his chest. "Easy. Just like practice. I should have done this on my own years ago."

"Uh-huh, right. Me too." Russet makes a face and flexes his arm.

The team laughs. Kiel throws a nut at Veit. Veit swats it from the air and pretends to be offended. My spirit rises. This is what I want. Not life in a palace. This is my true kingdom. This is my real family.

We continue up the cliff face. The rain increases between the first and second ledge. Ice begins to form between the second and third. Between three and four, I notice a serious problem.

The cold front that blew in left thick ice sheets on the rock. The rain shifts from cool liquid drops to small pellets of snow. I cannot see above me or to the side, but Burkhart has stopped moving. My core temperature drops. My fingers cramp, and I have difficulty belaying the rope. If I don't start climbing soon, my limbs will tighten up, and I fear my ability to ascend will be compromised.

The rope begins to pile up across my hands and body. Burkhart is descending. I pull as much rope tight as I can before being completely tangled in it. Aedan and Burkhart land on the ledge.

"What's going on?" I turn my head between the two men. "Why did we stop?"

"Too dangerous." Ice crystals have formed across the stubble on Aedan's face. He pulls a sheepskin overcoat from his satchel and buttons it up to the base of his chin. The curtain of white powder falling from the sky blurs his face. "Get warm. We need to regroup."

Burkhart puts on a sealskin coat and hunkers down by the cliff face. I move to the wall and sink to a crouch. Wind thrashes the snow in swirling eddies around our bodies. I squirm into my overcoat and wrap a thick woolen scarf around my neck.

"Where the hüle is Gio?" Burkhart rubs his hands together and stoops next to us. "Aedan called for us to fall back."

Kiel, Dieter, Russet, and Tizian throw on their extra garments and move to where we sit.

Veit stands at the wall, staring up into the snow. "Gio's not on the rope anymore." He tugs, and the rope spirals down the fel in a whooshing thud. "What should I do?"

"Get over here," Aedan shouts. "Put your coat on and get warm."

Veit leaves the rope and yanks a coat from his haulbag. He wraps a wool scarf around his ears. Someone pulls out a blanket and drapes it across our heads. The eight of us press as closely together as possible. But the moisture has soaked through our clothes, and the temperature continues to drop.

"Where is Gio?" Aedan's voice is filled with anxious fury. "I know he heard my command."

Gio doesn't appear. We lean in closer as the blizzard works to flush us over the edge. The snowstorm intensifies.

"We've got to get off this rock."

I am not sure who said the words. My face is buried in my knees. My teeth clatter. Icy wind blows up my skirt, trying to force its way through my woolen bloomers. As much as I agree with the statement, I am not sure I will be able to move.

"Conditions are too poor. Exposure on the cliff face will lead to another death. We stay put and wait out the storm."

I recognize Aedan's voice.

Each of us takes our turn on the outside edge of the huddle. I lose track of time. When I am pressed against the wall, surrounded by warm bodies, I think there is a chance I will survive. When it is my turn on the outer edge, when the wind whips at my back and slips beneath my coat to run its glacial fingers across my flesh, I am certain I will die. At one point, I feel an arm wrap around my shoulders. Kiel pulls me close to him. Burying my face in his shoulder, I welcome the warmth.

I pray to Orna to keep Gio safe. Maybe she doesn't give a scheiz about me, but I hope she still cares about the men on this team. We cannot lose any more brothers. I am unsure how we could come back from another loss.

Eventually my mind goes numb along with my body. I float in and out of a dream world, one filled with steaming mugs of tea and thick blankets laid out before a hearth. My body sways. I follow the rotation—into a bit of warmth, out into certain death.

"Everyone get your headlamp." Dieter digs in his bag as he says the words. "If we all ignite our lamps and put them in the center, maybe a little extra warmth will be generated."

With my small energy reserve, I remove my lamp and set it on the ground. My hands shake so furiously that I can't strike a match. When I finally ignite the red phosphorus tip, the wind snuffs out the flame before I can blink. Finally, Russet and Burkhart get their lamps lit. I don't feel any warmth, but the flicker of light makes me feel less icy.

With the help of Kiel using his hands to block the wind, I light both of our lamps. I hold the device in my hands and feel the tiniest bit of warmth seeping out.

Eventually the wind stops. The snow drifts lazily from the sky, switching from lethal to serene in minutes. A bitter chill remains, but we can see and won't get ripped off the cliff face. I stand and hop from foot to foot, shaking my arms. Hot needles stab my flesh.

"We need to get down." Aedan points to Tizian and Veit, who are clearly in some stage of hypothermia. Veit's lips are blue. Tizian shakes harder than the rest of us combined.

Dieter steps into the huddle. His lips, like the rest of ours, are unnaturally blue. Maybe we are all in some stage of hypothermia. "What about Gio?"

"We will figure out a rescue plan for him later," Aedan says. "For now, he's on his own. He had a spare rope with him. He knows how to rappel. If we don't get these two and ourselves down, we're all going to need rescuing."

Dieter nods. We descend slowly. Rappelling one at a time to each ledge. We reach the bottom just before nightfall. Other carriages have arrived. Medic tents have been erected. Nurses and doctors race forward. I am ushered into a tent and stripped down to my bare skin. I crawl into a makeshift cot. The nurse piles blankets on me and stuffs hot water bladders into my joints. She hands me a steaming mug. I shake violently, splashing warm tea onto the comforters.

Dieter is placed in the adjacent bed. I hear the metal cot rattling as his body convulses. We are in worse shape than I imagined. I picture Gio frozen on the cliff somewhere high above us. Is he the latest victim? Funny, kind Gio who doesn't deserve to die in this manner. Who will care for his mother and sisters?

The nurse leaves. I have no way of knowing how the rest of

the team is doing. I turn my head but don't see Dieter. He has concealed himself beneath the pile of blankets.

"Stand guard," a deep voice commands from the other side of the tent flap. "Let no one in until I leave. Understood? No one."

Prince Otto pulls aside the entrance flap and steps in. He is dressed in a thick fur cloak with riding boots that go to his knees. I smile, flattered that he came to see me, to make sure I am okay. He nods solemnly and turns to the pile of blankets on the other cot.

The prince reaches the edge of Dieter's bed and drops to his knees. He pulls back the blankets and flings his body across Dieter's trembling form. Confusion hinders my already foggy brain. I see Dieter's arms rise and wrap around the prince's neck. Dieter is shaking. Prince Otto is telling him that everything will be fine.

The truth clubs me in the head. Dieter and the prince disappeared into the forest at base camp. The prince does not want to marry, not just me but anyone. I recall his words that we are both outcasts, both abominations in the eyes of the law.

I shake my head. Prince Otto is in love with Dieter. I want to laugh. I want to skip. I feel happiness welling within, warming my icy core. I will never be forced into anything with Otto. He can live his life. I can live mine. We can keep each other's secrets till the day we die.

He pulls away from Dieter and looks in my direction. "Are you okay?"

I nod, a silly grin on my face. "Great. Fantish."

"You can't tell anyone." He moves toward me, his eyes full of concern. "Please."

"Otto." I grab his hands and feel tears well in my eyes. "I wouldn't dream of it."

He leans forward and hugs me. I feel his warmth, his generosity, his vulnerability. "At least it was just the elements that tried to kill you. And not a teammate." His lips tickle my ear. I feel his smile.

"Yeah, at least that." No one killed me, but we haven't escaped death yet. Gio is still out there. This climb was as cursed as the others.

I sit up. "Otto, could you bring me my skirt?"

"Of course." Otto leaves the bed and moves across the room. He lifts the still-damp garment and hands it to me.

I reach into the pocket and remove the offering from the päter. I have to know. During the climb, I'd imagined the bundle to contain a beating heart, someone's eyeball, Ellias's tongue...

With a shiver, I untie the bit of yarn. It opens to a small pile of dirt. Sighing, I toss the bundle onto the table between the beds. Something clinks. I run my finger through the dirt and then yank it back when something bites. A drop of blood has formed from a razor-like cut. I peer at the offering. A few small shards of glass poke from the dirt.

The queen's window.

"What is that?" Otto leans forward, gathering the glass into his hand. "Is this—?"

"From the queen's tower," I whisper, my eyes widening.

I imagine the open tower door. The päter's wink. He wants me to know they know. I shake away the foreboding dread before it can settle and pull the covers tighter around me. I am going to survive this night, but I am still freezing. And the image of someone watching me in the queen's tower doesn't help to bring me warmth.

27

Something crashes outside the tent. I shoot up in bed. Someone opens the flap and peers in, but their headlamp blinds me. The figure walks forward and removes the light, holding it in his hand and shining it on the canvas corner.

"How are you?" Burkhart lumbers to my bedside and hovers over my startled form.

I rub my head. My temples throb. I feel a slight burn in my fingers and toes, but I think I escaped in better shape than most. Burkhart looks like he just came in from the city—not like he spent a miserable afternoon on the side of a deadly cliff.

"I'm okay." I meet his gaze. Inquiring about my condition is the nicest thing he has ever said to me.

He turns to Dieter, who has not moved. Burkhart goes to his cot and lifts the blankets. Dieter is curled beneath them, shivering. He drops the comforters.

"I need your help." He tosses a leather bag at the foot of my bed. "Only you, Kiel, and I are in any shape to climb."

"To climb?" I sit up straighter, pulling the blankets up to my chin. "But it's dark. And cold. And..."

Burkhart's lip begins to curl. Whatever disdain for me he'd shelved comes creeping back in. "And Gio is lost up there. Get up. We leave in fifteen." He points to the bag and exits the tent.

I drop my face into my hands and shake my head. Gio could be anywhere between here and the top. He could have frozen and fallen off the cliff by now. His body might be an icicle wedged into some slot canyon or shattered on one of the upper ledges like a wine glass bumped from a tabletop. I can't bear to witness another broken body. I am also not sure if I can bear exposure to the cold for that long.

Knowing the team would come for me if necessary and not

wanting to prove Burkhart right, I roll from the cot and light my headlamp. I pull on a dry pair of wool bloomers from the bag. Next I find a small pair of hosen and a thick coat. Of course, there are no spare climbing outfits for women. I tie my harness and lace up a dry pair of climbing boots. I bite my lip through a smile. No skirt tonight. It might be temporary, but it feels like progress.

I grab the päter's offering—including the shards of glass—and stuff it into my pocket. I open the tent flap. The night air smacks me in the face with a frozen palm. Beneath the overcoat my body trembles. The camp is dark besides two other lights flickering at the base of the Disillusion Route. Burkhart and Kiel are already waiting. Kiel will belay Burkhart. I will belay Kiel. And then one of them will belay me from the top. I tap my sling, praying that Gio is still alive and that I will be too by night's end. Thankfully, it is not yet raining. We attach the headlamps to our hats.

Kiel touches my hand. Burkhart sighs and turns toward the cliff as if he has seen nothing.

"We will have another chance," Kiel whispers as he kisses my head. "Maybe it won't be as soon as we'd hoped, maybe new obstacles will be placed in our path, but we will get out of here. We will be together. We will be free."

I nod and lean into his proffered embrace. Kiel is warm and strong. I don't need a man in my life, but I do want one now. I want Kiel. I want to be free to choose my destiny.

"Nice hosen, by the way," he whispers into my hair before pulling away. I kick one leg into the air and laugh.

Burkhart grunts. "Klettag."

"Klettag und," Kiel replies with a grin.

Burkhart begins to climb. Kiel gives slack, heaving extra lengths of coil free each time Burkhart reaches a bolt so he can secure the rope for the rest of us. I stare up at his light bouncing through the night fog. It reminds me of a time when I was a little girl. My father took me on horseback to the Point of the Tolvalus to try to catch a glimpse of the majestic creatures that breed off our western coast and, if it was a clear day, to strain my eyes for a peek at the eastern shore of Kobo.

The free end of the rope drops from above. I prep to belay Kiel.

"Klettag," he says in a firm voice.

"Klettag und." My voice chatters from the cold. As I pull in Kiel's slack, my mind wanders to a warmer, happier place.

We left before dawn that day, my father's headlight bobbing up and down in front of me as the horses slipped through the dark woods. We stopped for lunch beside a clear stream in the middle of the Dangof Forest. I took my shoes off and let the minnows nibble my toes. We played in the water, skipped rocks, and tied braids of marsh grass into our horses' manes. Then we mounted our steeds and continued through the thick forest. Hours passed before we finally burst out onto a barren point of rock. Jagged limestone cut its way into the Straits of Hidar. We stood atop it, staring at the choppy water, eyes fixated on every burst of wave or dark splotch on the horizon. Finally, we saw them—a pod of tolvaluses not a hundred yards from shore. Big dark forms rising from the water to breathe.

"You're up!" Kiel shouts from above. "I'm ready to go on my end!"

I rerig my setup to go from belaying to climbing and begin.

I struggle over the edge of the first rock shelf. My energy reserves are depleted. My arms are as limber as a hunk of gemwood. When I finally haul myself up, I lie on my stomach, gasping into the icy stone. Kiel drags me into a seated position and wraps his arms around me. Burkhart removes a leather canteen from his rucksack and passes it around. Collectively, we shiver and sip lukewarm tea. I nibble at some dried fruit, although I am not hungry. Too soon, Burkhart rises to his feet and motions for us to do the same.

We repeat the belaying cycle. When it's my turn to climb, I stand on creaking knees and move to the rock face. My fingers feel like they will snap at the middle joint as soon as I bend them. They don't, but my hold on the rock is precarious. The gloves keeping my fingers from turning black and crusty also keep them from fitting into small cracks or safely grasping tiny crimpers. We make it to the ledge where we'd waited out the storm earlier.

Above the shelf, things get dicey. It would be one thing if we were actually ice climbing up a wall of frozen water. Equipment exists for that. There is a strategy. Climbing a stone wall with a thin layer of ice is just stupid.

With only a few minor slips, we make it to the final rock ledge before the summit. There has still been no sign of Gio. We drain the last of the tea. No one speaks. The stretch from here on out is treacherous, even in good conditions. Standing at the base of the final pitch in the freezing dark, it feels like I am lifting a knife to my throat and piercing the flesh. Burkhart sets off. Then Kiel. And finally, it is my turn again. If it weren't for a fist-sized block of ice in my chest, my heart might be thumping. I feel little other than resigned obedience and an acceptance of death. My lamp illuminates the icy rock in front of me. It bounces off the fog creating the illusion that I am in a cloudy tunnel, not suspended thousands of feet in the air.

When my father and I saw the tolvalus so many years back, that was the moment I knew I had to be true to myself. Those creatures taught me that freedom was more important than contented ignorance. Nothing told those whales where to go, what to do, who to be. They belonged only to themselves. I stood on the edge of a different cliff, my hand in my father's, and I knew I would never be the woman I was expected to be. I knew my path forward would be difficult. A few weeks later, I said goodbye to him for the last time. He kissed my forehead, promised to bring me spiced chocolate from Kobo, and sailed away, the orange sails of his ship carrying him from me for eternity.

The warmth that had graced me while thinking of my father vanishes. Thoughts of his death let in the frigid air. I see my breath in the lamplight. I see the slick ice coating my next hold.

A shout rings from above, and I cling to my current position.

A thud filters down, accompanied by another yell. Glancing up, I have a second to respond before a large chuck of ice crashes past my head. I fling my arm to the side and grip a horn of rock. I stretch out my left leg and find a toe hold. Then I pull my body to the side as more ice and rock tumble from the fel.

I brace for impact. I brace for a perfect cut to find its way onto the rope. I brace for the moraine and the decree that my death was an accident. My arms tremble as I grip the horn. My fingers begin to slip. My legs quake. Finally, the ice slide stops. I tug on the rope. It is tight, unsevered.

"You good?" Kiel's voice echoes down to me.

I take a deep breath and wiggle the fingers on my right hand. "Yeah. About to start climbing again. See you soon."

I glance into the cold darkness. This time I ignore the wall crack and make my way up the arête. It is slippery, and I am exhausted. I feel the occasional tug of rope as my belayer—probably Kiel—helps pull me up the route. There is still no sign of Gio. Either he free-climbed to the top, knowing it is warmer and someone would come to rescue him, or he is now just a name in a history book that children will skim over and forget.

Clouds hang so heavy I cannot see more than a few inches from where I place my hand. Fog hugs me like a blanket soaked in some virulent disease. I reach upward, searching for a hand-hold, but all I feel is empty air. Using my legs, I push off and heave myself up. I have reached the Celebern Fields.

Cleos, the star that normally warms this place by day, is hidden behind the horizon. Azura is out, bathing everything in a blue haze. The blokkenshon looms like a suspended shadow in her light, obstructing our view of the meadow. We stow our gear next to the boulder and don the extra layers of clothing from our rucksacks. I take a step around the blokkenshon and gaze upon the Celebern Fields. Mist seeps across the meadow, snaking its way through the tufts of solanas grass all the way to the trees at the far end of the field. Specters materialize in my mind, tormenting me with visions of death and torture. I shake the phantoms away and search for some sign of Gio.

"Do you want to lead the offering?" Kiel turns toward Burkhart, who gazes out across the field.

"Nide." Burkhart keeps his eyes ahead. "They don't actually listen. Waste o' time."

Kiel makes an agreeing noise. I nod. There's something we all agree upon. I peer out into the midnight fog. "I guess we should spread out."

Kiel touches my shoulder. I lean into him, wishing we could search together. I don't relish the idea of probing the mist alone.

"I'll go left," Burkhart says. "Kiel, take the center. Klarke, go right. We'll meet at the edge of the woods at the far end. Don't go in until we're all together with a rope ready unless ye want to end up stuffed down a crack. If anything goes wrong, use your flare."

Shadows play tricks on my brain as I set off through the solanas grass. It is so quiet, as if all sound except my heavy breathing and beating heart has been sucked into a void. Cold air presses against me. My headlamp illuminates the dirt at my feet. Occasional orange lumps peek out from the ground. I want to stomp them all.

I can no longer see the other two lights bobbing in the darkness to my left. I am alone, except for the mental ghosts. Goosebumps prickle my arm. My spine tingles. It is the cold, not the undead, but alone in the dark, it feels like it could be anything. Turning my fear into anger, I drop to the ground and yank one of the solans from the dirt, dusting it off before stuffing it into my pack. I will eat the root later in my room. Beneath the roof of the Rektburg. I will share it with Lena. With Rayna. With Silias. It is a small act of mutiny, but it takes only one enraged sailor to burn a ship at sea.

I stand and shout Gio's name. The night air consumes my words. Eventually I reach the woods. Gnarled trees form a natural barrier to protect us from the fissures beyond. The trees are so thick here they block Azura's blue light. The forest is as dark as the sea floor.

Kiel and Burkhart's lights are small glints across the mead-

ow. They're performing a better search, and it will take them a
while to reach me. I should go back. Gio could be unconscious,
hidden beneath long blades of grass.

As I turn, a sharp and high noise flutters through the trees. A
rockfall? A shout, maybe? My skin prickles. My throat tightens.
Whatever the sound, it came from a person.

"Gio," I squeak, pressing through the front line of the forest. My voice sends me leaping for cover behind a fallen log.
A spider web wraps around my face. I shriek and slap myself,
trying to remove the silk and its owner. Even the headlamp
struggles to pierce the heavy darkness.

Burkhart said to wait, and although I recall Ellias's warning
that the woods are treacherous, Gio needs my help. He might
be in immediate danger. I set out. The forest duff is thick. I
stumble twice but always keep a hand on a branch in case the
ground gives way. When I find Gio, I will send up my flare, and
Burkhart and Kiel can safely retrieve us.

I fight through the forest, brushing away limbs that tear
at my clothes and cheeks. Ripping vines from branches and
swatting bugs from my face. Large limestone boulders begin to
appear mixed in with the trees. The woods thin, morphing into
a forest of stone. I walk through monoliths of rock reaching
toward the sky like the fingers of a giant who has been buried
alive and is trying to escape from his grave. Fog swirls between
the stones, creating a lazy river of souls. I shiver.

Fifty yards ahead the earth gives way to a gaping pit. I move
closer, thinking I have reached the cliff's edge, but beyond the
yawning depression, I see more trees. And then I notice a faint
light glowing from within the cave. I think I hear voices. Argu-
ing voices.

"Gio?" I call, leaning over the edge. "It's Klarke. I'm here
to help."

The light vanishes. The cavern plunges into darkness. What
if it isn't Gio up here at all? I bend down to pick up a rock,
ready to defend myself, and notice the purple ferns everywhere.
Just like the ones the päters carried from Laren's tower. Just

like the ones the man with the two-toned eyes had. My heart thrums against my ribcage. Blood pounds in my ears.

"Klarke!" A dark shadow slithers up through the rocks.

I let out a scream, so shrill I almost die from embarrassment. "Gio, what the hüle? What are you doing here? What is this place? Who were you talking to?"

He slinks over the cavern's edge, stepping into the light. The tip of his nose is black. He is frostbitten but doesn't seem to care. "Shall I answer those questions in order, or does the inquisition continue?"

I sigh and lean against one of the limestone monoliths. Exhaustion sinks in now that my mission is complete. The cold feels deeper. The aches and pains squeeze and sear into me. I shake my head. "You're okay then?"

"I'm good." He leans on the rock next to me and rubs his hands together. "A bit cold. Tanks for coming to the rescue."

He doesn't answer a single question. I want to be cross, but I chalk it up to madness brought on by freezing temperatures and lack of sleep. Rummaging through my bag, I pull out the flare.

"What are you doing?" Gio's face tightens, almost as if he is angry or scared. "Not here."

"I need to let the others know you're safe. You might be fine, Gio, but we aren't." I move to strike a match against a rock, but he knocks it from my hand.

"Not here. You don't want the others getting hurt trying to find us, do you?" The words have a hint of malice laced through them. He bends down to retrieve the match, and something falls from his pocket. A small green sack. The contents spill onto the ground. Clear crystals, each about the size of a pea, glisten in the light from our headlamps.

Gio crashes to his knees and gathers the fallen contents. I bend down to help, but he shoves me away. I fall backward, landing hard on a rock.

"Ow!" I rub my backside and glare at him. "What has gotten into you?"

Purple leaves bulge from the top of his rucksack. Have the päters sent him on some secret mission? The wink behind the mask. The black gemstone. White crystals. I think I should be afraid, but it's Gio. I am just so confused.

I pull another match from my pocket, now more concerned about my safety than that of the others. Shifting my body from Gio's gaze, I strike the match and light the flare. Pink fireballs shoot into the air.

"What the scheiz, Klarke? I told you not to do that!" He stuffs the crystals into his pocket and turns on me.

"What are the crystals, Gio?" My mind forms a theory but doesn't want to commit. It can't be. I think of the description in the text by Dr. Vitus. *Flüstodapul, an odorless white powder, perhaps originating in crystal form.*

"Tell me the truth!" Rage wells in hot tears at the corners of my eyes. It can't be Gio. He can't be part of this. Ellias? Gerd? I lean over, about to be sick.

Gio looks like a cornered pig facing a butcher with a knife. His eyes dart back and forth. A tic throbs in his temple. I don't know this Gio. The Gio I know is funny and calm—someone you can count on to lighten the mood or ease tension. I take a step back, hoping Kiel and Burkhart are close.

"Okay, okay. It's veisel," he whispers. "I figured out there's some up here, so whenever we climb, I sneak over for a fix. I have a problem, Klarke. Please don't tell anyone." He scratches his neck and lifts sad eyes to mine.

"Veisel is made from the mohnblut plant. Mixed with by-products from the tar factory." I swallow and take a step back. "You're lying."

"Nide, nide, nide," he hisses. "That's not what I meant. I didn't mean veisel. This is a mineral that helps you break your addiction. That's what I meant. That's why I risked my life for it. To save myself." He brightens.

Mineral. Flüstodapul. "You risked my life. And Kiel's—" I am about to explode, to call him on his falsehood, when Burkhart emerges from behind a boulder.

"You're alive."

Gio shoots me a look. I drop my gaze to the ground. Kiel appears next, racing to Gio and embracing him. I decide to keep Gio's secret until we reach base camp. My life is still in danger so long as I'm relying on him on the face of the fel. I will confront him when we're down. I will get the truth, and if he is responsible for any of what happened, I will ensure he pays the same price as King Adolar.

The four of us rope together and pick our way through the forest. Gio fills Burkhart and Kiel's ears with a lie about getting lost and turned around and how the cold nearly drove him mad. My boots crunch the frozen ground.

I keep looking over my shoulder. I could have sworn I heard voices in the cave. And I know Gio lied. But no one else could have climbed Fitzhan. That requires skill beyond what any adel could learn in the gym.

And how did Gio learn of the crystals? If they are indeed Death's Whisper, then that knowledge could only have come from the king. And what connection did Gio have to the päters? Those päters were not carrying the purple ferns with anything other than intention. They knew something about them and were using them. Gio is bringing items back to the palace—to the päters and the king—without the knowledge of the Ascenditures.

Oh gods. Is that what Ellias uncovered before—

The others stop, but I don't notice in time. I bump into Kiel's back and stumble to the ground, bracing myself with frozen limbs. My wrist crumples beneath my weight. My forehead smacks against a sharp rock protruding from the ground. Pain blinds me in a flash so intense I think I might pass out.

Kiel drops to his knees. "Did something break?"

"I don't know." I suck in a desperate breath and fight tears. "My wrist. My head."

Kiel lifts me into his arms and stands. I utter a ragged scream before my head lolls forward. I know he is exhausted—at the end of his rope—yet he takes a step forward, cradling me gently as we push through the woods. We move through the forest, finally breaking out into the silent meadow. Kiel sets me down to take a break. He moves away to speak with Burkhart. I sniffle into my sleeve. Snot and tears freeze on my face.

"Take this." I glance up to see a crystal resting in Gio's gloved hand.

"Nide!" I shove his hand away and drop my head.

"It'll take the pain away. You'll be able to climb."

I won't be able to do anything if I take it. Eyeing him suspiciously, I reach for the small mineral and sniff it. It has no smell. Odorless, just as the description said. I don't intend to eat it, but I do want to sneak it back and show it to Otto.

"It won't hurt you." Gio shakes his head, grinning. "See?" He pops a crystal into his mouth. My eyes widen. I watch him chew and swallow. He then reaches into his pocket and pulls something out. He stuffs it into his mouth and then crouches next to me. "I'm all good."

"What was the second thing you ate?" I narrow my eyes. It doesn't make sense. That mineral has to be Death's Whisper, and yet Gio just ate it. I watched. I grab beneath my wrist and close my eyes as a wave of pain so deep I can barely keep my vision clear and my thoughts straight washes over me.

"It was a snack," he says. "The crystals make me hungry. Just eat it, Klarke. It'll make everything better."

I lean over and vomit into the solanas grass. My hand is shaking from the cold. The crystal falls into the dirt.

Gio squats next to me and shoves me to the ground, then presses on my injured wrist. I scream, and he thrusts the crystal into my open mouth, then covers my lips with his hand. I wiggle and cry out, but I don't have the strength to move him. I taste nothing as the crystal dissolves. Almost immediately, the pain subsides. I feel nothing, not even the cold.

Gio sighs and stares at me with an uncomfortable intensity. He releases me.

"What have you done?" I can barely form the words. The effort zaps my energy.

"You feel better, don't you? No more pain."

"No more pain," I whisper.

He looks back and forth between my eyes.

My breathing slows. The world grows darker. But I feel okay. I feel at peace.

"I just have to know that it's working." His eyes widen. I see fear. Sadness. Pain. "It has to work."

I tilt my head. His words don't linger long enough for me to question them. I can't arrange them into a sentence. They float through the air, unattached to meaning.

Kiel returns and lifts me back into his arms. It is as if the air reached out and elevated me onto a tendril of wind. My vision begins to blur. I close my eyes, and the discomfort leaves. I exist now only in a senseless bubble.

Emptiness fills me. I want to panic, but my brain is unable to send those signals. I try to speak, but words won't form. Gio was right that I don't feel pain, but I also feel nothing. I am not even sure if I am still breathing. I'm dying, but I am not afraid. Peace cradles me in tender arms. Is this what my mother felt before she passed beyond the darkened sea?

Kiel pauses for another break and sets me on the ground. I peer at the dirt on my fingers and see an orange solan poking out beneath the base of the solanas grass. I smile; at least I think I do. If I am to die, wouldn't it be nice to send this one final fiek-you to the king?

With lumbering force, I pull the raw tuber from the ground and lift it to my lips. I open my mouth and bite down. I don't feel the crunch. I don't experience the fibrous, earthy taste. I finish the solan, beaming proudly, and flop onto the ground. Warmth spreads from my stomach out into my limbs. Pain returns to my arms and head. Cold penetrates my clothes. I hear shouts coming from my friends. I welcome it all, especially the pain. Pain lets me know I am free. It lets me know I am alive.

28

Gio tried to kill me. Somehow, the solan reversed whatever the crystal did to me. Through the pain, I try to merge disjointed thoughts. My wrist throbs, though I don't think it's broken. I take stock of my situation, but nothing makes sense.

"I just have to know that it's working. It has to work."

Burkhart and Gio walk ahead through the meadow. The grass and mist part around their bodies. Gio peers over his shoulder. His look is as confusing as the rest of the scenario. I'd expect him to be angry or guilty. Scared. Instead, he stares blankly, as if I am a moss-covered stone or an insect crawling up the bark of an oakenwood tree.

Kiel lumbers beside me in silent thought. I don't speak, and he doesn't force me to. We've secured my arm across my heart with Burkhart's scarf so it can't move. Even so, it takes us double time to cross the fields.

It is still as dark as a whale's belly when we reach the cliff edge. Fog whirls in and out between our legs and lazily back into the meadow. The exhaustion that has been concealed in my bones creeps to the surface. We've been awake too long. Cold for too long. Wind screams over the cliff edge, carrying a knife's blade of icy air. Shivers grip my body as it cuts through my clothes. I press into Kiel, and he pulls me close.

"We should lower Klarke." Burkhart's voice is tight with fatigue. He sighs and rubs his hands together. "She'll be no use on the rock with that wrist."

I want to argue but don't. Of course I can't climb.

"Gio will rappel first to make sure Klarke lands softly on each ledge," Burkhart continues.

"Nide!" I shake my head and glance at Gio, who gives me the same unelaborated stare. "I...I'd rather have Kiel."

"Yes," Kiel says. "I'd be more comfortable with that too."

"Fine." Burkhart turns to Kiel and then to Gio. "I'll bring up the rear. Let's get off this fiekin' mountain."

My teammates add rope to my harness, giving me support around my lower body as well as the top. Kiel rappels first. Then I am lowered over the edge. I never imagined a scenario where I placed trust in my life in Burkhart Craddus, but now he is the only person keeping Gio from finishing what he started.

I sway in the wind like a cargo box being lowered from a ship's hull. Occasionally the wind pushes me into the cliff. Since I am not climbing, my muscles are not producing heat. By the time I land on the first rock shelf, I have nearly frozen into a solid block.

Kiel helps me into a seated position. I shake violently as if I have been struck by lightning, and the electricity is coursing through my veins. He runs his hands up and down my arms to create friction.

"Let's move," Kiel says after Gio and Burkhart drop to the hard stone. "Klarke's temperature is dropping. She can't stop shivering."

He helps me to my feet, and we move to the edge. After he rappels, I am lowered again. The wind slips between the layers of my clothes. I gasp for breath as the chill digs into my skin. Between the pain from the cold and the searing in my wrist and head, all I want to do is sleep and not wake until I am beneath the covers in one of the tents. I must have gone out for a second because the next thing I know, Kiel is shaking my shoulders and furiously rubbing my body. I open my eyes and try to smile, but he is a little out of focus.

He lifts me in his arms. Other voices say things, but their speech is slow and slurred. Is Burkhart drunk? He must be. But how? The ground drops out from beneath me. They are lowering me to the next ledge. I try to fill my lungs with air, but I can only take choppy breaths. I think I might suffocate, but the thought doesn't scare me. It doesn't affect me much at all.

Somewhere between rest stops, I quit shivering. I might even feel warm, but I am not sure. I don't feel like moving or lifting my head to check. I open my eyes, but all I see is fuzzy darkness. How is darkness fuzzy? I don't know. I couldn't say.

My back bumps into something cold and solid. The drunk voices filter into my mind. Maybe they aren't drunk. Maybe they are speaking to me from beneath the water. I say something to them, but I can't understand my words. All I know is that I have once again left the ground and am floating in the air. I am a bird. Or I am sinking. I fall asleep. I am not aware of anything until something warm is stuffed beneath my armpits. It's nice, like the hugs my mother used to give me. A garbled voice says something, and I am lost in a dreamless void.

I awaken to the face of a strange woman hovering over me. She pulls something from beneath the covers and replaces it with something warm and pleasant. I sigh and take a deep breath. My chest hurts. My wrist hurts. Most of all, my head throbs. I move my good hand to touch the injury and feel that it has been wrapped. I also feel bare skin. My fingers trace down the length of my arm to my stomach. Someone has removed my clothes. I am naked beneath the covers, with hot bladders of water shoved in all the nooks and crannies of my body. At first I feel exposed, then grateful for not being dead. And then I remember what I shoved into my rucksack up in the Celebern Fields.

Bolting upright, I nearly faint as thick darkness collapses my vision. The moment passes. I stare around the room. My clothes have been neatly folded on a makeshift table. My pack rests at the foot of the bed, seemingly untouched. Even though I am allowed to eat the solans at King Adolar's table, I can't imagine he'd be thrilled to know I was sneaking my own stash. Sighing, I lie back on the cot and give the startled nurse an apologetic smile. After she tucks the blankets around me, she promises to return in an hour to change the bladders and then exits the tent.

"You going make it?"

My head lolls to the side. Dieter stares at me from the adjacent bed. His skin has regained some color, and he is no longer shivering.

"Apparently. And you?" I pull the covers around my neck to keep out the chilly air. Even with the water bottles' heat and the blankets' warmth, I feel cold.

"So they say." Dieter coughs and closes his eyes. A raspy breath escapes from his lips. "Sure as hüle doesn't feel like it, though."

My head explodes in a burst of pain. I close my eyes and fight tears. "Sure as hüle doesn't." When the episode passes, I open my eyes and see Dieter still staring.

"He's a good man, you know. He won't hurt you." Dieter's lips pinch into a thin line. His eyes narrow, but not in an angry way, more like he is trying to battle some deep emotional pain. "I know you'll do what you must do. Just don't hurt him. Please."

"Huh?" It takes me a minute to catch up with the conversation. "Oh. Otto. Right." The prince must have told Dieter that I know. As supportive as I want to be for the happy couple, I am preoccupied with my own issues. Kiel is getting married. Gio tried to kill me. Hypothermia nearly claimed my life. Dieter's secret love hardly seems important. "Sure. I won't hurt him."

Dieter nods and rolls over to face the wall. Maybe he wanted more from me. Maybe he thinks we share some special bond and needs affirmation or consoling. Maybe I need the same. After scrolling through the list of things weighing me down, I realize I could also use a friend.

"I know how you feel."

He rolls over.

I bite my lip, wanting to retreat into my aloof cave. Instead, I take a deep breath and let it go. "Kiel is engaged to the king's niece. I am engaged to a man I don't love, who doesn't love me. I have been blamed for the deaths of men that I had no part in.

And late last night, atop the one bright spot in all of Ectair, a man I thought was my friend tried to kill me."

Dieter's face blanches. His eyes grow wide. "What?"

"I haven't told anyone, not even Kiel. But I have to tell someone in case he comes to finish the job." My heart beats in my injured wrist. I wince and try to catch my racing breath. "I don't think Ellias's death was an accident. Neither was the avalanche on Mount Bonen. One of us has been behind the murders, Dieter. And behind one of us lurks King Adolar. Releasing the arrow. Tightening the noose. I am the next name on his list. I wasn't supposed to survive."

Dieter's eyes have become saucers. He props himself on his elbow and leans toward me. "Who, Klarke? Who is doing this?"

The tent flap opens. Brittle wind races in, swirling around my head and causing tremors to attack my body. Aedan, Russet, and Tizian step into the tent. I see their faces brighten when they notice Dieter and I are awake.

"Thank the gods." Aedan rushes to my side and rests a hand on my forehead. "You were in bad shape, Klarke. Really bad."

Dieter gives me a questioning look, but I shake my head. None of these guys, I try to say wordlessly. He nods, grasping my message.

"Tanks to Kiel and Burkhart, I am still alive." I leave out Gio's name. I can't bear to give him false credit. "How are they?"

"Recovering." Aedan pats the covers by my shoulder and smiles. "Everyone will be back to full speed in the next few days. Even Gio. It's amazing you guys found him. The rescue story has spread across Kietsch. People are loving it. Future princess saves desperate male climber."

I would have given anything to hear those words a few weeks ago. I smile at Aedan, but it is not genuine. Thankfully he stands and moves to Dieter's bed. Turning my head toward the wall, I let hot tears fall. Gio's betrayal goes beyond leaving me feeling angry and vengeful. Gio was family. He was a brother. His betrayal hurts as much as the deaths of those he caused. He tried to kill me tonight. Not a faceless murderer, but my own kin. My eyes sting with the burning tears. My back heaves, and I accidentally let slip a painful sob.

This time Russet sits on the foot of my bed. He rests his hand on the covers at my back. "We're okay, Klarke. It's all going to be okay."

But we aren't. And it isn't. We might all be alive now, but over the next few days, the Ascenditures will grieve another loss. Another body will be sent to sea. Another oath will be recited. The question now is, will it be me, or will it be Gio?

29

Aedan declares that no more solans or ulrind flowers will be collected until vintazite passes and the ice drips down the rock face into the Sevier River. King Adolar doesn't argue. In fact, he looks pleased. I am unsure what to make of his reaction.

I think of the solan stashed in the back of my wardrobe. I am uncertain what happened at the cave on the far side of the fields, but I know two things: Gio tried to kill me, and the tuber saved my life. I don't yet know why, but I have added it to my ever-growing list that something big is happening within the kingdom, of which the citizens are unaware. Something that ties together the king, the päters, and my dead mother.

Because vintazite has officially been declared, the annual harvest masquerade ball will be held the following evening. Adels from across the kingdom will attend. Wealthy merchants from Kietsch will try to behave as if they are closer in status to royalty than to the peasants they normally mingle with. The Ascenditures will be invited, leaving me both anxious and excited. One part of me desperately wants to see Kiel. To tell him everything. The other part of me doesn't want to be anywhere near Gio.

Nightmares of cold, faceless figures in the mist keep me up most of the night. On the day of the ball, I sleep in well past dawn. The covers are drawn around my face, and even though the fire is crackling in the hearth and I am sweating beneath the down, I can't find warmth.

When I finally roll myself from the bed, I find my dress on the ornate chest by the footboard. The fabric is a soft yellow, the color of light and starshine. The color of the flowers high up in the Celebern Fields. Instead of great poofs and gaudy frills, the dress lies smooth and soft with understated elegance. Beside the dress a black and gold mask stares with vacant, eyeless slits. Small, dazzling citrine stones have been artfully attached, and as I hold it closer to the fire for a better look, the gems catch the blaze and sparkle with chaotic light. My internal ice begins to melt. Smiling, I think of Lena and know she made this dress and mask to fit my body and my whole being. I remind myself to thank her the next time I see her.

The day passes quickly. I stay in my room, eating the food brought to me, and then crawl back beneath the covers, ready to fetch the hidden tuber if I have been poisoned. Midday, Lena appears and draws a hot bath. It still unnerves me to have someone see me without clothes. Even more bothersome is having a fellow human being wash and tend to me like I am some sort of goddess.

Once I am bathed and dried, she begins to work on my hair. I close my eyes, relaxing into the pull of her fingers and the soft hum of her voice as she sings a folk song from Dor Drillingt, the grouping of islands off the Eastern shore of Ectair, where she is from. The song speaks of an unlikely hero, a young boy sent out to find food for his starving family. The sea berates him. A storm rolls in. The fish swim away each time his small boat approaches. But the boy never gives up, and by the end of her haunting ballad, he has caught enough fish to feed his village for a month.

"That was beautiful," I say as the song ends. "You have a gift, Lena. You should be singing in the theaters, not curling hair and washing feet."

She blushes and tugs a stray strand of my hair into place. "The theater is a place for the educated. I could never afford professional training. Besides, I am content where I am."

Content. I ponder the word. It is neither overly positive nor negative. It just is. Content with life sounds like you've settled, or compromised, or given up on your dreams. I am an Ascenditure. I have been elevated out of poverty and live in a palace with servants who bring me food and brush my hair. I am betrothed to a prince, and yet I am not content. Should

Lena demand more, or should I settle for less? Am I insatiable? Selfish? Unable to be happy?

I can't answer any of those questions.

"It is okay to struggle, just as it is okay to find peace with a situation." Her soft hand stops pulling on my scalp and rests on my shoulder. "Neither is more correct than the other."

Maybe the biggest difference between Lena and me is her level of maturity. She is wise beyond her years, while I can't see beyond the next minute of my day.

Lena finishes my hair and applies makeup to my face. A few times she steps back, wrinkles her nose, and wipes something away. When satisfied with her work, she helps me into the gown and hands me the mask. I pull the disguise over my face and feel safer behind its anonymity.

"You look beautiful." Lena guides me to the beveled mirror by the wardrobe and steps back.

I look at myself. The yellow gown hangs like silken water around my form. My hair is knotted and curled, forming an elegant trail down my right shoulder. Small white flowers have been woven in with pink ribbon. Beneath the mask, my eyelids have been accentuated in dark, smoky shades. For the first time, I believe I could be both a climber and a princess.

A knock sounds at the door. Lena opens it, stepping back to allow Prince Otto into the room.

"Wow. You are stunning." He smiles. The warmth in his eyes makes me feel calm and confident.

I hug Lena before I leave and kiss her cheek. She turns bright red and takes a deep bow. Wrapping my arm through the prince's, we make our way across the cavernous palace halls down to the great chamber along the back side of the Pentengen. Voices and music rise from below. We enter the Balhalle to the cheers and banalities of the kingdom's nobility. The pressure of so much attention makes me want to turn and flee, but Otto squeezes my arm and leads me to the head table at the far side of the room. King Adolar is already seated. A young brunette, no older than I am, sits by his side. Two empty chairs await us. I focus on the king until we take our seats and the celebration returns to normal.

The head table is elevated on a stone dais. Beneath our feet, long rectangular tables with wooden benches occupied by lords and ladies, businessmen and climbers, ship captains and governors, parliament, and military commanders form parallel lines across the hall. Beyond the tables, a wide swath of the floor has been cleared for patrons to dance.

Arched windows line the back wall, looking out into a sprawling garden along the rear of the Rektburg. Five-pointed chandeliers imbued with emeralds and heavy with candles hang from a vaulted ceiling. Murals and gold cover everything. Tucked away in an alcove to my right, the musicians play harps, flutes, fiddles, and lyres. The music is soft and elegant. Later, it will become more celebratory. Upbeat. Eager.

I feel out of place until I spot Aedan and Russet laughing as they crash pewter goblets together. Smiling, I see all my teammates, minus Kiel, surrounded by eligible Ectarian ladies, each desperate to claim a climber for their husband. My skin prickles when my eyes find Gio. He stares back at me through a plain dark mask. I shudder and lean into Otto. He takes my hand in his and kisses it. It is a simple gesture—not romantic—but I appreciate the comfort and friendship nonetheless.

"You're safe," he whispers. "Gio can't hurt you tonight."

I sigh and press my cheek into his shoulder. I filled Otto and Dieter in on what happened on top of Fitzhan. Otto immediately wanted to alert someone—at least Silias—but I objected. I trust no one at this point. Maybe not even Kiel. Otto conceded, as long as I agreed not to go anywhere on my own.

"Not tonight, but when?" I keep my eyes on Gio. This is the first I've seen him since that night. Gio's eyes are on the king. "How does one just sit around waiting to be killed?"

"I'll see what I can do. I will have Gio followed. We won't just sit by and—"

A commotion at the front of the room draws my attention and cuts off Otto's statement. A woman's commanding voice echoes through the hall. Two figures dressed in traveling cloaks stride through the doors of the Balhalle. Guards shout from behind for them to stop, but they ignore the demands.

"What is this?" King Adolar places his goblet on the table and shoves back his chair.

I turn to Otto, who shrugs.

"I am Naisae, the captain of the Parvanatari, Ainar's climbing team. We are emissaries sent by King Gyalzen of Ainar." The woman now stands only a few feet from our table. Her skin is the color of the dark clay along the creeks in the Dangof Forest. Ebony hair falls down her back in long, thin braids. I've never seen such a beautiful woman in my life. I've only heard that people from Kobo and other parts of the world had dark skin.

"Gyalzen?" King Adolar's face blanches. He clears his throat and bangs a heavy fist on the table. My wine rattles against the crystal. "Guards! Arrest these traitors immediately!"

The woman and her comrade appear confident. I scan the face of the man standing next to her. He looks to be around my age with short, messy black hair and a stocky build. Strong. Laughter lurks within his angled eyes. He grins knowingly at me. She merely sighs and takes another step forward.

"We are not here to cause trouble. We simply wish to extend an invitation." Her eyes drift to me and soften. She smiles and gives a slight bow of her head. I glance at my plate, unable to hold her mesmerizing gaze.

"My lord wishes to mend the broken relationship between our kingdoms. It has been too long since trade merchants trekked across the Bridge of Worlds. Too long since our ships have passed in harmony on the sea. Too long since we could rely on each other in times of need."

King Adolar's face looks like a dam about to break. His knuckles flex with white anger. "You have only your king to blame for that, stranger. I will not have an animal from the north ride into my kingdom making demands."

"You may refer to me as captain, sire. I am only an animal on the side of a mountain. There I am the fiercest of beasts, the alpha in a pack of volves." Ignoring his racial jab, she turns a humorless smile on the king. Beneath her cloak, her strong muscles flex. "Which brings me to my purpose. You have selected a woman to be on your elite Ascenditure team. That act of progress leads King Gyalzen to believe you may be ready to parlay. The League of Ascension will be hosting next year's climbing tournament in Kobo. What better way to break bread with a supposed enemy than for both of our teams to come together in representation of our kingdoms—of historic Galvaith—and climb in a practice competition to prepare for the Kobo games? To show the rest of the world that peace is possible."

I realize I am holding my breath. This woman is a climber. All I want to do is pull her aside and ask one of the million questions racing through my mind. There are other climbing teams and competitions? Ainar has a climbing team? Women are allowed to climb in Ainar? Not only that, but her king trusts her enough to send her on this dangerous mission. Even though I know nothing about her, this woman who keeps glancing in my direction is everything I want to be.

"Absolutely not." All sound has vacated the cavernous room. All eyes dart between the king and his perceived adversary. "I will not send my men into hostile territory so that you and your heathen brethren can consume their flesh at your winter feast."

The woman laughs softly. "If you will not send your men, then send your woman. I assure you she will not be harmed."

The darting eyes veer toward me. I shrink into my yellow gown and focus on a mole on Otto's wrist. The woman steps onto the dais. Gasps come from the crowd. She kneels in front of me at the table and takes my hand. Her fingers are dry and cracked like mine. I stare at the fissures, feeling a connection I've never felt before.

"Fram Ascher." Eyes the color of midnight bore into me, but though full of power, they emanate only kindness. She is middle-aged yet shows no signs of softness. "You have grown into such a beautiful and courageous woman. Your father…"

She trails off and lets her gaze drift toward the king. "He would be proud." She sets a small, battered box on the table before me. I lift the lid. It is full of spiced chocolate. The gift he was supposed to bring back from his last voyage.

"From Kobo," she whispers.

I lean forward. "You knew him?" It is as if we are the only two people in the room. The word *father* compresses my heart; my stomach stirs. It hurts. It delights. And the chocolate...

She nods. A guard grabs her, yanking her arms behind her back. The woman doesn't try to fight. It looks like she expected this from the moment she walked through the door.

Before he can be secured, her partner darts forward, tossing a squishy, smelly blob onto the table in front of me. "Fisch-bomb!" he shouts.

I slide my chair away as a guard grabs the man's arms. He laughs. It stirs something in my memory. Peering from the fish entrails to the curved smile of the intruder, my heart twists in painful recollection. It can't be. That boy died on the ship with my father...

"Losan?" I lean forward, desperate for another look at the man, but the guards have already dragged him across the hall. "Wait!"

"Take them away. Lock them in the dungeons." The king shoots daggers with his eyes as the prisoners are led away. When they disappear beyond the doors of the Balhalle, he takes a seat and the music resumes. A servant appears and wipes the chum bowels from the tablecloth.

"I think I know that man. A lifetime ago, he was my friend." I grab my wine and down its contents, beckoning toward the servant boy to top me off. "And that woman. Did you see her, Otto? She was beautiful. She was strong. She is the first woman I've ever seen who embodies my dreams."

He leans forward to block his father's view of me and chuckles. "Klarke Ascher idolizing someone?" His expression hardens. "If what she said is true, then Gyalzen wants a truce. My father will never go for it."

"We'd be so much stronger together. Not living in fear. I'm tired of living in fear." I shake my head and watch as three people approach the table.

"Lord Hector. Lady Arnette." King Adolar's voice booms; his confidence and bluster return. I lean forward and watch as a tall man draped in green and gold approaches, removing his mask. A woman wearing a beautiful blue gown curtsies to the king and moves beside her husband. Behind them a smaller, more petite woman stands with her hands folded politely across her abdomen. Her long brown hair flows past her waist like a silken waterfall. When she removes her mask, I am taken aback by her beauty. Only when Otto squeezes my hand so tightly I think the bones might break do I realize who this woman is. I feel the color drain from my face and think I might be sick. All thoughts of Naisae and the man who might be Losan vanish.

"Lady Gelta," King Adolar says smoothly. "My dear niece. You are lovelier every day. If you were not my kin, you would be my queen."

I choke on a sip of wine. He gestures with his hand, and the moment I thought couldn't get worse blackens into night.

It doesn't matter that he wears a mask. I know that closely cropped dark hair. I know that sharp jawline and those sparkling brown eyes. Beneath the yellow fabric my knees thump together. My chest heaves. Behind my mask, tears form. I hope they blend in with the twinkling of the citrine stones sparkling in the lamplight. Otto releases my hand, instead wrapping his arm around my shoulders. My body goes limp, and I allow him to hold me in place. It is as if I am beneath the water, unable to move, staring up at light, at air, but unable to reach it.

"Lady Gelta, may I introduce you to Kiel Abel."

I hear the words through the dense water, but I don't know who spoke. I am drowning. I can't breathe.

"Please, take this evening to get to know each other. The bond between husband and wife is eternal. Something to be cherished."

The beautiful brunette daintily offers her hand. Kiel flicks his gaze at me. Something beyond pain ripples through his eyes, but he tames his emotion. He takes her hand, smiles, and leads her from the table. Out toward the dance floor. He places his hand on her waist. She rests her hand on his shoulder. I snap myself back into a conscious state of mind. It's a game. And if I don't shape up, I will lose.

Taking a deep breath, I chug the wine in my goblet. I lean into Otto and exhale slowly. "I should be better at this."

"Don't be sorry," he whispers back, his mouth nuzzled against my hair. "I know how you feel."

We look out to the table where the Ascenditures are seated. A jester dressed like Rüdiger with billowing sleeves and a silly hat with dangling bells and ribbon appears to be teaching Russet and Veit to juggle. Russet keeps dropping the little round hofnuss on the ground, but Veit seems to have gotten the hang of it. A busty woman sits on Dieter's lap, giggling at something he says. She keeps moving Dieter's hand beneath her skirt. He keeps sliding it away.

"At least Dieter's not interested in women. Kiel might like me, but he is still a man. Eventually his feelings will shift, and Lady Gelta will steal his heart." The words hurt as they leave my mouth. They are barbed with thorns of despair.

"You don't think Dieter will be forced to marry as well? Forced to have children to keep his secret safe?" Otto shakes his head. I feel his body tremble next to mine.

I sigh, watching Kiel move across the floor in a way only I want to move with him. "This is wrong. We have to change the rules."

"We will. Together, I think we can do anything."

I lean farther into him. He kisses my head.

The food is served. Oozing pork sausages. Mashed potatoes piled high on silver platters. Apple crumble and spätzen noodles with cheese. Skewered fruit drizzled in something red, sticky, and sweet. If I had an appetite, I'd devour it all. Instead, I devour more wine. The king and his young mistress leave to dance. I glare at his crown as he walks away and then move my scowl to Kiel and his future bride sitting at a table.

"She's prettier than me."

Otto sets his glass down and chuckles. "But she can't climb mountains."

"Oh, right. Like that's what appeals to a man. Look at her. She is graceful and elegant. I bet she doesn't have scabbed knees and bruised elbows beneath all that fabric. She is everything I am not. The perfect definition of what a woman should be in Ectair."

He doesn't respond immediately. His gaze moves around the room before coming to rest on me. "Do you know how many eyes are on us right now?"

I straighten, trying to appear more like a princess than a bitter drunk.

"I don't mean that you should behave differently. What I am trying to say is that all these people are watching me, and what they see is a man who is tough and regal. A man who is everything they are not—the perfect definition of what a man, and a prince, should be." A small smile quakes at the corners of his lips. "If they only knew. But my point is, you cannot judge a person by what you see on the outside. Most of us are masters of deception, social chameleons. But not you, Klarke. You are exactly the person you portray to the world. That is why my father fears you so much. It is also why, no matter how many scrapes and bruises cover your body, you are still the most beautiful woman in the room to Kiel. You are also the most beautiful woman to me, not that it makes much of a difference."

I smile. It turns into a laugh. I almost snort wine through my nostrils.

"Besides…Gelta is quite dull. She is my cousin, you know. On my late mother's side. A total bore. She used to whine every time we'd do anything."

He sets down his goblet and scrunches up his nose. "My legs hurt, Otto," he says in a high-pitched falsetto. "I'm tired. This saddle itches. This horse smells funny." He lowers his voice again. "Trust me, Kiel won't find that attractive."

I wrap my arms around Otto's neck and pull him into a hug. "Tanks ye."

We embrace, and some of my misery melts away. For all the scheiz that has been shoveled into my path, the one bit of good luck, the one mistake King Adolar has made, is placing Otto and me together.

✷

The party continues well beyond midnight. Drunker than a Kaiwan mule, I stumble across the dance floor with an equally inebriated Otto. We laugh and lose our balance. At one point Otto takes a mandolin from one of the musicians and plays a lovely—though off-beat with the rest of the music—tune he says he wrote for Dieter.

I clap my hands and giggle while others glare at our growing inebriation. We are numb to everything other than the moment. People are watching. They might be judging our ability to rule the kingdom. That thought makes me laugh even harder. Drink even more.

"I have to make wee." I stop mid-dance and try to focus on Otto.

He chuckles and sways, pointing toward the doors to the Balhalle. "Garden's closer than the privy."

"I'll be right back," I say.

I bump into Kiel on my way out. Gelta is nowhere to be seen. He is sipping a glass of water.

"At least she is pretty," I slur. "You'll make beautiful babies." Clutching his sleeve to keep from falling over, I let out a garbled giggle. "Good for you."

Kiel rolls his eyes and grabs me by both arms. He looks mad. "This isn't what I want. I hate it as much as you do."

"Sure. Let's see what you think in a month. In three. Next year. I'll be dead." I lift my palms upright and shrug. "And you. You'll be safe. And happy. And that makes me happy."

"What are you talking about?" He runs a frustrated hand across the top of his head. Behind him, Gelta approaches. "Klarke, I want to be with you. Nothing is going to happen to you. Nothing you can't come back from. You are the strongest person I know."

He is wrong. About all of it. I wave my finger in his face. "Gio. It's Gio. He killed them. He tried to kill me. And the king. They haven't succeeded, but they will. I am strong but not strong enough to win."

Gelta slips her petite arm around Kiel's and gives it a tug. She eyes me with contempt like I could be a slug smeared on the side of a wall. Beneath his mask, Kiel's eyes widen. They might be filled with fire. I went too far. I don't remember what I said, but it was too much. Blowing them both a kiss, I turn, keep my balance, and find the door that leads out to the back garden.

The night is cool and calm. Clear. I can see the stars. Millions of them twinkling above me. Azura peers out from behind Kara Do. I find a bush, wanting to continue slinging mud at every female stereotype this kingdom forces upon us. A woman should be polite, tidy, modest. I hike up my dress as high as it will go and laugh as I attempt to urinate like a man.

"I'll let you finish."

The cool night freezes. The stars above die out, leaving only darkness. I drop the yellow fabric to the ground, no longer feeling cheered or warmed by its color. The speaker carries no hint of malice in his voice. No hate. No pain. No anger. That is the most terrifying part of it. The emptiness. The void where human emotion, any emotion, should exist.

"Why?" Turning slowly, I face Gio. He has removed his mask. It dangles by a ribbon in his left hand. Those vacant eyes peer at me. "Why Ellias? Why Feiko?" I must say their names aloud. If I am to die, I at least want to force this monster to relive his crimes. "Gerd?"

He shrugs. The gesture is as empty as his eyes. "I no longer love to climb."

"That's it?" I storm forward, tripping over my dress. My head throbs, both from the booze and from the injury that occurred when Gio last tried to kill me. "You don't like climbing anymore, so you switched to murder?"

Again the blank stare. "For years I've risked my life to collect the king's tubers. To gather ulrind. To fetch the other things that hide up there. And tonight I'll risk my life again for a man I loathe almost as much as the mountains he instructs me to climb. The monarchy holds my life on a sisal rope dangling over the gaping trench of Miter's Waste, waiting for me to screw up so they can slice the cord in one emotionless hack."

The statement is cold and matter-of-fact. Detached. "That's all of us, Gio. That's what we signed up for."

"The solans are just a cover. There's other stuff up there. Ellias figured it out. That's why he had to go." Gio takes a step closer. His hands remain at his sides. "I didn't hate him, didn't wish him ill, but control of my life was forfeited the moment I held the golden rope in front of the entire kingdom and swore fealty to this gods-forsaken profession. Just like yours. That rope was my freedom from poverty, but also a noose that strangled whatever conscience cowered in the bowels of my body."

"Gio, stop." His monotone scares me. I want to be brave, but I also want to live. I don't want to die out here. Not like this. "What's up there? It's Death's Whisper, isn't it? And what is the purple fern?"

"They've made me the villain. I didn't want those boys to die on Bonen. That's why I told you to back out. If only you'd backed out." He lets out a deep exhalation and shakes his head.

Tears stream from my face. They burn like acid. My stomach churns. Rage congeals in my blood. "We're your family. You don't have to do this. Stand with me. Fight with me. We can beat him. You've done unspeakable things, but King Adolar is the true villain of this story. You will pay for your crimes, Gio. And I will never forgive you. But I need your help in telling the truth. I need your help to bring him down."

"Family." He shakes his head and lowers his voice. "He has

Lisel, Klarke. My sweet sister. For months now. If I don't do this…I can't let him hurt her."

My heart drops. Liselotte is only ten, pretty and shy. I think of her soft skin and the dimples in her cheeks. If the king has taken her, then she is already gone. "Let me help you. I'll find her. I live in the palace now. If she is here, I'll save her."

"Only your death can do that." He takes a deep, ragged breath. The fleeting moment of emotion evaporates.

"My death? Why? At least tell me that." I remove my mask and cast it aside. I want Gio to see my eyes. To see me as the person he once cared for.

"I do only as commanded." His exterior almost cracks. He shakes his head to cast aside any tears or emotion. "I didn't want this either, Klarke."

I sniffle. My heart trembles. "We were friends. We cared for each other." It hurts. My pain is greater than my fear.

"I am an Ascenditure now." He steels himself and stands tall. "I will persevere in honoring those who have fallen before me, fighting against those who wish us harm, and *above all*, serving my benevolent king." He recites the final part of our oath. "I will not fall. I will not fail. I will *not* betray my kingdom. I swore an oath, Klarke. I will keep my promise."

"You also promised to honor those who have fallen before you and to fight against those who wish us harm. Fight, dammit." My fists clench. The anger erupting inside me has burned away some of the drunkenness and is warming me against the frigid winter air. I wipe my tears.

He lowers his voice and again steps forward. "And above all, to serve my benevolent king." He raises the mask in his left hand and rips the ribbon from its side. I turn to run just as the garrote slips around my neck.

30

Fear mutates into pain. Searing agony grips my neck. Glass shatters in my brain. I reach for the ribbon and dig my nails beneath it, trying to tear it from my skin. Gio has pulled it so tight that I can't get a good grip. I hear him grunting and breathing hard. The same noises a wild hog makes when it gores a fawn to death.

My brain screams. Clouds roll in. The ribbon cuts into my throat. I let my body go limp, hoping the deadweight will throw him off balance. As I buckle and hit the ground, Gio stumbles, releasing one side of the silk band.

I suck at the air as my vision returns. Clawing at the ground, I try to drag myself forward. Away. The ribbon finds my neck again. I choke, cough, gasp. A hand wraps around my curls and jerks my head. Stars flood my vision—stars and the promise of a black forever.

But that is not my future.

My legs are untethered. I kick one back like a horse would kick a stable boy and contact his groin. Gio groans and releases me. I pant. My injured wrist balks at the weight I place on it. My neck is in the perfect position to accept the garrote once again.

I leap forward beyond the black forever. Footsteps pound the ground behind me. Branches slash at my cheeks. Air burns my throat and lungs. Deeper into the garden I press, leaving the light streaming from the palace behind. It provides a false sense of safety anyway.

I burst from the trees into a clearing full of small stone statues atop marble pillars. Etched faces glare at me, snarl. Some have horns. Others, wings. I am mystified and afraid but slink into their midst, disappearing behind their protective shapes. Gio is close. I hear his breathing even over the thrashing of my blood.

On the pedestal in front of me sits the perfectly carved image of a climber in a figure four position. The move is relatively useless in actual climbing, more of a technique used by the greats to show off. The left hand of the climber is high above his head. The other hand is grasping a hold at his side. The left leg is threaded over the right hand, with the crook of the knee resting against the crook of the elbow. I've seen only one climber use this technique for anything other than pointless bluster. Ellias. Ellias could do anything.

The sculpture is rectangular and about the size of a fireplace log. I step forward and pull it from the base. It is heavy. Ignoring the pain in my wrist, I get a firm grasp and take a deep breath.

"Klarke. Whether it's me and now or someone else and later, your time is up. Come out and end this, or you will be running forever."

Gio's voice is like a frozen finger with a long, jagged nail running down my spine. His words wiggle in one ear, but before they can burrow into my brain, I purge them out of the other. I would rather look over my shoulder than at the back of my eyelids.

Gravel crunches. A hand comes into view. I position my legs apart and lift the statue. Ellias. Ellias in his signature move. The side of Gio's face appears around the nearest sculpture. I swing the statue with every ounce of strength I possess. Something pops when it hits his cheek. Crunch, snap, crack. And then a wail of pain.

"King Adolar has a daughter," I scream as Gio writhes on the ground. Someone has to know. If I am to die, let my murderer share the truth. I don't care how it happens. "She is in Ainar. Find Obid. He'll know what to do."

I toss the statue and run into the darkness. Back toward the palace. Back to Kiel and Prince Otto. Footsteps slap the path behind me. With sinking horror, I realize Gio is on my heels.

The ten turrets of the Rektburg rise over the trees. Head tucked low, I move like a rabbit chased by a volf. My feet hardly touch the ground. Fear fills me with light dread. When vestiges

of lamplight break the barrier of darkness, I push myself harder. I crash into the cobbled courtyard, startling a pair of lovers
lying behind a berry-filled Salal. The woman screams. I keep
running.

Lords and ladies surge from the yawning back doors out
onto the terrace. Despite the audience, Gio grabs my hair and
yanks me to my knees. I scream and collapse, hitting the hard
stone with his and my weight combined. Blood drips from his
face onto the pale-yellow dress as he loops the ribbon around
my neck. My eyes bulge. The crowd watches. I can't tell what
they want. Do I see pleasure in their eyes? Vindication? Hopelessness?

"Die," Gio hisses. "I need you to die. Die for Lisel."

My head is on fire. My neck might soon snap in half. I can't
breathe. I can't think. Someone leaps through the throng, hur-
tling toward me. The figure rams into Gio. The ribbon releases
its stranglehold. I fall forward, lapping at the air and grasping
at my throat.

"What in my name is going on out here?"

I lift my face from the muddy stones long enough to glare
at the king. I don't have the energy to keep it up, so I drop my
cheek back to the ground and pant. When I cough, blood flecks
the nearest stone.

"Let go of him, Kiel! What do you think you're doing?"
King Adolar marches forward. He is an incredible actor. If I
didn't know better, I'd believe his surprise.

"He tried to kill Klarke, your majesty." Kiel's voice shakes,
intoned with fear, anger, and disbelief. "We all saw it happen."

"Is this true?" King Adolar turns back to the steps. I see a
few nods. Many don't respond. I hate them all. "Dear me. A
man has just tried to kill the princess-to-be. That is treason of
the highest order. Guards! Guards!" The king's hands fly into
the air. He rushes to my side and kneels. A finger runs along
my neck. I flinch.

"Get my doctor!" he shouts. "Now!"

Chaos erupts. Someone helps me to a seated position. Dr.

Helmut arrives. He gently touches my neck and shoulders. Kiel tries to reach me but is intercepted by a weeping Gelta. I shake my head, not wishing trouble for him. He has done enough. He saved my life when everyone else was willing to watch it fade.

Gio is surrounded by palace guards, invisible now to the rest of us. I have so many questions I want answered. I am certain his penalty will be death, but before the trial, maybe I can get something useful from him—something to help me destroy the king.

Nausea spirals up my throat. Someone grabs my hand. Otto. His eyes burn holes into everyone around us.

"Don't let them put anything in my mouth," I hiss. It hurts. Every syllable of every word scalds my throat.

"I won't leave your side." He takes a seat next to me and squeezes my hand. I watch the swarm of guards milling around my attacker, my face still pressed to the ground.

"What the—?" Otto straightens. His pulse quickens.

I lift my eyes. Silias carries a sword big enough to slay an ox. He moves down the steps. The other guards fan out. Gio is forced to his knees, head and neck extended.

"Nide!" I scream though it comes out as a raspy cough. I grab my throat to try and ease the pain. My head throbs.

"Don't speak," Dr. Helmut instructs. He rubs my forehead. "It could do further damage."

I feel helpless and afraid. Otto leaps to his feet, racing toward the guards. "Stop. I command you."

Silias turns. King Adolar rests a hand on Otto's shoulder. Otto glowers at his father. King Adolar's eyes brush over me, lingering a little too long before coming to rest on Gio.

"Gio Vinzenz, you are accused of the attempted murder of Klarke Ascher." King Adolar lifts his crowned head to the ogling mass. His scowl is almost believable. "Does the accused deny the charge?"

Gio is facing the ground. I can only see the top of his head. It moves side to side, a loyal servant to the end. He whispers something. I think it was Liselotte's name.

Gasps. Women clutch their hearts. Men clutch their women. I lean over, again consumed by the need to be sick. Gio is not innocent and deserves punishment, but the king is covering his tracks and the truth. With Gio dead, he will never have to answer for his other crimes. With Gio dead, there will never be justice for those who died on Mount Bonen, or for Ellias and Feiko, or Rosalie.

"With this confession, I find it unnecessary to wait for a trial to determine this man's fate. As king of Ectair, I sentence you, Gio Vinzenz, to death by beheading on this, the first moon of vintazite in the year of the great harvest."

"Father, please." Otto steps between the king and the condemned man. "What if Klarke is not the first? Don't you think we should wait? See if there are other victims. I implore you to reconsider."

I muster one final ounce of strength and crawl to Gio's side.

The king's nostrils flare. Madness radiates from him. "Step aside, foolish boy. And someone remove this hysterical woman."

"Give me something," I seethe at Gio in a low whisper. "Give me something, you coward."

His head remains bowed. He won't look at me. "Find Lisel."

"I promise."

Hands begin to pull me away. Before they succeed, Gio sneaks something into my hand.

"Take this to Obid. I'm not alone. There's another."

Otto takes my arm and pulls me back to the crowd. I glance into my palm at the small clear crystal Gio has given me. The crystal from the cave. Death's Whisper.

There's another.

The king brushes past us and nods at Silias. I force myself to watch. Silias lifts the great sword above his head. Gio neither fights nor trembles. He has accepted his death. I, on the other hand, have not.

An order is given. The blade falls. I hear a thunk. See crimson liquid. Gio's severed head lands on the ground and rolls away, down the slope into the dark garden below. It leaves a thin trail of blood. Despite the warm light coming from the palace, the darkness pressing in around us, and the ever-present green from the trees, shrubs, and mosses, all I can see is red.

31

J ust like every other day in Ectair, it is raining. Pelting drops of cool water splash against my skin and against the cliff face the anxious climbers are about to ascend. The rock slickens, each mossy handhold growing more precarious as the storm continues. I could make this climb with my eyes closed and one hand tied behind my back if I had to.

But I don't have to, because I am already an Ascenditure.

Today I stand behind the competitors with the rest of the team, watching, as if in a mirror, as if sent back in time, as the eight eager climbers—all men—stand at the base of Vether's Fel. Gio's spot is up for grabs.

Next to me, seven other figures are visible through the misty morning, ready to belay. Aedan. Burkhart, Tizian, Russet, Dieter, Kiel, Veit, and me. Seven men and one woman. Behind us a small crowd of onlookers has gathered. Beneath the white canvas tent, the three judges sit.

I hear a *thunk* in the back of my brain and wince. See Gio's head rolling into the garden. Coming to rest at the base of the Salal. It's been only a week, though a year might have passed, and I wouldn't know. I try to force the thoughts away. Gio is dead. His secrets and answers have washed out to sea with his empty corpse. Obid is also gone, still on the ship to Ainar, so I haven't been able to ask him about the crystal or about the things I uncovered in the queen's tower—namely, the identity of Ramanata and where I can find it or him or her. I intend to press the prisoners from Ainar for information, but what could they know and how can I access them? I should have some semblance of peace now that Ellias's murderer has been brought to justice, but I don't.

There's another. Gio's words are burned into my brain. Another what? Murderer? I recall the second voice I heard in the cave atop Fitzhan. Is it one of these men? Even with Gio gone, I watch my back more than ever.

Ahead of me lies a new mountain, a higher summit, a deadlier climb. But this is what I do. This is what I live for. Part of the sickness may have been purged, but the plague is just beginning. I won't stop until the entire illness is eradicated from Ectair. I won't stop until King Adolar is dead.

The gong sounds.

"Klettag," the unnamed climber before me says.

There is power in a name.

"Klettag und," I repeat rotely.

I count down from sixty in my head. The gong sounds again. The climbers begin their ascents. I've invested no time in getting to know them. Part of me feels guilty; the other part feels grateful that I won't lose a friend when the king decides to kill whoever wins today. I hear a bell ring from high above the fel. That was fast. Must be a good climber.

Eight other bells ring a few minutes later. The competitors descend together. A man my age named Haydrich who hails from Merket lands on the ground, unties his sling from the rope, and throws his hands in the air. A smile as wide as Miter's Waste lights up his face. I can't bear to look at him. I wish I knew that feeling. The one where victory is sweet and accomplishment doesn't come weighted with consequences and terms.

"Next time," I say to the dejected-looking boy I just belayed as I untie from the rope. "Head up." I can't finish the rest of Ellias's statement.

The crowd cheers. The judges collaborate. I glance up as a small twig drops from the oakenwood tree above and lands on my shoulder. A pair of dark eyes stare down at me.

The girl is around eight, with long brown hair tied in a messy braid and a serious expression. I know who she is. She has climbed a treacherous trunk and is perched far out on a limb. Instead of looking afraid that she has been caught where she shouldn't be, she gives me a wink and then disappears into the thick canopy. Despite the rain, despite Gio's fate, the failures of my kingdom, and all the things making me feel hopeless, I smile.

There may not have been a woman competing for a spot on the team today, maybe not again for a few years, but it will happen. Someday.

"I'll be right back," I whisper to Veit. "Give Haydrich my regards." He shrugs and rolls his eyes.

I race to the base of the oakenwood trunk just as the young girl lands on her feet. When she sees me, she takes off running. I follow. Through the woods, over fallen logs, beyond slippery stones, and gurgling streams. She has more energy than I do, but I know the importance of endurance today. I don't let up.

After a bit, she latches on to the trunk of a massive pine and shimmies up. With a grin, I follow. She is in my domain now. Forty feet up she stops and leans against the trunk, her legs straddling a thick branch.

"You're Gerd's sister, aren't you?" I perch across from her, wiping the sweat from my forehead. Trying to still my pulse and regain my breathing. "He was an amazing climber and an even better friend. He told me about you. And about how much you love to climb."

"He was really good, wasn't he?" she whispers.

"One of the best." My voice cracks and I don't try to hide it. "One of the best I've ever seen."

She nods and begins plucking pine needles from the tree. She releases them. We watch as they fall to the layer of detritus on the forest floor.

I scoot forward on the limb. "Marike?"

"You know my name?" She eyes me warily. "Am I in trouble?"

I laugh. A real, honest laugh. The joy it brings makes me want to cry. "No, Marike. You aren't in trouble. I want to make you an offer."

"What kind of offer?" She bites her lip. Her hair is askew and full of leaves. Her clothes are matted in layers of unwashed dirt and oil. Her face is covered in soot, masking a rash that is breaking out across her cheek. I see so much of me in her—a hunger for something greater. A need to grow beyond the small pot she has been planted in.

"I want to train you to climb. I want to be your mentor. Someday, I want you to be an Ascenditure. If you're anything like your brother, you will be one of the best. Would you like that?"

Her eyes narrow. There is a fierceness in them that makes me proud even though I know nothing about this kid. I wonder if this is how Ellias felt when he first encountered me up a tree. I imagine him watching me right now, his bald head glistening with raindrops. The wrinkles around his eyes shifting upward with the corners of his mouth, which is slightly hidden behind his beard.

"The trainee becomes the mentor. Give 'em hüle, Klarkey girl. Show the world what you're made of."

"Is this a joke?" Marike folds her arms across her chest and continues to give a piercing stare. The needles block most of the rain, but a thin drizzle falls on our hair and faces.

"No joke." I wipe the moisture from my forehead and lean against the tree. "Someone once believed in me. They believed in a better world. Now I believe in you, and I want to believe in a better future. I've lost a lot lately. I am struggling to find hope. But when I saw you in that tree earlier, I felt it. I felt all the things that the world is trying to take from me." Tears well in my eyes. I want to fight them, to appear strong to this girl who doesn't yet trust me. But I can't fight them any longer, and kids are too smart to be fooled by thinly veiled acts. I think of Naisae from Ainar sitting in the dungeon beneath the Rektburg. Strong. Proud. Independent.

"Seeing you today reminded me of something. This burden isn't mine alone to carry. If I make it such, then they will win. But if I share it, if I train other talented, strong women to rise above what society has forced upon them, then it doesn't matter what happens to me. The fight lives on. The battle isn't lost. Join me, Marike, and I will make you an Ascenditure. But more importantly, I will make you matter. And in turn, you will make others matter."

She toys with her lip, tugging on it with her fingers. I am unsure if my babble made any sense but after a moment, she smiles. I smile back and reach out my hand. She takes it. We shake.

King Adolar may have won the first battle, but the war is just beginning, and I am coming for him with an army he misunderstands and is ill prepared to face.

Untying one of the pink ribbons from my hair, I pass it to Marike. She ties a perfect little bow around the green sleeve of her dürmel. Green to represent that she is destined to become a brideprize. I stare at the ribbon, pink against Marike's dress. Pink used to be a color to demean me. Now it means strength. I think green represents hope. Add that to the list of notions I intend to redefine.

ACKNOWLEDGMENTS

First, I must thank my former agent, Shannon Orso, who passed away during this book's development. This project was our baby and might not have happened without her, and certainly wouldn't have been as strong without her dedication and love for Klarke and the world of Galvaith.

Thank you to my husband, Andy, for your enthusiasm, encouragement, and love. You inspire me each day to be a better person and writer. Thank you for lifting me up (literally) when things feel too hard, for believing tirelessly in my dreams and abilities, for bringing so much light and color into my life, and for being an incredibly creative sparring partner.

To Nathanael Gold for supporting me through so much of this project and my career. Your belief in me and my stories made it possible to pursue my dreams. I am forever grateful.

To Natalie Wright for being the greatest writing and podcasting partner I could have asked for. Thank you for the emotional support, the late-night calls, the tipsy rants, and for helping me keep my head up in this challenging industry.

To Daniel McNeil for teaching me to climb, how to write about climbing, and in doing both, helping me climb out of a difficult life period.

Thank you to my agent Lizz Nagle with Victress Literary, and all my agency siblings. You all are the best champions and cheerleaders a writer could have.

To my mom, Carey, my dad, Walt, and my sister Alexis for being there for me from day one and encouraging me to be creative, kind, and passionate, and that what I contribute to the world matters. I love you all and couldn't have asked for a better family.

Thank you to the team at Regal House Publishing for bringing my idea to life and creating the beautiful book you hold in your hands. To Darynda Jones for the mentorship on this project. To Sierra Blair Coyle for chatting with me about your experience as a professional female climber. A hearty thanks to Bill Poston, Lauren Darby, Kinsey East, and Anthony Jacobs for their ongoing marketing support. To my long-time best pal Adrienne Godschalx for the critiques and inspiration. To Adam Bassett for bringing the world of Galvaith to life in the maps you see in this book. And a big shout-out to the Certainly Winners group of writers for your moral support and encouragement.

And finally, to all the friends, family, and readers who have supported this journey but I did not list, I see you, and I am forever grateful for your support and confidence. Thanks for giving me a reason to share my passion for storytelling. I hope you all enjoy reading *The Ascenditure* as much as I enjoyed writing it.